DOVE ALIGHT

DOVE
ALIGHT

KAREN BAO

VIKING

VIKING
An imprint of Penguin Random House LLC
375 Hudson Street
New York, New York 10014

First published in the United States of America by Viking,
an imprint of Penguin Random House LLC, 2017

LIBRARY OF CONGRESS CATALOGING-IN-PUBLICATION DATA IS AVAILABLE
ISBN 9780451469038

Printed in U.S.A.
Set in Apolline Std
Book design by Nancy Brennan

1   3   5   7   9   10   8   6   4   2

FOR THE FRIENDS WHO BECAME FAMILY

DOVE ALIGHT

1

I'VE BEEN ALIVE FOR SEVENTEEN YEARS, BUT I collected most of my identities in the past two. Stripes, Girl Sage, Fay, Moon's Most Wanted.

Phaet. The one name I've carried all this time has fallen into disuse. I only hear it now from the people who knew me as the silent, unthreatening girl I used to be.

Most days, it's hard to keep track of the people calling my various names during strategy meetings, political rallies, and slapdash training sessions for new rebel soldiers. Dovetail's twenty-six thousand members know *about* me, but they don't know me. Otherwise they'd understand how only a few of them can overwhelm my senses. Although they might imagine me idling on the job, perhaps dreaming about past or future days, I'm really figuring out which way to turn my head.

Today, though, chaos liberates me from my usual responsibilities. The Dovetail fighters in the ships around me are shouting over the intercom even as they steer their Pygmette speeders through a laser storm, driven by survival instincts and their mission to free the Moon—and, eventually, the Earth—from the Lunar Standing Committee's grasp. From restricted expression, surveillance, rigged elections, and killings. Long before the revolt, we'd all gotten sick of the killings.

In their panic, my comrades don't ask me for orders; they simply react. I'm just another pilot to them—and to our Committee-loyal enemies, who see a ragtag cluster of ships, more rebels they must reduce to a bloodstain on the lunar regolith. I'm one more pawn to flick off the chessboard.

That's all the Moon has become. A vast, tricked-out chessboard.

A blast of purple light stings my eyes, and I slam on the rightward thrusters. Our ship—a two-person Pygmette—jerks to evade the laser. A loyalist Omnibus ship, which can hold up to two hundred people, zips off to the left. Alex, my copilot, sends a missile chasing after it and curses colorfully when he misses.

"That laser could've shaved off our hull, Dove Girl," he quips in his odd Earthbound accent. "Don't get us shot down when we're almost there."

Alex's speech differs from *his*, but the similarities dredge up old memories and make me ache for someone who's half a million kilometers away. I like Alex, but at the least convenient times, his mannerisms and even his sense of humor cut to my heart, highlighting the hollowness left by Wes Carlyle's absence.

"Base VI is in the next crater over . . ." Alex glances backward. "And someone's behind us. Someone who's not a friend."

Checking the rearview screen, I see a five-person Destroyer ship tailing us, one without a red stripe across the nose to indicate Dovetail affiliation. From that angle, the loyalist crew could use us for target practice.

Get it together, I tell myself, *and don't let anyone get that close again.*

Jamming my thumb down, on a button, I pull the Pygmette into a 180-degree turn; Alex sends another missile careening into the enemy Destroyer.

The craft tumbles onto the dull gray regolith and comes to rest belly up, like a fruit fly's carcass. I start to sigh in relief but stop mid-exhale when a pulsing pain rattles my cranium. I shouldn't have stayed up half the night planning and expected to fight at dawn without an on-and-off killer headache.

Alex doesn't notice my grimace; he seems preoccupied with events in his own head. Our recent victory forgotten, he shifts around in his seat as if it's burning.

"The closer we get, the more I want to turn back," he says, helping me steer the Pygmette into the shelter of a small crater overlooking Base VI. "Hasn't been long enough since I booked it out of the Singularity with my tongue all tangled up. Didn't even warn my lab friends that I had to go."

Three months ago, Alex Huxley, Earthbound spy, steered a limping Pygmette—or "Pig," as he angrily called it—onto Base IV, the sole settlement under Operation Dovetail's governance. After we revolted against the Committee, our home base was nicknamed the Free Radical.

Alex bolted as soon as his employers in the renowned Base VI Astrophysics Department scheduled a speech analysis test for him, and I understood why as soon he opened his mouth. He leaves *h*'s off the beginnings of some words and *r*'s off the ends of others; he usually forgets to pronounce his *t*'s and overemphasizes them when he remembers. Although Alex says his accent betrays both his Caribbean childhood and his Odan adolescence, all I hear is strangeness. When Alex is calm, he imitates Lunar speech well enough, but he would've lasted about five minutes under pressure from the authorities.

Returning to Base VI—commonly known as the Singularity, because it's a "black hole" of physics and astronomy research— has put Alex on edge, and in such close quarters, his mood affects mine. With my heartbeat in my throat, I adjust the camera above the Pygmette's windshield so it peers over the edge of the crater in which we've hunkered down, and the Singularity's majesty comes into focus on the dashboard's video feed.

The nine-thousand-meter-wide dish of a telescope, hollowed into the Crater Daedalus, stares out like a blank black spider's eye. Researchers use it to look immense distances into space, at places so remote I can't wrap my mind around the numbers of kilometers. A thick metal ring containing living and working quarters surrounds the satellite dish, which is in turn surrounded by a thinner copper tube called the Pandora Particle Accelerator, or PaPA. Inside, scientists are studying matter's fundamental components, seeking more and more specific answers to the question, "What *really* makes up everything we know?"

Unlike the other five bases, which started out as food and energy production stations, the Singularity was constructed primarily as a research post and isolated on the Moon's Far Side. To threaten its scientists, as we're doing now, is a crime.

I try to ignore the twisting feeling in my gut. "Hardly any loyalist ships above Singularity," I say into my headset. "Only two, maybe three Destroyers near the satellite dish."

As we'd predicted. We scheduled this attack the day after an enormous dispatch of Singularity Militia to Earth; the Committee's fighting a two-front war now that its Earthbound ally, Pacifia, has engaged its longtime rival Battery Bay in the fight for the Earth and Moon. The loyalists' multitasking is probably their only weakness, and we'll continue to exploit it.

"Cool. Just a few ships? That means Alex got the date right." The whine of active wing artillery blurs Yinha Rho's words. Now the leader of Dovetail's armed forces, my friend and one-time

Militia instructor must command our entire military operation as well as fight in it. Her Pygmette cruises behind ours, releasing projectiles.

Hands steady on the controls, I steer us up and out of our hiding place, over a rocky rill, and into the enemy's line of sight. A dozen more two-person Pygmettes, three Destroyers, and two much larger Omnibuses follow.

"Thank me again later, Yinha," Alex drawls. "Once you make sure my head's still in one piece. Shouldn't be hard—Medical's got tape and glue at the ready if something gets past my helmet."

I give him a thumbs-up and an uncomfortable smile. Several weeks passed before I learned the difference between his amusement, which he covers up with sarcasm, and genuine annoyance. When he's entertained, his long, curling eyelashes shiver, and his dark skin subtly flushes.

"Lovely. Now we're all picturing Alex's fractured skull," Orion says into our headsets. His Pygmette pulls ahead. "Just what we needed before an invasion. Tell me, Alex, do all Earthbound get sidetracked this easily?"

Next to me, Alex stiffens, and we hear Yinha groan. Although Orion has never liked the Earthbound, I'd have thought my old Militia friend would avoid creating tension for the duration of the mission . . .

Flash. A white beam thinner than a strand of hair slices through my vision; it seemingly scalds my brain. A scream passes between my lips.

"We're okay, Dove Girl, we're okay . . ." Alex mumbles soothingly.

But I'm still rattled. Even after I shut my eyes and rub them hard, I see a reddish gash in the blackness.

"That one barely missed us!" shouts Nash, another Militia veteran in the Pygmette with Orion. "A hair to the left, and this Pig would be cinders by now."

Whatever people's opinion of Alex, his nickname for the smallest Lunar ship has stuck.

Another ray, silent like lightning unaccompanied by thunder, flashes in front of our Pygmette and cleaves through the Destroyer to our left. The shark-shaped ship tumbles downward and crashes, scattering bits and pieces over the lunar surface. Fleet members cry out, murmuring our fallen comrades' names—Levy, Nijima, Mayuri, Rhea, Asgard. No one I knew well. But listening to our new recruits' screams brings me to the edge of grief, and I ride it over. Names turn statistics into people, the people who are dying every day for Dovetail's cause.

Even as a storm of sorrow gathers in my heart, I resist the urge to mute my headset. I need to be here for Dovetail's recruits, who are experiencing the sensory overload of their first real battle, or are readjusting to combat after years on hiatus. Many began their service five months ago, when Dovetail instituted a comprehensive military recruitment and training program. First there were volunteers. Then there were draftees: able-bodied individuals age eighteen to forty, preferably ones who'd completed Militia training. Whether they remember how to fight is a different matter altogether.

Soon we forced seventeen-year-olds to join—and then sixteen-year-olds. If we continue to sustain losses, Dovetail might have to go even younger, to fifteen: Cygnus's age. My brother. With the way he's been since Umbriel and I pulled him from the Committee's clutches, I can't let that happen. Dovetail's leaders might grant him an exemption for reasons of mental health, but I won't count on their mercy.

Then turn this battle around, I tell myself.

White flashes are fracturing the sky at greater frequency now. They originate from a point on Base VI's outskirts, where sub-atomic particles circle the settlement at near light speed. When I realize what's happening, every instinct tells me to turn back and order everyone else to follow. Instead, I call out: "They've weaponized the particle accelerator!"

"*What?*" Yinha's voice crackles in my headset. "The atom smasher?"

"It's a big, circular tube lined with electromagnets," Alex drawls. "They're probably adjusting those to aim at us."

Ingenious. But it makes me sick. Instead of producing knowledge, the Committee's cronies are engineering death.

"Shave off altitude now, and fast." Alex sounds annoyed, not panicked in the slightest. "Fly close to the telescope dish so they'll quit lobbing protons at us."

I fire exhaust upward, and our Pygmette drops below the Crater Daedalus's lip with gut-wrenching speed. Sure enough, the PaPA ceases firing; even the Singularity's loyalists still have the sense not to shoot at the most powerful radio telescope ever built with the most advanced accelerator in existence. That would only endanger civilians.

A headset feed fizzles out, and ship fragments fly into my line of sight. *Another ship down,* I think, chains wrapping around my heart. In retaliation, a Dovetail ship takes down a loyalist one, sending it crashing into the regolith, but those brave teammates meet with two missiles to the left wing.

As the second ship goes down, I have to reach inside my helmet to wipe my eyes.

Our breathing labored, our minds rattled, we push on. Because the soldiers' sacrifices have cleared the way forward, it feels anticlimactic and *wrong* when Dovetail reaches the entrance at the telescope dish's lowest point. Like we've discarded our comrades' lives to get here.

The airlock gates open downward, feeding us into the Singularity's center. That's one success today: despite everything that went wrong on our journey, the undercover Dovetailers stationed here have managed to hold up their part of the plan.

Our nine Pygmettes, two Destroyers, and two Omnibuses descend inside, taking turns riding an elevator leading into the hangar. The Singularity's Defense Department is smaller than that of the Free Radical, and since most of their Militia is on Earth, we'll never have a better opportunity to invade.

At least that's what we've been told.

I touch our Pygmette onto the elevator, and it begins to jerk us downward, away from the stars and into the unknown.

2

AS SOON AS I STEP OUT OF THE PYGMETTE, dense laser fire bars my way. It's as if the whole base is clustered here, fighting us.

Overwhelmed, I duck behind the fuselage and nearly crush a small, ashen-faced Dovetailer who's clutching a Lazy—a deadly weapon that can shoot violet lasers—for dear life. He must be a year or so younger than me and fresh from our "training" program.

"G-g-girl Sage, don't make me." He grabs my sleeve, his fingers stiff from terror. That paralysis could kill him in battle. "Don't make me walk into that."

But he can't stay here either.

I take his trembling hand and stare into his unblinking brown eyes. "We're going to *run* into it. Stay with me, all right?"

Hand in hand, we dash into the laser storm, from which there's sparse shelter. The hangar is nearly empty of ships, and the ones that I see are old models, hardly spaceworthy. Their wings are bent at strange angles and wires poke through gashes in their hulls.

The young soldier and I let go and roll under a Pygmette with a busted windshield. As we catch our breath, I take a hard look around, my hopes sinking with every damaged vessel I see. So much for adding to our fleet. Even if Dovetail takes this base, we can't use its ships. I should've expected this. The Singularity garnered fame for its research, not its Militia; that's the domain of Base I, the Moon's capitol, and Base III, home of the Moon's uranium mine.

This place has no shortage of hostile humans, though. They're concealed at the moment, hiding in dark corners and under ships, but they're blanketing the place in violet. We have to break through the hangar and into friendlier territory or this mission will fail, leaving us imprisoned or dead.

"Did the General call all the troops back from Earth, or what?" Nash shouts from above me and the scared new recruit. She's crouched under the ship's dashboard to avoid getting hit through the cracked windshield.

"Not all of them," I say, surveying the black-suited loyalist soldiers spread throughout the hangar. If the gore disturbs them, their glassy opaque helmets don't let them show it. "But someone's commanded them to shoot everything they've got."

"Hmph. Let's hope this really is everything, and there isn't more ammo around the corner."

On every side, hundreds of Dovetail troops pour from the two Omnibuses and then scatter, shouting and flailing, their haphazard training forgotten. Ours isn't an army; it's a swarm. Some troops aren't young anymore, and they lack the youthful Militia's rapid-fire responses. Others, like the boy still trailing me, are so young they should've stayed home. Most fighters wear old Militia jackets and pants that we've sanded down to a dull gray color—it's meant to be silver, but we didn't have the resources to dye it. Other Dovetail troops fight in colorful civilian robes, which trumpet their presence and offer little protection from enemy weapons.

A few meters ahead, Yinha raises her fist, attempting to rally the Dovetailers. She has switched her Pygmette to its indoor combat settings; it's shed its outer shell, and its wings have folded in. "Hold the ranks. Shields up! Advance!"

Get up, Phaet. This is what you're here for. Shield in one hand, knife in the other, I lunge from my hiding place as the loyalist troops surge forward. Now that they've broken cover, their numerical advantage hits us full force. They have enough troops on the floor to crush any hope of breaking through, and several more units perch atop spaceships, firing down from above.

"Sage! Help!" the young soldier screams. A Militia soldier's gloved hand wrenches his head back, and the soldier's laser finds its way into his chest.

Before I can think, my half-meter knife buries itself in his attacker's shoulder. The female loyalist soldier sways, then collapses, taking the boy soldier down with her. She'll wake up screaming in pain, but at least she'll wake. No one can say the same for the boy. I've seen enough laser deaths to know that my companion is gone.

Muting my headset, I empty my lungs in a cry of despair.

Nash doesn't miss it. She drops down from above me, draping a strong arm around my shoulders to pull me to safety and then to embrace me.

"Phaet, you were there for him. You tried, you really did." Her dark, familiar eyes ground me in the moment, make me notice the things that are constant, not changing.

"I was supposed to protect him," I whisper. I should be protecting *all* of them. But it's getting harder.

Our already-small attacking force dwindles. Unless we can show ourselves to the Singularity's residents, and they give us the support we've hoped for, we won't survive—let alone take the base.

More Dovetailers follow Nash and me into the open hangar. As she falls back to let me lead, a cone of them gathers behind me, pushing me deeper into the melee. Featureless enemy helmets are all I can see; the blankness makes it easier to fight them. When I think of them as human, I make mistakes.

My knife sneaks between plates of armor, sinks into flesh and blood, injures many but kills none. Before every battle, I remind myself that I've murdered one person—an unknown Lunar recruit who died on Saint Oda's shores—and that one is too many. I swore not to increase that number, but as the weeks drag on, it's getting harder and harder to keep that promise.

I survey the scene. A few loyalist troops have fallen back; the ones that haven't push on despite nonlethal but surely excruciating gashes and projectile wounds. They're good fighters—better than ours. Only experienced soldiers can fight through those injuries.

Grateful for the visor over my face, I let panic arrange my features into a desperate grimace. My knife bites into a forearm and a shoulder muscle, knocks a laser blaster out of an enemy's hand.

"Oi, Dove Girl, give me a hand here!" Alex's voice sounds from inside my helmet. I see him three Destroyers ahead, perched atop the ship's left wing and facing down a squat enemy soldier. "This pest could use a nap, don't you think?"

With my left hand, I get out my tranquilizing gun and send a dart, known as a "Downer," into the soldier's kneecap. He lunges at Alex but stumbles as his leg goes numb. Alex side-kicks him into the fuselage; soon he's slumped against it like a drunkard, unconscious.

"Brilliant." Alex pushes the soldier through the hatch on top of the ship. "I'm using his fingerprint to fire this baby up . . . We'll fly into the hallways soon."

True to his word, Alex makes the Destroyer heave backward. He slides out through the repair door on the ship belly's left side and rolls when he lands. Each second stretches out, long and suspenseful, as the ship picks up speed. The wheels begin to whistle—and then the forked tail tears into the hangar doors.

Crrrunch! The doors buckle, and the troops nearest them push the totaled Destroyer away to reveal a circular hole about two meters in diameter.

"Out! Into Defense!" Yinha barks, satisfaction lacing her sharp words.

Some of us on foot, some in converted Pygmettes, we burst through the jagged hole in the hangar doors and run straight into the Defense Department's hallways—and another conglomeration of Militia troops. Our steps are accompanied by the flat, female voice of a computer: *"Attack on base. Terminate all experiments and proceed to the nearest rendezvous point immediately. Attack on base. Terminate . . ."*

"Get Phaet into the hallways!" Yinha hollers over the noise. "And make sure everyone recognizes her!"

Since the fighting in Defense is at such close range, the loyalists don't dare create a laser-storm. Dovetailers shove their way through the dilapidated military stronghold. The place is a low-ceilinged warren of hallways with historical firearms on display as if in a museum.

Finally, we make it into the Singularity's interior, which is dark like a planetarium. The first department on our right is Astrophysics, the front door a glowing blue hemisphere with a panel that slides back to allow entry. It's a model of a giant star, millions of times as massive as our sun. White eddies swirl across its surface: storms that could engulf a nearby planet.

Alex sprints ahead, enters something into a keypad next to the star-door, and pounds on it for good measure. Seconds later, it opens, and two women in their late twenties gesture for us to hurry into the dimly lit, low-ceilinged entryway, taking shelter from the battle. Inside, they flash us the Dovetail sign with their hands: thumbs interlaced, fingers spread wide like wings. They have similar inquisitive eyes and short bobbed haircuts, but one has electrically pale features while the other is tan-skinned and black-haired.

The Singularity's crawling with Dovetail allies, Alex told us during the briefing. *Some of my coworkers can't wait a second longer for freedom.*

When Alex bends down to crush the pale woman in a hug, I realize she's sitting in a metal battery-powered hoverchair with landing cushions that float several centimeters above the ground. The metal of the chair probably interacts with the base's grav-magnets, which repel the water in our bodies and create the illusion of greater gravity. In this woman's case, it allows her to hover. Her right hand rests on a joystick attached to the armrest.

The tan woman leans forward and whispers something in Alex's ear.

"Friends," Alex calls to us, "meet some more friends. This is Rose Mu"—he points to the pale woman—"and Mitchell Mu"—the tan one. "They were Astrophysics' cybersecurity team until about a minute ago. I wouldn't have survived a week here without them."

Rose glides alongside me, smiling and squinting slightly. She looks familiar; I suspect I've seen her in old news broadcasts. Her eyes, a misty blue gray, are fringed by lashes like frost, and they make the back of my neck prickle. One front tooth looks recently chipped, something that the Singularity's Medical Department should've fixed as soon as it happened. They probably haven't because the Committee reduced supply shipments after small incidents—a secret meeting here, an assault on a lone Militia soldier there—began to crop up.

"Phaet?" Rose touches my forearm, fingers light like moths. "The living legend."

"Stuff it, Rose," Alex says. Turning to me, he mutters, "She cracked Battery Bay's top classified network at *fourteen.*"

My jaw falls open, and I stare, dumbfounded. That's why I

recognize her. She must've won some Committee award, and I watched the televised ceremony. That makes Rose one of the genius hackers we were hoping to find here.

Rose disregards Alex's comments and my astonished face. She gestures toward her sister. "Mitchell probably wants to say hello too, but she's shyer than I am. Also more focused, and less fun—"

"Come on, Rose," calls Mitchell, jogging next to Alex. "Let's fight now and make friends later."

She sounds . . . tired. Weak and hungry. Both women do, in spite of their excitement. Their faded lavender robes hang loosely on their frames. Taking a peek through the translucent door, I see that the other Singularity residents look similar, and know that this place doesn't have enough food for itself, let alone for Dovetail. My heart sinks.

"Down this hallway," Alex calls. "Let's capture some Committee cronies!"

Rose floats nearer to Mitchell and Alex, who are gathered around a wide air vent in the floor. Yinha and I stand guard as the three of them pry up the grate—Rose grabs an edge with her left hand and pulls her hoverchair's joystick back with the right. One by one, Alex, Mitchell, and Rose disappear inside. They'll begin tracking down the Singularity's leadership, which our reports indicate has hidden in one of the interconnected scientific departments.

The rest of us exit Astrophysics the way we came and move farther into the base's claustrophobic interior. Since the radio telescope built atop the colony imposes spatial limitations, Base VI lacks IV's wide corridors and expansive domes. The comparatively tiny Atrium is a cylindrical room a hundred meters in diameter and five meters high. Along the perimeter, different scientific departments' sliding doors open into labs and boardrooms. As a whole, the structure resembles a small-scale panopticon.

I run in the front line. The transparent alumina helmet some Materials engineers designed for me means the Singularity's residents can instantly identify me. Their eyes, and then their fingers, point at my hair, which is more than half silver now. The fading color doesn't concern me, though Dovetailers have said they're worried that I'm in poor health. It makes me look as weary as I feel.

The transparent helmet was the brainchild of Sol Eta, Mom's former colleague in Journalism and Dovetail's public relations coordinator. "Instant recognition!" she said. "Seeing the Girl Sage's hair will galvanize everyone around you."

The Singularity's civilians react as we hoped. "The Girl Sage is here!" they shout. "Dovetail's come for us!"

But the patrolling Beetles punish them for it. A Sergeant several meters in front of me smacks an awestruck teenage girl across the face with an Electrostun gun. Blood dribbles from her left nostril. "Quit that talk and get back," the Sergeant barks. "They're *terrorists.*"

A nearby boy—probably the girl's friend—tries to pull the much bigger Sergeant away from her. The Sergeant zaps him with his Electrostun, turning back to his black-suited Militia troops before the boy's head hits the floor. The girl screams; the Sergeant ignores her too. "Get Theta first," he tells his unit.

But the crowd rushes in, enraged by the loyalists' assault on their own. Civilians wrench Lazies from soldiers' hands, drive fists into chest armor, shout for bystanders to join in. Our allies look almost comical next to our enemies—exhausted, undernourished, pathetic—but sheer numbers turn the battle in our favor. Although their reckless fervor endears them to me, it makes the scene painful to watch.

The soldiers that evade assault are firing violet lasers my way. But I'm prepared. When I squeeze my left hand into a fist with my fingers *around* my thumb, microscopic mirrors swing out of my suit's gray fabric. Although my skin heats up, the clothing reflects the brunt of the laser blasts back at my attackers.

This uniform is the most valuable thing I own—and my first real engineering project. Three months ago, a Committee attack sent a Dovetail satellite crashing down near the Free Radical, shattering its ultra-thin, reflective solar sail. I spent long nights in an engineering lab, breaking the fragments into even smaller pieces and attaching them to my Dovetail uniform. An engineer helped me perfect the mirrors' flipping mechanism, and my brother wrote code so I could control my suit with hand motions.

Cygnus. I must return to him, to my sister, and not empty-handed.

The lasers reflected by my suit either strike or blind my opponents, forming a pocket of open space around me. I take advantage of the visibility to fire a Downer into a loyalist's thigh. As he collapses, knocked out by the tranquilizer, I wrench the ballistic shield from his hands. Hunkering down behind it, my back protected by my troops, I set my gun in long-range mode and pick off enemy soldiers, targeting the ones with civilians in chokeholds or handcuffs. My heart beats steadily, and I'm grateful for every pulse. How could I live without this suit? It works so effectively that Asterion Epsilon, the newly elected leader of Dovetail's territory, wants a suit made for every member in active service—eventually. The cost in time and materials will be enormous.

Is my life worth more than other soldiers'? I don't like to think so, but the proof is right here. The loyalists' violet lasers gather most thickly around me.

Protected by a ring of Dovetail soldiers, I run to the Atrium's center, where a stark black sculpture about three meters high rises from the floor. It roughly represents a black hole, a real "singularity" in space-time. Two rings of white metal intersect, one oriented vertically and one horizontally, with nothing but darkness in the center. I grab one of the rings, using momentum to swing myself back and forth until I'm up and standing on top of it.

The situation looks promising. Dovetail troops have surrounded pockets of struggling civilians, protecting them from loyalist Militia. We've taken the hallway's center and pushed the enemy back against the walls.

Okay, I think. *Time to talk. Deep breaths. Shoulders down. Look at their hairlines so that you seem to be making eye contact.*

"Militia of the Singularity," I call. My high-pitched, timid voice echoes through the cramped space. The Dovetailers here have hooked up my headset to the speaker system, and it makes me sound more authoritative than I feel. "You're outnumbered. Your leaders have left you for dead. Disarm now, or Dovetail will turn your own weapons against you."

The few Beetles left standing respond by training their Lazies on me; their violet laser fire glances harmlessly off my suit. They look at one another, befuddled and scared, and check their belts for other weapons that might work.

"Base VI is ready to join IV as a free city." I've practiced this speech dozens of times, but my tongue still threatens to trip over every word. "You are the Moon's best Physicists, Mathematicians, Software Engineers, and more. Dovetail welcomes you with open arms. You . . . you've chafed against the Committee's restrictions on your intellectual freedom for long enough—assigning you experiments, censoring your publications, disrupting your children's education with Militia training."

I see nods, the sparks of repressed anger in their eyes. It gives me hope—and the courage to keep speaking.

"So I beg you: take action against the Committee. Help us capture Hopper Gamma and bring her to justice." According to hearsay, the woman who replaced the Singularity's deceased, feral-eyed dictator Wolf Omega as representative is tamer—and smarter—than her predecessor. "Help us send the last of the loyalists fleeing to Base I. Are you with us?"

A meek chorus of affirmation, punctuated with a few strong yells. I've reached the script's end, but the situation calls for improvisation. "You can say what you mean now—you don't have to be afraid." I suck air into my lungs and put wind behind my words. *"Are you with us?"*

This time, their shouts are so powerful that they resonate in my bones. As I dismount from the black hole statue, the Singularity's population begins striking the last Militia stragglers with fists, feet, knees, and elbows. Just as we hoped, the base's meticulous order has disintegrated, leaving the place not only messy but vulnerable. Dovetail will have to restore it, on our terms—or the base might not last another day.

3

ACROSS THE ATRIUM, THE THREE-METER-HIGH doors to the Nuclear Physics Department blow off their frame. Sizzling and shining, the metal blocks send a throng of civilians and several Dovetail fighters stumbling backward.

After that, dead silence.

When the curtains of smoke lift, they reveal five Dovetail members and Mitchell and Rose clustered around where the department entrance used to be. Dovetailers from the Free Radical restrain prisoners in magnetic handcuffs; half of them have already given up struggling. In front, Alex holds the chain around a short, elderly woman's wrists with his left hand. His right wields a Lazy, the tip jammed against the captive's forehead.

Hopper Gamma, the interim Base VI representative. Her face, with its button nose and weak jaw, is youthful, not what I'd expected of Wolf Omega's replacement. But I'm careful not to underestimate her. Because she headed InfoTech for decades in Base I, the Moon's capital, Hopper's mind is a labyrinth of secrets. Those child-like eyes are piercing and clear.

"Great place to hide, Nuclear, with all those giant magnets and lasers sitting around." Alex sounds bored, but there's an electric current running beneath his words, an intensity that I almost never hear from him. The old woman in his grip whimpers. He sneers. "Don't worry; we won't kill you. Dovetail's after the puppeteers, not the poor minions tied to the strings."

Sol Eta asked me to deliver the final victory speech, but Alex begged me to let him do it. I surrendered the duty without hesitation. My mind is still whirling from my words earlier. Phaet Theta didn't know how to shout. But this person I've become? She has no choice but to propel her voice into every crevice in people's minds.

Now Alex hands Hopper off to two Dovetail fighters. "Load her up—we'll take her home as a souvenir."

The soldiers grasp our prisoner's elbows and sweep her off to the side.

"I rotted on this base for more'n three years with the lot of you," Alex says. "Worked as a data monkey till my eyes bled. These two"—he points at Mitchell and Rose—"made it bearable by hating it too. Cobalt in the next solar system over? Committee wants it for *weapons*, not pretty blue face paint, as some of us may have hoped." Grim chuckles from the crowd; Rose laughs a bit too loudly, and Mitchell shushes her. "The Dovetail life's better. Take it, or we will take you out."

Stepping to the front of the crowd, I toss a grenade-sized firecracker upward. It spins like one of my daggers, exploding at its zenith in a small flare of black, silver, and red—the colors of the rebellion.

The girl named after the Dove star has marked Dovetail's territory.

But after the embers float down, there aren't cheers. No movement. Just thousands of eyes staring at the black hole statue, which is now lit.

"We are disappointed in you, Base VI." The voice is slick, smooth, spine-chilling. The center of the black hole projects a hologram of four shadowy figures, towering above us and filling up the pitifully

small space. The four faceless Committee members who aren't here. To see them dwarf the stars drains away every bit of happiness I have.

We should've disabled signal transmission from Base I, the capital, as soon as we got here.

"Despite your intelligence, you have joined the side of chaos. Of increasing entropy," Hydrus Iota, the Base I representative, goes on. *"We only wanted to restore order to the Moon and bring it to the Earth— so that no climate or resource wars ever happen again. Anywhere."* What about the catastrophe happening right now? I want to interject. *"But you do not want the same perfect world. And because of your astounding betrayal, we will never let you forget that you are surrounded by instruments of our power."*

He lets the words sink in, lets us picture the nuclear, chemical, and biological weapons orbiting the Earth and Moon, lets us imagine the chaos if they used one here.

"I'm with you, Committee!" shouts a man's voice from the back of the crowd. Senseless loyalist.

"We want you back!" someone else hollers. "No more hunger, no more chaos!"

Soon, other voices—those of dissent—overtake the loyalists, but their words echo in my head. They think life was better before, when they weren't hungry and afraid of what Dovetail would bring . . . I can empathize with that. But having the Committee back? That's the easy way out, and it'll only lead to tyranny.

Suddenly, the entire base shudders; small dust clouds fill the air, as if in a moonquake. People drop to the ground and cover their heads, a reflex honed through many emergency drills. Fear roils through me again—a moonquake killed my father, and so many of my worst memories are associated with them. But this isn't a moonquake. After the first tremor, there are no more.

"A mini-nuke!" people are calling. "They dropped a mini-nuke on Recreation!"

The Committee's shadowy heads nod, once. *They attacked the base*, I think in horror. *They attacked the base, in the spot where children play.*

"*That is all . . . for now,*" Hydrus says.

The holograms disappear, and for many moments, the only sound I hear is the pounding of my own heart.

Afterward, there's hardly celebration. Dovetail's soldiers, shaken by the Committee's threat, carry body after broken body—rebel and loyalist alike; they all look the same—to the Singularity's Medical Department, which is both understocked and understaffed. Some loyalists manage to zip away on Pygmette speeders, and Yinha barks at us to let them go. No point in risking more lives to capture aging rich people who (we hope) can't help the Committee much.

I help move an unconscious Militia soldier out of the way; I support her feet, while a balding man with a patchy beard and deep-set frown lifts her by the shoulders. "About time you Dovetailers arrived," he says, cracking a smile. "You'd better start shipping water and food over here or we'll have to visit the Free Radical and take it ourselves."

He's joking, but it puts me on edge. Dovetail counted on restocking our dwindling rations with this base's supplies. Instead, it seems we've got to provide for them too. How many hungry mouths did we add to our ranks by taking the Singularity? Dovetail will need to capture another base, and soon. The thought makes me hang my head in exhaustion.

"I thought the Singularity would have . . . more," I say dumbly. "More of everything."

The man scoffs. "You think the Committee would let us keep

our supplies once we started making trouble? They took the food we grew, the clothes we made, sent it all to the more obedient bases. What was left the Beetles hoarded away in the Defense Department. Took some to Earth when they fled yesterday, and they're running away with the rest as we speak."

Earth. I think of Saint Oda, where finding food was as simple as walking through Wes's backyard or wading into the sea. Where clear water bubbled up from the ground. That city's an ash heap now, but Earth is still a planet of plenty, a planet that could help us . . .

If only Battery Bay, the rival of Pacifia, the Committee's ally, hadn't rebuffed our every communication with either radio silence or a sharp warning not to contact them again. Messages communicating our goodwill haven't undone decades of distrust. Friendly Lunars? To the Batterers, that's an oxymoron.

"Sage," the man says, lifting me out of my rumination. We've reached Medical and drop the Militia soldier off nearby. "Look at this base, at that flag. Isn't she a beauty?"

Slowly, I raise my eyes. Civilians are unfurling Dovetail's banner from the ceiling: a silver-and-red bird on black fabric. Silver represents the Moon, black the empty space surrounding it, red the blood shed by the Committee. I hook my thumbs together and spread my fingers over my heart, pride filling me up. My little sister, Anka, whose name means "phoenix," created the banner design.

A majority of the Dovetail company will stay here to strengthen our hold—mostly new recruits and their superiors. Alex, Yinha, and I board the one Omnibus bound for home. The Dovetail leadership needs us there, and my family needs me. Or is it the other way around? The longer this war drags on, the more I depend on them to help me feel something again, especially after battle. To dissipate the numbness. I keep them safe, and they keep me human.

4

THE OFFICERS' DECK OF THE OMNIBUS BUZZES with conversation. Across the aisle from me, Yinha speaks with Rose, who's traveling home with us to the Free Radical to advance Dovetail's espionage efforts. Yinha's stopped taking notes; with a half-smile, she listens to Rose's soft voice and watches her slim white hands gesticulate. Rose uses them often when she talks, more than compensating for her legs' stillness.

Yinha's never looked so . . . *okay* after a battle. Perhaps it's Rose's hacking pedigree, the fact that she and Singularity recruits like her give us an edge against the Committee. Or maybe it's something else. If Rose can make Yinha smile despite recent bloodshed, then she deserves a place among us.

Nearer the flight deck, clustered in a ring of seats, several Dovetail officers send rapid-fire updates to our leaders on the Free Radical. We've captured the most important loyalist leader, Hopper Gamma. Some lesser ones have fled to Bases I, II, III, and V. An amazing victory, but we'd be foolish to dwell on it, lest the Committee take back lost ground while we're distracted. Already, the Dovetail leaders are discussing our next moves.

More battle. More death. The thought of killing again sickens me.

Suddenly, I am not only alone but also devastatingly lonely.

Seeking someone—anyone—for company, I cross the narrow, low-ceilinged room, applying little downward force on the floor so that in moon-grav I don't bounce too high and hit my head. Two-thirds of the ceiling's lights are off to save hydrogen fuel. Alex sits alone in a dark corner, next to a window. Through it is dark, unknowable, unending space; Mars, a small dot, flashes rusty red amidst the blackness.

Alex is applying black dye from a narrow cylindrical object to a stack of bound paper: the ancient Earthbound writing method. His hands and feet are too big for his body, making him look clumsy when he's not fighting. He's tall, but he looks shorter sitting down because of his disproportionately long legs. He crosses them, one foot bouncing up and down.

To avoid annoying him, I sit down a meter away without saying a word.

"You know, Dove Girl." Alex doesn't lift his eyes from his work. "I write with pen and paper to repel snooping eyes, not attract them."

From the inflections in his voice, I know Alex is trying to amuse me. With rebels and loyalist hackers engaged in a snooping war, non-digital records are more secure than handscreen and HeRP files. Information about strategy, about leaders, soldiers, and their families—that is, information about anyone—has become more valuable than drinkable water, and both sides know it. Even though we have cut off Base IV from the Committee's network, knocked out all their cameras, and put up multiple firewalls, Dovetail still encrypts every communication, of which there are few. Ninety-nine percent of our discussions happen face-to-face.

"What disruptive things are you putting in there?" I mean to tease Alex, but my voice sounds morbid. The Committee punishes the crime of "disruptive print" with quarantine, imprisonment, heavy fines, and execution by laser fire, as I learned a year and a half ago. After my mother penned Dovetail's manifesto and got caught, I had to watch the government destroy her life one step at a time—and was powerless to stop it.

"I'm recording how it feels to fight." Alex sounds downcast as well. "Sights, sounds, smells—and emotions. The conflicts beneath our skin, the ones Journalists leave out of articles, because they're 'subjective' or too difficult to wrap up in words. I'll give you an example. Medium hate feels hot, but intense hate feels cold. Did you know that?"

I'd rather avoid such emotions altogether. But, like anyone, I fail. Often.

"There's gotta be someone you hate with all your atoms and more," Alex says. "Even you, Dove Girl."

Especially me. I medium-hate the Committee members, the General, Corporal Cressida Psi for tormenting my family; my head heats up when I think of them, so much that I can almost hear gray matter sizzling in my skull. But at the same time, I understand their reasons for doing what they did. In some sick way, I even empathize. They love order; they think the only way to preserve it is by holding power over countless individuals. They're evil, but they truly believe they're working for the common good.

The only person who turns me frigid with hate is the *thing* who seduced Wes's sister, Murray; killed his teammate; and convinced Wes's father to send me on a suicide mission after old secrets came to light. Then, because he couldn't have me ruin his perfect reputation on the Moon, he decided to destroy me—and nearly succeeded, luring me into the Committee's clutches under the guise of helping my brother. Remembering Lazarus Penny numbs my conscience with frostbite; hate twists my features at the mere thought. Were he around, I might slide a dagger between his ribs and not feel a thing.

Alex scoots away from me, holding his hands up in self-defense. "You see what I mean? As soon as you remembered your little devil, you went from peace 'n' hearts Dove Girl to the scariest ice queen I ever saw."

"'My' little devil is your philosopher of a former teammate." My voice is a monotone; my tongue refuses to utter his name aloud.

Alex snorts. "Lazarus, a philosopher? He spends too much time admiring his own face to have any left for navel-gazing." Then Alex's face turns serious again. "He's had a hard life, Phaet. No one taught him what love is. Not even his parents. He fled to Saint Oda looking for it—showed up covered in scars both on his skin and beneath it. But he left their abuse far too late. All he wants is to come down on the right side of history, with the Committee, and he confuses that wish for being loved by the world."

I look away, and Alex stops talking. It's too strange to think of Lazarus as starved for love, as having longings of his own. My ears seem to reject any sympathetic words for the charming snake who betrayed me and everyone I care about. *Who has he gotten in with now?* I wonder, my heart thumping with anxiety. The Committee, most likely, but he could also be hiding on a Dovetail base . . . or even on Earth.

"I understand your hypothesis about temperature dependence on hate intensity," I snap at Alex. "We can move on."

"Nerd," Alex mutters.

"Recording feelings still seems . . . unnecessary. To me."

"Even for posterity?" Alex blows on the ink to dry it and snaps his notebook shut. "Ariel Phi's a Lunar like you, yet he thinks it's worthwhile." These past few months, Umbriel's twin brother and Alex have spent hours talking in their free time. Probably about abstract, impractical issues like these.

"Someday I'll write a story that'll transport people into our minds and souls," Alex continues. "They'll live as we live by reading my words. Nitty-gritty details don't have to be true, but the feelings do."

I blink at him, wondering how anyone could think of posterity when day-to-day survival is so uncertain.

"Planning gives me something to live for." Alex crosses his long legs on the bench. A stray beam of sunlight sneaks in through a window, highlighting every pinch in his facial muscles. "City's gone, family's dead. You still have a brother and a sister, Phaet, so you don't know how dry and empty life is once they've wiped all your blood off the face of the Earth. Every last drop."

I wince, aching for him. When Pacifia and the Militia jointly invaded Saint Oda nine months ago, the Pacifian army murdered Alex's family. They surrounded their grain and vegetable farm, spraying fire onto the crops at the edge, and then moved in and killed survivors.

I remember those flaming fields. I took the smoke into my lungs.

And I hate that Alex's suffering makes me feel fortunate. Will the guilt ever leave? Even if I saw the Odans settled again, and safe, I'd know that innocents—including Alex's entire family—died due to my oversights.

"I'll tell you a secret, Dove Girl. Before I met you, I hated you. The Lunar castaway who brought the wrath of the Committee and Pacifia down on Saint Oda? I thought it was typical selfish demon behavior, and I was going to write you off forever."

"I've been wondering why you didn't," I whisper.

Alex shrugs. "You were an idiot, not a fiend. And on top of that,

Wes cares about you, and he doesn't care about just anybody."

Wes . . . I must've meant something to him when we trained in Militia, laughed together while drunk on the stars above, traversed the Earth's wide ocean, shared a kiss that tasted like smoke. But half a year has passed, and we've had more important things to do than reminisce, especially when remembering is so painful.

"Wes is the only person I have left," Alex says. "My Astrophysics friends—and don't tell this to Rose—they're amazing, but they mostly just helped pass the time. They don't *know* me; I couldn't *let* them know me. Not like Wes. If he wanted me to help you out, by God, that's what I've got to do."

Part of me wants to change the subject, to forget Wes, at least for the time being. Another part—the masochistic part—enjoys this conversation. It proves that Wes is real, not some golden being my brain conjured up.

"I wish we could hear from him," I say. "Even if it was computer code saying he's all right."

"He'd probably write us in zeroes and ones," Alex says, a small smile on his mouth. "Using binary just to mess with our heads."

"Or to show off," I agree, remembering Wes's technical brilliance and occasionally irritating jokes.

Dovetail has discontinued communication with him. The loyalists had infiltrated the Odan Earth-Moon communication system and could use anything we said as a weapon. It was for everyone's good, but to me, it felt like sawing off an arm. Maybe he experienced the pain too, but we had to hide it. We had no choice.

"I worry all the time that he'll bite it before I see him again," Alex says, face serious. "Makes me almost want to die first, be the first to find peace."

I nod, knowing the feeling.

"It gives me a real fright, every time the thought crosses my mind. I can't go on, having one person to care about, because when he's gone, what'll keep me here? But after I write this thing, the people who read it will become *my* people, and I won't be alone anymore."

Alex looks out the window, squinting into the sun. When he turns to me, the sarcastic mask is back. He adds with a yawn, "Then again, there's that nap I want to take for the rest of today."

As if on cue, his eyelids droop.

Reaching across him, I lower the window shade so that he doesn't dream of fire.

5

WE STEP OUT INTO THE FREE RADICAL'S
arched white hallways, and the Dovetailer onslaught begins—the
calling of names, the frenzied gesturing, the waves of bodies surging into our ranks. A pageant of muted colors mixes with the soldiers' uniforms. The civilians' once-vibrant robes are tattered and
faded, but the unguarded joy on their faces is as bright as anything
I've seen.

They embrace family members and friends, eyes damp with
tears of relief. As I scan the crowd for my own loved ones, I narrowly dodge the palm-sized, hand-stitched Dovetail flags they
wave. They don't need to apologize for making a ruckus or worry
about saying or doing the wrong thing—not anymore. Seeing
them smile and hearing them shout make me feel like everything
we've endured together—the pain and sickness and death—was
worthwhile.

After what happened three months ago, it feels strange to see
people's faces at all. Militia snuck an aerosol bomb into the Omega
apartment complex's air filters. When it exploded, mutated anthrax spores flew everywhere, infecting hundreds, killing forty-six,
and necessitating Omega's complete isolation. Everyone became
feverish with either disease or fear, donning Medical face masks
to avoid breathing in the spores. The quarantine has worked, but

paranoia lingers. People have only recently started gathering in groups again. I still dream about the swollen scarlet lesions on the victims' skin, their wheezing breaths, their robes soaked with sweat from stratospheric fevers. My adrenaline spikes when I see dust motes floating under the lights.

The stream of memories halts when a round-faced, black-haired girl—taller than she used to be—leaps from the crowd to hug me.

"You made it!" Anka's skinny arms squeeze all the air out of my lungs, but I'm so grateful to feel them around me again. Every time I return from combat, they tell me that I'm home. Really home.

A second set of arms enfolds us both.

"You're probably sick of us tackling you," Umbriel says. "But this whole seeing-you-alive thing? It never gets old."

He pulls back, careful not to touch me for too long. After I told him about Wes, our friendship has remained steady, but we tiptoe confusedly around certain things.

"You'd quickly get sick of the alternative," I say.

He snorts at the morbid joke.

"Don't say that, Phaet," says a quieter voice. My brother stands two meters away, jostled by the people brushing by. His shoulders are hiked up to his ears, and he doesn't meet my eyes. I feel rotten for not having noticed him at first, but these days, I have trouble recognizing him. He hunches over like an arthritic man, and without his trademark big, crooked-toothed grin stretching his mouth, his face seems like someone else's.

I unbuckle my weapons belt and give it to Umbriel before approaching Cygnus. When I hug him—carefully—he curls up tighter around himself.

"S-sorry," he stammers. "It's crazy out here. Anka said I could stay in the apartment—"

"I said you *should*—" my sister says.

"—but I wanted to see you. Took a calculated risk. Anyway, welcome back."

He cracks a shy but toothy smile, and I rejoice inside like I do whenever something brings his old self to mind.

My family and I walk into the Atrium. The towering wall screens that once displayed flashing propaganda are now blank. We've razed the concave security mirrors, which reminded us that our every move was being watched, and done away with the wall cameras. To add color to the bleak dome, Dovetail has hung posters with messages referring to ongoing shortages, like SHOW TROOPS YOU CARE; EAT ONLY YOUR SHARE. Other posters display the silver-and-red dove that Anka designed, now as ubiquitous as the Committee's six-star emblem used to be.

"Phaet! Phaet, over here!" A tall, thirty-something man in a white lab coat waves, one arm flailing high above people's heads. His usually slick side-parted hair is ruffled, and the tips of his large ears are reddish from exertion. A mask covers the lower half of his heart-shaped face, leaving only his dark brown eyes visible. Eyes that frantically dart around every few seconds, searching for someone that's not here. "Have you seen my sister? Is she—"

"Yinha's safe, Bai," I say. "She's reporting inventory in Defense, but she should come out soon."

Bai Rho expels a breath that I suspect he's held all day and collapses against a pillar. He looks as exhausted as if he'd been in battle himself, but I know he's been working on his biodefense project in his Nanoengineering lab. "Yinha's perfectly capable, but every time she goes on a mission, I lose it."

"We all do," Umbriel says, squeezing Bai's shoulder. His black eyes dart to me, and there's anger in them—perhaps at the thought that I've just gotten back from hurting people. Possibly killing them. He confronted me about it as soon as I joined Militia a year and a half ago, and we haven't quite resolved the issue.

Bai goes on. "And it's gotten worse since Ida—" Her name hangs in the air like smog. The skin around Bai's eyes tightens with pain, and his mind seems to jam. *Since the anthrax attack*, I think, my heart aching for him. Ida Omega, Bai's partner, was one of the forty-six who didn't make it.

Ida. I almost see her, a tall, square-jawed woman in a lab coat, her long brown hair gathered in a messy ponytail. I suspect Bai never takes off his mask because it lets him hold on to her.

Umbriel drops his hand.

"Well, that's all in the past," Bai says. "I'm going to find Yinha now. But before I forget—can you, Phaet and Umbriel, meet in the greenhouses tomorrow morning, roundabouts 7:00? Before the base-wide assembly? Asterion and my assistants will be there too."

"The greenhouses?" Umbriel says.

"I've got . . ." He glances at the pulsing crowd. The average Dovetailer won't know about his project until completion. It's safer that way. "Something to show all of you. Something promising."

Umbriel turns to me, and we nod at each other.

"A way to make the plants produce twice as much food?" Anka says. She laughs, but there's a hungry glint in her eye.

"If only defying mass and energy conservation were my specialty." Bai turns to me and Umbriel. "But you won't be disappointed."

Saying good-bye to us with brisk hugs, Bai shuffles off toward Defense to search for his younger sister. Each step raises his pant leg hem, allowing a peep of plastic prosthetic ankle.

"Guy's gonna wear himself out," Anka says, watching Bai go.

"Running around all day, inventing stuff all night."

I glance at our brother, who's standing in the spot Bai vacated. He leans against the pillar, oblivious to our conversation. Cygnus's mind frequently leaves his body these days, wandering off to somewhere only he knows.

I look back at my sister, at her piercing but worried eyes. "Bai needs that, Anka."

Many people do. To avoid the pain until the world lets them feel it in peace.

6

UMBRIEL'S LONG, THIN FINGERS HAVE NEVER worked more carefully, not while cultivating plants, not even while thieving. The things he was picking then couldn't kill him on contact. Hands shielded by elbow-length latex gloves, he coaxes scarlet jequirity seeds from brown pods, which hang from vines that crawl all over Greenhouse 17's floor. The elliptical seeds, each about the size of my pinky toenail, have a black spot at one end that looks like an evil eye.

If we can find a way to use abrin, the poison in the seeds, to target bacteria like anthrax, it could stop another mass killing. Abrin would enter bacterial cells and paralyze the organisms until they die. But the poison doesn't discriminate. Ingesting three milligrams—or "migs," as Bai and his assistants say—can kill an adult human. I once napped near a jequirity patch; within a few hours, I was too woozy to realize it could do me in. Asterion Epsilon pulled me away and saved my life.

To prevent contact with or inhalation of the toxin, Umbriel wears a full face mask and bulky insulation suit. Despite the danger, I'd rather see him in this than the Dovetail military getup, which he'll practically live in after he finishes training next month. Asterion—who works several rows away in his own protective suit—cajoled me into wearing orange nylon coveralls and a face mask that covers my nose and mouth too.

A renowned Chemist before he became a freedom fighter, Asterion is developing ways to synthesize abrin in the lab so that we no longer have to extract it from plants. Bai, an engineer, works on distributing it.

"Sometimes I wonder if harvesting this stuff is worth it, Phaet." The mask muffles Umbriel's deep voice. His left hand twitches, as if he wants to cover his handscreen's audio receptors. That's unnecessary now. The Committee's eavesdropping ceased as soon as Dovetail set up a firewall, which requires a full-time team of ex-InfoTech workers to maintain. "What if it gives more people rashes during harvesting than it saves after a bio-attack?"

"We need to defend ourselves," I say, shuddering. "We can't have another Omega."

Umbriel sighs. "Right. If we do, we'll run out of penicillin."

Since Dovetail lacked a cure for the mutated anthrax bacterium, we put the victims on the antibiotic and hoped for the best. The forty-six died because our best wasn't enough.

"The Committee might try another disease next time," I say.

"Yeah," Umbriel says. "Did you hear the new report from the Graveyard?"

He means Base III, the site of the Moon's major uranium deposits, where many adults work in mines or refineries and die young of radiation sickness. "Came in earlier today. We've got to look out for botulinum *and* drug-resistant *E. coli* now."

I wince, picturing the ravages of those diseases from images in my Earthbound Studies textbooks. Drooping eyelids, open sores, lumpy rashes, fevers . . .

The first set of greenhouse doors slide open with a *whoosh*, and Bai Rho enters the holding cell. He rolls his eyes impatiently as robotic arms zip him into the protective suit that we're all wearing. When it's done, he reaches into his pocket, cups his nitrile-gloved hands around something precious, and rushes into the greenhouse. There's more haste than usual in his limping gait, and his goggles strap has one kink in it, like a Möbius strip. "Thanks so much for coming, everyone. The 3-D printer finally coughed up exact replicas."

When he's focused, Bai's sharp voice carries as much authority as Yinha's. Umbriel and I share an excited look before wading through the jequirity vines toward him. Asterion's already there. The eagerness that lights up our leader's gold-tinged eyes doesn't disguise the fact that his bronze skin looks sallow and his graying hair has receded. Still, his face hasn't lost the friendly, fatherly roundness that gained him Dovetail's trust in the first place.

Five other Harvesters and two more Chemists join our cluster. We all lean over Bai's outstretched hand, looking through the digital magnifying glass he's holding. It's set to one thousand times magnification.

Several dozen tiny objects nest in his palm, each smaller than a dust mote. For a second, I think they're the bodies of insects, but on second glance I see they're more streamlined and have a strange reddish-brown tint. Each has two pairs of wings and a long, snout-like tube. They're made of copper, a metal unaffected by the ceilings' grav-magnets.

"Each nanodrone carries a small fraction of the three-mig lethal dose of abrin," Bai rattles off. "They'll spray it through these tubes. The toxins in one spray will kill a pocket of infectious agents, and nothing bigger, so they can't harm us. Each drone holds three doses. The design team couldn't pack in any more without sacrificing aerial buoyancy."

The Harvesters nod slowly, their foreheads wrinkled in concentration. I'm still acclimating to Bai's frenetic intellectual energy. He taught me how to operate the machinery in Nanoengineering, so that I could cut up the solar sail and attach the mirrored fragments to my uniform. He coached me and looked over my shoulder as I used the laser knife, keeping one hand on the emergency Off switch in case the tool skidded in my hand.

Back then—before the anthrax attack, before he put on his mask—I remember thinking that he looked young for someone in his mid-thirties, and I couldn't help but find him attractive in a brainy sort of way. Those thoughts still cross my mind. Then I see Bai's ever-present mask, remember Ida's death, and feel guilty about it all.

"Couldn't you increase the abrin concentration so that one drone would kill off more than three bacteria colonies?" I ask.

Asterion shakes his head. "We can't increase the concentration, or the abrin starts precipitating as a solid."

"And we can't make the drones any bigger, or they might damage equipment and lose accuracy . . ." Bai trails off. "At least we got the batteries working. Miss Phaet, you're a fan of plants, right? The drone batteries are like tiny photosynthesizers, using light as energy."

Hearing Bai talk about his work—and relate it to my humble education—reinvigorates my admiration. It makes me want to *be* him. He became an engineer after an accident that took him out of Militia, and quickly became head of his own research group. Most members stayed with him when he joined Dovetail. Before I dropped out of Primary to enlist in Militia, I'd hoped to do something similar, but in the Bioengineering Department.

I've probably gone starry-eyed. *Snap out of it,* I tell myself.

But Bai's not paying attention to me. He's facing Asterion and speaking more quickly than before. Something dark creeps into his voice, and the rest of us lean away, sensing tension in the air.

"The drones are almost ready, Asterion. I mean it this time. We should begin mass production soon. Who knows when the Committee might sneak more diseases onto Dovetail territory?"

"It's unlikely to happen soon," Asterion says. "They need to regroup from their losses on the Singularity, and we don't have enough copper to—"

"We didn't think an attack was likely the last time either," Bai says, his eyes narrowing above his mask.

"This base wasn't verging on starvation last time." Asterion holds his ground. "I'm sorry, Bai, but Dovetail can only deal with one crisis at a time."

"They can't catch us unprepared again. I won't let them." Bai closes his eyes, thinking hard, and then speaks in a quiet, threatening voice. "Why am I so much more concerned about biodefense than you? I've got less left to lose."

Asterion seems to choke on whatever he's about to say and exhales, looking overwhelmed. He raises a gloved hand to rub his temples but remembers that he's handled jequirity and drops it. "Let's talk about it later today. After the assembly."

Dovetail's leader turns to me. "You and I need to leave for the briefing, Phaet. Andromeda's already waiting."

I'm still not used to people asking me to go places instead of receiving summons from the Committee via handscreen.

"Bye for now, Phaet." Umbriel raises his gloved hand to touch my shoulder, but snatches it away when I shake my head at him. "You've been around these killer plants long enough for one day."

I give him a smile, a bittersweet one. Maybe he wishes I were working next to him in the greenhouses like I used to. I miss those times too, but we can't erase my new duties as Mira Theta's heir, as the Girl Sage.

Something has to change. Biodefense drones full of lethal poison? Scrounging for food on other bases? What has Dovetail come to? Have the leaders ruled out all other options for winning this war? Battles, one after the other, have occupied my mind, blotting out the big picture. Despite our small victories, the Committee's violent acts are draining us of hope.

Dovetail needs a big idea, a new paradigm for fighting the war. And I, the Girl Sage, the one who gave them courage to revolt in the first place, have to give it to them. Picking my way through the rough terrain, I start running possibilities—big, crazy ideas—through my mind.

"See you later, Phaet," Bai calls, waving. "Asterion, I'll come by your office this afternoon." It's a statement, not a question.

"Apologies in advance if there's a line," Asterion says, leading me toward the exit.

I glance once more at Bai, then at Umbriel, as we leave, both of them in white face masks. For a brief, frightening moment, I can't picture what they look like underneath.

7

CYGNUS FITS ANOTHER HANDSCREEN TETRIS
block into place, seemingly oblivious to the crowd assembling below us on the Atrium's ground floor. In a few moments, I'll have
to leave him here with Anka and move down one row to sit with
the half a dozen Dovetail leaders in the center of the second-floor
balcony.

My brother has preferred Tetris to chess ever since we pried
him out of the Committee's clutches. In handscreen chess, when
pieces are taken, they disappear from the board with a tiny *zap*.
Not a healthy thing to hear if you still relive the big zaps the Committee gave you. Anka and I live day by day, observing what keeps
him tranquil and what makes him withdraw—or worse. Even
though we know he hates crowds, we had no choice but to bring
him here and hope for the best. We've learned not to leave Cygnus
alone, with no one to turn to.

I say good-bye by squeezing his shoulder, eliciting a quick shrug
and a brisk "See ya." Then I scoot forward, into my assigned seat
in the spotlight.

Once there, I survey the assembly below us, the churning mass
of bodies. Only half the ceiling lights are switched on to conserve
solar energy; the Committee's severed the Free Radical from the

Moon-wide power grid, and we've yet to hook up our system to the Singularity's.

Facing the masses, Dovetail's major players sit all in a row: Asterion, our leader; Andromeda, his second-in-command; Sol Eta, who oversees public relations; Yinha Rho, director of our armed forces; and now Rose from the Singularity, at the end of the leaders' balcony.

Then there's me, the teenage Girl Sage. Sometimes, appearing in public with the others makes me feel like I'm filling in for my mother, that small, secretive word-spinner. In my mind, she stands taller than her followers. She started this movement, and we have no choice but to see it through to its conclusion: freedom. Although I'm the youngest by a decade and a half, I *will* speak out if needed. I've done it before.

The other children of the revolution, some older than I, have been placed in less visible locations. Chitra Epsilon, Asterion's seventeen-year-old daughter and a newly minted soldier, sits behind her father. Looking weary from today's battle, she has a bronze-skinned face full of angles, hair shaved close to her scalp, and wary amber eyes—so unlike her sister Vinasa, one of my first friends in Militia. If not for the spaceship accident that stole her life, Vinasa would be here now. And Chitra might not look so terrified.

Twenty-year-old Callisto Chi also sits behind her mother. Andromeda had the sense not to place her near my family. The transition from Committee darling to a rebel hated by her peers hasn't treated Callisto kindly. Over the past year, her brown-blonde ringlets have become a frizzy beehive and her predatory stride has slowed to a shuffle. Even her sneer has vanished, giving way to a dull mask of professionalism; I wonder what she does all day, since Dovetail barred her from military service. Umbriel thinks the restraints on her have broken her mean streak, but I'm not so sure. If Andromeda hadn't revealed herself to be a Dovetail member, Callisto would still be fighting for the Committee alongside her hulking boyfriend, Jupiter, trying to finish me off at every opportunity.

Shuddering at the thought, I turn my attention back to Andromeda Chi, otherwise known as Lady A. Unlike her daughter, who crosses her arms and pretends to ignore her mother, Andromeda appears more alive than ever, thanks to the mask of cosmetics she applies before public appearances. Full-figured and red-cheeked, Andromeda illuminates the Atrium, filling her role as "mother of the rebellion." Maybe it helps make up for her strained relationship with her own child.

While the public's gaze seems to suit Andromeda best, it's Asterion who must speak. Although Asterion seems comfortable in the greenhouses—*settled*, even—he gets shifty and nervous during his public addresses. Though he was a renowned Chemistry principal investigator for decades, carrying the hopes of tens of thousands on his shoulders has taken some getting used to.

". . . even with the addition of manpower and equipment from Base VI," he says now, a sweat stain forming on his lower back, spreading across his robes, "we cannot recover from our losses. Half the Committee's troops are down on Earth, fighting alongside Pacifian soldiers to recolonize the planet. However, because we've taken Base VI, the Committee will likely order Militia back to the Moon in droves."

My ears pick up concerned shuffling and murmuring from the motley crowd. Many people combine colors in their outfits—Phi green pants with a Kappa ultraviolet tunic, for instance. It's part fashion statement, part necessity. After the Free Radical's secession, clothing production ground to a halt, food production fell, and all resources went to Dovetail's army. Despite the fact that they voted for this redistribution, the civilians have grown grumpy and thin from rationing.

At least it'll be easier to pack everyone into hiding spots if the loyalists invade. I keep nasty jokes like this to myself, even though they'd make my friends laugh.

"We need more soldiers, more hackers, more weapons. Any resources you can spare, any skills you can lend us . . ."

Dovetailers have heard some variant on this speech time and time again, so they're only half listening. People mill around the huge collection bins on the Atrium's far side, dropping off scrap plastic, discarded rubber, and fruit and vegetable rinds for composting. In the dome's center, Nash and several other soldiers run a draft booth for the Dovetail armed forces—as I predicted and feared, because of today's losses, we lowered the minimum age to fifteen.

The volunteers enlist first. Boys and girls queue up behind the booth, tugging their frowning parents along. They're fifteen, like Cygnus. Children. When I enlisted in Militia at that age, people thought me insane. But insanity has become the new normal.

". . . the Singularity can't provide us with additional food and water."

"Mr. Asterion reminds me of the beggars in Shelter," Anka whispers behind me, "asking for help from people who can't even help themselves."

My sister's right. Dovetail needs aid, but this base is tapped out, and the Singularity won't help either, not when our friends on the Far Side are even hungrier than we are. We can no longer rely on any part of the Moon for manpower or raw materials, which leaves planet Earth. And with approximately half of Earth fighting for the Committee . . .

That's it. Battery Bay is our only hope.

You have to tell them, I think. Asterion has always valued my input more than the other leaders. He's the only one who feels like a friend.

". . . I am so sorry to decrease the water ration again," he's saying now, "to three liters per person per day . . ."

Angry murmurs arise from below, and hundreds of faces droop in disillusionment. Before I can change my mind, I stand on shaking legs, one hand raised. Sol Eta taps Asterion's shoulder and points to me. Although I refuse to look down, I know that thousands of eyes are watching my every move.

Asterion pauses his pleading speech and turns my way. My heart flutters in my throat. Here goes everything. "We need an Earthbound ally. Soon."

Below us, the crowd stops churning. Asterion slowly takes a seat.

"We've tried that." Sol speaks dismissively into the microphone, her low, powerful voice belying her small size. "As you and everyone else know."

Since we freed her from Committee imprisonment, her golden hair has grown out into a jagged pixie cut that highlights her square jaw and glinting eyes. Like Andromeda, Sol thrives when people are watching her. Given her life under Committee rule, this ease makes sense. When she worked in Journalism with Mom, Sol appeared on Committee-sponsored newscasts every other night.

"I mean, literally, that we need to travel to Earth and *get* a city to help us," I clarify. "Sending message after message, as we've been doing, is useless. Dovetailers need to fly in, bringing goodwill by the shipload, or they'll keep ignoring us."

Across the floor, brows furrow and eyes blink in confusion.

"The Earthbound are . . . different." I describe how the Batterer Parliament met in person, even though their elaborate video technology would've allowed them to communicate remotely. Then there were the Odans, who didn't even allow electronics in the public sphere. "To them, digital communication indicates a lack of dedication. Yes, our hackers might've had to work hard to ensure secure delivery, but the Earthbound think it was an insult, like we couldn't be bothered to meet with them in person."

Asterion rubs his chin, considering my words. "Who do you propose should go on this . . . this hypothetical mission?"

"You or Lady A," I say. "Yinha. One or two more fighters. And me."

There's a hush. Behind me, Anka looks up, frowning. Even Cygnus has furrowed his brow. *You're leaving?* their eyes seem to say. *Again?*

Sol wrinkles her nose and breaks the silence. "We'd endanger you and other high-level personnel in a mission that might net us nothing."

Rose pipes up. "Um. We should also estimate the energy it would take to facilitate the alliance. Literal energy from transporting payloads from Earth to here."

She speaks into an old security pod, which amplifies her voice. The audio experts must have sent them out to enable discussion. Instead of chucking the Committee's spying devices into orbit as the ruling body has done with its trash for decades, Dovetail reprogrammed the pods to perform administrative tasks.

I shift my weight, my legs like gelatin. "We can't keep starving ourselves and sending younger and younger children off to fight. My mother started Dovetail to give Lunars a better life, and this is not it!"

Hundreds of heads nod in agreement.

But some people speak against the idea, saying that the Earthbound are too unpredictable, or else too weak, to help us.

Frightened chatter fills the Atrium; Asterion, Andromeda, and Sol murmur among themselves. Sol fears nuclear attacks and the disorder arising from splitting the leadership; Asterion and Andromeda see no other choice. Two for three out of the leaders, but I need to convince the masses.

"Have you ever met an Earthbound?" My question catches the audience's attention, and the noise dies down. "I've met many. Yes, they are different from us. And they are different from one another."

I search the front of the crowd until I catch Alex's eye. Although the Dovetail leadership knows he's from Saint Oda, we haven't told the public for fear of backlash. "But they want the Committee gone as much as we do, maybe more, and if they add their might to ours, we'll have the fighting capacity to follow through."

I fold myself back into my seat, drained. The crowd's babble starts up again, and I hear a frustrated, girlish sigh behind me. Glancing back, I watch Anka study the huge Dovetail banner hanging from the Atrium's opposite wall. I can almost see the red-and-silver reflected in her eyes.

"You want to leave again," she says. "This time you have friends on Earth waiting for you."

She's right. If Dovetail sends an envoy to Battery Bay, I'll see a host of familiar faces. That city shelters the hundreds of Odan refugees—including Murray Carlyle, Nanna Zeffie, Emberley, Jubilee. And Wes. The happiness rising up in me seems to have no place amidst my feelings of anxiety and frustration.

The Dovetail leaders' circle breaks open, and this time Asterion speaks: "Lady A and I support a Batterer alliance, but I defer to all of you: let us vote on the matter."

A wave of whispers passes through the crowd. Referendum votes have happened before, as when we decided to attack the Singularity. Without the use of our handscreens, aside from offline games and word processing applications, Dovetail members vote by raising their hands.

First, those who don't support seeking Batterer help vote. Shaking with nervousness, I keep my hand firmly in my lap as about half the people raise theirs. Scattered individuals glance my way, looking unsure, and put their hands back down. Security pods buzz around the Atrium, getting the tally. One thousand five hundred and ninety-three people vote no, including Sol Eta. In the audience, Umbriel Phi's hand shoots up, and his twin Ariel's follows. It feels like betrayal, them voting against my idea, but I know they've got reasons for doing so.

Two hundred and thirty-seven people abstain, Atlas Phi, the twins' father, among them. His skin hangs more loosely around the bones of his face now, and his hair is grayer than mine.

As for the yes votes? One thousand eight hundred and thirty. Among the Dovetail leaders, Andromeda, Asterion, and Yinha support seeking an alliance. As do I. My triumphant hand trembles in the air, shaking with happiness that I shouldn't logically feel.

Soon, several other leaders and I will travel through Committee-controlled space to a war-torn Earth so that we can plead with a hostile nation . . . and I absolutely can't wait.

Somewhere on Battery Bay are scores of Odan refugees, people who took me in as one of their own, believing I was a runaway Pacifian slave. People who are homeless now because I kept the truth from them. The prospect of facing them as the Lunar I am assuages some of my lingering guilt, but it doesn't make me feel like smiling.

But I'll see Wes again. The moments I've played over and over in my mind—against my better judgment—can't sustain me anymore. Does he remember the reckless joy that overtook us when we kissed, and the gut-wrenching sorrow when it ended?

Maybe he doesn't want to remember. The most practical, Wes-like move would be to forget, as I've tried and failed to do. This is wartime, and we're soldiers. I'd be a fool to take a kiss as a promise.

Yet, in spite of my doubts, I look down at my cold, empty hands and hope that they won't stay that way much longer.

8

I SCORE ANOTHER SIDE KICK ON UMBRIEL'S abdomen, knocking his center of gravity backward. The scratched and yellowed foam mat breaks his fall. As he gathers his long legs under him, he leaves a slick of sweat on the spongy material.

"Close off your fighting stance—turn more to the side," I say, wiping sweat off my own forehead. "Otherwise, your vitals are wide open."

Frustration sharpens my words. Fear, too, for what would happen if he were facing, say, Jupiter Alpha or another Beater. He and his brother survived their first battle—the Committee's most recent attempt at invading the Free Radical last month—but because I asked Yinha to have mercy on them, they were stationed far from the front lines.

I can't keep asking her to play favorites.

"Don't drop your fists, Umbriel!" I say, ducking a cross punch. "Keep them up by your face."

With each piece of advice I dole out, I remind myself of Wes, except that I'm more awkward and less funny. A year and a half ago, in this training dome, he was the fighter everyone tried to imitate. Now, it's me, and I wish he were here to help.

Umbriel drops his head, puts his hands on his knees. "I don't ever want to take someone down for real," he says.

He's still upset about the draft, about the fact that he'll have to fight loyalists no matter what. "Umbriel," I say, "at this rate, you won't even be able to defend yourself, let alone do any damage."

"Damage," Umbriel scoffs. "As if they were things, not people."

Other new recruits, spread across the floor executing exercises with and without weapons, sneak glances when they think I'm not looking. Since the new ones are training under time pressure with an irregular schedule, there are gaping holes in their abilities, and they spend hours in open workouts like this trying to fill them. Better to find weaknesses and correct them than die from them in battle.

The training dome has become my old Militia classmates' favorite haunt: near the dome's center, Nash leads two dozen trainees in a plyometric workout, forcing them to squat, lunge, jump, and touch the floor in quick succession. Near the climbing wall, Orion watches more advanced recruits hold up their laser blasters for minutes at a time to develop steady aim. High in the bleachers, Callisto Chi surveys the scene like a sniper, her pimpled face cupped in her hands, her narrow eyebrows pulled close together.

When Umbriel is steady on his feet and willing to fight, I return my attention to him. My body, my opponent's body, and nothing else. He engages me with a slide forward, a fake, and a cross punch, one I duck and counter with an upward elbow strike that grazes his chin. Now that I've closed in, I use my shorter limbs to put him on the defensive. We spar for another minute or so—I always lose track of time when I fight someone—before I hook my foot behind his leg and knock him off balance again.

"Give me a break, Captain," Umbriel says. By mentioning my old Militia rank, he's doing more than teasing me. He's reminding me of the violent soldier I became . . . of the soldier I still am.

But then he bends over again, hands on knees, eliciting a worried look from Anka. My sister perches low on the bleachers, sharpening dagger after identical dagger with a file. Although I find it unnerving for a thirteen-year-old girl to play with knives, she's gotten good at wielding them. Cygnus flinches at the mere sight of blades, so he's turned to the side, one foot tucked under his bum, reading something on his handscreen. No, not reading. Staring at it.

"Maybe my brother will finally score on you when you get back from Earth, Phaet," Ariel calls from his corner of the mat. After tripping him one too many times in our last match, I parked him there to practice footwork.

"Speaking of Earth . . . why'd you two vote no?" I ask.

Ariel slides forward, steps to the side, and slides back, teetering as though he'll fall over if someone so much as breathes on him. "Too much history between us and the Earthbound," he says. All his Primary studying under the Committee has left its mark. "Assuming your mission succeeds and you bring some Batterers up here, the culture clashes will drive both sides insane."

Umbriel tries to surprise me with a roundhouse kick, but I counter it by sliding close to him and jabbing him in the chest.

"I didn't even think that far ahead," he says, massaging the area where I've hit. "On the trip down, the loyalists will turn space into a shooting range. If something takes out you and Andromeda, will Dovetail still function? Never mind *us*." He gestures at himself, Ariel, my siblings. "Plus"—he lowers his voice—"I know you have your own reasons for risking your life to get down there."

Wes. I can't deny that.

"Umbriel, if Dovetail has to, we'll find people who can lead." Anka examines the razor-edged blade of a dagger, admiring her handiwork. "We found people after Mom, and we'll keep doing it if Phaet . . . you know."

"That's a horrible thing to say, Anka," Ariel scolds. But I disagree. Though they sting, Anka's words ring with the practicality of preparing for the worst: me, as Alex would say, biting it.

"Don't tell me what to say," Anka snaps. "I've got forty kids running war supply bins to give *you* decent weapons, and you just sit around, bored to death, whenever you're not in this smelly gym or blabbing to Alex Huxley."

"Seriously, Anka?" Ariel says, his cheeks turning emergency-light red. "Would *you* rather be fighting?"

Umbriel walks to his brother and takes a fighting stance, right foot behind the left, body turned to the side to minimize the surface area facing his opponent. "Come on, Ariel. Time to put all that shuffling practice to work."

"But . . ." I start to protest. Ariel's less advanced than his brother, and fighting Umbriel could reinforce his bad technique.

"He's sick of losing to you," Ariel jokes, golden-brown eyes lighting up when he smiles. He takes a fighting stance, his hips almost squared to Umbriel, and Anka observes the twins with a scowl.

Biting hard on my lip, I watch the two of them trade blows. Although they have the same long limbs and intimidating height, Umbriel is more comfortable in his gangly body, easily ducking his brother's clumsy punches. As if he fears losing his balance, Ariel hardly tries to kick.

Back in the old days, Ariel filled his time with studying and secretarial duties in the Law Department, while Umbriel worked officially in Agriculture and unofficially as a thief. Their different interests show in their fighting. I silence my urge to interrupt whenever one of them—usually Ariel—makes a mistake that could be fatal in real combat. Frankly, it happens every few seconds.

Behind me, I hear the shuffle of footsteps and the whisper of someone's breath.

"How does it feel, showing these boys what 'training' really means?" The voice is full of sweetness but not sincerity.

Callisto. She must have stepped down from the bleachers when Umbriel and I were sparring. Stiffening, I turn to her and look into her acne-scarred face. I'd rather avoid acknowledging her existence. But experience has taught me never to let her out of my sight lest she literally stab me in the back.

"I could get these beanpoles in shape while you're away," she says, glancing at the twins. "Make sure their first deployment isn't a one-way trip."

The boys pause their sparring match to give me anxious looks, but I shake my head and gesture for them to keep practicing. Then I face Callisto again, wishing some green recruit would accidentally barrel into her and take her out of earshot. She must want something; otherwise, she wouldn't have approached me after months of ignoring my existence.

"What are you doing here?" I say.

"Taking time off from work." Surveying the floor, Callisto plants her fists on her hips like a conqueror, but the gesture seems grandiose. Her yellowish tunic and trousers match—a rare sight these days—but they're too big, and parts are stained brownish, giving the unfortunate impression of a bruised banana. "The training dome's a good place for remembering better days."

I imagine she's reminiscing about our Militia training, when she and Jupiter Alpha placed consistently near the top, until Wes and I overpowered them. When she still frightened people. Maybe she sees the invisible trophies of past victories in this place.

Me? I only see what's changed. Dovetail recruits, slogging through drills or thrashing in simulated combat, have replaced neat rows of Militia trainees executing burpees and jumping jacks.

How can we send these novices off to fight the Committee's lethal Beaters?

"Phaet," Callisto says, and I'm surprised by her honest, even-toned pronunciation of my name. She doesn't spit it out like a fish bone, the way she used to, or call me names. "Take care of my mom on Earth. Okay?"

Protecting Andromeda is my duty, which makes Callisto's request redundant. But there's a hint of longing, of brokenness, in that word, *Earth*, and it makes me curious.

"There's one open seat in the Destroyer," I point out. Andromeda, Yinha, Alex, and I will go to Earth together; we wanted to take as few people as possible in case anything goes wrong. "Why didn't you ask for it?"

Callisto snorts. "Like grits the leaders would say yes. They don't trust me, and they won't let me prove that they *can* trust me."

"How so?"

"Equipment inventory reports, every single day. That's all I'm good for now. If I get the numbers right, I've done my job. If I get them wrong, fuses forbid, they'll think the Committee stole our stuff—with my help." She sighs, pausing to let her frustration impress itself on me. The corners of her mouth pull downward, and sadness clouds her eyes, sadness that a stranger who doesn't know better might think was real.

"But they're wrong to doubt me." Anger rumbles beneath the smooth surface of her voice, and I remind myself not to take it as a threat. She can't hurt me—not here, not now. "I can't go back to the Committee, not after they almost killed me for being my mother's daughter."

Like they almost killed *me*. She doesn't point out the parallel between our lives, but we both know it's there. She's probably manipulating me—for what, I don't know—but pity for her creeps into my heart, pity I don't know what to do with.

"Why are you complaining to *me*?"

"Because you're the only one who's guaranteed to listen."

The back of my neck prickles. My former archenemy knows me well. Girl Sage. Dovetailers don't call me that for nothing. I guess my habit of observing events before participating in them gives off the impression of wisdom.

"Jupiter," I say. "What about him?"

"He's tried to contact me. Bribed a guard to deliver handwritten messages. I didn't want to read them, so I turned that guard in."

I raise one eyebrow. In Militia, Jupiter and Callisto were so in love, walking around Defense with their arms around each other, staring into each other's eyes for what seemed like minutes at a time. Things I can't imagine doing with anyone in public. Even Wes.

"I picked my side in this war, and I'll avoid anything that could make me regret that." Callisto watches my face, perhaps searching for sympathy. I put up the usual wall. "Sorry. I didn't mean to talk so much. But you heard me out." She pauses. "Thank you."

Behind us, Ariel blocks a punch from Umbriel and returns it with a growl—but misses. I notice Alex standing to the side, coaching Ariel, and Ariel's mouth tightens in concentration. Although a love of words and history unites the two, Alex seems to intimidate Ariel. Or at least put him on edge.

Alex calls a time-out. The twins wipe their sweaty foreheads on their sleeves, nod to my siblings, and, Alex in tow, head out the training dome doors. Since Dovetail's shut off the plumbing to Defense, they must go to Market to pick up their precious water rations.

"Speaking of listening, here comes someone who *doesn't* . . ." Callisto's gaze drifts sideways, and she gives something in her field of vision the stink-eye—Sol. "I should get back to staring at spreadsheets. You keep it together now, Phact."

Taking leave with a bow of the head, she sidles across the training floor in the opposite direction. I'm left with a feeling of something unfinished: she didn't ask me to improve her standing in Dovetail. But she didn't have to—I gave her what she was after, without meaning to, and I feel sorry for her when I realize what it was.

Attention.

9

SOL ETA'S BLONDE HEAD DRAWS MANY EYES
as she strides toward me and my family. In her clean orange robes,
she's a flare in a sea of sweat and grime. Following Sol like a bright
comet tail, lavender robes fanning out behind her, is Rose.

The name Sol calls out surprises me. "Cygnus!"

My abdomen clenches.

Anka scoots to her left so that she's sitting in front of Cygnus,
shielding him with her much smaller body.

Sol halts in front my siblings and takes a seat across from Cygnus. He continues staring at his handscreen as if she's not there.

"Listen up, kid." Her eyes are cobalt blue, without a hint of any
other color. "This is Rose, our new arrival. Dovetail's putting her in
charge of a huge hacking task, and I'm putting her in charge of you."

Cygnus blinks at the two women, and then jabs his thumb sideways at Sol. "She's allowed to do that?"

I swallow my confusion and look Sol in the eye. "You're in charge
of public relations," I say. "This isn't within your jurisdiction."

"But it is." Sol's smile is white, perfectly symmetrical. "Since
Cygnus's return from Base I, he hasn't contributed to the war effort.
Dovetailers may wonder why we risked so much to extract him if
we're not putting his abilities to use."

"Because I'm a *person*." Cygnus's legs tense, as if he's ready to run should Sol attempt to punish him for talking back. "And my sisters didn't want me to die."

"Or keep getting abused by higher powers," Anka says sarcastically. She means the Committee—and people like Sol.

Sol purses her thin lips. "If Cygnus won't work with Rose, he'll be drafted with the others his age to begin basic training next month."

Cygnus's eyes clench shut, and he shakes his head. Wearing a sorrowful expression, Rose looks between my brother and the door from which she and Sol entered.

"He must have medical exemption," I say. Cygnus's draft slip, and the accompanying weapons-intensive training, might as well be a ticket to a psych ward. If we could afford to run psych wards. I don't let myself imagine what would happen to him in battle.

"Dovetail's amputees are going back out to fight as soon as they learn to walk again," Sol points out. A smug smile stretches her mouth. "We don't have enough people. Period. *No one* can sit out anymore, Girl Sage. So let's discuss Cygnus's assignment."

I bite my lip to hold back a frustrated cry, while my sister fumes in silence. Not even Anka can come up with a biting retort against Sol now.

"Um, hi, Cygnus." Rose tucks a strand of platinum hair behind her ear and laughs awkwardly. Her soothing voice diffuses some of the tension. "I was a Cybersecurity Officer in the Singularity's Astrophysics Department until yesterday morning, and now I'm . . . what was it, Ms. Sol?"

"Dovetail's Director of Strategic Intelligence," Sol says tersely. "Rose will lead hackers in accessing Committee communications and seizing their digitally controlled weaponry."

"Yeah," Rose says. "Tunneling through cyberspace to control real space."

My brother edges away on the bench, gaze shifting from one woman to the other. "What does that have to do with me?"

"Well, we're under pressure from Committee hacks, and you'd . . ." Rose squirms, then throws up her hands and turns to Sol. "I said I could use another pair of coding hands, but I didn't expect them to be attached to . . . Sol, look at him. I can't ask him to . . . This isn't right."

"This is necessary, Rose." Sol crosses her arms. "You will find a way to work with him."

They want him to hack again? After what happened the last time? My brother broke into the Committee's most secure systems; in return, they beat him, captured him, and subjected him to months of unspeakable torture. He hasn't touched a HeRP since his return. Although he won't get captured again under Dovetail's protection— at least, I hope not—I know Cygnus may relive his experience, over and over, if he tries to crack a single loyalist network.

"Leave my brother out of your cyber war, Ms. Sol," Anka says through her teeth, threatening in her anger.

"He's sacrificed enough," I add lamely.

Sol clicks her tongue. "Don't you understand, Phaet? Cygnus *needs* to do this. Because of you."

Taken aback, I wait for her to continue.

"You and Ms. Andromeda, Yinha, and Alex will cruise toward Earth in your Destroyer—through the orbital paths of nine hundred forty-six Committee-controlled weapons and fifty-seven macro satellites that could track you or crash into you. Now, Rose, what does that mean?"

Though I wouldn't have thought it possible, Rose's skin blanches even whiter. "Well . . . we'll need to digitally control as many of those objects as possible. To know where they are, if the loyalists are altering trajectories, if there's spyware involved."

"Phaet, your mission means that Cygnus needs to do this. It's for *you*." Satisfied, Sol turns to my brother, knowing that she's cornered me and made *me* seem like the demanding one. Maybe she's punishing me for today's base-wide meeting, for advancing an agenda with which she disagreed. "Now, Cygnus, what if you could save your sister's life out there?"

My brother pulls his knees into his chest and rocks back and forth on his sit bones. "I . . . I don't know," he says. "I don't know if I can do it. I haven't gone near a HeRP since . . . since Phaet and Umbriel pulled me home."

Sol tries to organize her features into a comforting expression, but her flared nostrils give away her impatience. "We all need to contribute," she repeats.

"I *know*," Cygnus snaps. "You don't think I feel like grit sitting around, not hacking or fighting or even *composting*? Believe me, I fight the Committee every day, but in here." He raps his temple with a fist.

Rose's left hand flutters up to cover her heart.

Sol clears her throat. "Let's look into different medications for you."

Anka and I simultaneously shoot glares at her. We've heard Cygnus screaming in the night, seen him leap back from electrical sparks no matter their source, and felt his mind and heart leave the room and travel far, far away at the slightest provocation.

"Ms. Sol, I don't think it works like that," Rose says.

"Yeah," Cygnus says, twisting his hands together in his lap. "It doesn't."

Sol frowns; I hope we've embarrassed her. Her next words prove me wrong. "My apologies, Cygnus. But these are orders. Find a way to take them."

"Fine." Cygnus's eyes meet mine, and I detect a spark through the fog. "I'll try. But to protect Phaet. Not because *you* told me to."

My little brother's words fill me with love. I'd worried that the Committee had sucked his sweetness away, but it's still there, buried inside him.

"Good." Sol rises and brushes imaginary dirt off her orange robes. "Rose, he's all yours. I expect a progress report early next week." She turns her back to us and high-steps her way through a cluster of troops straining through push-up drills.

Rose shakes her head as she watches Sol go. Then her hand reaches deep into her pocket and pulls out a spotless red apple the size of a toddler's fist.

"Cygnus, this isn't a banana—I heard you love those—but I thought you might like it." She offers the tiny apple to my brother, and my vision loses its angry red tinge. Cygnus's assignment might open up old wounds, but Rose won't rub salt into them.

"Thanks," Cygnus says. Once his eyes would've gone round at the sight of whole fruit, a luxury item. Now they remain unfocused, fixed on past horrors only he can see.

※ — ※ — ※

When we sit down to Theta-and-Phi dinners nowadays, three people are missing: Mom, who's dead; Umbriel and Ariel's mom, who betrayed us all; and Cygnus's old self, who shows little sign of returning.

We eat in the Phis' white-walled apartment, which was my siblings' and my second home growing up. The meager decorations— a digital photo frame here, a wooden cube sculpture there—are gone, since Atlas swiftly donated them all to the war effort. Even the table has been recycled into weapons or ship parts; we sit on the cold linoleum floor, cross-legged.

At least the meals are shorter now, simply because there's less food, so we have less time to take in the pain of it all. Anka and Umbriel have cooked up some oat porridge using a blend of precious seasonings that Mom came up with, but it just doesn't taste good in mush form, and Anka tends to overcook things to kill off all the bacteria that are living in them. At least the mush is a bit spicy: Umbriel snuck into the defunct Culinary Department's pantry, found cinnamon sticks at the bottom of a cabinet, and smuggled them home. He hasn't lost his thieving impulse, nor his need to take care of us.

Atlas used to cook when we were children; now he just eats, his hand tiredly spooning food into his mouth. A former Law counselor, he's all but useless now, and does manual labor in the Defense Department. Like his father, Ariel looks . . . bored, which is pretty much his expression whenever he's not talking to me or Alex. We once competed with each other for the top spots in Primary rankings, but while my mental energy is focused on strategizing, he can only train and train—a mindless pursuit.

As long as I've known him, Ariel never had interest in making food, and it's sad to watch him become so listless. Cygnus, who's sitting with one foot under his bum, has lost all of his passion for eating—even bananas—and I'm too busy to pick up so much as a spatula. That leaves Anka and Umbriel. I'd never expected my baby sister and best friend to take care of us all.

Anka slurps down the last of her food and sets her bowl on the floor. She took only the dregs of the pot, arguing that she doesn't burn as much energy training as me or the twins.

I suddenly feel guilty about my own sizeable portion, which I've almost finished, and about the fact that Anka's taken on Mom's role of providing, of sacrifice.

Cygnus's spoon stops halfway to his mouth. He slides his bowl sideways so that it's in front of our sister, wipes his lips on his sleeve, and says, "Thanks for fighting for me today."

Then he clumsily climbs to his feet, long legs unfolding like an egret's, and walks down the hall, presumably to be alone in one of the bedrooms.

Tears filling her eyes, my sister leans her head on my shoulder. Umbriel reaches across the circle for her hand, and Ariel pats his brother on the back. With Cygnus taking awful new orders, me running off to Earth, and all of us afraid of the future, there's not much to say. But that's okay.

The conversation is gone, but the love remains.

10

THE NEXT DAY, WE'RE OFF, AND EVERYTHING
starts out well.

Then, several kilometers above the Free Radical, the decoy ship
explodes.

Dovetail has sent two unmanned Destroyers ahead of us into
space to distract the Committee's patrol ships, which hover dis-
tantly above our home base. One of the enemy's missiles has just
blown a Destroyer apart, sending parts spinning into space.

Shrapnel from the blast sinks into our Destroyer's hull. As the
carbon fiber knits itself back together, I suck in a breath; Dovetail
has lost yet another vessel from our dwindling fleet.

"Rats." Rose's voice crackles in the intercom. We're approaching the altitude where the radio signal will get cut off, and I dread
the moment when we'll no longer hear her. "That one's our fault;
we should've seen the Committee missile coming."

In the background, Rose's coworkers raise their voices; I catch
the words "Theta kid" and "junk on his HeRP."

Cygnus. My mind leaves the ship and fixates on my brother.
Has he had a nervous episode on the job, putting our ship at risk?
Worry rolls through me, then anger. Not at Cygnus, but at Sol for
forcing him back into hacking.

"Hold on, Destroyer," Rose says to us over her team's bickering. "I'm having personnel issues." She cuts the connection.

"Phaet," Yinha says. "I'm sorry about Cygnus, about—"

"Steer," I tell Yinha, more harshly than I'd intended. She shouldn't be distracted by my family's problems, and Rose better come back on soon—we'll be vulnerable until she does. I'm sitting copilot, adjusting Yinha's flight path to avoid lasers and missiles. Behind me, Alex mans the right wing weapons. Andromeda sits to his left. She doesn't speak—our hectic journey seems to have subdued her—but she occasionally works buttons and levers, contributing everything she remembers from her long-ago Militia training.

"All done arguing. For now." Rose's sweet voice sounds not a moment too soon, but it's shrill now. Just how bad were the "personnel issues"? And how did Cygnus react to people's criticisms? "Yinha, there's a trio of warheads coming up at eighty-nine meters per second—Committee controls these, so watch out!"

At Yinha's hands, our craft dodges one, two, then three nuclear warheads careening in orbit around the Moon. I shiver when I see them. The long, narrow capsules serve as a constant reminder that the Committee could destroy an entire base or Earthbound city at their leisure.

"Now there's a satellite approaching from behind, one you could use as shelter. It's ours." Rose's voice grows fainter as the radio signal fades. In less than a minute, we'll be on our own.

"The Terrestar— there she goes!" Alex shouts. "Get behind her!"

We beeline for a battered-looking satellite a few hundred meters away—an Earthbound relic sent up during the twenty-first century to map the Moon. Dysfunctional but left in orbit, its two cross-shaped aggregations of solar panels connected to a prism. Loyalist ships shoot at us and miss.

Taking shelter behind the Terrestar, we follow its lopsided orbital path and gain a huge lead on our pursuers. The loyalist fleet's shots either burn or shatter the solar cells; with no friction to slow them, the photovoltaic glass fragments zoom away. As we begin to detach, Alex launches our largest missile at the Terrestar. It rips off an entire section of solar panels and pushes it toward our enemy. The loyalist ships turn tail and flee in different directions as the Moon's gravity catches the solar panel chunk, pulling it downward. But one doesn't fly away fast enough; within seconds, the Terrestar fragment crashes into the regolith far beneath us, taking the loyalist Destroyer with it.

"Really cool aim, Alex," Yinha says.

"My aim can't be cool, because I'm a hotshot," Alex mutters.

Yinha groans. "Your puns burn my ears every time."

Rose's throaty laughter echoes in our headsets—and then the radio signal fades into a *zzzz* sound. Andromeda tsks, berating Alex in her regal way to take the flight more seriously. But I exhale for a long time. If Alex is still . . . Alex, that means we're okay.

Peeking at the rearview feed every few minutes, I watch my home base shrink behind us until it's a patch of white bumps clustered against a crater wall. Most of the people who need me are there, on the Moon. But not all of them.

We've made it past most of the Committee's satellites, which can detect Moon-Earth communications. "It's safe to tell the Batterers we're coming," I say. "And the sooner, the better. We don't want to enter their airspace only to have them think we're attacking."

Alex begins fiddling with the communications system dashboard. "I'm setting this up to connect with the Batterer Diplomacy Ministry. I'd better have the right frequency."

"If you're not able to reach the Batterers, we could always fly a white sheet behind us," Yinha says, only half kidding.

Alex takes his hand off the dial and turns to Andromeda. "Fire away."

"To our friends on Battery Bay," Andromeda begins, "we are approaching your city from space on a lone Lunar Destroyer ship. The four of us come in peace. Although we fly a repurposed Militia vehicle, we represent the Lunar fighters who are struggling to free the Moon from the Committee's despotism. We, ambassadors from Operation Dovetail, wish to land on your noble soil and engage in diplomacy."

The Batterers' quick response strikes dread into our hearts. *"Thank you for your message,"* says a flat female voice. *"We will return your communication as soon as possible."*

Great. It's automated. My hands tremble on the controls.

"The Diplomacy Ministry must be overrun with other tasks," Andromeda grumbles.

"Have a little hope, Lady A," Alex says. "The Batterers might not have heard us, but if the Sanctuarists intercepted the signal and know we're coming, it'll be a jolly day down there. Maybe even for Wes's bullheaded dad."

Yinha scoffs. "Interception? That's pretty unlikely. Even if they hear our message, how will they protect us from the Batterers' homeland defense?"

"Er . . . They'll convince the military not to kill us before we land," Alex says. "But I can't guarantee we won't get arrested. Or manhandled."

"That doesn't sound so bad," Andromeda says, with an awkward burst of laughter. *I didn't know Lady A had a sense of humor.* "Each of us has already been arrested or manhandled, even me. We'll just have to take our chances."

I repress a shudder. On my last visit to Battery Bay, soldiers handcuffed Wes and me, and marched us to the Diplomacy Minister himself for questioning. They thought I was lying about my Odan citizenship and nearly threw me overboard. *What'll they do when they find out I'm a Lunar after all?*

Before I can imagine too many ugly scenarios, we meet the resistance of the Earth's upper atmosphere. Here, the air is thin and scalding hot—it can't sustain life, just like the Moon's surface. But even this place contrasts with the cold, rocky world we come from. As the Moon fades into a pale silver circle behind our ship, I wonder how long I'll be suspended between these two worlds.

But are the Earth and Moon really that separate? Are they two worlds, or one? Increasingly, Lunar problems are Earthbound problems. Dovetailers and Odans, we are all victims of the same tyrants. One world, indeed, the Earth and its natural satellite. Like trees on opposite edges of a forest, people living on both celestial bodies are tangled up with one another in spite of the kilometers between us. Like my family and Wes, taking up space in the most guarded part of my heart.

11

"IT'S ALMOST AS SHINY AS I REMEMBER," ALEX says from behind me. "When I snuck onto Battery Bay and lifted off, the lights burned holes through my eyes."

"But it's so lovely," Andromeda says.

From up here, Battery Bay looks like some supernatural being's glittering thumbprint, bright against the otherwise black Sea of Japan. The scarlet sun peeks out above the horizon. The mobile metropolis's glow is patchier than before—some of the city's structures were damaged during last year's clash with Pacifia near Saint Oda, and others must have been hit more recently. According to our reports, two months ago, Battery Bay began waging war against its nemesis's Asian land-based allies.

I guide the Destroyer downward, letting wind currents carry us sideways to save fuel. Yinha's entrusted me with steering, claiming she needs "a break." In my peripheral vision, I see her hand picking at a loose string on her glove. She's avoided Earth for over a decade. Now it's rushing up to meet her.

The craft slows when I open the wing flaps. *Get the landing gear out now and head for the runways by the tip of the oval,* I imagine Wes's voice saying. I must stay methodical despite my mounting anxiety and excitement at seeing him again—at finding out if he's still with us, if he's still the same.

Did he or another Sanctuarist intercept our message? Are they looking out for us? Or will the Batterers think we're a Committee-allied ship trying to bomb them?

Now we're flying parallel to the ocean waves, toward the city's eastern tip. The sky grows redder, and we project a bright white peace sign into the clouds with our headlights. *The Batterers can't miss that*, I tell myself.

Yinha opens a parachute behind us. When it catches on air, we all pitch forward in our seats, sliding unstoppably towards the white light cutting through the windshield.

✴ — ✴ — ✴

Flanked by a club-shaped Batterer aircraft on either side, our Destroyer meets the tarmac with two head-lolling bounces. I fire our front thrusters so that the forward-moving exhaust will slow us. Many moments after we've stopped, my pulse still pounds in my fingertips.

"Do not open your hatch!" someone shouts.

Batterer soldiers in teal-and-gold uniforms cluster around; the officer in charge, who must have given the orders, is a pointy-chinned man small enough to pass as a ten-year-old. When about twenty of his troops have formed two rings around the Destroyer, he shouts, "Evacuate your ship! These are orders from the Battery Bay Coastwatch!"

Andromeda fearlessly clambers out of the hatch, and the others follow. Keeping my head down to hide my face, I walk with them into the fragrant, somehow brittle autumn air. The first pinkish rays of morning sun, whole and nurturing, surround my body. A breeze picks up a stray yellow ginkgo leaf; it flutters over my shoes like a broken-winged butterfly.

The entire inner circle of Batterer soldiers has their handguns raised. Heart rate surging, I try to ignore what's in my peripheral vision: no less than three muzzles pointed at my head alone.

"Names and documentation!" the officer barks.

They didn't get our message, I think, my heart sinking. *And that silly peace sign wasn't enough.*

Andromeda reaches for her handscreen, but Alex smacks her arms down. "That'll scare the grits out of them, Lady A!" he hisses. Turning to the officer with his hands up, he broadcasts his accented drawl for all to hear. "Alexander Huxley, Andromeda Chi, Yinha Rho, Phaet Theta. We're Lunar outlaws and existential threats to the Standing Committee, you see, so they're not terribly keen on giving us documentation. Put those guns down and you might find us quite charming."

The tiny officer turns to a thin pole of a woman, probably his second-in-command, and whispers rapidly. She whispers back, and he nods.

"You're from Earth, boy," he says. "The Sanctuarists informed us that one of the alleged Lunar rebels would be."

The handgun muzzles droop by a few centimeters, and my anxiety ticks down a notch.

"We saw from your light signals that you 'came in peace,'" the officer says, "but specialists thought it was a ruse."

"Why didn't you engage us in battle, then?" Andromeda asks.

The rings of soldiers open up a meter-wide path, and Battery Bay's Diplomacy Minister Costa advances through the gap. Behind him, two of his aides size us up through their dark sunglasses. Short and pale, Costa wears a tight gold suit that contains rather than covers his fleshy limbs. Instead of hair, a clear fluid that ripples like water sits atop his pink scalp. I never found out if it was a projection or a liquid within a membrane. Does he sleep with it? What about when he wants to go swimming?

Snap out of it. My mind's wandering, just when I need my wits about me.

Once the bizarre-looking Minister reaches us, the Batterer soldiers close the ring again.

"We did not attack because of your Sanctuarist friends, who claimed to detect your incoming message using their rudimentary equipment," Costa says, extending a hand with gold-painted fingernails for Andromeda to shake. She gingerly grasps it, wrestling a frown from her face. In the most formal Lunar introductions, people speak their name aloud so that it shows up on the other person's handscreen, and handshakes in casual settings never last more than half a second.

"But that didn't mean I would let any Lunar ship land on our airstrips." Costa pumps Andromeda's hand up and down, adding his other hand for good measure. "Even if you were supposedly allies. Apologies for the Coastwatch's martial measures."

"No need." Yinha clears her throat and extends her own hand to take the burden off her superior. Still smiling, Costa grabs her hand and wrings it.

"I'm eager to hear how you can contribute to the war effort here," he says.

"With personnel and lots of enthusiasm," Yinha replies.

"Excellent!" exclaims Costa. He lowers his voice; Andromeda and I lean in to hear his next words. "Prime Minister Sear's party— *my* party—has a supermajority in Parliament, and he wants to install a friendlier regime on the Moon. If all party members vote for his agenda, we'll have over half the representatives' votes, and be ready to work with you toward our common goal. The trouble is maintaining party discipline. Each representative's district has a different complaint these days, because of this godforsaken war with Pacifia."

What in the universe does that mean? Yinha and Andromeda seem as confused as I am by Costa's babbling. Nevertheless, he continues down the line. When he reaches me, my befuddlement gives way to paralyzing fear. Heart pounding in my ears, I keep my eyes on my boots and dangle my hand out in front of me.

Costa doesn't take it. "The last time I saw you, you were Odan," he says in a voice too bright and loud to be sincere. Lower, he continues, "Who are you really working for?"

My tongue feels like a slug. I hadn't expected Costa to *rejoice* at seeing me, but I wasn't prepared for an open confrontation before my superiors.

"I . . . I . . ." I stammer, before my vocal cords go still. Then I try again. "I'm Dovetail. And a friend to Saint Oda. They're not mutually exclusive."

I look to my crewmates for support. Andromeda and Yinha fidget, while Alex smirks, giving nothing away.

"I wish I could believe you," Costa says, patting my hand like I'm a child. "But I won't be surprised if you've changed into a Martian at this time tomorrow."

He's joking. I let out the breath I'm holding but wonder if other Batterers will put my deception behind them so easily.

Chuckling, Costa scoots back from me and addresses everyone again. "Before we allow you into the city, we require one more verification—from the Odans themselves. Bring them in."

The Odans? Indeed, five silhouettes are approaching, looking out of place in their loose, homespun clothing. My mind skids, unable to believe it's happening. That *he* could be walking toward me.

The Batterers form two lines again, leaving a narrow aisle for the Odan procession. As I watch them, my cheeks ache from the big, dumb smile on my face. I lower my head to hide it, but then feel silly. I'm not ashamed of how happy I am to see him. He should be the first to know.

The five Odans move closer, and the faraway city glow illuminates their faces: three new, two familiar. The three young Sanctuarists, barely out of boyhood, look terrified. In contrast, Odan Sanctuary Coordinator Carlyle exudes confidence; he draws himself up to his impressive full height, every centimeter of his body alert.

On his left, a smaller figure glides across the tarmac with all the coordinated grace I remember. Rays of sun glance off his coppery hair, dyeing it scarlet.

The Odans study us as intently as we do them, and anticipation makes my entire torso feel like a big, beating heart. I shift my gaze to meet the newcomers' eyes, one by one, until I find a pair like burnished steel. The world around me goes quiet, and so does the racket in my chest. There's only an overwhelming sense of peace.

"It's them, Minister." Wesley Carlyle's voice is as shy and melodious in life as in my memories. He watches me, a small smile playing across his lips. "They're the ones we've been waiting for."

And at once, I'm right where I belong.

※ — ※ — ※

Well, not exactly. There's too much space between us for my liking. Yet he's everywhere to me. My imagination fills in the gap with his woodsy scent, the feel of him in my arms, the eight freckles across his nose that I can't quite see.

Wes is wearing a grin so big his face can hardly contain it and shaking his head in disbelief. I stifle a laugh. *I'm real*, I want to say, *and so are you.*

Wes's father nudges him in the ribs, and Wes glances sidelong at Costa, who's saying something that couldn't possibly be more important than our tacit communication. I force myself to pay attention to the minister's babbling.

". . . Lunars, yes, but Lunar *rebels* . . . I should usher you to Parliament, they'll expect us soon. There will be a closed session, of course, because of security concerns."

Coordinator Carlyle marches forward. "You've arrived in time for—"

Andromeda cuts him off, holding up one hand, palm facing him. "Minister Costa, we'll need accommodations." She glances at the three weary Dovetailers, her face taking on a motherly expression that catches me by surprise. "And food."

Costa forces a smile. "Supplies are low, but allies will receive the best our city has to offer. We'll transport you to the waterfront international hostel—a beautiful house; it serves all our guests—after you formally introduce yourselves to Parliament."

Sensing that our superiors are otherwise occupied, Alex strides over to Wes, comes to a standstill, and punches him hard on the shoulder. Walking forward, I pull a sour face, which Wes doesn't miss. He winces but says nothing to Alex.

"*That* was for bungling your Moon exit, you dimwit." Another punch. "*This* is for putting pressure on the rest of us." Alex stiffly extends his arms for a hug. "And *this* is because I can't help but forgive you."

As they embrace, thumping each other on the back, Alex hoists Wes half a meter into the air and spins him in a circle, as he might a girlfriend. There's an amused snort behind us. It's Yinha, her expression mocking, her arms crossed.

Momentum takes Alex in a jagged trajectory toward me; he plops Wes down on his feet half a meter away. "Now you spin *her* around. Go on, I know you want to."

My cheeks turn into twin hotplates. With Alex towering over us and grinning, I can hardly look at Wes, but my eyes betray me: I sneak a glance. He's rumpling his hair, and perhaps because of his nervousness, it stays rumpled and doesn't fall back into place.

Instead of performing a grand gesture that would catch our superiors' attention, Wes reaches for my hand. His scent has changed, from fresh pine to wood smoke. In running my thumb over his palm, I learn how tough these months have been for him. His skin is dry, the muscles beneath ropy and strong. A hard pebble of skin sits at the base of each finger. And his face . . . it's darker, thinner, more worn. It can't have been easy to defend the Odan refugees on a floating war-city, but he seems to have succeeded so far. And I'm proud of him, proud of every scar he bears.

Our superiors' small circle breaks apart. They're coming for us. Wariness darkens Wesley Sr.'s expression; his son releases my hand. Normally a look like that from the Sanctuary Coordinator— from anyone with power over me—would chill my bones.

Today, though, my joy has left no room for fear.

12

A HOVERCRAFT THE SIZE OF A SMALL WHALE
arrives to spirit us toward the center city, its pill-like outline dark
against the brightening sky. Painted teal with gold stars around the
nose, the vehicle is shaped like a kidney bean and gives the stiff
impression of official importance. We climb inside the open top,
which is made of tinted glass, and take seats on the cushioned U-
shaped bench hugging the vehicle's walls. Wes sits dutifully next to
his father, and I squeeze in between Andromeda and Yinha. The
driver retracts the ceiling over our heads and floats us upward.

En route, we spend less time moving than bobbing amidst
other hovercraft. These vehicles, which range from an eighth to
half the size of ours, span the color spectrum from neon green to
muted gray. The smallest ones roll through the air like tires. Above
us, a hovercraft like a segmented worm parts the air: it's tens of
meters long and packed with people, probably a commuter tram.

Due to the high volume of traffic, my senses have more time
to soak in Battery Bay's sights, sounds, and—yes—smells. Exhaust,
smoke, a hundred cuisines blending together. There's a big, confus-
ing world out there; it's frightening and overwhelming. Part of me
wants to hide from it, but part of me wants to explore every conti-
nent, every island of this mysterious waterlogged planet.

"You hungry?" the driver asks. He's a small, blond man with

a square chin and a prominent nose who speaks in slightly broken English. "Roti in overhead compartments."

"Famished," Yinha says. "Mr. Driver, you have your priorities straight. Thank you." She takes down a huge insulated lunchbox and hands a paper package to each Dovetailer and Batterer. Wes and Alex's Odan comrades sneer a bit at the processed food, so different from their people's homegrown fare, but accept the packages anyway. Wartime turns even the pickiest eaters into omnivores.

When I unwrap my roti—green curry encased in flatbread—a wave of savory and piquant scents overwhelms my nose and fills my mouth with saliva.

"Go on," Wes tells me, biting into his roti with the side of his mouth. "It's not half as spicy as it smells."

But when I chomp down, it's like biting into lava. Green, fibrous lava that tastes like spinach, chicken, garlic, cumin, coriander, and a barrage of other spices I don't know. My eyes tear up, and Wes smiles sheepishly. That smile alone makes my heart seem to sputter.

I'd almost forgotten what a good liar he is. At least this time it was harmless.

After swallowing and swigging water, I find I actually like the curry. Then guilt dulls my appetite. Dovetail hasn't had meat, even the lab-grown stuff, in months. My siblings have probably forgotten what vegetables are. Still, I finish my portion; wasting food would only exacerbate my guilt.

"I'm sorry there so much delay," says the driver.

"I thought you cosmopolitan folk called this time of day 'rush hour,'" Wes points out, wiping his smirking lips with a cloth napkin.

"Wrong name. Everything slow down. Many hovercraft lanes close after Pacifia bombs—this things take long time to fix."

"Mr. Driver, sir," I say, eyes still smarting from the spicy food.

"If there are fuel and food shortages, why are people still behaving like they did before?"

"Eh?" he says.

I repeat my question, more slowly this time.

"*Oh*," the driver says, drawing out the word. "Battery Bay travel more, take more from poorer ally cities, make *them* have shortages. Still, everything more expensive here since the war start. Everything, I tell you."

I polish off my roti and fold up the paper wrapper, looking for a compost bin. Unfortunately, the hovercraft doesn't seem to have one; the Batterers toss their wrappers into a trash chute, and, biting my lip, I imitate them. *Wasteful Earthbound*, I think to myself. The Committee was right about that.

"We are trying to stabilize the economy," Costa says, turning to face Andromeda. "We came here to the Sea of Japan to pick up raw metals for manufacturing; two days from now, we sail to the Philippine Sea. Our land-based allies there will have the crops we need."

"See?" the driver says to us. "When we dock I'll buy overpriced mango."

"At least Parliament funds cover your vehicle's fuel costs," Costa jokes.

The driver nods. "So glad to be Parliament employee. If government stop paying fuel, I stop driving."

Shortages across the Batterer alliance don't bode well for us. I'll need to convince Parliament that Dovetail would make good use of their limited resources—but how? My sense of dread grows as we fly past patches of damaged skyscrapers. Most have missing windows and lean to one side, with several or more floors caved in. The worst look like toothpicks snapped in half. Repair crews buzz around the buildings in hovercraft outfitted with cranes, staying within public no-go zones marked by blinking orange lights.

The traffic jam eases as we fly along the edge of Battery Bay's enormous park, an area of forests and grassy fields several kilometers wide and walled in by skyscrapers. From here, the neighborhoods grow more multifaceted: storefronts with curved architecture, stone statues of women with fish tails and men holding three-pointed spears. The structures at ground level are made of brick, metal, stone, concrete; some have existed for ages, while others seem as if they were constructed yesterday.

At an intersection, a small vehicle painted black and yellow like a wasp cuts us off. The hovercraft driver slams his fist on the center of his steering wheel, causing our vehicle to emit a horrible squealing noise.

"Urban planning geniuses didn't think to make one lane for government only?" Alex's flat tone sounds condescending, but I know he doesn't mean to be haughty. Wes sighs; Costa blinks, unsure what to make of Alex's question.

"You mean . . . Parliament members occupying their own lane? We are not the Lunar Standing Committee. If we didn't live like the rest of our people, how could we govern them?"

I bite my lip to keep from asking more questions. Battery Bay's leaders not only go out in public and battle for one another's votes in Parliament, they sit in air traffic that not even a pigeon could weave through. Would the Committee ever consider putting up with such inconveniences? And after years of living under their iron-fisted rule, does anyone in Dovetail understand what the word *govern* really means anymore?

13

"ABSOLUTELY NOT!"

The Batterer representative stands on a balcony across Parliament's enormous spherical hall. She's dressed in a white pantsuit with an enormous teal flower pinned to her lapel, her orange curls plastered to her scalp with some kind of gel, so that they look like frozen ripples in a magma sea. The indignation in her face makes me regret opening my mouth in pleading speech. I've fed Parliament comprehensive data on our shortages, the anthrax attack, and the deaths of Dovetail's members, but that painful information may yet prove insufficient. *Maybe numbers weren't enough.*

"My fellow members of Parliament," the woman says, "I beg you: do not waste food, fuel, and ammunition on off-world revolutionaries with questionable intentions. Do not succumb to the cries of a child chosen to garner your sympathy."

As the woman's rejection sinks in, the hall wavers before my eyes. Will all of Parliament detect my vulnerability?

A thick metal arm connects Minister Costa's balcony, upon which we stand, to the wall. Right now, it's extended to place us in the room's center. Andromeda sits next to me, Yinha periodically whispers in her ear, and Alex scribbles in his black notebook.

Prime Minister Sear, the head of state, stands behind us, occasionally pacing back and forth. I can almost hear him breathing down our necks. Mine in particular—I feel like he watches me with one eye and the rest of the room with the other. Although he's simply dressed in a dark gray suit, his towering stature and the falcon profile shaved into the side of his head make him stand out. His silken tie gleams like melted gold. Like every representative in the room, Sear sports an accessory that indicates party affiliation; about half wear gold, and the other half wear teal, like the woman who spoke out against me.

The fact that I've been here before doesn't put me at ease. The spherical blue-green hall feels empty without the usual herd of reporters and lobbyists. They were shut out after Parliament called a high-security closed session.

More representatives speak against me, citing Battery Bay's failed mission to democratize the Moon thirty years ago. They don't trust that Dovetail's small revolution will be worth thousands of young lives.

Fifteen minutes ago, during my own speech, how did I not anticipate these arguments and counter them? All my words feel like a waste now. Wes, who leans his elbow on the edge of Costa's balcony, catches my gaze. He rolls his eyes, and I hold back a laugh. My heart doesn't beat faster; it . . . warms up. That alone dissipates some of my frustration and exhaustion. We've stolen several glances at each other since entering Parliament, but I've generally confined him to my peripheral vision. In front of all these people and their cameras, letting my eyes settle on Wes would be akin to printing my feelings on a banner and hanging it from the ceiling. Those feelings belong to us, and us alone.

"The situation's worse up there now compared to when the Battle of Peary took place," one of Sear's aides mutters to her colleague. "And still these representatives don't want to get their hands dirty. I smell party politics, or reelection schemes . . ."

"There might not be Batterers around to reelect them," another aide shoots back.

Across the hall, Representative Harrington of the Mississippi River Delta stands up to speak. He's a balding, pasty man who's dyed the stringy remains of his hair jet black. The faux gold lily pinned to his lapel gives me confidence. Instantly, he deflates it, announcing, "These particular Lunars' intentions might be good, but cooperation on a large scale is impossible."

I hold back a grimace—why would he argue against his own party's agenda? Then I remember what Costa said on the runway when we first arrived: now that the war has expanded, each district has its own goals.

"The Moon's residents are as different from us as the Pacifians. Their thirst for scientific progress has eroded their humanity. They neglect their poor, confining them to inhumane living conditions. To maintain the population, they tell women to have at least one child, but no more than three."

Each of Harrington's points feels like a punch in the gut. Peeking around the hall, I see nods of agreement. The worst Batterer prejudices against Lunars stare us Dovetailers in the face. And we can't argue against them, because they're based on fact.

Andromeda shoots to her feet, looking personally offended. "Those are things Dovetail will change, sir—"

The Batterer man plows on, ignoring her, and she sits back down unsteadily. "They have alien family values—none at all, in fact. Their last names are Greek letters, rendering the family unit unrecognizable. Brother betrays sister; parents keep secrets from children."

Next to me, Andromeda and Yinha bristle. I have to speak again. But would that make things worse? I feel like a child cowering in the dark—nothing like the white-haired girl from the Chinese folktale Yinha told me once. One whose mere appearance struck fear into evildoers' hearts, and whose words drew sympathy from the good.

"Representative—" Sear says. Glancing at our faces, he narrows his hawkish eyes at Harrington. "Representative, enough!"

Harrington sneers back at the Prime Minister. The two men must have clashed for years; I can almost smell the acrimony between them.

"Sear, I could argue for days about the Lunars' degeneracy," Harrington says. "And we're still debating whether to trust them with an *alliance*?"

Despite my exhaustion, part of me roils with grief and rage. There's a furnace buried inside me, and it roars to life every time someone denies someone else's humanity, denies that every life is worthwhile, denies that my parents could have loved me.

"If they cannot even feel *affection*—"

Without thinking, I spring to my feet. "Stop!" I say into the microphone hovering in front of my face. Amazed at my own rudeness, and fearing the consequences, I watch its tiny propellers spin and speak through clenched teeth.

"You've got us all wrong. My parents fought Committee rule, *knowing* they would die for it. Why do something so . . . suicidal? They did it so that my brother, my sister, and I could grow up safe. They did it out of love—first for us, then for everyone who ever suffered under Committee rule."

I take a deep breath and sweep my eyes over the room. "I hope Representative Harrington's views don't represent the entirety of Battery Bay's. Because if they do, Dovetail will not ally with you. You wouldn't deserve it."

The hall goes so quiet that I hear cloth rustling as representatives and their aides shift and squirm. Their beady eyes inspect me for signs of weakness. Across the hall, a tall, brown-skinned aide with bright auburn hair grimaces at me, muttering something into a microphone at his neck. I glare at him until his lips are still. Then he turns sideways so that he's no longer facing me. *That'll show him*, I think with mild satisfaction.

When tension stretches the mood so thin it might snap at any moment, Prime Minister Sear gestures for me to sit down, his dark eyes glinting dangerously. The representatives chatter to each other.

"We should have stopped her, Lady A," Alex whispers to Andromeda. I doubt he means for me to hear. "We can't expect a yes vote now—we can only hope they won't boot us out."

With an electronic system and scoreboard, Parliament votes on whether or not to send troops to the Moon. The room lights up red; the proposition has lost, 490–242. Although Sear supported us, many members of his party must have voted with the opposition. I *know* I'm devastated, but the sensation doesn't register in my body. I see the crestfallen expressions of Andromeda, Yinha, Alex, and, yes, Wes—and imagine the fear on my siblings' faces if they knew how vulnerable this will make them. And yet, I don't feel a thing.

Head held high, I walk behind the Dovetail members as they exit the auditorium. As we're streaming out our balcony's door, Sear grabs my upper arm. Alex notices and tries to turn back, but Sear's Batterer guards restrain him. The lights in the hall are dimming, and the falcon head shaved into Sear's scalp looks more and more as if it'll attack me next. Trying not to panic, I turn my attention to the debate beginning in Parliament—something about hastening the city's departure for the Philippine Sea, since Pacifian allies fill the Sea of Japan and Pacifia itself is approaching from the north.

"Was that story about your parents the truth, or did you lie to us again, *Odan girl?*" His fingers tighten around my arm. "You were an escaped Pacifian engine room slave the last time I saw you."

Panicking, I shake my head.

"Which question does that answer?" His breath smells of basil leaves and red meat. "Last time, our city bent to your will—yours and that boy's."

I squirm, struggling to escape his grip. If he weren't the Prime Minister of Battery Bay, I'd try to kick my way free.

"I'm not done, girl," Sear growls. "I promised Battery Bay to eliminate the Pacifian-Lunar threat, and they will vote me out if I fail. Many of my party's representatives have long hoped to fight the Committee and finally crush Pacifia. We could have formed some kind of alliance today, but it's fallen to pieces. My own party split with me—because of *your* words." He shakes my limp arm, furious about his tenuous grip on political power—like any Committee member. Even though he's an elected official, responsible to millions of citizens, that commonality terrifies me.

"You are permitted to accompany your countrymen to the hovercar," Sear says. "But do not enter the international hostel with them. Find another place to sleep. The hostel, a place of diplomatic goodwill, does not tolerate malicious intentions. Or liars."

He releases my arm, and I back away, restraining myself from rubbing away the pain.

"If the guards see your face there, they will notify me immediately. Get out of Parliament."

From down the hallway, I hear a hovercar's engine revving up. But I'm too shocked to move.

"*Out!*" Sear thunders.

I rush from the hall as if speeding away will erase all that transpired here today. Everything went wrong, and it's nobody's fault but mine.

The same hovercraft that brought us here whisks us away. We're heading to the temporary Odan settlement, where we'll exchange intelligence with Wes's father and the other Sanctuarists. Just what I need—more people who despise me. If I hadn't been so ignorant and selfish last year, they'd still live on their beautiful islands. I led the Lunars and Pacifians right to them. By the time Wes and I finagled a survival plan involving booby traps and a Battery Bay intervention, we could only save the people—not all of them, and not Saint Oda itself—from obliteration.

"Great," Yinha says. "Now we'll have to find Phaet a place to sleep." She looks at me. "Thanks to Sear. Not you."

"He is hothead," the hovercar driver comments under his breath.

"He's punishing you unfairly." Andromeda frowns like a mother whose child has been sent home from Primary. "I have half a mind to tell him all the things you've accomplished—and more."

Her concern surprises me—maybe she's started liking me more since we took off from the Free Radical. Or she's always liked me, but couldn't show it in front of Callisto.

"Don't," Yinha says. "We don't have the leverage to argue with Sear over Phaet's accommodations."

Alex's hand lands heavily on my shoulder. "For your attempt to deal with Parliament, Dove Girl, you can stay with the Odans in the park. I'm sure Wes won't object."

I suck in a breath, embarrassed and nervous at the prospect.

Wes starts glaring out the window, as if the adjacent party bus full of teenagers is annoying him. "Keep insinuating things, Alex, and I *will* object. To you. At a meal. With a bottle of green chili sauce. In your food."

Alex chuckles, and Wes turns to me, smiling despite the threat he just made to his friend. "I'll talk to my father and the rest of them first, so you won't scare them, Phaet."

His words remind me about the events in Parliament, and my burst of happiness ebbs away.

Whatever might happen in the future, today was disastrous, and I made it so. I couldn't slip into my "Girl Sage" persona—words rolled off my tongue before I thought them through. The wrong words. But even if I'd said the right things, would it have made a difference?

14

THE HOVERCRAFT LANDS AT THE PARK'S EDGE.
Wes and Alex disembark and hike toward the Odan camp. I'm sad
to watch Wes go so soon after seeing him again, but I know our
next reunion will happen in a matter of hours.

The sounds of the wood help alleviate my sudden loneliness.
Insects stridulate in their leafy hiding places, their wings' whirring
cycling between soft and loud. Trees twist and tangle together, ob-
scuring our view of the sprawling meadow upon which the Odans
have erected nylon tents provided by the Batterers. Although their
hosts initially offered the refugees accommodation in the international hostel, the Odans refused, preferring to live close to nature. The city has left an astonishing amount of green space unde-
veloped, perhaps to counter their vast carbon emissions. They're
lucky: they didn't have to build an air filtration system, like the
Lunars had to do on every base.

I step outside, into midday sunshine and onto packed soil.
Squinting, Andromeda waves through the door of the hovercraft,
and the driver says they'll be departing soon.

Yinha jumps down and taps my shoulder. "You sure you don't
want to sneak into the hostel?"

"I don't mind it here," I say, shrugging. The hovercraft lifts off,
stirring up leaves and sending shivers through the trees. "I owe the

Odans a visit, in any case. . . ." And then something brushes over my foot, and I scream.

It's a snake, skinny and green. As long as my leg, it has black beady eyes and a forked tongue that makes terrifying hissing noises.

"Phaet, don't move!" Yinha's shaking, bewildered by this Earthbound creature. She's ducked behind a tree in fear. "Stay still—Wes and Alex will be back soon. . . ."

Running footsteps. Someone's coming from deeper in the woods, drawn out by my cry.

"Why be afraid?" says a soft female voice. "That snake's not even poisonous."

A voice I remember very, very well.

※ — ※ — ※

Yinha and I jump. Out of habit, I raise my fists and slide one foot behind the other in a fighting stance; the startled snake slithers away into the shadows. I shield my eyes from the sun with my hand. As my pupils adjust, I make out the outline of a tall figure hiding in the shadow of a pine. She's wearing a dark brown dress that camouflages her body, but her pale face and hands give her away.

"Murray?" I say, as Yinha slinks farther behind the tree.

Murray steps forward, expression unreadable.

"You're back, Fay." Her mouth hints at a smile, but then she frowns, eyes narrowed. "My apologies. *Phaet.*"

I lied to her. To all the Odans. And now they know. Most won't confront me—they're too peaceful for that—but will look at me with a mix of pity and anger. It will hurt just as badly.

"Why aren't you in the camp?" I stammer.

"It's suffocating me." Murray steps out of the shadows. "Everybody knows what I'm doing at every minute. Not at all like home."

I can see Murray's whole body now. She's changed: no small brown nightingale perches on her right shoulder, and she no longer holds herself as if the bird were the center of her universe.

Murray notices me staring. "Lewis flew off during the big fight last year. I don't begrudge him. If I'd had wings, I would've done the same."

Unable to look Murray in the face any longer, I rest my eyes on a streak of grayish-brown fur that nearly blends into the oak tree trunk behind her. An eavesdropping squirrel.

Murray follows my eyes . . . and her gaze lands on Yinha.

She shouldn't have come here.

Murray shrinks from Yinha as if she were a predatory animal. When Murray's hair blows into her field of vision, she pushes it back, hand lingering over the laceration scar on her right eyelid. Her feet begin shifting in a frantic dance. Whether she'll advance or flee remains unclear.

Yinha stares back at Murray, hands up to show they're empty. She steps out from behind the tree and takes one, two slow steps forward. As she approaches, Murray inches backward, into the shelter of the trees.

I reach out to pull Yinha back. But Murray's already tied her down with her gaze.

"Demon soldier," Murray says from the shadows. "*Why?* Why did you come back?"

Her glass shard of a voice cuts the air. Even from here, I see lightning in her one undamaged eye. I brace myself for the explosion. Any second now.

Yinha hangs her head. She's never looked so small, so vulnerable. "So you remember me too."

"How could I forget?" Murray says. "What more do you want from me?"

My mind reaches back to the moment I found out that the soldier who crippled Wes's sister is the same one that trained us in Militia. When I first realized the connection, it tainted my thoughts for days, like formaldehyde in the mind.

Murray's eyes dart about, looking for an escape. "I have to go," she says. Then she spins a hundred eighty degrees and strides into the woods.

＊ — ＊ — ＊

It doesn't take long to catch her—because of her damaged vision, she has to pick her way over roots and brambles with care. Yinha and I call out to her.

We follow Murray until a boulder-lined stream bars her way. Sensing she's trapped, she spins around and presses her back against a mossy rock that stands taller than any of us.

"Tell the demon woman to leave me alone, Fay." Her voice sounds oddly childish. "Please."

"Her name is Yinha, and she tried to help you." If Murray's the child, I have to be the parent.

"Help?" Murray scoffs. "I see half of what everyone else can, and *she's* the reason for it."

I hear Yinha breathing hard behind me.

"If it weren't for Yinha, you wouldn't see or hear or breathe at all," I say. "She knocked you out so her squad wouldn't kill you. Militia could've expelled her for not shooting you dead."

"Shh, Phaet," Yinha says. She edges in front of me—it's not hard, given her small stature. "I messed up, Murray. No excuses.

I've spent eleven years regretting that mission and cooking up what else I could've done to save you. I took myself off active duty and haven't harmed an innocent person since. This . . . is my first time on Earth since it happened."

Rarely have I heard her commander's bark reduced to a whisper. It makes me nervous, as if the ground under my feet is trembling.

Murray's indignant expression doesn't change. "Regret it all you want. That doesn't make it *fair*."

Yinha takes a deep breath and stares right into Murray's eyes. "I know. It'll never be fair. But maybe it will get better." She shakes her head. "I'm sorry. Sorry as I'll ever be about anything."

Murray's angry expression yields to a puzzled one. "When I saw you, I thought you'd come back to kill me. That was my first thought, even though you're with Fay." Yinha shakes her head, speechless. "How silly," Murray continues. "Maybe you hit my head too hard back on Saint Oda."

"I shouldn't have hit you at all," Yinha says. "I'm done hurting you, forever."

"Then why are you here? What more do you want?"

"From you?" Yinha cracks a half-smile, and just like that, my cool Militia instructor is back. "A conversation would be enough."

Without a word, Murray begins walking back into the woods, and we follow. On Saint Oda, I noticed that every time she threatened to boil over with emotion, she took to the rocky footpaths overlooking the sea, hiking for hours until she was calm again.

Here in Battery Bay, it's harder; understory shrubs grow thick and twisted beneath the colorful oak and maple canopy. I recognize witch hazel, with its asymmetric veined leaves, and the globular cones of swamp cedar. Twigs catch on Murray's tangled waist-length hair, but she doesn't seem to notice. She still holds one shoulder lower than the other; Lewis always favored her right side.

Birds chirp around us, but none of their calls sound like his.

The thin path leads under a stone bridge. A stream flowed through here once. When we're gathered underneath, sheltered from the sun, Murray stops walking. *How Lunar of her,* I think. *It's as if she's hiding from the Committee's eavesdroppers.* But the closest she's ever gotten to the Moon is the highest peak on Saint Oda. Her caution comes from years of hiding secrets—but from her watchful parents, not a tyrannical government.

"Your name's Yinha," Murray says. "Am I pronouncing that correctly?"

Yinha leans against the tunnel wall. "Well enough. No one in my family remembers how to say it in the original language. We only speak English on the bases."

"So, Yinha. One would think you'd try to forget me. Why are we speaking?"

Yinha scratches her head, grimacing. Finally, she says, "It's a selfish reason. Believe me, you don't want to hear it."

Murray crosses her arms. "Now I've got to."

Yinha gives her a look that says *you asked for it.* "I was a soldier, and now I train them for a living. I've sent so many killers out into the world."

"And now you want me to say that being a war machine hasn't cost you your soul. Is that it?"

"No. I need to know I'm more to the world than that—a war machine."

Murray rubs her eyes with both hands. The bridge's shadow is deep; I can't tell if she's crying or not.

"Odans love their enemies," I offer. A cliché that I'd heard Odans say again and again.

"*Love?* Mercy will have to suffice." Murray paces back and forth within the confined space, and then stops in front of Yinha.

"You let me live. But I want you to understand what my life has been like."

"That's fair," Yinha says. She swallows nervously.

And so Murray tells us the story of her long recovery from trauma, of finding solace in nature because it never judged her like people did. Of meeting Lazarus Penny and rejoicing that he, this man who'd survived a hellish childhood and become a respected protector of Saint Oda, loved her despite her imperfections, perhaps even because of them. Then he left for the Moon, followed by her brother. And when Lazarus ended things with her, she went through the same pain again, this time alone.

"But I've made sense of Lazarus now," she says as the sun begins to slip through the trees. "Broken people can only love in a broken way."

Yinha's nodding, deep sorrow etched onto her face. And I feel it too.

Soon after, Wes returns for me, saying that I can sleep in the Odan camp. We leave Murray and Yinha and step into the afternoon sun. As we walk away, the leaves crunching under our feet block out the whispers sounding from under the bridge.

15

DISTANT MUSIC, PERCUSSIVE YET MELODIC, wakes me after dark. I'd come to the wooden gazebo after leaving Murray, intending to nap for half an hour, but the day has already gone by.

There's a tiny earthquake in my stomach. Hunger aside, though, I feel excellent. My limbs are floppy, but in a comfortable, well-rested way. I roll onto my back, and the jacket with which some-one has covered me falls to the floor. I rub crumbly rheum off my eyelashes and nearly yell when I see Wes's face hovering over mine.

"Good morning," he says. "But more precisely, it's closer to bedtime."

I sit up, shocked—the Free Radical and Battery Bay are in different time zones, and I've dozed through the afternoon and evening as if they were night, lying on a pile of blankets in an oc-tagonal wooden building with a roof but no walls. The city lights surrounding the unlit park blot out the stars; the full, golden Moon hangs in the sky.

"Is Yinha here too?" I say.

"She kept putting off pickup. The hovercar driver turned in for the night. He'll fly Andromeda here tomorrow so they can talk with my father. The driver's not working until morning—tonight's a holiday for some Batterer cultural groups."

"Speaking of cultures, do your parents know you're . . . with me?" We're alone together, even though I'm underage—something Odan propriety would never allow.

Wes adjusts the legs of his cotton pants. He wears tough Batterer military boots under flowing Odan clothes, and the juxtaposition is striking. Modernity and tradition, war and peace.

"Monitoring my interactions with you has slipped far down my family's list of priorities. In any case, most of the camp is asleep—Odans still rise and set with the sun."

He stands and holds out a hand to help me up. When my palm meets his, a shiver ripples through my torso and down my suddenly watery legs. I dismiss it and pull myself to my feet, squeezing his hand tighter before letting go.

"So we don't have to sneak around," I say. "That's one advantage to being nocturnal."

As soon as the brazen words leave my mouth, I want to take them back. Wes just laughs, and I don't know what to make of it. "Come on, I want to show you something."

We put on wool Odan jackets and knitted hats that flop over the tops of our heads like mushroom caps. Then Wes leads me between two rows of tents. After several seconds, he stops and points to a large green tent lit from within by candlelight. I see two silhouettes inside, heads bowed together, and hear the faint mumble of voices as they whisper to each other.

The shorter figure—Yinha—pats the taller figure's back. Murray's shoulders are hunched. There's austerity between the two women, but also an intimacy that only occurs between total strangers, someone you might never see again.

". . . after he broke off the engagement—through my *brother*, no less—I felt worthless," Murray is saying. "Like God created me by mistake. If Lazarus preferred demon girls to me, was I destined to be alone?"

"He doesn't *prefer* people, Murray, he *uses* them," Yinha says. "But most men aren't like that, I think."

"You think? You don't *know*?"

Yinha's shadow looks downward. "I—well, I mean, most *people* aren't like that."

We've eavesdropped long enough. I'm proud of them—Murray, for confronting her past mistakes and present fears, and Yinha, for trying to understand.

"I didn't think Murray would ever talk to Yinha," I say to Wes. "Or that Yinha would talk too. Let alone talk like this."

Wes beckons, gesturing to me to keep walking. At the edge of the Odans' camp, we turn right and walk onto a field of cut grass, the sharp green blades reflecting moonlight.

"Is this it?" I say. "What you wanted to show me?"

"Patience, sagacious one," Wes teases.

We walk across the lawn, shoes slipping on the moist grass, step onto the street bordering the park and into a cloud of scarlet paper lanterns. Flutes and pipes play atop a background of thumping drums, like a runner's heartbeat. Most of the celebrants look East Asian, like me, but a number of other ethnicities are also present. Children dressed in embroidered silk chase each other through the dense crowd, narrowly missing the food stalls that line the road; each one hawks pungent delights advertised in characters I can't read. Munching on fried goodies, adults turn their faces toward the full Moon. Some even have binoculars.

I see why it catches their interest; I couldn't have drawn a more perfect circle in the sky with a compass.

What's going on? Why has Battery Bay's East Asian population stepped out to gaze up at my homeland—with *happiness* on their faces? The sentiment is infectious; my own mouth curves into a crescent of a smile.

"Seems like they're engaging in moon worship," Wes whispers to me. "A tad ironic, given the Committee's recent tricks."

Trying to orient myself, I turn toward the glass skyscraper at the end of the lane. One façade serves as a video screen, so bright it almost blinds me. Standing dozens of meters tall, a white-faced, red-cheeked woman in a floor-length red dress drinks a magic potion, and begins to rise into the night sky. She flails her wide sleeves and tosses her knee-length black hair, but gravity refuses to pull her back down.

On the ground, a handsome man, presumably her husband, extends both hands upward, as if trying to catch her. Then he takes a bow off his back and shoots arrows, trying to bring his wife back down to Earth, but to no avail. The woman keeps rising until she lands on the pale yellow Moon. There, she folds her hands in her lap and sighs. In front of her, a white rabbit leaps across the foreground.

"*Yao yuebing ma?*" says a childish voice nearby. Startled by the foreign language, I turn away from the light show and look for the speaker.

Standing next to me is an Asian boy with a bowl haircut and a missing front tooth. He reaches into a plastic bag and offers me a round yellow pastry with an intricate flower-petal design on top. Obeying my rumbling belly, I nod. The boy places the cake in my hand and skips away to rejoin his friends.

Several people around us are eating the same kind of cake. I break off half for Wes and take a bite from my portion. The yellow exterior crumbles away on my tongue; sweet red bean paste, like the kind Mom used to make, fills the pastry's interior.

Wes bites into his half with the side of his mouth. The tic is more awkward and endearing than I remembered. His face lights up when he tastes the pastry.

"This holiday makes little sense to me, yet I'm rather enjoying myself," he says.

A tall girl in a red pantsuit approaches us, a huge pink lily pinned onto her short, asymmetrically cut hair. Her smiling lips are coated in dark red pigment. "You're new here, eh?"

"Yeah." I pronounce the word like an Earthbound—*yee-ah*—not *yah*, like a Lunar.

She tips her head back, laughing. Shiny hair swishes around her face. "Visitors are easy to spot, always craning their heads up to see how tall the buildings are."

A hovercar towing a glowing red banner decorated with golden symbols splits the air above us; it blares fast-paced instrumental music featuring a flute-like instrument. Wes and I clap our hands over our ears, and a frightened elderly woman on the street buries her head in her husband's chest. He hugs her close, and they burst into giggles, like children.

The girl laughs again, shaking her head, and turns to me. "Do your folks back home celebrate so . . . bombastically?"

I shrug; I'm not sure what we're celebrating.

The girl blinks at me, confused. "Sorry, I shouldn't have assumed. You . . . look like one of us. Chinese, you know? This is the Moon Festival."

But I'm not one of you. My face heats up in embarrassment, even anger—anger at the Committee. Despite the way I look, I probably have less of China in me than the average Odan. The Committee ensured that by eradicating "ethnic rituals" in the name of "Lunar unity."

The girl points to the Moon. "That's as full as it'll get this year, see? Legend says there's a lonely woman with a pet rabbit trapped up there for eternity, and her husband can only get a glimpse of her tonight."

Wes taps my elbow and shoots me a wicked grin. Embarrassed, I cross my arms and look down at my boots. The girl reads our faces, purses her lips, and diffuses the awkwardness by speaking again. "You know, the story came out of China centuries ago, yeah? The Chinese diaspora all over the world passes it down through the generations."

But I'm not from this world. With a stab of panic, I realize that I've all but given away my Lunar identity. How soon until the girl picks up on the clues?

Wes covers for me. "We're from a small city in northwest Europe. An island," he rattles off. It's only half a lie, and the girl seems to buy it. "This is new to both of us."

I scan the area for an escape route. A couple of stalls over, two flashes of green catch my attention. A man with eyes like spring shoots leans against the counter of an open bar. The red paper lantern light accentuates his unnaturally auburn hair, which I suspect is dyed or a wig. Several young women invite his attention with their eyes, but he approaches only one. Her pale face lit by a tipsy glow, she wears a tight, knee-length gold dress and oversized teal ribbon around her waist. Smooth golden hair encircles her neck like a silk scarf. Gold and teal—the Batterer flag colors, the colors suffusing Parliament Hall. This woman must work for the government.

Could it be? Beckoning Wes, I move toward the green-eyed man, leaving the girl behind us, puzzled. Wes waves a good-bye over his shoulder, thanking her.

By the stand ahead, the green-eyed man orders a bubbling pink drink for the woman and strikes up a conversation. Wes and I duck behind the corner of the bar and peek out from underneath the tent's fabric, training our ears on the exchange.

". . . I got off work, and I heard that Parliament had a closed session, oh?" The man's words come fast and slurred, spoken with a flawless Batterer accent. His familiar voice sounds like warm water running through my fingers. "So much has happened since I ducked into that cubicle this morning."

Lazarus Penny. Why is he on Battery Bay? My heart pounds faster. Roiling blood scalds my veins. Every muscle in me longs to break cover and attack him—if not for Wes's steely grip around my wrist, I'd already have done it.

But I can't let months of hating the traitor strip away my wits. I focus all my attention on the Batterer woman.

"Well, aren't you behind on the news, eh?" she says. "The rest of the hostel's staff couldn't stop talking about how the Moon people landed here on the same day as the Moon Festival. The cleaning staff has been so distracted and sloppy."

"What a pretty coincidence, though all this must befuddle them." Lazarus Penny sweeps a hand over the scene: food frying and spattering oil everywhere, blinding light shows, children chasing each other in circles. *That hand tried to kill me.* "Where in the hostel are they staying? Have you given them a lovely view—or put them on a lower floor to stave off vertigo?"

That ruddy hair . . . Could he have been the aide giving me dirty looks in Parliament this morning? *He knows we're here, he knows we're here—*

The woman giggles. "I couldn't possibly tell you where we've lodged them. Security reasons, of course."

Why does he want our delegation's exact location? Will he attempt to capture us? Kill us? Or is something even bigger on his mind? I slip a dagger into my sleeve. Wes squeezes my hand hard—it's just short of being painful.

"You're still wound up from a long day at the concierge desk," Lazarus says to the woman. "Bartender! A round of *baijiu*, please, for me and the lady."

The woman toys with a strand of hair that's come loose from around her neck. "Oh, you're too much of a gentleman—sorry, your name is . . ."

The right side of Lazarus's mouth pulls up, showing that single sharp canine. "What would you like it to be?"

Winking at him, the violet-haired bartender deposits two glasses of clear liquor on the countertop. The blonde receptionist chugs hers and slams the glass down with an "Ah!"

Lazarus brings his drink close to his face but doesn't sip. His eyes shift across the scene. The woman might think he has a wandering eye that she must tame, but I know that he's watching for threats.

His eyes seem to catch something, and he retreats deeper under the awning. He whispers to the woman, making her laugh, and orders another drink for her. She guzzles it down like the first two. They start whispering again.

What are we missing? Struggling to see and hear, I lean farther out of our hiding place, into the light. I'll need to take a step forward if I'm to—

"Don't!" Wes yanks me back into the shadows.

My dagger falls from my sleeve. Lazarus's green eyes spot it—and narrow. Wariness contorts his face.

I've all but lost us this round.

"What's wrong?" The woman looks in the knife's direction, but her unfocused eyes fail to see it.

Lazarus dumps his drink into a nearby potted plant, puts a

slender hand to his forehead, and straightens to leave. While he's distracted, I grab my dagger back. "The libations are clouding my mind," he mutters, and strides away, just slowly and crookedly enough to pass for a drunk.

The woman gathers her things and stumbles after him. "I have some painkillers at my apartment. It's not far."

"Lead the way, madam." Lazarus grabs her and places her in front of him like a human shield. They zigzag through the throngs of people, drunken giggles bubbling from her mouth. Wes and I tail them, but with difficulty: dancers waving long red ribbons almost run us over, and a baker holding a tray of the yellow cakes barely avoids dumping them on our heads. For a moment, we lose Lazarus and the woman—but just a moment.

"There!" Wes points at two figures shuffling down a quiet block lined with row houses. Hopping from shadow to shadow, we tail them. Lazarus turns to look back, and we squat down behind a star-shaped bush before he glimpses us.

Too soon, the woman hustles Lazarus up to her building's front door and feeds a key card into a slot at eye level.

"Fuse," I swear.

Wes pulls an insect-like bit of metal from his pocket and peels off the adhesive backing. "Batterer toy," he whispers. "It's a tracker." Wes holds the bug to his heart as if praying. "Please work, little spider," he says, and lobs it.

It lands on the doormat in front of Lazarus, sticky side up, and adheres to his shoe when he steps forward.

The woman slams the door behind them. Although she has shut out the city's chaos, she's locked herself in with a snake.

16

WE MAKE OUR WAY BACK THROUGH THE
Moon Festival celebrations, which rage on as brightly as ever. But
they no longer fascinate me. They're irritating distractions from
the rapidly deteriorating situation.

On our walk back toward the park, we try to warn no less than
seven Batterer policemen, policewomen, and soldiers about Lazarus,
the impending threat. The first three brush us off, and the fourth
takes thirty seconds to explain that Battery Bay's security apparatus
is already overtaxed. The big city doesn't have one-tenth the Committee's surveillance capabilities, I realize with a jolt of frustration.
It'll be near impossible for them to root out an enemy in disguise.

"I'll go mad if they keep this up," Wes mutters. "In all senses
of the word."

Still, we keep trying; worry widens his gray eyes so that he
looks half-crazed, and I shudder to think of the impression *I* must
give off. My voice squeaks when I open my mouth, and my lungs
seem to take two shallow breaths every second.

The fifth and sixth Batterers—middle-aged foot soldiers—seem
too exhausted to process our words, and the seventh—a young
policewoman—tells us that a traitor would not have made it into
the Batterers' midst, given the city's "advanced" security system.

Beaten down, we slip into the forested park. Yinha meets us

at the edge of the Odan camp. After we warn her about Lazarus's presence, she hurries away to the hostel to pass on the message to Andromeda. Maybe the Batterers will listen to *her*.

We've done all we can. In a rock garden near the camp, Wes and I sit on a massive boulder and watch Lazarus's tracker feed on a Batterer rollout touchscreen. Three hours later, the blinking green dot hasn't left the woman's apartment building.

The pounding anger I felt in the street has yielded to dull dread. Lazarus has probably pried Dovetail's temporary address from the drunken receptionist, down to the exact room number at the hostel.

Wes lets out a long sigh. "All this trouble because one rotten egg made it up there." He means the Moon. "You know, Phaet, I want to go back. I was more useful to Saint Oda, and now the goings-on in the sky are . . . personal to me. What do you think?"

He's considered this for a long time. Although I want him back on the bases, I'm torn: he should stay where it's safer, on Earth.

Unsure what to say, I rest my eyes on the bonsai specimens to our right. Midget pine trees stand straight and proud, their needles as long as my eyelashes. The trunks of several elms zigzag in a Z formation; a juniper grows on a downward cascade so that its branches scrape the ground. Five spruces cluster together in one pot, their roots spread over pebbles and under moss.

"I might be biased," I confess.

"Isn't everyone?" Wes shrugs. "My mother wants me to stay here, to protect the Odans, and my father thinks the other Lunar agents can handle the Committee. And with that . . . *turncoat* here on Earth, well . . . I've got to eliminate him from the equation." He grimaces at the mention of Lazarus. "But this sorry business of wondering if the other spies have gotten caught, wondering if *you've* gotten hurt or captured or . . . it's got to end, Phaet."

So I wasn't the only one.

"You worried about me," I say, growing aware of the heat radiating from his body. "I assumed you'd try to forget."

"Trying to forget someone is the surest way of remembering everything about her." Wes shifts his position so that he can look me in the eye. "Doesn't seem like you succeeded with me."

He's right, and we both know it. I gather my knees to my chest as if trying to protect myself from—what, exactly? "Every time Alex opened his mouth, it reminded me of you," I say, feeling like someone's lit matches under my skin.

"If he were eavesdropping on us, he'd feel terribly guilty or terribly amused." Wes shakes his head, smiling. "I didn't need help to remember what you sound like."

I can't help but look at him in wonder.

"Going to the pier before dawn, before the Moon set in the sky, and listening to the waves—that was enough."

His words are so gentle, so vulnerable. They have to be true. Unable to stop myself, I lean toward him, reaching for his hand, seeking shelter in his warmth. Our foreheads touch, and then the tips of our noses.

Wes doesn't kiss me, but he doesn't move away either. "Phaet . . ." he whispers. "Is this the best idea?" The vibrations from each syllable pass through the air from his lips to mine.

His words make me long to be *normal*. What if we could fall in love without fear creeping behind us, ready to pounce and steal our happiness? What if we could focus on something other than strategizing, fighting, and *not dying* when we're together?

"For survival, no," I say, inching back. I don't know whether to be disappointed or relieved. "For life, for making the most of the time we have . . . who can say?"

My mother taught me the difference between "surviving" and "living" when I was a child. She must have been talking about enduring Committee rule, keeping our heads down during the day and fearing that Beaters would visit at night. But she was also talking about times like this, when we're with someone radiant and can only worry about his light fading.

"What would you do if you had all the time in the world?"

Besides spend much of it with you? The question surprises and then annoys me. Wes knows I always try to contain my optimism.

But then I remember what Alex said on the ship: how his plan to tell stories in the future gives him a reason to live. How the promise of *something* keeps him going.

"You mean . . . if my dozens of enemies don't take me down before the revolution succeeds?"

"Right—if the world becomes a friendly place, and you're still in it. And you no longer have to fight to stay alive."

I shake my head, thinking of the classes I'll never take, the technologies I'll never invent. Of everything the war has erased from my future. "Hope is dangerous these days," I say. "And too many of my dreams have died."

"That's too bad." Wes sounds disappointed. "Someday, I want to adopt some sort of Lunar public health measures on Saint Oda, but in a form closer to nature, one that people will accept. Maybe using concentrated alcohol from potatoes or rye to disinfect public facilities. Stuff like that. When we rebuild the city, we'll have so much room to try new things."

Despite the chaos around him, Wes, like Alex, has still made time to concoct new ideas. *Ideas for Earth, where he belongs.* So what do *I* want? "*If* my family and I make it through . . ." Again, my mind draws a blank.

"Didn't you want to be a Bioengineer?"

I give him an incredulous look—he remembers my old, pre-Militia ambitions better than I do—and burst out laughing. "Yes, I planned to design the ultimate nutrient-packed fruit, or the perfect assortment of gut bacteria so that kids in Shelter would quit getting diarrhea. And I wanted a Committee prize for it."

He chuckles, shaking his head, before touching an index finger to his temple. "This is a random thought—I don't know where it came from. But you're methodical and smart and good at taking care of people."

"I try."

"What if you became a teacher? In Primary Biology, or something like that?"

Thinking of the fear that arrests me every time I speak in public, I shake my head and mock-zip my lips.

"Yes, you'd be talking, but to children. Besides, it seems like you've found your voice in the time you've been away. Telling Parliament off, telling your Dovetail friends what to do, telling me what you're thinking."

To my surprise, Wes puts a hand on my upper back, and then drapes his arm across my shoulders. I tremble all over again in spite of its warmth.

Is this the best idea? I want to return the question he asked earlier, but don't want him to let go of me.

"Do you think the change is for the better?" I ask, settling into his embrace, testing it out. All the muscles in my body loosen, and my heartbeat slows to a steady *ka-thump, ka-thump.* These days, I never feel so calm. Not even when I'm sleeping.

"It doesn't matter what I think," Wes says. "But you seem to have less weighing you down now."

He's right. Now that I've said what I needed to say, I feel as if my body's made of air. Sitting and shivering on the boulder together, we watch the big gold coin of a moon set in the night sky. We speak rarely and quietly, only giving voice to our thoughts when lingering looks and clasped hands prove inadequate.

Souls, like bodies, need space, and Wes's doesn't intrude on mine.

As the sun's first red rays peek out from behind a skyscraper shaped like a pyramid of pebbles, I begin to think that maybe this is it. People as different as the old couple on the street and the lonely lady on the Moon have experienced this, what's between us. Something so common, and yet so special, because it finds people two at a time. I don't try to capture the feeling in words—an impossible task—and neither does Wes. There's no need. The air is full enough without them.

17

AFTER SUNRISE, THE BOULDER WE'RE SITTING ON BE-gins to rumble. Battery Bay is firing up its engines, ready for its journey southward toward more secure territory. I lift my head from Wes's shoulder, rub my eyes—and wish I hadn't.

Smog and clouds blanket the island city. Only the lemon-colored emergency lights continue to shine; all other colors have disappeared. Wheel-shaped hovercraft fly overhead, pulling illuminated banners behind them: PACIFIAN FORCE DETECTED NEAR HOK-KAIDO. BATTERY BAY NOW ON YELLOW ALERT.

Shockwaves of anxiety pulse through my chest. *Please, please let this be a false alarm.* Checking the tracker map, I see that Lazarus's blinking dot has vanished. He must have destroyed the tracker or moved out of range.

Wes stirs, and in a voice heavy with sleep mumbles, "G'morning, Phaet."

Cursing our luck, I shake my head. No, it's a bad morning, as mornings go, because it cut short one of the best nights.

His eyes snap open, taking in our surroundings and the empty tracker map. Every muscle in his torso tightens. We stagger to our feet and dash through the garden, toward the Odan camp. As we run, more hovercraft zoom over our heads: CITY NOW EVACUATING TO THE KOREA STRAIT.

The move makes sense. Battery Bay has land-based allies scattered throughout the former territories of Japan and South Korea; this move will put us right between the two. It's risky, though. Pacifia was a land-based city in China before it floated away, so the Pacifian alliance in the southwest is strong. If they plan to attack, they'll have an advantage. The plan seems too perfect, too perfectly timed. Did someone alert Pacifia that Battery Bay planned to break for friendlier territory today?

The auburn-haired Parliament aide . . . Lazarus. He knows all of Battery Bay's plans to defend itself—and that means the Committee knows too. They probably gave him a ship to pilot to Earth, and he must've conned his way into the city.

Yellow lights all over the city shut off, and red ones turn on, the light bloody against the shiny metal façades. A sparse rainfall begins, the droplets combining with our sweat, leaving our cotton clothes heavy and stuck to our backs.

In the campsite, Odans are shouting one another's names and hustling loved ones into tents for shelter. Before long, Batterer officials force them out again.

"Red alert," says a young man in a blue uniform with gold buttons—a policeman. Instead of a right eyebrow, he has a tattoo of a dragonfly's wing. "The Bay's on lockdown. We need to escort you indoors."

Emberley, Wes's younger sister, squares her shoulders, facing off with him. "We *are* indoors."

"By 'indoors,' we mean a bulletproof shelter," the policeman replies.

Mrs. Carlyle glares at him; she's angry that he's using the cold language of war around her innocent daughter. I respect her devotion to the pacifist Odan tradition, though it seems inevitable that her endeavors will fail in these troubled times.

The policemen march us into the rain, toward the international hostel. The Odans' moccasins slosh through ankle-deep puddles; heads turn back to the abandoned tents. As we scramble out of the park, several adults hold their children closer to shield them from the unnatural, violent things surrounding us: law enforcement hovercraft painted gold, metal guns holstered in belts, low-flying military aircraft overhead. Other parents look right through the spectacle, as if weary of such sights. In the smog, the red emergency lights are like evil eyes following us through the narrow streets.

When we reach the hostel, Wes, Alex, and I split off from the Odans and head for Dovetail's new quarters. After Yinha warned her about Lazarus, Andromeda took shelter three floors above the rooms we were initially assigned. Public safety officers in teal and gold rush about the lobby, a chapel-like space lit by a dozen silver chandeliers shaped like jellyfish. They usher diplomats into vehicles, switch on emergency lights, pull workers from the front desk and kitchens and direct them toward safer locations. I was worried that security would block me from entering the hostel, but when I see the chaos, I relax: they'll never catch me in this mess.

The elevators are shut down, so we take the stairs, scurrying up flight after flight. I gulp down air to mitigate the lactic acid burn in my quadriceps, determined to treat the endless climb like an exercise in Militia training—I can't let the others beat me.

At last, we burst into a hallway, its ceiling molded into shapes that resemble upside-down waves. Yinha pounds on the frosted glass door to Dovetail's new suite; Andromeda opens it, and we rush inside.

The suite has thick teal shag carpeting and a high dining table that extends out of the pale blue wall. An aquarium installed in the ceiling houses red, orange, black, and white goldfish. We gather our weapons, strip off our street clothes, and don our Militia gear. Despite how crowded it is, I give only a passing thought to modesty.

"Just to clarify, you won't *use* those weapons except in self-defense, correct?" Andromeda sounds like a parent trying to keep her children under control. She paces as she speaks. "We've presented Dovetail as a movement founded on nonviolence, and I can't have Battery Bay vloggers film you actively killing Pacifians when we haven't even declared war on them."

"Can't guarantee we'll sit this out." Wes pulls on tattered black gloves and flexes his fingers. "Alex and I still have our Odan Sanctuarist duties."

"I'm officially a Dovetailer," Alex says, "but he's got no good reason to listen to you."

"True," Wes says.

Andromeda paces back and forth, talking more to herself than to us. "To think you've risked your lives since you were practically children . . ."

She stops and slumps onto an ornate couch. An open suitcase lies by her feet. With pensive eyes, she looks out the floor-to-ceiling windows at the sea. I see faint yellow lights in a neat grid and the outlines of wings—a wall of aircraft heading our way.

Behind the menacing array of planes, the gargantuan city of Pacifia, with its familiar jagged outline, approaches Battery Bay. Cubic concrete buildings squat on either side of the wide boulevards, and the monorail winds around the city's perimeter like a lasso.

"Look at that eyesore, Phaet," Andromeda's eyes never leave the window. "I can't help but wish we had brought more people. It's easier to face with a crowd behind you."

Somehow I know she isn't talking about just any Dovetail members. "Callisto?"

Andromeda's mouth presses into a line, and she nods almost imperceptibly. "If it weren't for her reputation, I'd have asked Asterion to allow her to accompany us."

Her confession doesn't shock me—she's a mother, after all—but it makes me queasy. "Do you trust her?" I ask, remembering our strange conversation in the training dome.

Andromeda presses her knuckles against her heart. "In here, I do. In here, she's a little girl with a toy sword who said she'd protect me no matter what. But I fear that she's a Committee child through and through, that she wouldn't have joined the revolution if I hadn't. Bringing her here was too risky. I have to show Dovetail that principles run deeper than blood."

I don't have the heart, or the nerve, to point out that Callisto didn't join Dovetail for Andromeda. She joined to save her own skin after the Committee linked her mother to the rebels. Dovetail would let her live. The loyalist side would have shown no mercy.

"Enough talk." Andromeda looks out at Pacifia, the ever-approaching goliath. Her fingers toy with the handle of her suitcase. "Everyone, gather your things. We're heading to Battery Bay's lowest levels, beneath the water line. It's our best hope of survival."

Her calmness under pressure unnerves me. *She's hiding her anxiety*, I realize. She spent four years as a Dovetail mole on the Committee; of course there's a wall between her feelings and her face. After all this time, Lady A is too cold, too politically proficient—it's why Dovetail chose the transparent, earnest Asterion to lead us instead.

I move to Wes's side. "Should we go belowdecks?" I whisper to him.

"We won't be any safer down there. Pacifia's attacking from underwater, from the air, and on the sea's surface, all at once," Wes says. "And they're just a few minutes out; we'll never make it underground in time. But we can try to find an empty suite in the hostel. The Odans and Andromeda can stay there. The rest of us will fight."

He and I share a long look. As a Sanctuarist, his duty is to repel invading troops and keep the Odan refugees safe. As a naturalized Odan citizen who's partly responsible for their current homeless state, I feel obligated to join him. My allegiance to Dovetail shouldn't stop me; my mother's revolutionaries wouldn't have me at all if the Odans hadn't saved my life.

What would you do if you had all the time in the world? The memory's a sucker punch to the gut. Neither of us anticipated that our time could end today.

Looking out at our foes, I see shiny, aerodynamic carbon-fiber ships with pliable midsections hovering over Pacifia like schooling skipjacks.

"*Lunars,*" I say, and sheathe an extra dagger in my boot. Shoving aside my distaste for laser weaponry, I walk to the room's desk, where we've laid out a Militia weapons stash, and grab a Lazy. "Laser for laser. Reciprocal self-defense."

"Phaet, we cannot let you out there," Andromeda says. "You will take shelter with us underground. Please. The Moon needs you."

"The Pacifians are sending submarines," I say. "It's more dangerous belowdecks. Stay in the hostel."

She blinks. "We'll stay, but I can't let you fight."

"You let her go to the Singularity," Alex says. "You *made* her go."

"That was different," Andromeda counters. "That was a controlled environment; she had hundreds of troops to protect her. I doubt that your Militia training provided adequate information about foul-weather oceanic combat, Phaet."

"I will choose when and how I risk my life."

Andromeda opens her mouth in surprise but rapidly recovers. "I never said you couldn't."

A thrill zips up my spine. "Then I choose to protect the Odan refugees. They lost their home because they took me in when I had nowhere else to go. Lady A, the way you try so hard to keep me safe? That's how I feel about them."

"I owe them one too," Yinha says softly. "I don't want to commit insubordination, but—"

The entire building tips a degree or two, causing everyone to stumble.

"Did the enemy just send a *tidal wave* at us?" I say, on my hands and knees.

Wes shrugs and extends a hand to help me up. He's remained steady, leaning against the wooden desk. "Consider it your introduction to floating city warfare."

18

THE PACIFIAN AIRCRAFTS' HIGH BEAM HEAD-
lights pierce the vapor-saturated air. Even the weather is on their
side: the rain has thinned to a drizzle that'll sharpen the enemy's
aim.

Small water scooters straddled by gray-suited Pacifian foot soldiers snake across the ocean. Although we can't see beneath the
gray-green waves, we know submarines are approaching, deep underwater.

Clipped to ropes and pulleys, I perch on the outside wall of
the hostel's seventieth floor, about two-thirds of the way up the
building. To avoid revealing that there are Lunars fighting among
the Batterer troops, I'm wearing a Batterer soldier's dark teal uniform over my mirrored suit and carrying an unwieldy Earthbound
handgun as long as my forearm. The hostel's ocean-view balconies
have retracted, leaving a smooth surface that's difficult to climb
and easy to slip off. Like the rock-climbing wall in Militia training,
however, it has ridges that can serve as handholds.

Our mission: protect the Odans who have taken shelter on
this floor, deep in the building's interior. The Sanctuarists have
rigged the place with booby traps, but it's hardly secure. At this
moment, nowhere in the city is safe. Enemy aircraft could strike
high floors, while submarines attack belowdecks. And the foot

soldiers on water scooters are headed straight for "ground" level.

Hating myself for what I'm about to do, I raise my borrowed Earthbound handgun. *Bang!* The shot sends a Pacifian soldier tumbling into the ocean. The weapon's kicking recoil—and my own guilt—crushes the air from my lungs.

I hate this, I hate this, I hate this.

But he would've killed the Odans and me.

I did it because I had to.

Along with the Sanctuarists and about a hundred Batterer soldiers, I must prevent enemy foot soldiers from infiltrating the hostel. Dozens of Pacifians have hopped off their water scooters and are climbing the exterior wall. I send three more bullets downward and score one hit. The unfamiliar gun handles like a twitching rodent, throwing off my aim.

To make matters worse, the two-hundred-meter drop between my feet and the black waves strikes terror in me every time I look down. Never mind that my rope's automated belaying mechanism will catch me if I fall too fast, or that the magnets strapped around my ankles glue me to the metal wall. The water is there, and I can't swim.

"Heads up!" shouts a Batterer soldier.

"They put a fizzing *plane* on the roof!" Yinha cries.

A flash of lightning rattles me to the bone; it illuminates dozens of foot soldiers sliding down on ropes just like ours. From hundreds of meters away, they look like innocuous bugs. Up close, they'll be lethal. I try shooting at them with my Earthbound gun, but due to rain and gravity, the metal bullets slow their upward climb and fall back down before they reach their targets.

"Phaet! On your right!" Alex shouts.

I scoot to my left as something whizzes by my ear. The grenade that was meant for me hits a Batterer soldier two floors below, blowing a hole in the hostel wall and tossing the soldier's mangled body into the air. I watch the corpse fall into the ocean with an insignificant splash, unable to tear my eyes away.

Focus. Swallowing bile, I reorient myself and assess the situation. With the advantage of gravity, the Pacifians have an easier time hitting us than vice versa. I have to rectify that. Taking a deep breath, I begin climbing and signal for Wes and Alex to do the same. Despite the risks, we need to take the higher ground.

"They're descending too quickly!" Wes shouts. "And they're killing every soldier in their way."

The enemy is but forty meters above us. I can't let them reach this level. Even if it means giving away our identities. Clipping my Earthbound handgun to my belt, I take out my Lazy and point it upward, knowing its ammunition is immune to rain and gravity. A continuous violet beam leaves its muzzle. I swing my arm in a wide arc, shooting the entire line of soldiers.

I shut my eyes, too, knowing that if I open them I'll take my finger off the trigger. When I do, I see a row of burnt bodies thrown about by the wind, like dead spiders dangling from their webs.

19

"WONDERFUL," ALEX SHOUTS FROM BELOW ME. Not even the wind can dissipate the bite in his tone. "Blastedly, phenomenally great!"

"Phaet saved us," Wes points out. "For at least the next thirty seconds."

"Anyone who saw that beam knows there are Loonies on board, Loonies fighting against Pacifia," Alex says. "Loonies who can *only* be Dovetailers."

There's no room in my head to care about what's coming next. *I swore I'd never use lasers to kill.* Not after watching one end my mother's life. I want to hurl my blaster outward, to be swallowed by the ocean, but that would be suicide. Instead, I slide the cursed thing into a belt loop and vow not to use it again. My grip on the wall slackens, and I slide downward a meter and a half. I'd plunge into the sea if not for the magnets on my ankles and the rope around my waist.

Alex is still raging. "And now we've got a plane headed straight for—"

There's a colossal *clang* as a midsize Batterer hovercraft magnetically latches on to the wall, right on the seventieth floor. It's an older steel model with a bubble-like shape and rectangular wings that point diagonally upward.

Smaller, newer, more aerodynamic Batterer military hover-craft, painted in a blue-and-gray camouflage pattern, instantly surround the rogue vehicle to investigate. It takes off again, ripping out a chunk of wall, spraying metal and glass into the air. Fragments ping against my helmet, settle into the fabric of my Batterer uniform.

"Hang on, that's not *really* a Batterer vehicle," Wes mutters.

I've got grudging admiration for whoever's inside, Pacifians or Lunars. Without their deception—without our *stupidity*—they never would have gotten this close. And now they've left a gaping hole in the hostel wall. I scuttle toward the opening and breathe a sigh of relief when I see half a dozen Batterer soldiers already inside, fending off the enemy. Alex pulls himself up over the ledge and joins the troops. Wes swoops in too, using his rope as a pendulum.

Hovering in the air just out of range of the Batterer guns, the stolen craft's hull opens like stiff flower petals unfolding, curved metal segments lifting back to reveal a hovering platform that holds perhaps thirty black-clad Lunar soldiers, Lazies at the ready.

The tall, slim flight leader stands. Pinned to his jacket is a SPECIAL AGENT badge instead of a Militia rank insignia. As a flash of lightning bleaches everything bone white, he leaps across from the platform into the hostel.

Blinded by the flash, I shoot at him and miss. No one else fares any better. But his followers choose less opportune times to make their exits. I nail one in the groin before seeing that the leader has taken off into the hostel—straight toward the Odans' hiding place on the other side. He doesn't spare a glance for the Lunar soldiers fighting and falling behind him.

This one clearly operates on his own, and I'm 80 percent sure of his identity. The other 20 percent is trying to deny that I'm right.

"Hold down the turf!" I shout to the Batterer soldiers. "Wes, Alex, we've got to stop the leader."

My friends and I tail the tall Lunar soldier into the hallway. He runs in an unpredictable zigzagging pattern, so our shots miss and hit fine wallpaper or expensive-looking lava lamps instead. Footsteps echo behind us, and I curse internally as I realize that at least five Lunar soldiers made it past our Batterer allies. Now *we're* the ones dodging bullets.

The tall Lunar soldier tosses a small hand grenade forward at the double doors—and everything goes orange. Heat slicks against my suit.

The soldier runs into the center of the room, and Alex, Wes, and I dive behind a couch a moment before the other Lunar soldiers make it inside. Two people wearing what look like wool rags are already hidden there; they scream when we join them, but make room once they recognize Wes and Alex.

As the smoke clears, I behold a once-beautiful aquamarine room that resembles Dovetail's quarters several floors below. The floor-to-ceiling window showcases Battery Bay's interior. Buildings are burning, and instead of the organized traffic in the midair freeways, there's swarming and explosions of aircraft. Terrified Odans huddle against the walls behind makeshift barricades of plush couches and mahogany tables.

Finally in sight of his victims, the soldier lifts his visor. Lazarus's green eyes glare in the half-light. He's ditched the auburn wig; sweaty black hair sticks to the brown skin of his forehead. As he stalks forward, only the balls of his feet touch the ground.

Hate, the frigid kind, locks my joints in place. Although he's as handsome as ever, he's left behind his mask of civility. I prefer him this way. No more pretending not to hate me and mine.

"The Standing Committee has provided me with a list of individuals who must be brought to justice," he shouts. "And entrusted me with their eradication."

Let me guess: Dovetail's messengers are on that list, and the Committee will compensate him handsomely for getting rid of us. It's brilliant—using his rage and desire for vengeance to get him to kill those he would kill anyway—for their riskiest work. If he weren't poised to take lives, I might feel amused that the player is being played.

"Five of them hide among you," Lazarus says. "Inside this room. With your cooperation, I will exterminate those five, and only those five, before I leave. If anybody dares to interfere, he or she will be discarded."

Lazarus Penny leers at the trembling Odans. "Shall we begin?"

"You will not begin anything!" cries an Odan man near the front of the huddle. He has a full gray beard and spectacles. "We are Odans, Lazarus, guardians of all God's children. We protect our own people. We protect those who are not our own. We protected *you*—until you became a demon."

And then they excommunicated him.

Lazarus winces—he's always hated reminders of his past. "What did I say about cooperation?" A flash of silver, and his Lazy is pointed at the Odans, daring one of them to protest.

"No . . ." Alex murmurs beside me.

We can't let Lazarus shoot, even if it means giving away our position.

Rocketing to my feet, I lift my visor. "We're here," I call out, willing my voice not to betray my fear. "We're cooperating. Leave your people alone."

"Excellent. As it so happens, the first name on the list"—Lazarus twirls his left hand around to point an accusing finger at me—"is Phaet Theta."

Turning his back to the Odans, he raises his Lazy—

My left hand clenches into a fist, thumb under my fingers, as Lazarus squeezes the trigger. The violet laser beam burns through my Batterer uniform, hits my mirrored suit, and bounces back at him. His speed saves him—he ducks, fast, to evade it.

"Bury that man," growls Wes's father.

Wes and Alex spring to their feet, weapons at the ready. Lunar lasers streak the air; the Sanctuarists' poison darts shoot out to meet them. Several Militia troops stop moving, their feet caught in booby traps. A Sanctuarist throws a chair upward, breaking the glass separating the ceiling's aquarium from the living area. Glass shards, pebbles, false seaweed, and goldfish rain down on the Lunars.

But despite their efforts, the Odans are no match for their foes, who have armor that can stop bullets and weapons made for killing. Even though they've entangled several Militia members in ropes, other Lunars soon cut them free. Lazarus's troops charge through the Odans, batting them away or shooting them with their guns; they don't bother to finish them off, knowing they'll die anyway.

Seeing several Lazies pointed my way, I throw myself to the floor and dig a dagger out of my boot. Alex and Wes rush the soldiers from behind, smashing their helmeted heads together two by two. The distraction lasts just long enough for me to disappear behind a marble countertop, squatting to hide myself.

"Where'd she go?" the Militia soldier nearest me hollers.

I inch forward on my elbows like a worm and slash her hamstring. She keels over, crying out in pain. When a nearby teammate rushes toward her fallen body, I give him the same treatment.

Crash! A cold wind shudders through the room, chilling me through my uniform and spraying us all with rain. The floor-to-ceiling window has shattered—and a small Pacifian hovercraft is beelining toward us, its headlights two red beams in the murky space. The craft's body is boxy looking, its wings triangular; it seems to be a convertible set up for open-air combat, since all the seats are exposed to the elements.

Around me, the chaos has thinned, perhaps because the Odans and Sanctuarists know Lazarus has won this round. I pull myself up to get a better view, putting my back against a wall.

The Odans' temporary hideout has been destroyed. Chairs are tipped over, broken. A wall mirror, smashed. The ceiling's lotus-shaped fluorescent lamp swings from a screw. Twisted bodies litter the floor, glittering with a dusting of shattered glass from the smashed window. Family members bend over the fallen, pressing their warm foreheads to chilly brows.

Otherwise, the floor is empty; the remaining Odans have fled to the hostel's lower levels, or into other buildings. The few remaining include Wes's parents. Wesley Sr.'s expression is brittle, stony; Mrs. Carlyle sobs, muttering to herself, one arm around each of her younger daughters. They both stare in horror at something outside; I watch Mrs. Carlyle's lips move: *He's got her, he's got her.*

Even without names, I know exactly whom she means. In front of the smashed window, Lazarus stands, feet planted in a wide stance, Murray's neck caught in the crook of his elbow. Her pale skin chafes against the black canvas of his sleeve with every shallow breath. Threads of her hair whip around their heads, as though binding them together. Her thundercloud eyes are wide, their frenzied storm visible even from a distance.

But she's not struggling. Does she think fighting is useless?

Or does part of her still want to be in his arms? It makes me sick, how from far away he could almost be her sweetheart, hugging her too hard.

The hovercraft docks.

"If anybody shoots," Lazarus says, pointing a Lazy at us, "I will strangle her."

He steps onto the hovercraft, yanking Murray along by the neck, nearly gagging her. Even if she wanted to, she couldn't scream.

20

WES AND I START SPRINTING BEFORE THE
hovercraft detaches from the hostel wall. But the vehicle is accelerating too, gliding away toward Pacifia at the command of the pilot,
who's securely tethered to his seat.

They take off.

By the time Wes and I reach the edge, the hovercraft's a meter
and a half out from the hole in the wall. I don't think twice about
leaping across the gap, though it's hundreds of meters above the
city streets. Neither does Wes. The protests from our allies and
his family don't reach our ears, blocked out by the storm and the
frenzy of our rage.

The craft rocks twice as we land on its edge. Our boots slip on
the wet metal.

Two Pacifian soldiers' bodies are strewn across the rear seat of
the craft; perhaps they were shot earlier in the battle. I decide that
they're dead and not a threat. Glancing backward, I see two Lunar
soldiers leaping after us—one doesn't make it and falls, shouting,
toward the ground. The other sticks her landing, but I shove her
hard and she goes the same way as her colleague.

"Phaet, behind you!" Wes shouts.

I duck under the rifle butt meant to brain me, straighten, and
see that the pilot's seat is empty; the pilot has left the craft on auto-

pilot to attack me. Wes wrestles my assailant for a moment—then strikes his forehead with the underside of his wrist, knocking him out. To be safe, we heave him overboard. There's no time for guilt. These soldiers are part of Lazarus's larger scheme.

Ahead of us, Lazarus pushes a struggling Murray toward one of the rear seats, seemingly unfazed by the loss of his accomplices. She kicks at his knees and tries to bite his forearms. The hovercraft circles around the hostel and jets across the roiling dark sea, toward Pacifia.

"Excellent work, Phaet," he shouts. "Wesley, I knew you would follow me, as long as I had her. You cannot help but lead me to one another."

Murray claws at him halfheartedly. "Lazarus, you're better than this. I *know* you are . . ." Even if she could run, she has nowhere to go. The craft has floated ten meters or more out to sea. Lazarus handcuffs her, wrestles her down, and chains her to an armrest. The dagger in my hand feels flimsy compared to his strong, sure limbs, but I watch, waiting for the right moment to use it.

"The name Wesley Carlyle was second on the extermination list," Lazarus says. "I'd known he was on Battery Bay for some while—"

I throw the dagger at the back of Lazarus's neck, aiming for the spot between his helmet and torso armor. He ducks out of its path, and the weapon clinks against the hovercraft's side.

I freeze, astonished.

"—but I bided my time, knowing Phaet Theta would be unable to stay away. *Affection*—isn't it a puzzle?" Lazarus laughs, a charming, too-perfect laugh, and picks up my weapon. *No one taught him what love is,* I remember Alex saying. "I was correct. She arrived, as predicted—with three more of my targets in tow."

Alex, Yinha, Andromeda. I bite back a frustrated cry, infuriated that we made his deadly assignment so easy. Behind me, I hear Wes's breath, quick and ragged. His fear multiplies my own.

"Marina is just a bonus," Lazarus says, raising my weapon to Murray's face. She doesn't whimper or scream. If she cries, her tears are invisible in the rain.

"A bonus?" Her expression is pleading. "You are not your mother, Lazarus—I know you . . ."

He stiffens, glares at her, and drags the blade across her left cheek. "My despicable mother. You want me to grace your ears with stories of her? Want to hear about how after my father left, she denied me food and sleep until I learned to fight, to read, to bring honor to the Penny name?"

Murray shakes the blood off her face as if it's just water. "When we were together, you never laid a hand on me, never made me feel small . . . please."

Stony-faced like his father, Wes unsheathes a long serrated knife from his belt. I dig out my last dagger and hide the blade in my sleeve.

Lazarus keeps his eyes trained on Murray.

"I have become so much more than she ever expected of me, and none of you will bring me down again."

Murray's face is bleeding profusely; she must be in terrible pain. Still, she tries to kick Lazarus and misses. He straightens into a relaxed fighting stance, one foot back, dagger hand raised to his chest.

Murray starts yanking on the handcuffs. Within seconds, they rub her wrists raw. Wes and I rush forward at the same time. At close range, Lazarus can't effectively use his Lazy. Instead, he takes full advantage of the dagger I've all but handed him. He slashes and splits the air, forcing us to avoid his right side. I squat down to keep my balance, utilizing my lower center of gravity, while

Wes ricochets off the seats, the dashboard, the hovercraft's left and right sides. We attack with knives, fists and feet, elbows and knees, but to no avail. We're unable to dislodge Lazarus from the craft's center, the most stable part of the vehicle.

A small Batterer military hovercraft, painted in blue-and-gray camouflage like the others, catches up with us. Its artillery points our way, but the crew can't fire at Lazarus while he's so close.

"Amateurs," Lazarus says, his blade grating against mine. "You're both so out of shape. Love has made you soft."

He raises the dagger and drives the blade into the back of Wes's unarmored knee.

Wes's howl of pain nearly knocks me off balance. He kneels on one leg, blood dribbling from the other. It mixes with the rain, leaving a scarlet sheen on his armor.

Has affection made me weak? My frustration growing, I thrust my dagger at Lazarus's midsection. He slithers out of range, drawing another, longer blade from his belt. Even with the help of Wes, whom I once thought unbeatable at close-range combat, I can't punish Lazarus for his many betrayals. Can't save Murray, who's suffered too much.

"You couldn't face us on your own?" I imagine I'm Callisto, taunting him into distraction. With Wes down, there's no other choice. "Had to wait until Pacifia and the Militia arrived?"

"*I* brought them here!" Lazarus lunges at me, aiming one knife at my neck, the other at my midsection. I twist down and away, showing him my back; the lower blade slips between my armor's plates and punctures three centimeters of flesh, narrowly missing my spine. I let out a screech that sounds like a wildcat's, a wolf's— anything but human, anything but *mine*.

Lazarus swipes at my belly, and I wriggle out of the way, back throbbing with every movement. "I . . . informed them"—he aims at my head—"that this was their . . . golden day. To . . . destroy Battery Bay . . . before it fled, or formed an alliance with the likes of *you*."

Just as I thought. Lazarus orchestrated the attack, knowing Pacifia would lose its opportunity to pin the island city down after Battery Bay moved southward. I kick at him, doing little damage. The small Batterer hovercraft, piloted by some unknown ally, still cruises beside us, but how can it help when Murray's chained up? We're halfway to Pacifia. If we don't defeat Lazarus soon, we'll touch down and get swarmed by soldiers. They'll kill Murray first, while we watch.

A gust of wind rams our hovercraft from the side. The vessel lurches, causing Lazarus to lose his footing. Wes and I cling to the railing, our eyes meeting amidst the flashing light and falling rain.

The autopilot can't adjust fast enough. The hovercraft loses several meters of altitude. Lazarus slips backward, toward the side of the ship where he's tethered Murray. Eyes cast down, she picks at her handcuff with a wire. Maybe her cleverness could save her, save us all.

As Lazarus slides, the Batterer hovercraft fires needle-like explosives at him. But he reaches Murray; to make things worse, Pacifian craft engages the Batterer one from afar, and our allies must leave us.

We can turn this fight around on our own, I tell myself. *We have to.*

"Get to the controls!" Wes's voice grows weaker—he's losing too much blood. "We can't let this thing touch down!"

He draws the Lazy from his belt, takes aim at Lazarus, and fires two shots, both of which miss due to a combination of opaque rain and our enemy's cursed agility. I scramble toward the pilot's seat, slipping on puddles and stumbling across the rows of seats. The glass is so cracked it looks like it's been frosted over, like it's ready to shatter.

"Stop shooting, Wesley," Lazarus says. "Now."

Panicking, I look over my shoulder. He's grabbed Murray by the waist; he tugs her to her feet and swings her body like a shield, blocking any further bombardment. He presses his dagger's blade against her white throat, and blood from her cheek dribbles onto the glinting metal. She stands still, fist closed around the handcuff-picking wire, her eyes as clear as I've ever seen them. Clear, and full of terror.

Wes keeps his finger on the trigger. "Let her go," he begs. "If you ever loved her, spare her. People will remember you as merciful, not cold-blooded."

Lazarus blinks, and for a second, vulnerability emanates from those acid-green eyes. Then they turn hateful again.

"I couldn't love her, because I didn't know how." His voice is soft; it breaks several times with emotion. "And my legacy is already ruined—because of *you*."

Wes lunges forward, Lazy in the air.

I reach the pilot's seat. The controls are unfamiliar: a ball implanted in a socket for steering and dozens of wheels, levers, and buttons. Earthbound technology complicates everything.

The ball-and-socket is locked to steer us in a trajectory toward Pacifia. I hunch over the driver's seat, flip a switch to Unlock, and spin the ball clockwise. With an almighty jerk, the hovercraft tilts to the right. I hear a body tumbling, look back, and see Lazarus pulling himself up by the railing; he's contorting his limbs to dodge Wes's laser fire. Perhaps he stumbled because he was wielding two knives at the expense of holding on. And now he's dropped one.

Murray still looks petrified, but she's upright, alternately picking at the handcuff with the wire and banging it against the railing as if she can crack the metal like an eggshell. Across the craft, Wes holds on to the ship's side with one hand and wraps a foot around a lower rung. He aims the Lazy and fires. One violet blast hits Lazarus in the calf, and he mewls like a cat.

"Lazarus—I can't lose her," Wes hollers, raindrops rolling down his face like tears. "My family—"

"Your *family*," Lazarus spits. "That word is a conglomeration of empty sounds. I never belonged to one, unlike every other human I've known. The Sanctuarists were the closest thing I had to a brotherhood, before they discarded me." Now he only has the Committee, who have no capacity for love or honor. "I owe you nothing. I owe the world nothing."

He explodes into motion, pulling himself to his feet and lunging at Murray, who's screaming her brother's name. She's given up on picking the handcuff's lock. Again and again, she yanks at it—blood pours from her wrist. Even from here, I can tell that several bones are fractured.

Wes shoots at Lazarus's head but misses, burning zigzag patterns onto Lazarus's unhurt leg. Emitting another cry, Lazarus trips and falls—but not without purpose. I see his predatory smile as his knife drops—toward Murray's chest—into her heart—

Frantic, I spin the steering ball to the right. The hovercraft flips over, and Wes screams hoarsely, wordlessly.

I clench my eyes shut, fight the rising bile in my throat, and slam my palm over the ball to stop the spinning.

The sky is above me again. I open my eyes and look over the edge of the craft.

Lazarus keeps falling—down, down, toward the sea, until a black parachute snaps open above his head. I watch the dark dot drift until fog rolls in to conceal it.

He'll be back, I think, dread hitting me in a sickly wave. *He won't stop until we're dead and the Committee has won. Until he has their "love."*

Murray dangles from the side of the craft, where he left her. Chained to the railing, her bloody hand is raised as if in triumph. Her legs seem to kick, like she's swimming through the wind. A nimbus of dust-colored hair, darkened now by rain, surrounds her scarred, peaceful face. A maroon stain blossoms like a flower across her chest.

I imagine pouring all that blood back into her body. It's as feasible as piecing together the hostel's shattered windows or reaching through the clouds to pluck Lazarus's black parachute out of the ocean.

Nothing that's happened here can be undone.

21

WES PERCHES ON THE HOVERCRAFT'S RAIL-
ing, holding on with one hand. His other limbs are tucked into a
ball, and he looks over the edge at his sister's body, tossed about by
gusts as if she were made of paper.

I pull the hovercraft into a U-turn, set it on autopilot, and cross
the deck to Wes. Shock mutes the feel of icy rain hitting my face
and the throbbing of the gash on my back.

Murray Carlyle. A guiltless girl—gone, because of chance, or one
man's evil, or our own inadequacy. Or all three.

My fingers curl around Wes's wrist, the one that's clamped
down on the railing. "Come down? Wes?"

He doesn't move. His eyelids are swollen and red; his breath
comes in bursts. One hand reaches down and grabs the chain tethered to his sister's handcuffs; he heaves upward. The muscles and
tendons in his neck strain against the skin. I clamber onto a seat,
grab the chain, and tug with what strength I have left.

It takes too much time to pull Murray back on deck, and yet
too little. I can't bear to look at her bloodied clothes and her open
eyes. They're a dull, flat gray now. The sparks have disappeared.

Wes cradles her head to his chest, slides her eyelids shut, buries
his face in her hair. Only when he's hidden himself do his shoulders

start to shake. I'd hold him if it didn't mean intruding. After I lost Mom, my first impulse was to run from everything that breathed. My love for her belonged to her alone; why should I share that grief with anyone else?

Boom. A massive explosion, somewhere on Battery Bay. I look backward and gasp as Parliament's meeting hall implodes, the sea urchin folding in on itself amidst a red-and-orange cloud. The city of Pacifia has edged close to its archenemy; fighter planes and water speeders jet toward Battery Bay, ready to do even more damage.

A painful cry escapes Wes's mouth, drawing my attention to our hovercraft. I can't hold back anymore. My leaden hand finds his shoulder in stops and stutters; the other rubs circles into his back. He holds Murray closer and shakes harder, wraps his arms tighter around her. And I watch, helpless.

"Come on!" The familiar, amplified voice is from a Pygmette below. Its top hatch is flipped wide open. In the turmoil, I must not have heard it approach. Yinha's waving one arm and steering with the other. "Jump! You're losing altitude—jump before you crash!"

"We have to go, Wes," I whisper.

Yinha's Pygmette is almost level with ours. Below, the battle at sea rages.

"Destroy this craft, then." Wes lifts his face to the sky. "She'd want her ashes scattered across the water."

I cross back to the controls, turn the hovercraft to face Pacifia, push the thrusters as far as they'll go, and lock in the settings. It will accelerate from here.

Yinha loses a meter of altitude relative to our position. I can't see her face, but her hands slip and shake on the controls. Blood vessels and tendons crisscross the backs of her clenched fists.

We stand, climb over the railing, ready our feet, bend our knees. Then, hands locked together, we jump.

※ — ※ — ※

The Pygmette sags beneath the weight of three people. Wes and I catch our breath, watch our former hovercraft roar toward Pacifia. Enemy lasers, missiles, and bullets strike the hull, but none can stop the craft's kamikaze advance. A side panel breaks off and spirals downward. As the engine overheats, the vehicle catches fire.

A missile blows off the left wing, and I hold my breath. The hovercraft loses more altitude and beelines for lower Pacifia, where horizontal black smokestacks belch coal residue.

It makes contact.

Right over the engine rooms.

22

FLAMES SPURT FROM PACIFIA'S HULL, THEIR
reflections shimmering orange and white in the waves. Murray's
pyre. Blinking raindrops from my eyes, I picture the remainder of
her body catching fire, sinking into the ocean like countless others
around her. She shared her life with so few, but her death with so
many. I hope she'd have wanted that.

The collision leaves a gaping hole in Pacifia's steel-paneled hull.
As Yinha flies us toward Battery Bay, dodging broken aircraft fragments, a surge of Batterer ships flies past us in the opposite direction. The blaze by the Pacifian engine room draws their heat-
seeking missiles. More explosions sound from the floating city's
interior.

Fumbling, I apply an adhesive bandage to my back and bind up
Wes's leg wound, which he doesn't seem to feel. In the distance, a
siren cuts off the thousand screams: a citywide alarm sounding on
Pacifia. It slides upward in pitch and volume, dipping back down
every few seconds as if catching its breath, reminding us that twenty
million Pacifians are trapped in the city as its engine rooms go up
in smoke.

The civilians never meant to hurt us, yet they are the ones
who suffer.

Soon, we're flying over gray skyscrapers rather than gray water. Battery Bay is barely recognizable: the hostel, many of its windows missing, its steel frame exposed and crooked; the huge rectangular park, chasms dug out of the green and forested spaces by Pacifian bombs; airways emptied of hovercraft, save the occasional ambulance soaring along at many meters per second above the posted speed limits. A choir of Batterer sirens pulsates under the screaming Pacifian one.

Yinha looks over her shoulder at me. "Murray?" she whispers, quietly so that Wes doesn't hear. He sits behind me, staring ahead, arms wrapped loosely around my middle.

I shake my head no.

The ship lurches, and a cry whips through the hazy air. Witnessing Yinha's grief shatters my heart all over again, but I reach under her arm and hold the joystick steady.

Yinha pilots us several kilometers, to the part of Battery Bay that faces away from Pacifia. Here, the damage is less extensive. We head for the tallest building in the city, an elongated loop of glass tinted teal and gold, the colors shifting and glinting even under the cloudy sky. Nicknamed the Needle's Eye, the structure has an elongated looped spire that rises from the top, its tip piercing the clouds. Across hundreds of floors, there are only a few broken windows.

Yinha takes the craft up in a slow, graceful curve. We approach the observation deck, some four hundred meters above sea level. Hundreds of people have gathered, but they clear out a space for us to land. Yinha occupies it after two wobbly attempts. She powers off the craft, puts her head down on the dashboard, and lies there, shaking.

I wish I could cry too. I wish I could feel something—anything.

With every blast of wind, the Needle's Eye leans, the structure slanted like the raindrops as they fall. It creaks as it bends, but it doesn't break. Wes hunches over in his seat behind me, making himself as small as possible. Like me, after Mom died, wanting to disappear. At least I could run to the greenhouses to be alone. All Wes has for shelter is me.

Finally, Yinha climbs out of the Pygmette. She offers a hand to help me up. Mist coats the inside of her visor.

I reach back to squeeze Wes's hand. His limp fingers tighten around mine. Then I switch the Pygmette to its space settings to give him some privacy, and disembark, following Yinha. The craft's opaque carbon-fiber shell closes around Wes like a cocoon.

Batterers are fighting for space at the observation deck's edges. Andromeda pushes through them to reach us, the binoculars around her neck bouncing with each step. I blink, shocked, as Dovetail's second-in-command takes me in her warm, soft arms.

"We've been searching the sky for you. We almost sent out scouting ships, but this poor visibility would've made it a waste."

She's right. I can barely see Pacifia's looming outline through the haze; from this distance, the aircraft of both sides, hovering around Battery Bay's other end, look identical. Shiny specks, fading in and out of their stormy surroundings.

"Where are the boys?" Andromeda asks.

"Alex is still out there," Yinha says. "Wes is in the ship. His sister . . ." She blinks—hard—and turns away.

"Finally free," I say, using the Odan euphemism for death. Murray's free now, indeed. Free from shame, from her damaged body, from her ever-present memories. Even Andromeda, Lunar born and raised, understands my meaning; she bows her head in that embarrassed way people do when mourning a stranger's pain.

"Free from what?" Yinha snaps at me. "Are you saying she's better off?"

Without waiting for an answer, she looks toward the horizon, face unreadable. I follow her gaze and find myself staring at the blurry contours of Pacifia, at the blaze that's taken over the lower hull. It looks comically small from this distance, as harmless as an ember-tipped match.

The clouds begin to part, and the mists thin. Pacifia's siren wail stops, and a low hum rumbles out of the engines that haven't yet burned. The Pacifians' clunky bombers pull U-turns in midair and head homeward. On the water, countless speeders do the same, leaving white arrows of foam on the dark sea's surface. Pacifia has begun its retreat.

"The rain may put out the fire," Andromeda says, "but wind will spread the embers."

I grasp her deeper meaning. What's begun here today will set off a chain of consequences across Earth and the Moon. Battery Bay must take up arms against the Committee, or let the Pacifian and Militia joint attack go unpunished. After so much human suffering, Dovetail will get what it wants.

The realization meets only numbness in my mind. I watch Pacifia limp away until the horizon is as empty as I feel.

※ — ※ — ※

The Parliament building's ruins lie smoldering behind the military procession. Battalions of Batterer soldiers march down the wide avenue, boots crunching on rubble. Shiny, rain-slicked black tanks are interspersed throughout their ranks; officers carry flags from all over the Batterer alliance, flown at half-staff to mourn the lives lost in the recent battle.

Prime Minister Sear stands on a balcony overlooking the scene. He speaks reassuring words that don't matter to me. So many other noises are swallowing his voice that it's not worth the mental effort to pick apart his meaning.

Squarish old spaceships fly above the army's ranks, plunging the troops into shadow. Batterer craft run on the large side, ranging from Omnibus-sized to the length of a small skyscraper oriented horizontally. The vehicles have been refurbished in a rush following Parliament's unanimous declaration of war against the Lunar-Pacifian alliance. Rust coats the seams in the metal; many vehicles sport dents from the last time they were used: thirty years ago, in the failed diplomacy mission to the bases.

"They're gonna attack the Commmittee with *those*?" On my right, Yinha works her jaw. "They're relics. Heavy steel exteriors, no self-repairing mechanism. Pilots are probably out of practice too."

Relics? Alex would say. *Don't you mean* coffins? He's with Wes and the other Odans in what's left of the rectangular park, participating in a mourning ritual for Murray and the other dead.

"At least it's something," I mumble. "We got the alliance we came for."

Under Committee rule, we didn't hold funerals. Hours after someone died, officials picked up the body, burned it, and mixed the ashes into the greenhouse soil. The deceased continued to serve the bases, and the rest of us moved on. Excessive emotion earned official admonition, as it "hindered progress" and "disrupted order." I didn't know then that the Committee had ordered many deaths and wanted us to forget them too. After Dad's, Mom ordered my siblings and me never to cry—not even inside our apartment.

That's why the Odans baffle me. All of them, even the disci-

plined Sanctuarists, have removed themselves from the larger
world for hours to honor their dead. *They need to live*, I imagine
Mom saying. *Not only survive.*

A wave of gasps runs through the crowd, pulling me away from
my troubled thoughts. The Batterers tilt their heads back, pointing
upward.

A small open hovercar, painted orange and packed with yelling
civilians, flies under the spacecraft, above the foot soldiers. It trails
a black cloth banner with a blinking white skull and text that reads:
CUT TIES TO PHONY ALLIES. Another hovercraft follows, bearing the
message, THEY'RE NOT DOVES, THEY'RE WAR HAWKS. A third: DOVE-
TAIL SACRIFICED OUR LIVES FOR THEIR CAUSE.

A burning sensation breaks through my numbness. Anger. Do
the Batterers really think we staged the Pacifian attack to enlist
their nation's help? I push back against the surge of feeling. Such
unfounded hypotheses are bound to surface in a place with a vocal, multifaceted population. Still, this one hurts. They're accusing
Dovetail of the same double-dealing that we're trying to fight.

Three meters to my right, a preteen boy with a long blond
ponytail tugs on his father's sleeve. I barely make out his words—
they're muffled by Sear's booming voice.

"Can't they get in trouble for interrupting a military procession?"

His father's wearing a ponytail too and has a curling beard several centimeters long. "Parliament's shut down, police are digging
people out of the ground—the conspiracy theorists can do what
they damn well please."

Yellow emergency lights begin flashing, followed by beeping
from the PA system. Panic and exasperation well up inside me; I
hold back a groan. Another attack? On every side, people crane

their heads toward the sky, but the soldiers on the street march onward, trying to look unfazed.

Then a crackling public announcement rocks the city. *"Unidentified falling object is approaching the Needle's Eye at terminal velocity."*

No! Amidst the screaming, milling crowd, I scan the sky, but too many clouds obscure my line of sight. Though the Needle's Eye is far away, I feel a slow ache build in my heart. It's one of the few architectural beauties on Battery Bay that's remained intact, and it's full of people that won't get out in time.

"Object is a sphere less than a foot in diameter. We have reason to believe it originates from the Moon. Evacuate the area immediately."

23

A FLASH OF STEEL PLUMMETS FROM THE clouds. Filmed by remote-controlled vlogger cameras broadcasting to civilians' roll-out screens all over the city, it lands on the observatory of the Needle's Eye, stirring up a mushroom cloud of dust. Shrieks and screams drown out the sound of impact. But there's no thunderous explosion, no splintered metal or raging fire or bodies tossed about.

After the dust settles and the crowd clears, I see that the object has split down the middle, like a walnut cracking open in the neatest possible way. A conical light beam shoots upward from the opening, and a giant, high-resolution projection of the Moon forms high above the city. We tip our heads back to watch.

As it rotates, each base becomes visible—I and II near the North Pole; III, IV, and V scattered across the Near Side; and Base VI, the one lonely settlement in the center of the Far Side. We can even see the satellites orbiting the Moon, like wasps circling their hive.

Below the projection is a timer—this seems to be footage from 16:32 Lunar time: yesterday afternoon. The Batterers' screams yield to stunned silence. Too afraid to watch the fake Moon, I look at their faces instead.

That's when an almighty *boom* shatters the peace. Heart pulsating in my chest, I search the area for the source. But Yinha taps me on the shoulder, gestures to the fake Moon with a quivering finger.

A spherical aurora is expanding above a familiar crater on the Moon's Far Side. It looks like a dandelion, bursting with silver tufts. The light stings my eyes, but I can't look away from the beauty of it, and the horror.

The dandelion cloud rises and dissipates, leaving behind a crater full of fire, blackened metal, shattered glass. The enormous radio telescope and particle accelerator, blown to bits.

This has to be an animation, I tell myself, hoping beyond hope. *Not real footage.*

But then the shot zooms in—to the blood-soaked bodies buried underneath the debris, limbs swelling as the water in them vaporizes in the absence of pressure. Crushed bones, melted skin, blank minds. No one, not even the Committee, could fake such gore.

Black text wraps around the silver Moon. AID THE DOVETAIL INSURGENCY, AND WE WILL DESTROY YOU.

Fragmented thoughts collide in my mind, unable to form a coherent whole. *Bomb. Who would call us an insurgency?*—the Committee. *The Far Side . . . the Singularity.*

Back when Dovetail took the Singularity, the Committee made a terrifying threat. And now they've followed through.

Something's wrapped around my cold forearms: Yinha's trembling hands. Even as I watch her desolate face and hear her shouted words, I find myself unable to feel, as I did watching Murray's last moments. As if by holding back emotion, I can deny what I've seen here.

But it's real, and all the numbness in the world won't erase it.

Base VI is gone forever.

✳ — ✳ — ✳

"What we have witnessed was a crime not only against innocent Lunar civilians, but against all of humanity." Prime Minister Sear's voice cuts through the empty air. The broadcast screens show him leaning on a podium, muscles coiled in anger as if he's ready to spring. This time, I listen to every word.

The Batterers filling the streets and watching on their roll-out screens mostly look terrified, though a few are full of grief, and still others are furious. Parents grasp children's hands; couples turn to each other for comfort. I witnessed a similar scene right after the Free Radical wrenched itself from Committee rule and prepared to fight. Change the Batterers' clothes, wipe off their face paint, and they'd look almost Lunar.

"We must join the fight against injustice, millions of miles above our heads," says Prime Minister Sear. He's leapt on our tragedy, using it to advance his longtime political agenda. His single-mindedness doesn't anger me. I've learned to expect such things from people with power, whether they're Lunar or Earthbound.

"We cannot stand by while their sham government commits mass murder! If the Committee eradicates Dovetail, we will be their next target. We cannot wait until that day to fight back!"

Applause, whistles, and flag-waving from the growing crowd. Sear has turned his people's fear into indignation and determination; impressed, I make a mental note for the next time I give a speech.

News stations all over Battery Bay begin to broadcast interviews with Parliament members. As I walk, I watch people's roll-out screens over their shoulders.

"Representative, what do you make of the Lunar Standing Committee's threat?" asks a reporter.

"They want to deter us from allying with Operation Dovetail," replies his interviewee, a young, expertly groomed Parliament member. "Battery Bay does not cower before threats!"

Another screen, another journalist: "Representative Harrington, yesterday you denigrated the Lunar people, calling them degenerate. Have you changed your position on the Dovetail insurgency?"

The stringy-haired bigot who tore apart the alliance proposal looks shaken. "Whatever a people's moral deficiencies, they do not deserve to be killed by their governments."

He talks robotically, as if hating every word that passes between his teeth. Though he doesn't want to help Dovetail, he'd be a fool to speak out against public opinion.

Pushing through the crowd behind Andromeda, I hear segments of more news reports: "The Standing Committee constitutes an Earth-wide threat and must be deposed." "If the Committee defeats the rebels, they'll destroy us next. We must fight them." "My constituents are afraid for their lives, and we must take down the cause of their fear—the Lunar government."

It took an entire base's murder to bring these people to our side. But it's worked. Maybe the Committee didn't think we'd react to their atrocities by uniting instead of disintegrating.

"Come this way." Andromeda motions for Yinha and me to follow her. "The Batterers are reaching consensus in our favor. We need to figure out our next move."

We hustle down a side street until the wide rectangular "park" comes into view. It no longer deserves that name. Black water sits in depressions dug out by Pacifian bombs; the great lawns look parched, pockmarked. Trees have been ripped out of the ground or torn limb from limb; leaves blown away, branches singed black. Even the squirrels and pigeons must have perished in the attacks.

The three of us stare at the devastation for a long moment before venturing into the burial grounds.

24

"WE NEED YOU BACK. ALL OF YOU." ASTERION'S DIS-
tressed voice plays from the Sanctuarists' makeshift computer.
We're in a sheltered cave near the park's center. It was spared much
of the destruction that wrecked the surrounding area.

In the background of the audio clip, there's the hum of spaceship engines and the tremolo of conversation. Asterion sent the
message at 03:48 Lunar time: several hours ago. We'd have used
Dovetail's communication mechanism to intercept it—HeRPs
with signal connections to the Free Radical—but Alex insisted that
the Sanctuarists' smaller, more convoluted network was safer from
Lunar or Pacifian spies.

It's dark here. The chilly air smells like rotting leaves and
damp fur; dirty water fills small pockets in the bumpy granite of
the cave floor. The blue light from the screen, which runs off the
power of an emergency generator, casts a sickly hue on the skin
of everyone assembled—me, Yinha, Andromeda, Alex, Wes, and
Wesley Sr.

We sit in a semicircle, facing the monitor on the wall. Wes's knee
touches mine, and I hope the contact comforts him as it does me.
You're with me now, it seems to say. Each instant we're alive, the universe is granting us one more second together. Then, impossibly,
another and another. Given recent events, I'm grateful for every one.

"I wish I had a better way to deliver both the terrible news," Asterion says, *"and the good news too."*

On Wes's other side, his father sits, body angled protectively toward his son. His back is hunched in a C-curve. One hand shields his forehead and eyes from view. The grief in his posture—and the love—sends shivers up my spine. This man sent his fifteen-year-old son to the Moon, sent me on a suicide mission after I proved to be Lunar. But he looks incapable of hurting anyone now. His oldest child's death seems to have snapped something inside him.

"The Singularity. It's . . ." Asterion takes a deep breath before confirming our worst fears. *"It's . . . gone. Bombed out. Small thermonuclear warhead with twelve kilotons of explosive force, but it was enough to exterminate the settlement. Committee pulled the bomb from lunar orbit, sent it crashing down. Evacuation from the base was futile. Over thirty thousand dead."*

All those lights snuffed out, in one instant. My mind struggles to wrap around the number, but it unravels each time I try.

Alex is shivering, mumbling to himself. "Leavitt— Lovelace—" Some of the thirty thousand dead, the ones he cared for most. I think of Mitchell, Rose's black-haired sister, who remained on the Singularity after the invasion, of her sharp eyes sparking with unanswered questions. Incinerated. How has Rose reacted to the news?

Wesley Sr. tugs on his sleeve. "Be still, agent."

Alex shakes his head, refusing to look up. I look at Wes to see how he's taking Asterion's revelations. His face is blank, as if the words haven't yet entered his ears.

"We should've left more important loyalist prisoners there as a deterrent . . ." Yinha muses.

Andromeda shushes her. "It wouldn't have done any good."

I wonder if she's right.

Asterion begins talking again, his voice more businesslike this time.

"*Here's the real reason we need you. Dovetail had no choice but to attack Base II ahead of schedule.*" He tells us that loyalists were preparing to storm Base I's underground neighbor, Base II, known colloquially as the Dugout, to root out Dovetailers. So we beat them to it.

Andromeda tenses up, but the weariness on her face remains.

"*The invasion succeeded,*" Asterion announces. "*As of 02:12 today, the Dugout is Dovetail territory.*"

I blink dumbly at the cavern wall. After such a tragedy, the enormity of Dovetail's success feels like a lie. An illusion someone could wipe away at any moment.

"*The cost to Dovetail was minimal,*" Asterion's recorded voice says. He describes cutting power from the Dugout, causing chaos and letting Dovetail invade with minimal damage. Most of Dovetail's troops and influential people like my siblings have been moved to the Dugout, as have our prisoners Jupiter Alpha and Skat Yotta, to deter nuclear attack.

We exhale in relief—and wonder.

Bit by bit, I let myself believe that it's true. Dovetail proved itself stronger and smarter than anyone could have foreseen. The Dugout is ours.

My family's there now. Has Cygnus adjusted to his new surroundings? Is Anka still able to take care of him?

She's strong. I know she can.

"*Now for the less thrilling news,*" Asterion says. "*The loyalists attacked a fleet of our ships flying from home*"—Base IV—"*to the Dugout, and we lost food as well as personnel. A shipment of Bai's drone prototypes was also destroyed, so the new territory is biologically vulnerable.*"

But we'll be back to help soon enough. The Dovetail envoy

will soon fly to the Moon, passing through contested airspace and a belt of nuclear weapons.

"*With thousands of loyalist troops returning from Earth,*" Asterion says, "*I need your help to lead our forces, Yinha. Andromeda, we need you—you and your practical advice, even if it's the last thing I want to hear sometimes.*" This elicits a sad chuckle from Andromeda. "*And Girl Sage, we need you to put the light back in Dovetail's eyes. Come home. And bring as many Batterers as you can—*"

"*Sir, we've finished the weapons inventory.*" A young woman's voice interrupts. She sounds far away.

"*Coming,*" Asterion calls. Turning back to the recording microphone, he says, "*I have to go. Reply as soon as it's safe.*"

A *click*, and he's gone.

Taking the Dugout was no small victory for Dovetail. Losing all of the Singularity was no small loss for humankind. I want to celebrate and mourn, to give both events the weight they deserve, but all the people who'd do either with me are otherwise occupied. Andromeda has taken up the microphone to record a reply. Leaning over her shoulder, Yinha occasionally interjects with comments. Alex ignores their feverish whispers, instead watching Wes plead with his father.

"Please," Wes says, "I have to go back up there."

He's coming with us. A burst of happiness makes me feel weightless, but only for a moment. I want Wes to stay with me, but I can imagine how painful it'll be for him to leave his grieving family. And how dangerous our journey into the sky will be.

Wesley Sr. presses his thin lips together. "No. You will not leave this city. It would crush your mother—"

"Come off it, Senior," Alex says.

"You will stay on Earth as well, Huxley," Wesley Sr. says. "There's enough work for you here on Battery Bay."

"We've helped set off a civil war up there," Alex says. *One that killed his friends.* For both boys, the Lunar conflict is personal.

"He's right," Wes says to his father. "The Lunar war exists in part because of our actions. Didn't you teach us to finish what we started?"

"I . . . After Marina . . ." Wesley Sr.'s chest deflates. It makes him look terribly small, especially because we're all sitting on the ground. "It can't happen to you, son."

Wes stares at his hands. He's toying with his shoelaces, winding and unwinding them around his wrist. "If I'd gone back earlier and thrown the Committee out, maybe she'd still be here." His father remains silent. "When I go to the Moon this time, I won't be alone. I've got Alex . . . and Phaet." His knee nudges mine. "This time, I'll save Saint Oda for good, just like you and Mother always wanted."

"We don't expect you to be a hero or a savior—not anymore," Wesley Sr. says. "We just want you to live. That's what she and I have decided."

Wes looks into his father's face—not as an underling or a child, but as an equal. "It's time for me to make that decision on my own. Even if it's one of my last."

Wesley Sr. stares at his son, blinking in surprise. Then he puts an arm around Wes and thumps him on the shoulder. When Wes returns the one-sided embrace, his father crushes him in both arms.

"I've never been prouder of you, my boy." Wesley Sr.'s face is buried in his son's shoulder, but I can still hear his voice cracking with emotion. "Or more afraid to lose you."

25

"UP YOU GO, MISS."

As the Batterer officer boosts me into the *Champion*'s cramped cabin, I take a last look at Wes, who's boarding an identical vessel off to my right. It takes everything in me not to scream his name. *You'll see him again on the Moon*, I tell myself. The Batterers will have to guard his life until then.

To prepare for liftoff, our clumsy Earthbound spaceship is oriented vertically, its tail pointed at the ground, instead of horizontally like a Lunar craft's. The *Champion* is a meter longer than a standard Destroyer but twice as heavy; with squarish stabilizers, it's shaped more like a chubby manatee than a shark.

Yinha's already inside. She cranes her head back to look at me, her lip curled up as if she's smelled something awful. Perhaps it's the old cotton cloth covering the seats, or the oxidized iron on the dashboard.

In a few minutes, we'll be en route to the Dugout, where everyone important to me and the rebellion is stationed. I wish we could pilot our own Destroyer there, but the Batterers deemed it too dangerous: Committee ships would target a Dovetail vessel first, and this time we lack decoy Destroyers to throw them off. So Yinha and I are aboard the *Champion*. Andromeda is in another ship, and Wes and Alex are in yet another. The Batterers spread us throughout their fleet so that enemies will have trouble capturing—or killing—all five of us at once.

As the ship fires up, preparing to launch, metal rattles all around me. Yinha grips my arm, squeezing her eyes shut as we lift off. The vehicle trails smoke and roars like a typhoon—as other ships join us in the air, the din escalates, and my head begins to pound. The two pilots and four other crewmembers gesture at each other. Their mouths move, but I can't hear a word.

Crack. Pain pulsates through my skull; the ship's sudden movement has smashed my head into the metal wall. When I open my eyes, black spots block out the center of my vision.

"What's going on?" Yinha shouts at the pilots. "Hey, Batterers, you just dodge something?"

My vision clears; I look through the windshield and see missiles about half a meter long streaking toward us.

"We've reached the belt of weaponized base satellites," a Batterer pilot calls. "And someone's activated the tactical nukes."

The Batterer fleet disperses. Yinha's fingers tighten around my arm; neither of us has ever sat in a ship under attack and been unable to pilot it to safety. We've both studied the bases' miniature nuclear weapons and were prepared for the Committee to use them, but we're stuck now, depending on the less-knowledgeable Batterers to get us through this barrage alive.

Embedded in satellites, the warheads can be fired at spaceborne objects with great accuracy. They have slightly more than a critical mass of uranium-235 under enormous pressure, resulting in a few dozen tons of explosive force each. That's more than enough to vaporize a ship.

"Disassemble hull's outer layer!" calls the lead pilot.

A crewmember jams his finger on a red button. The *Champion*'s covering peels away like an onion skin. Metal pieces shoot outward, knocking three missiles out of the way. They silently explode into shiny arrowheads as we roar past, our hull one layer thinner.

Behind us, another Batterer ship isn't so lucky. A missile collides with its left wing. The uranium atom fragments react with the oxygen in the cabin, and the explosion sprays blinding orange flames into space.

Horrific thoughts crowd my mind: Andromeda could've been on that ship, or Alex and Wes. *Would the universe dare to take Wes away from me only two days after our reunion?* Yes, it would. I've never believed it's a fair place.

I can't control what happens to Wes's ship. But I must ensure this one makes it to the Moon. Sucking in a deep breath, I reassess the situation: the Batterer pilots are trying to shoot down the satellites. But the spherical spacecraft rotate too rapidly, spinning away on their orbital paths. Every shot misses.

"Forget the satellites!" I beg the crew. "Fly us close to Bases I and II. The Committee won't risk hitting their own stronghold."

They listen. Pressure builds in the engine; the spaceship jets northward, our pilots aiming us at the lunar North Pole. Within seconds, other Batterer ships overtake us so that we're no longer a single target.

By the time Bases I and II come into view, we're racing through a clear black sky, empty of missiles. The pilots let off exhaust from the front of the craft to slow us down.

To the north, a sprawling complex of semi-polyhedral buildings—Base I—hugs the Peary Crater's rugged rim. Known as the peaks of eternal light, the mountains behind Base I are almost always in the sun's spotlight. Only the most thorough lunar eclipses can cloak them in shadow. In contrast, the deepest, coldest craterlets south of the base house ancient black water ice that's only illuminated by passing satellites.

"The Dugout's the bump over there!" Yinha calls. "We're almost on top of it."

Peering out the window, the small lumps in the regolith look like badly buried treasure. The Dugout, built a decade after Base I, was constructed a dozen kilometers south of its predecessor as an emergency hideout. Due to its underground location, its residents can't enjoy views of mountains or even the black basalt "sea," Mare Frigoris, that spreads southward from the base in all its pock-marked glory. But many Dugout residents sampled Base I's grandeur, if only for a few hours at a time, before Dovetail took over. An underground passageway hollowed out millions of years ago by volcanic activity connects the two settlements, and the Committee's architects turned it into a metro tunnel. Dugout residents commute to Base I every day to cook, clean, and serve the highest echelons of Lunar society—or should I say "commuted"? Now that Dovetail's occupied the Dugout, the tunnel must be out of service.

Without more interference from the loyalists, the Batterer fleet circles closer to the newest chunk of Dovetail territory. Although the Committee's not attacking us anymore, uneasiness lingers in my gut. I know them. They're watching our every move.

26

FIVE THOUSAND BATTERER TROOPS SPILL
into the Dugout's dingy subterranean hangar, their teal uniforms
vibrant against the concrete walls. Enormous spacecraft dock; towering, storm-gray rovers that hold hundreds of personnel crawl out
of their bellies. The rovers' eight long legs are constructed to creep
across rough terrain. Their roofs nearly touch the exposed metal
struts crisscrossing the hangar's low ceiling.

After the Batterer pilots park the *Champion,* the crew, Yinha,
and I will have to wear pressure suits to walk through Defense, a
small department added to the Dugout almost as an afterthought.
The habitat is still leaking air into space because of damage sustained during the invasion.

While the pilots wait for a space to open up, I watch Alex help
Wes climb out of their ship. I long to disembark prematurely and
join them. Wes leans on Alex, tilts his head toward the *Champion,*
and salutes. *That was for me.* My heart suddenly feels too big for
my chest.

Someone taps my shoulder, interrupting my thoughts. Yinha.

"What I wouldn't give to know what they're thinking right
now," she says, pointing her chin at the teal masses of Batterer
troops. Of the faces I see, almost all are unreadable. But their hands

are shaking, their steps wobbly—I doubt their unsteadiness results from spaceflight alone.

"They look so professional," Yinha says. "But I can guess what's on their minds. All the usual questions: What if I suffer? Why should I—not my friends or family back home—risk everything for these strange people? Why, why, why? If there's anything I've learned from watching Earthbound, it's that they ask questions that don't have answers."

That wouldn't happen on the Moon, where we frame inquiries solely in the spirit and style of scientific experimentation. We would ask nothing that we couldn't answer by making observations, plugging data into spreadsheets, and running statistical tests. The Committee didn't appreciate anyone engaging with the big questions—for example, why things were one way, *their* way, and not another.

"What makes you say that?" I ask.

Yinha sighs, her face softening. "That poor girl, Murray. She had so many questions that day in the park, and she fired them at me like bullets."

I'd wondered about what they talked about but was afraid to pry.

"She wanted to understand. Why'd the Lunars attack Saint Oda, of all the cities on Earth? Why'd my squad kill her friend but leave Murray to live a smashed-up life? She said that the typical Odan answer—*it was God's will*—wasn't enough. She thought I'd give her something better."

"Did you?"

Yinha shakes her head. "I said that if we knew why bad things happened to good people, it would justify their suffering. It's better not to have an answer. Because once we can explain something, it becomes okay."

I give her a puzzled look.

"Remember how people used to obsess about whether preventing radiation sickness was even possible? Then Asterion made those Gamma-Gone meds, and now we only think about cosmic rays busting our cells for as long as it takes to swallow the pill."

She's right. Once we solve a mystery, people get all matter-of-fact about it. They publish some papers, implement new gadgets, and move on.

"A bit of mystery isn't so awful," Yinha says, as if reading my mind.

While we've spoken, the *Champion* has slid into a tight space between two identical ships. Yinha grabs her pressure suit from the wall of the hold, preparing to disembark.

"Murray was so disappointed," she continues. "She thought I'd tie up all the loose ends in her life, because I was there when the strings unraveled. Wherever she is now, wherever her atoms have spread—the sea or the sky or even space itself—I hope she has a better view of things."

"We'll give her one," I say, stepping into my pressure suit. How clearly would Murray see us, and how uncluttered would the skies be, if this war came to an end?

I accept that we don't know the answer. At least for now.

⁂ — ⁂ — ⁂

Outside the ship, Base II's Defense Department feels haunted. Dovetail's invasion has killed the power; only the red-orange emergency lights still function.

Clothed in a pressure suit, Yinha leads the Batterers and the recently returned Dovetailers past empty barracks, deserted mess halls, and gymnasiums full of crooked exercise equipment. Aside from a few scrapes on the walls, it's as Asterion said: not much damage. But the air pressure gauge in my helmet gives a frighteningly low reading.

Moving fast, I catch up to Alex, and together he and I flank Wes. I can't see Wes's face through his visor, but he leans on Alex, gait uneven, movements stiff, as he's trying not to break the new scabs over his leg wounds.

I offer him my gloved hand, and his palm lands in mine, heavier than expected. *How much invisible weight does he bear on those shoulders?* I wonder. *Will he ever leave it behind?*

27

THE FIVE THOUSAND BATTERERS INUNDATE the Dugout's decrepit main corridor. Like the other Lunars, I can't peel my eyes away from the soldiers—in their teal uniforms, they look like a wave that'll wash us away. Dovetailers whisper to one another and children clutch their parents' hands in fear, but none cry or turn aside. The Committee has conditioned us well, taught us never to show grief or fear. Civilians and soldiers alike hold themselves with robotic poise, even though I know they're disturbed by the Singularity's destruction and the subsequent arrival of scores of foreigners.

I sit with Dovetail's leaders in the center of the second-floor balcony, surrounded by other Dovetailers, all of us looking down at the Earthbound. Anka positions herself in front of me—we're the same height now—as if to shield me from the Batterer tide below. Cygnus watches the soldiers march past, his lips counting the rows. *He's improving*, I think to myself. He can look at the guns strapped at their hips without flinching. But has his hacking assignment gotten any easier for him?

I remember our reunion, when they came to Defense to see me during my shift. A hug from Anka, a quick squeeze on the shoulder from Cygnus, zero tears or shouts of joy. Maybe they're going numb too, not daring to hope or feel happiness.

Aside from the soldiers, there's not much to see. The Dugout's cramped interior lacks Base I's glamor and even the Free Radical's sleek minimalism. The floor plan follows the lunar lava tubes into which the base was built; the departments were constructed out of swells in the tubes. No windows disrupt the tunnel walls' matrix of concrete reinforced with steel beams. The Dugout looks like what it is: an emergency shelter, a place where not even sunlight can break in. Branching off from the main hallway, the tiny, sad underground greenhouses grow plants for food and oxygen by blasting them with overhead lamps. A gigantic emergency bunker burrows even farther down. The Committee ordered it built before the Battle of Peary, knowing that they needed a refuge within a refuge to survive our then-enemies' most advanced bombs.

Three beeps command everyone's attention. The corridor quiets, and all heads turn toward us.

Asterion, standing to my left, leaves the group. On his other side are Andromeda, Sol, and most conspicuously, Minister Costa, who wears a shimmering gold suit and turquoise tie.

Yinha's on my immediate right; Rose hovers next to her, her expression obscured by curtains of pale hair. Her runny nose is a red splotch on her white face, and she sips a steaming hot drink from a utilitarian insulated mug that I recognize as Yinha's. Rose coughs, and Yinha puts a hand on the small of her back. It gives me a start: *Are Yinha and Rose together now?* I feel as warm as if I'd sipped from the mug myself, glad that my friends have found love and companionship even in these trying times.

Older Dovetailers might not feel the same. They grew up hearing from the Committee that same-sex relationships interfere with birthrates and thus population stability, or some other nonsense. But it's about time they stopped believing those ideas.

Minister Costa clears his throat and steps forward, his water-hair wavering around his head, betraying his nerves.

"Today marks the first peaceful interaction between Battery Bay and an extraterrestrial people," Costa says. His shaky tone doesn't foster confidence, but the Dovetailers hang on to him with their eyes. His troops could lead us to victory. "We are united today not only by a common enemy, but by common principles."

There's a huffing noise behind me. I turn to see my sister crossing her arms and rolling her eyes. She fixes me with a raised eyebrow. I should tell her to behave, but I don't. *Anka's heard enough about principles*, I think to myself. *He needs to show us something real.*

Costa offers his friendship and loyalty, expecting ours in return. Behind me, Ariel is talking to Alex, holding Alex's paper notebook open between them. Ariel's chin hovers a centimeter above Alex's shoulder, and his eyes study the young Earthbound man with . . . something more than admiration. I'd suspected for a while that Alex's magnetic personality had attracted the intellectually restless Ariel even more than most.

And Ariel's feelings haven't escaped him; Alex looks both depressed and slightly ill at ease.

Umbriel smacks his brother on the arm, and Ariel stops talking just as Costa wraps up his speech to courteous clapping.

Below me, thousands of Dovetailers stare up at Costa with wide, desperate eyes. *Free us*, they seem to beg, *and we will do whatever you ask.*

28

THE BATTERER SOLDIERS HAVE A SOMEWHAT
icy quality about them, something I sense rather than see or hear.
They say "Hello" to us but "Hey there, oh?" to one another; they
make excuses to avoid sitting or conversing with Dovetail troops
in their free time, and groups of them guffaw with each other but
put on solemn masks when they notice our approach.

In the main hallway, Cygnus and I pass a trio of Batterer soldiers who stare at us for a heartbeat too long. At the sight of their
half-meter-long handguns, my brother shudders and reaches for
my arm. Up close, the weapons are still too much for him.

"What's wrong with them?" Cygnus whispers. We're en route
to his job in InfoTech so that I can catch up on what he and the
other specialists have been working on. Rose will update me on
space battle logistics too, which I'll need to know when I fly into
the skirmishes taking place between the Earth and Moon.

"They act like we're not here," Cygnus says. "And stare like *we're*
the nutcases."

"They may be homesick, Cygnus," I say. "Don't worry, we didn't
upset them."

I don't admit that the Batterers seem to dislike us, for some
mysterious reason, as much as they tolerate us. The thought makes
me uneasy. Being comrades-in-arms requires a stronger bond.

"Yeah." Cygnus releases my arm. "Homesick. Makes sense, I guess. The food's not much here, and the apartments are gritty."

True. The tiny quarters in which my family lives have such low ceilings that Cygnus bumps his head on light fixtures, and we can hear our neighbors' frightened conversations through the thin walls. A young couple with a two-year-old daughter, they're terrified that if she survives the war, she won't develop normal social skills because of the environment in which she's growing up.

A lone Batterer officer, about to cross paths with us, nods curtly at me. Recognizing him as the *Champion*'s pilot, I raise two fingers to salute him, but he swerves to the side, taking a meter-wide detour to avoid contact.

Cygnus plods along, watching his feet. "I'm homesick too," he says. "I miss our old base. But being here, away from where all *that* happened"—Mom's death, his capture, and so many other tragedies—"it's helping me."

I turn to look at him, my worries about the Batterers temporarily banished. "How?" The burst of hope in my voice surprises me. "By letting you forget?"

"I'll never forget," Cygnus says. "But I have to move on."

※ — ※ — ※

Rose seems to have slept in the InfoTech Department, or not at all. Her cold hasn't improved since yesterday, and her sister is still dead. If this meeting wasn't so critical, I would feel guilty for intruding upon her. No, scratch that. I feel guilty anyway.

Despite her obvious grief, Rose spares a smile for me and my brother as we enter the dark intelligence headquarters. Rows of desks with HeRPs stretch across the floor, strings of code swirling across the domed screens. A grim-faced hacker sits behind each one. The bitter scent of Three-Molar Coffee mixed with the stress-induced body odor of thirty information specialists hits me full force, and I blink back the tears that spring to my eyes.

As Cygnus takes his place in the second row, Rose waves me over to a corner where we won't disturb anyone. On the backmost, rightmost monitor, Rose pulls up a 3-D projection of the Earth, the Moon, and the hundreds of blocky satellites swinging in elliptical orbits around both.

"Sorry I've made the model so big," she says, sniffling. "My eyes aren't the best."

The entire diorama measures four human wingspans across—three, if the arms in question are Umbriel's. He and I have seen each other once, in passing, and I miss him despite the fact that we're geographically close again. He hasn't told me about his experiences here, and I haven't told him about the wonder and horror of Earth.

Earth. In Rose's model, the planet's about the size of my head, and the Moon so small I could grab and throw it with one hand. Despite being tiny as a fingerprint, the satellites look menacing, like fossilized cicadas and flies.

"As you know from all your flying around, space isn't flat." Rose pokes an icon on the HeRP, and the background blankness representing space shades over in gradations of gray. "The darker colors indicate greater gravitational force, and the lighter indicates less. See how the area near Earth is almost black, near the Moon is dark gray, and the area in between is nearly white? Gravity shapes the battlefield out there. Being in an area with less gravity is like being on a hilltop: it's easier to lob something and hit your enemy, who's below you, than to throw it upward."

I nod, transfixed. I've felt gravity's pull outside—invisible, inaudible—and have had to bend to its will, just as when Pacifian bullets rained down on us in Battery Bay, and we could not retaliate with the same weapons.

Rose goes on, the speed of her speech increasing with her enthusiasm. Some of the sadness leaves her as she talks. It's inspiring to see, but I can't forget that we're using these maps to kill and avoid being killed.

"These five points are the highest of the high ground, where the gravitational fields of the Earth and Moon cancel out, and it's equally effortless to attack either body." Extending her arms, Rose points at five spots far from Earth, near the Moon's orbit, each marked with a flashing yellow icon. The area around them is shaded white. "But only two of the points are stable. Put anything in an unstable point and it'll fall out of orbit. The satellites Turner 1 and 3, which the Committee launched a century ago, move with each stable point as the positions of the Earth and Moon shift. We took control of Turner 3 last month, and have since warded off denial of service attacks and other grit."

Rose glides into the band of metal satellites orbiting the Moon, and the light makes her skin look pearly. "Red tags indicate the thermonuclear warheads, and the tiny ones with green tags are active communications satellites used by the Pacifians. We've got a team of nine that reads and listens to everything that passes through there, and another team monitoring where the Committee's spies have hacked *us*."

"Battery Bay ending its movement to Great Barrier Reef!" shouts one of the information specialists. Her voice is low for a woman's. "Current coordinates eleven degrees south, one hundred seventy-eight degrees east."

"Duly noted!" Rose calls, trying to sound peppy. Turning back to me, she sighs and drops the mask. "We have people communicating with Earthbound allies and checking every city's location to prevent surprise attacks. Other team members intercept and decrypt Committee communications."

Once upon a time, Cygnus would've loved those jobs, and it saddens me to think he isn't doing them now. "What about my brother?" I ask.

Rose's pale eyes drift from mine, and pain, even guilt, flits across her face. "The first job I gave him—on the team that's trying to hack into satellite-deployed nuclear weapons—seemed to . . . remind him of things. He was running proxies, keyscramblers, and other network defenses . . ." *Like he was afraid of getting caught again.* "It almost crashed his HeRP."

I nod, remembering the near-disastrous flight from the Free Radical to Earth. As I'd feared, Cygnus was the cause of Rose's "personnel issues"—he must've failed to take control of the weapons barring our ship's way.

"So I switched him to orbit tracking. He watches each satellite's trajectory around Earth and alerts us if anything wobbles or veers off course. Minimal coding involved. He's good at it, very detail-oriented."

Rose looks up at me, searching my expression for something: forgiveness, perhaps, for assigning Cygnus a horrendous first task. I hesitate, and then give her a smile. She was only following Sol's orders and making him useful. But does orbit tracking fit the bill? It seems like a job Rose invented out of pity.

"Has he flagged anything important?" I ask.

"He's alerted us to a couple of things. False alarms," Rose says, and I feel the crush of disappointment. Before my brother's capture, he could've out-coded everyone in this room. Now, he's merely . . . here. Watching satellites move across his screen, serene concentration mellowing his expression. He sometimes zooms in on particular objects, studies them closely, and then zooms out again, seeming to conclude that everything is normal. He doesn't seem *useful*, but he looks . . . okay. Okay is better than I'd hoped for.

"Thank you, Rose. Thanks for accommodating him. And for meeting me today, after . . ." My voice trails off, and I wonder if I've said too much by alluding to Mitchell's death. During Committee times, talking about lost loved ones, even to give sympathy, was considered unproductive and thus disruptive.

Even though I hardly know her, Rose's gentleness makes me too comfortable. She's like Wes in that way. Around both people, I'm not afraid to speak first and think later.

Rose makes a hiccupping sound halfway between a laugh and a sob. "Cygnus is doing what he can. I wouldn't ask for anything more."

She doesn't mention Mitchell, and I'm secretly glad. Grief is personal, but war is business; the first can't interfere with the second if we're to survive. That's a hard truth, one that much of Dovetail has accepted, one that makes our hearts burst with unsaid words and unshed tears.

A truth that, as I soon learn, is ripping us apart.

29

THE MARKET DEPARTMENT'S POORLY LIT TA-
bles are dusted with crumbs and the ghostly slicks of evaporated
spills. It doesn't smell like anything in the cramped room, despite
the fact that hundreds of troops and civilians are eating at once.

My lunch is euphemistically called "oat-and-soy stew," a
lukewarm mush made from the freeze-dried crops the Batterers
brought up. The food should sustain me through this afternoon's
foot-combat drill for the latest round of draftees—with the leak in
Defense finally fixed, we need to make up for lost training time.
Still, the "stew" is so bland that as I eat, I open my senses to more
interesting stimuli. A conversation coming from the table behind
me, conducted in snappish Batterer accents, soon becomes impossible to ignore.

"Since when is bread made out of yams and cut into tiny cubes?"
The speaker is a female soldier, just a year or so older than me. "They
take our crops and turn 'em into cat food."

"Everything's too tidy here, you know?" says another voice,
this one animated and male. With young Batterers, even state-
ments come out like questions, I notice.

"The people too," grunts another male soldier. "So neat with
the way they do things, the way they eat, all nibbly like mice, the

way they walk—their arms hardly swing, have you noticed that? Hey, Barnett, pass the peas, eh?"

Interesting, if insulting. I sink lower in my seat, hoping the Batterers won't catch me eavesdropping.

"Five spuds for the first person to see a Loony cry," grunts a female soldier. She lowers her voice and whispers, "Living under six dictators for a hundred years must've taken the heart right out of them."

My mouth goes dry. How could she perceive us like that, and dare to express her opinion in public, even quietly?

"All those people died on Base VI and they're pretending it didn't happen," one of the men says. "Business as usual, polishing laser guns and training teenagers to die. Not even a ceasefire, eh? Nope. Nothing."

"I don't trust them." The girl lowers her voice to a whisper. "I feel sorry for them, but I don't trust them."

Her fellow soldiers all agree, saying "yee-ah" and "mmhmm" and "that's just it."

I get up, sort my waste at the compost and recycling bins, and jog to Defense, pushing thoughts through my mind. It'll take more than quiet cooperation to break through the Batterers' distrust. It'll take something that they never anticipated.

※ — ※ — ※

"The Batterers don't trust us. How will they fight with us, for us, if they don't trust us?" After training lets out, I pace around the abandoned loyalist apartment Wes and Alex have occupied. The walls are concrete, the furniture made of twisted copper spotted with oxidized patches. Threadbare yellow throw pillows slump against the armrests. A string of flickering orange lightbulbs the size of buttons dangles from the ceiling's center, like so many fires threatening to go out. A typical room in the Dugout, this one has no windows. I'm beginning to thirst for a glimpse of the stars.

The boys lounge on the copper sofas, looking like prisoners on Dovetail's own turf. Exhaustion glazes their eyes; dried sweat cakes their skin. Wes lies on his back. Alex scribbles in his book, a frown framing his mouth.

"I'd ask the Batterers what we're doing wrong," I go on, "if it didn't make Dovetail seem like the flailing excuse for a revolt that we are."

Alex ignores me, but Wes nods, twisting his hands together on his lap. Copper-colored stubble covers his chin and upper lip; his eyelids are pink and puffy. Since we got back from Earth, he's talked even less than I do, and it unsettles me. But I know he wants me around. If he didn't, he'd have already insinuated that I should leave.

"We think they're strange, but they think we're . . . machines."

Wes rubs his red eyes with a clenched fist.

"I can't concentrate in this ruckus." Alex purses his lips, throws his pen between his notebook's pages, and ducks into the apartment's one bedroom. "Keep it down out there, all right?" He slams the old-fashioned hinged door with a *clang.*

Wes shrugs, as if to apologize for his friend's behavior. Aside from training and meetings where Asterion requires his presence, Alex hasn't gone out in public all week. He seems more disturbed by the Singularity's demolition than anyone could've predicted—more so than Rose, who grew up there. But he doesn't talk about it, even though I think he wants to. He's only scribbled more frequently than ever before, preserving his memories on paper. When people are nearby, he curls around his notebook like a mother wolf, trying to shield the words from wandering eyes.

"You and Alex must have seen us Lunars as robots too at first," I go on. "As *inhuman*. There has to be a way to convince the Batterers that we're *people*."

Finally, Wes opens his mouth. "I'm about to say something, and you won't like it."

I wait for him to gather his words.

"After the fight on Battery Bay, the Odans had nothing. Many of our loved ones' bodies were missing. But we went to a clearing in the park, lit some dry wood on fire, and prayed for their souls. People who knew them talked about the wonderful things they'd done in life, and, if they were young, the things they didn't get to do." He sighs and goes on in a near-whisper, "I spoke for my sister. Said she found some measure of happiness in life but had many unfulfilled hopes. I told them that Murray wanted someone to know everything about her, and to love her more with each new thing he discovered."

Don't we all? Watching him, reveling in his nearness, I wish more than ever that this war would leave the two of us alone. So that maybe we could experience for ourselves what Murray wanted, without sickness and death and demolition distracting us.

"Death hurts, Phaet," Wes continues. "It doesn't matter who you are or how you grew up."

He's talking about himself, and me, and everyone who's ever lost anyone. *It hurts the same for all of us. The Batterers too.* Maybe we can convince them that blood, not metal wire, runs through our bodies. If we let ourselves feel—if we let ourselves be human . . . there's a chance.

"It's not shameful to say good-bye to your people after they've gone."

I frown, thinking hard. Dovetail is afraid to show our grief, afraid to seem weak, afraid that the Batterer forces will abandon us. All those lives were cut short on the Singularity, and yet, we've only tried to move on.

We should have stopped living our lives based on fear long ago. More than a year has passed since we began our fight for freedom, but we're still acting as if the Committee commands our every move. It's time to put an end to that.

Without speaking, I give Wes a quick hug. Then I shrug on my jacket and dash across the Residential Department to find my sister.

* — * — *

Anka's in our borrowed apartment, sitting on the living room's black plastic sofa, doodling on her handscreen. Cygnus's bedroom door is closed—he's sleeping, or at least trying to.

One lamp is switched on, and it throws yellow light on the sharp lines of my sister's left cheek and jaw, on the soft curve of her lips, which she's sucking in as she concentrates. I feel as if an invisible hand is dragging me back to better days. Anka looks just like our mother. She speaks without looking at me, squinting at her handscreen, engrossed in her work.

"What's so exciting? It's not every day my sister comes running home as if the Committee's after her. Actually, no. That does happen every day."

I let out a choked laugh. "Want to strike back at them? Even if it's an indirect move?"

Anka lowers her handscreen. "Go on."

"We need to smooth out the spikes between us and our guests." I explain to her what we need to do, my voice rising and falling, filled with hope and solemnity, the feelings that I'm done hiding from others.

After I'm done, Anka breathes out for a long time. "I can't make this alone," she says, "but I know who can help. Mom's old Journalist friends, maybe Alex too. It'll be ready tomorrow. And it'll be unforgettable."

30

34,543.

The numbers, white against a black background, appear on every wall screen that flanks the Dugout's main hallway. Thousands of eyes take them in, Dovetailer and Batterer alike. The ceiling lights are off, so the base is dark. At my sister's direction, someone has brought in dozens of O-shaped mood lamps from a Militia official's apartment. They glow yellow, like anemic candlelight, and the illumination makes the metal beams across the ceiling look as if they're burning.

HOW DO WE MAKE SENSE OF SO MANY DEAD? the screens ask. WE DON'T KNOW. WE CAN ONLY TRY.

"34,543—it's a prime number." Sitting on my left, Cygnus rocks back and forth on his tailbone, whispering to himself. "A palindromic prime . . ."

I'd shush him, but it was hard enough for him to come here. He should do whatever he needs to do to stay.

Anka has helped several former Journalists make a video to honor the Singularity's dead. The film screening at the vigil will begin in about two minutes. Out of respect, Anka, Cygnus, and I have changed into white Theta robes. I remember my mother telling me white was the ancient Chinese color of mourning—the Committee didn't manage to steal that knowledge from her, the way they stole the Moon Festival. We sit lined up like ducklings in a row, the green-clad Phis clustered behind us.

Wes tiptoes up to my family and sits down to my immediate right. I'm surprised that he's left his apartment, and even more surprised to see him all in white. Knowing the color's significance to me, he must have requested old Theta robes instead of the ultramarine Kappa ones he used to wear.

Wes is my family now. I'd be kidding myself if I thought otherwise.

Behind me, Umbriel clears his throat, and I sit in suspense, wondering what will happen. He's said he isn't angry at Wes, not anymore—but now that they're both here, will they get along?

"Uh, welcome back," Umbriel whispers, and extends a hand to Wes to shake.

Wes's eyebrows shoot up—he's probably surprised that Umbriel greeted him civilly—and then he breaks into a welcoming smile. "Thanks, Umbriel."

Ariel watches approvingly, nods at Wes, and then looks at me. *All clear,* his eyes seem to say. Then his eyes rake over the room as if combing the crowd for Alex, who said he'd take a spot in the shadows, out of sight.

"Psst. Wes. Remember me?" Anka whispers.

Wes releases Umbriel's hand and takes my sister's. "Anka, your art's everywhere on base; how could I forget?"

"The scraps collection bins and the weapons-sharpener teams were her ideas too," Umbriel points out, and Anka grins pridefully.

Wes faces my brother, observes his nervous knotted hands and faraway expression. "And I'm glad to see you safe, Cygnus."

My brother shrugs. "Safer than I *was*."

"With your sisters and this fellow around?" Wes points at

Umbriel. "I say you're covered. Free to work computer magic in peace."

"I'm getting there," Cygnus says. Umbriel gives Wes a forced smile, but it's a smile all the same. My heart warms at the sight of my family members—from both Earth and the Moon—knitting themselves together.

As if to make the moment more perfect, a simple melody begins to play—it's some kind of plucked string instrument, but I haven't heard enough music in my lifetime to identify anything else about the song. The screens flash the words: HELENE AND HYPERION YOTTA, TINY DANCERS. As I realize what's coming, my happiness ebbs away.

The text fades out into a video of two brown-haired children holding hands and hopping in a circle on the Base VI Atrium floor. The bottom right-hand corner shows the date and time, as well as the words DISRUPTIVE MOVEMENT. A security pod taped this, and someone—Rose, perhaps, pulled it from the video files.

KEPLER THETA. A smiling old man with several missing teeth appears on the screen. He's wrapped a cloth around his head in an elaborate design. InfoTech caught him on camera for committing an attire violation.

CURIE SIGMA, LEADING ASTROBIOLOGIST. A long-necked woman wearing wrinkled robes stands before dioramas of different stars' solar systems, pointing at planets on which spectra of organic molecules were detected. She's not guilty of anything, except being in the wrong place at the wrong time when the bomb hit.

As we get more glimpses into the lives of the Singularity's residents, my sister begins to tremble. She wipes tears away with clenched fists. Umbriel reaches out to comfort her, but she shakes her head. "I don't *want* to stop being sad. We have to feel something, don't you see? There's no one else left to be sad for them."

Beside her, I continue watching the video. There's a young man studying on his handscreen; a middle-aged Sanitation worker mopping her brow; a teenage couple, clad in lab coats, kissing in a dark hallway. I reel in tears before they spill over, imagining how hopeful, how determined, how *alive* they all must have felt. No one besides Anka is crying; Umbriel looks angry, Ariel crestfallen, and Wes guilty.

Why was it them? I wonder. *Why them, and not another base— or us?*

"They've shown twelve victims so far." Cygnus scrunches up his eyes, trying to wrap his head around the tragedy. "That leaves 34,531 more people." His face goes slack, and then lights up with anger. "So many died. Killing the Committee won't change that."

I catch my brother's eye and shake my head, brokenhearted. But his furious expression doesn't budge. I can almost see numbers funneling through his head, adding to his despair.

To give him some privacy, I turn again to the video. A tan young woman stands in front of a giant touchscreen with equations scribbled across it, looking regally at the security pod that films her. MITCHELL MU, ASTROPHYSICS EMPLOYEE OF THE YEAR. Watching Rose's sister, I sink deeper into sadness—as a rising scientist, she reminds me of myself, of my own unrealized dreams. Mitchell will never reach her potential. In theory, I still have a chance. I almost feel guilty for wasting it.

The next clip twists the knife harder. FRANKLIN PHI, reads the caption. BASE VI'S YOUNGEST VICTIM. The date the bomb dropped is in the screen's corner. Against a backdrop of Medical white, gloved hands snip an umbilical cord and lift up a screaming baby. Fast-forward thirty minutes: a flushed, laughing woman cradles the newborn boy to her chest. Within seconds, his screams turn to soft giggles. Then Franklin falls asleep, his head nestled in his mother's hand.

Franklin Phi came into the universe on the same day that he left it behind.

The tears come then, tracing lines down my face and spotting the white cotton of my robes. Warm strong arms and the aroma of smoke and wood surround me. I let my head drop into the curve of Wes's neck and shoulder. With him as my cocoon, I'm safe. He doesn't speak, doesn't tell me it's okay when it's not. One thing I love about Wes: he doesn't talk when there's nothing to say.

He stiffens, and I feel the weight of someone watching us. Umbriel. My friend nods, seeming to understand that there's nothing I need from him, and we three turn back to watch the screen.

A low, melancholy hum presses on my eardrums. Wes and I remain entwined until he shakes my shoulder to get my attention. I lift my head, and he points upward.

The film concludes with black text on a white background: ON JANUARY 17, 2349, OVER THIRTY THOUSAND STORIES WERE CUT SHORT. REMEMBER THEM ALWAYS, FOR NO ONE ELSE CAN.

As if I could forget what I've seen today. It's given me 34,543 more reasons to keep fighting.

The humming gathers strength behind us, swelling among the Dovetailers gathered on the balcony. In the front stand, Asterion, Andromeda, and her daughter all join in—Callisto's throat tightens repeatedly, as if she's swallowing tears. Several meters to the side and bathed in the faint lighting, Rose sits stoically, white and silver like a marble statue. Yinha stands close beside her, one comforting hand resting on her shoulder.

The Dovetailers sing a familiar melody but darker and heavier than I've ever heard it. Hundreds of lips move at the same time, putting new words to the tune we all know so well.

"Red blood falls on blackest seas
Children fall on bended knee
Only here is mankind free
Only here is mankind free."

※ — ※ — ※

When I realize what they're doing, tremors seize my spine and the tears dry on my face. The Dovetailers have appropriated "Luna," the bases' national anthem, and changed the words—but they've left the last line intact. In this context, it takes on a whole new meaning: Dovetail territories are the only places on the Moon where people can breathe.

More voices join in, and their sound fills the base. Soon, Anka is chanting the words out loud, and Wes is singing them in my ear. "Red blood falls on blackest seas . . ."

The Committee would have us sprayed with neurotoxic gas for this, I think, and I draw strength from our defiant act. Around the perimeter, soldiers in teal have added their voices to the chorus. Their backs are straight, their faces somber; those standing near Dovetailers join hands with them. The concrete floor upon which we sit vibrates with the music's vitality.

The song infects me. It takes root in my heart and wraps around my vocal cords. I feel as if I've never used them before.

"Only here is mankind free," I sing, shyly and out of tune. At last, the words don't stick in my throat like a lie. "Only here is mankind free."

31

THE BASE'S ALARM SYSTEM SHRIEKS AT 06:00.
It doesn't bother me at first, since it's less jarring than the human
screams that have constituted the background noise of all my
dreams since this war started.

But when I wake, and then pinch my inner elbow to make sure
I'm *really* awake, the digitized panic doesn't stop. Leaping out of bed,
I grab my sister first, my weapons belt and helmet next. Out of
habit, I've slept in uniform, leaving one less task to check off the list
in emergency gear-ups.

Anka and I each grab one of Cygnus's hands and pull him from
the apartment, out into a whirlpool of bodies. My brother clenches
his eyes shut, but his ears are wide open.

"To the bunker!" Anka shouts, gesturing wildly to our right.
"Remember the drill we did?"

Anka all but sprints down the hallway, taking right and left
turns as if she's practiced her flight dozens of times. Pride surges
within me as panicking people form a V behind us like a gaggle
of migrating geese.

On the sides of the Dugout's largest hallway, narrow slits have
opened. "Evacuate to the deep bunker as per Emergency Procedure Two," booms Asterion's voice from the base-wide audio system. "Enemy foot soldiers have been detected entering the metro

tunnel connecting Bases I and II. They may be attempting an inva-sion. I repeat, evacuate to the underground bunker."

I'd feared as much. Both the metro tunnel opening and the bunker are underground; they're on opposite sides of the base, the former at the north end of the main hallway and the latter at the south, beneath a shield volcano. I can't be both places at once.

As we run down the main hallway, we narrowly avoid crashing into Atlas Phi, his expression wavering between worry and grief, and the twins, dressed in their faded secondhand battle gear.

"Where do we go?" Atlas asks none of us in particular, his eyes darting from one face to another. "What do we do?"

"Come on." Anka leads us toward a cavernous hole in the wall, which used to be screened by blank white panels. Now a steady rush of civilians pours inside. "It's not so complicated. You and me and Cygnus are going in there, Mr. Atlas. Phaet and Umbriel and Ariel will go out to fight."

"About time we put that training to use, right?" Umbriel says, tone full of sarcasm. "Getting to nail a couple clueless Commit-tee puppets in the name of 'freedom.'" There's resentment in his booming voice, and for a moment, I worry that he can't be trusted in the field.

"Training . . ." Ariel shivers even as sweat trickles from his temples. "Something I should've done more of." Then he looks at Wes and me, his eyebrows raised in worry. "Is Alex feeling okay enough to come?"

"He has no choice," I say.

The twins' father turns to me and puts his hands on my shoul-ders. Once a tower of a man, he seems so much smaller now. He's all but leaning on me for support. "My boys . . . I never wanted them to fight for a living, and now they're fighting for their lives. For all our lives. Please, Phaet, bring them home."

"I'm an officer, not a bodyguard," I say. "But I will try."

I can't look Atlas in the eye as he steps back from me, sick with concern, and files forward. Cygnus stares at the twins' father as he goes, taking in the hordes of people entering the narrow spiral staircase that leads endless stories downward into the bunker.

"I can't. Go down there, I mean. No one can make me crowd in with all those people." He talks faster and faster, eyes shifting left to right. "I can't, I can't, I can't. I thought I could but it's not going to happen."

Terrified that his ghosts are coming back to haunt him—even though his life is in danger, *because* his life is in danger—I hold both his hands, squeezing them hard, and try to fix his panicked gaze with mine. "You will go to safety, Cygnus. You have to. The next time I see you, it'll be deeper underground, okay?"

Cygnus gulps, shaking his head.

Anka's face spasms with worry, but the expression is soon replaced with determination. "I've got this, Phaet." She grabs Cygnus's wrist with both hands. "See you soon."

With a sinking heart, I watch her lead Cygnus down into darkness.

※ — ※ — ※

The metro tunnel is one of the Moon's greatest architectural feats, one that schoolchildren learned about early and dreamt of seeing one day. Constructed out of a hollow lunar lava tube, it contains six defunct passenger trams: three on the tunnel floor and three suspended from the ceiling, an arrangement made possible by the minimal lunar gravity. The space in the middle is wide enough for a Pygmette to pass through, but too narrow for an invasion by ship.

Now that the trams aren't running, it's pitch-black inside, and we've chosen not to use our helmets' headlamps to avoid giving away our location. Instead, we rely on infrared vision: anything with a human body temperature appears on our viewscreens as a bright red spot.

"Prepare to engage infantry," warns Yinha's voice in my headset.

A red mass of soldiers in pressure suits picks their way toward us, clambering over and between the boulders in their path. In this territorial tug-of-war, every square meter will count. If we can push the enemy back far enough, Dovetail might be able to switch from defense to offense and infiltrate Base I. If we lose ground, Committee-aligned forces will swarm the Dugout and take control of everything and everyone I have left.

"This way." Wes points to a defunct tram to our right. "Let's take cover."

Crouching behind the car, ballistic shield protecting my open side, I peek my head out periodically, aiming Downers at the on-coming soldiers. Wes hoists himself onto a ledge near my head and uses a Batterer gun to try to puncture their pressure suits with metal bullets, which are denser and cheaper than the carbon-fiber Lunar ones. Alex does the same to my left. Four green Dovetailers— Umbriel and Ariel among them—cluster behind me and the Odans, also wielding our allies' weapons. Yinha's commanded us not to fire lasers for the same reason we've avoided headlamps: to keep our location secret.

Small groups of Dovetailers and Batterers are scattered across the area, ducked behind tramcars and boulders. Many tug at their pressure suits between shots; made of the same self-repairing car-bon fiber as the Militia's, these suits are all that separate our bodies from the near-vacuum outside. In our haste to prepare back in Defense, we didn't have time to do proper fittings before venturing into the tunnel.

Our bodies are all that stand between the enemy soldiers and the Dugout—we must repel them from the two old airlock gates that separate the tunnel from our territory's main hallway. If they breach those, it's a matter of time before they run down the hallway and descend into the bunker.

We have to push forward.

"All clear!" I shout into my headset, and break cover, shield covering my vitals.

"Advance to the next car down." Wes moves to the front of our unit, leading us on a slightly rightward trajectory. "That way!"

Our unit runs to the rear of the next car, trying to adjust our movements for moon-grav. One new Dovetail soldier pushes off the ground, soars a meter and a half upward, and gets sprayed by a combination of lasers and bullets, her suit's self-repairing function too slow to save her. Tattered and unmoving, her body drifts down to slump, lifeless, against the ground. In my headset, I hear Ariel's gasp and another recruit's muffled sobs.

"Leave her!" I bark, hating the callousness of my own voice. "Push on!"

We've reached the end of the passenger tram whose cars we've used as cover. From here, boulders will be the only shelter. Twenty meters separate us from the first enemy soldiers, who are positioned to attack a group of Dovetailers to our right. *How did they advance so quickly?*

I get my answer fast as one soldier *glides* toward us, trailing a cloud of gas from a cylinder strapped to his back. Three others follow in close order. Not all of the soldiers wear the cylinders—this frontmost unit, of about twenty, seems to be a specialized one.

"Pacifian propulsion packs," Wes says, sounding unsurprised. Long ago, Earthbound astronauts used the devices to aid mobility in space. On special occasions, Militia uses a variant: smaller modular propulsion units strapped to the arms and legs. Crouching to the side, I take another look at the soldier's pressure suit, which is bulkier and less reflective than the ones I'm used to. His comrades look similar. Wes is right: these suits must come from Earth.

"Come on, let's put an end to their flying about." He leads us rightward. A nearby unit of amateur Dovetail fighters seeks shelter behind him; Alex, Umbriel, and Ariel follow, seemingly eager to protect the jerkily moving new recruits.

"Wes!" I call out, keeping up with my team. He should know better than to move without my orders—now we all have to follow him to cover his back.

The tram tunnel's lights flick on, and though they're not bright, we can finally see our enemies. I switch off my helmet's infrared vision, cursing under my breath. I must put off dealing with Wes's strange behavior until after we get our bearings.

"These soldiers are either carrying Lazies or wearing Militia suits," Alex hisses. "Not both. Committee must've saved the better equipment for their soldiers. These are Pacifians."

Pacifians—fighting outdoors on lunar terrain? The Committee must've known this mission would have a high fatality rate and sent their allies instead of their own, more valuable Militia troops. Since the Pacifians brought less advanced equipment and lack space-deployed weapons of mass destruction, they have no choice but to obey their more powerful ally. I almost pity them, doing their side's dirty work. But that won't stop me from destroying them. Experience has shown me that if it means protecting Dovetailers, I will commit crimes for which I'll never forgive myself.

Not that hurting them is easy. Wes has positioned us directly in front of the gliding Pacifian unit, and we only manage to take down a few before they're upon us. The last two turn off their propulsion packs when they're above our heads and fire bullets downward as they descend. I manage to roll under a ledge, and Wes and Alex throw themselves to the side to evade the shots. But bullets hit another member of our unit, and he crumples slowly, until his body hugs the ground.

He was my responsibility. As leader, I needed to keep him safe. Him—and the other soldier who perished a minute ago.

The Pacifians continues to approach; the lead soldier is a tall man who creeps along like a fast-growing vine. Before I realize he's gotten so close, he descends on me, one gloved hand swinging a pickax at my helmet. I grab his wrist before he can smash the polymer standing between me and the lethal vacuum. When light from my headlamp shines through his visor and illuminates his face, I see two flashes of green.

The familiar sight poisons me with fear.

I let loose a silent, furious scream, lunging for the pickax. We wrestle to control it, but with my lighter body and limited mobility, I know I won't last long. When I swing the butt of my weapon around to bat him away, he delivers a hook kick to my head, sending me flying. My body arcs in a wide parabola, and I wrench the shield into place to catch the bullets fired at me.

I land on all fours, rocks bruising my shins, and holler into my headset, "It's Lazarus! Don't engage at close range—we take him down together!"

Wes knocks the head of the soldcr he's fighting into a boulder, splitting his helmet so that the vacuum sucks out the air inside. Opponent defeated, he turns, clenching and unclenching his fists.

He's acting as if he hasn't heard my commands. He watches Lazarus, and Lazarus watches him. I wish I could reel my words back in. From Wes's body language, I know he's abandoned our cause in favor of a more personal one.

Lazarus crosses his arms.

Wes points at him accusingly, threatening him more with that raised finger than he ever could with words. But I know that he's not here to threaten. He's here to destroy.

32

WES SPRINGS FORWARD, HURLING A HAND-sized metal disk at his foe. Lazarus ducks so that it sails over his head.

"Don't!" Alex hollers. He lurches in Wes's direction—I almost run after Wes myself—but then Alex remembers that he must stay with our unit, which is still under attack. "That devil's got a plan. If you—"

Snap! I look up, to where a crack is darting across the ceiling. A torso-sized rock above Alex's head jiggles loose and begins to fall. Throwing myself forward, I tackle him so that we roll out of its trajectory. Thankfully, we land among Dovetail soldiers, not Pacifian ones.

The boulder makes impact mere centimeters beyond my toes, and the tunnel shivers. *Could it be a moonquake?* On either side, Dovetailers pull Alex and me to our feet. *Or worse?* Whatever is going on, the shifting landscape could kill us without warning.

"Lazarus—isn't here—for me," Wes grunts between the blows he's exchanging with his adversary. "I'm here—for him."

Of course he would try this—why didn't I know? Why did I listen to him when he led us to Lazarus's unit? The rest of us could try to stop him, but more Pacifian troops have reached the clearing, and they cluster around Alex, the Phi twins, and me like ants around rotting fruit. Behind us, other Dovetailers are using laser weapons against the Pacifians, and I decide it's time we do the same.

"Circle up!" I call to the three boys, the only members of my team that are alive and still under my control. We scramble to our feet and form a ring with our backs in the center.

"I can't . . ." Umbriel is saying. "I can't shoot them . . ."

I switch to my Lazy and fire a beam in a wide arc to blind the enemy. The other three do the same.

The barrage of violet light makes some Pacifians twist to the side and burns through the weak spots on their pressure suits. Umbriel screams, horrified. One soldier tries to cover a hole I've made over his chest, but the suit's polymer doesn't have a self-repairing mechanism. He gasps once, twice, and then keels over, suffocated by the vacuum surrounding us.

The tunnel spins, the familiar guilt seizes me, and I try to think myself out of it. *He's Pacifian. If he'd lived, he would've done in one of the twins. He would've stormed the Dugout and gone after your family.*

The black mass of Pacifian troops advances farther. My team is still split. An adrenaline rush from that fact alone spurs me to put the immediate past behind me.

Inside the tramcar, Wes and Lazarus dart from side to side, leaping over the seats, at once pursuing and fleeing from each other.

"Get out of there, Wes!" I call, catching two bullets with my ballistic shield. "We can't help you—"

A grenade sails over my head, narrowly missing. Ariel, who's shadowed me out of both fear and loyalty, is at my back. Shouting, he dives under the tramcar to dodge the projectile.

"Umbriel! You and me—advance together!" I holler.

But Umbriel runs to take cover behind a boulder, letting loose a string of panicked words that rattle through our headsets. "Sorry, Phaet. I . . . It's not right. I can't. I can't. I can't." There's a dead soldier next to Umbriel, a gun shoved through his gut, and he can't look away.

Swearing, I scan the scene for a way I can help.

A tramcar window shatters, and Wes jumps out. But Lazarus follows and kicks him before he can regain his balance. Wes's helmet clangs hard against the tunnel wall, and he slumps to the ground. I watch, numb with fear; I hear static coming from his feed and then—nothing. His body has gone death-still.

If Umbriel hadn't . . . No, I can't afford to resent my best friend's insubordination until we're all safe again.

Wes will get up, I tell myself as one of Lazarus's underlings tries to stab me with a bayonet. *He always gets up.*

As Lazarus lifts the pickax to strike Wes's helmet, something shiny swipes at his calf. Wes gets to his feet, pressing one hand to his abdomen.

Lazarus looks down at Ariel, crawling out from underneath the car, dagger in hand. Lazarus laughs, teeth flashing white underneath his visor, and the sight unnerves me all the more because no voice accompanies it.

The mismatch startles me: a Sanctuarist-trained warrior, standing tall, against a green Dovetail recruit sprawled on the ground. I struggle to reach Ariel, but bodies, Dovetail and Pacifian alike, bar my way. More of our troops have penetrated this area of the tunnel. Several units have even advanced past us. They're hoping to reach Base I, and they might succeed. But to me, infiltrating Base I wouldn't constitute a victory unless my unit—all of it—pulls through this battle.

My headset buzzes; a Batterer leader is trying to communicate with me. "Turn back!" he yells. I blink, confused: why should our forces give up this opportunity? "Committee ships above the tunnel, loaded with explosives."

The Dovetailers ahead of us stop in their tracks. Behind me, Wes engages Lazarus and two Pacifians in an attempt to defend Ariel; Alex stands near him, as if unsure how to help; Umbriel cowers under a ledge, muttering to himself, shell-shocked and utterly useless.

I think of the falling boulder, and even though I refuse to believe it, I know what the Committee forces have come to do.

We have to evacuate the tunnel. My unit is nearer to Base I than Base II, but we can't run toward the former. Once we're in their midst, the Pacifians will make us prisoners, not conquerors.

I look upward, scoping out weak spots in the rock ceiling above, and give the order I know I must give. "You heard the Batterer officer," I shout. "Retreat!"

An explosion from the tunnel's center rocks the ground beneath our feet. Because there's a vacuum outside our suits, we don't hear a thing, but we can see cracks tens of meters long tearing through the ceiling. The upper tram tracks twist and snap, pulled apart by the impact.

On the ground, the Pacifians turn tail and scramble toward Base I. Lazarus's unit, which was giving us so much trouble a minute ago, retreats, letting Ariel break free and run toward me. But as they go, the Pacifians grab three, four, five retreating Dovetail and Batterer soldiers from other units that try to flee past them and toward the Dugout.

I run, followed immediately by Wes and Alex. Umbriel and Ariel, who lack the agility of veteran soldiers, struggle to keep up. Yinha's voice booms in my helmet, that fragile safe space around my head. "Committee forces are sealing off the tunnel by bombing it from above. Coordinates eighty-five degrees and forty-two minutes north, sixty-eight degrees and thirteen to fifteen minutes west are bad, bad places to be."

The tunnel is rumbling, crumbling, closing in on itself. As if the landscape, the Moon's molten core, is hungry for bodies. Dovetail, Batterer, Pacifian—it doesn't matter. The Committee would rather destroy this territory than see someone else take it. They would bury their own allies to accomplish that.

Panicking, I leap over boulders and crevices, driven now by a terrifying rush of self-preservation. My remaining teammates' footfalls, sounding behind me, offer reassurance . . . until those four sets of footsteps become three.

"Phaet! Phaet, please!" A voice screams in my headset. "Umbriel—someone!"

Twisting back, I see that a lone Pacifian among the Dovetailer and Batterer swarm has grabbed Ariel's utility belt and bent his reedy body into a headlock.

"Ariel!" Umbriel slows, looking over his shoulder to try to find his brother.

"Keep going!" Alex shouts, yanking Umbriel back on course. "We need to get inside now!"

Ariel may be Umbriel's brother, but he's *my* soldier. I break off from my teammates, run to Ariel, and swipe at his assailant with a dagger—but not before the Pacifian soldier slams a rifle butt into my visor with his free hand. The force of it wrenches my head back, and pain spikes through my entire upper body. Still, I manage to glimpse my opponent's face through his helmet—*Lazarus*.

I shake off the blow. Cracks have appeared in the polymer of my visor. My hands instinctively reach up to protect my face. It's a matter of time before the pressure differential between my aerated helmet and the vacuum outside builds to an impossible level. If he scores another hit . . .

Hit. Putting my weight on my hands, I kick both feet back into Lazarus's groin. Due to the low-gravity environment, he goes flying backward, and the force propels me forward. I land on my feet—but it's no good: he's still got Ariel by the neck.

Behind him, more chunks of rock tumble from the ceiling. Slinging Ariel over his shoulder, Lazarus turns on his propulsion pack and speeds into the midst of the debris.

"Come on, Phaet!" Alex's voice shouts in my ear.

Hating every movement I make, I half run, half stumble to the airlock. Dovetail has decreased the opening's diameter, making it just wide enough to crawl through.

Wes's hands are the first ones I reach for. Countless other pairs pull me farther inside, lift up my cracked helmet, clap me on the shoulder.

Umbriel's are not among them. He stares at the tunnel, into which the brother he's shared his entire life with has disappeared.

33

"WHAT THE FUSE DID YOU THINK YOU WERE doing?"

Still wide-eyed from shock, Umbriel hounds Wes through Medical's cramped lobby, spewing hot fury. His fist is tight around the handle of an emergency kit; none of us have changed out of our filthy uniforms, though Wes has thrown a white coat and gloves over his.

"Not to make excuses," Wes mutters, "but you could've been a *tad* more helpful back there." He's right—Umbriel's pacifism, and then his paralysis upon seeing so much gore, rendered him a liability rather than a contributing team member. I just don't have the heart to argue with him.

"It was my second real battle!" Umbriel roars at Wes. "And besides, I never wanted to kill. Or to see that many people get killed. I'm not an Earthbound war machine like you."

Alex and I look at each other worriedly, eyes meeting over the body of the unconscious soldier we're carrying. More teams of two hustle through the lobby's doors, carrying other wounded soldiers—their skin bloody, blistered, or both. We've run out of stretchers. I try not to gag on the metallic scent of blood, which permeates every corner.

"You led us straight to that sociopathic killer." Umbriel's practically breathing down Wes's neck.

"And now Lazarus can gain some of the Committee's favor back," I say. That's probably why he took Ariel—he probably needs to repair his reputation with his protectors after losing Wes and me on Battery Bay.

"How did you find him, mate?" Alex says to Wes. "And how did we not know?"

I shake my head, torn between sympathy for Wes's grief—I understand his need to avenge Murray—and anger at his recklessness.

"It doesn't matter." Wes can't meet any of our eyes.

"You're right. It doesn't," Umbriel says. "What happened happened all the same. My brother kept *your blasted head* on your neck and got captured. After that, who knows? Smashed by a falling rock? Killed by the Committee? Questioned in an electric chair?"

Ariel wasn't the only one. Within a few hours, we'll get official tallies of the wounded, dead, and captured. More than I dread seeing the numbers, I dread the expressions on people's faces when they hear the names.

Umbriel sets the emergency kit on the blood-smeared floor, almost slamming it down. "What'll I tell my dad? Actually, no—*you* should tell him. Can you even look him in the face?"

Alex and I lay our burden down on a towel on the floor. It'll serve as our wounded soldier's cot for now. I say nothing to stop Umbriel's tirade. Wes deserves it.

"Umbriel, you're creating a hostile environment for the patients," Wes says. Face frozen in concentration, Wes kneels by our soldier, a middle-aged female Dovetailer with multiple bullet holes in her leg. She's slipping in and out of consciousness.

Umbriel lowers his voice to a harsh whisper. "You think patching people up in here can make up for what you did out there?"

Ignoring him, Wes slices off the patient's pant leg to the upper thigh and props her foot on his lap. "Alex, tourniquet?"

Alex shoves the device in Wes's face as if punching him. The tourniquet is a polymer cuff connected by plastic tubing to a small hand pump. "Umbriel, I'm so upset about what happened—hell, Ariel's a bit like a brother to me too—but Wes's sister . . ."

Umbriel silences him with a glare.

Wes wraps the tourniquet's cuff around the woman's thigh and inflates it by pumping air through the tube, increasing the pressure on her wound to try to stop the bleeding. I sit by her head, murmuring to her to give her something to focus on, trying to keep her conscious.

"Your sister's *dead*, Wes," Umbriel says. "Running after her killer wasn't going to change anything—except maybe send my brother right after her."

Wes lifts his head slowly, staring at Umbriel, wrapping up his work on the injured woman. At first, his eyes blaze with anger, but then he lowers them, face filling with sorrow.

"I'm sorry, Umbriel. I could say it a dozen times and it wouldn't be enough. I'm sorry about your brother. I'm sorry that you didn't want to fight. I'm sorry Lazarus didn't get what he deserved. I'm sorry I was selfish and an idiot. But I didn't intend for any of that— or any of *this*—to happen." Wes gestures to the wounded and dying all around us. "The butchers on the other end of that collapsed tunnel can't say the same."

He starts walking to the next patient, and Alex follows, leaving me alone with Umbriel. My best friend turns to me, looking deflated. Vulnerability is replacing the anger in his eyes. "I should've tried harder to save Ariel. I ran away, Phaet." Tears leak from his eyes. "I failed my family. And I can't fix it."

His words remind me of how I felt after Mom's death, after Cygnus's capture. *Self-loathing and regret are no more productive than anger.* I hug him, wishing my arms could squeeze the poisonous emotions out of his body.

34

I STAY IN THE PHIS' BORROWED LIVING ROOM that night, knowing better than to leave Umbriel alone. Ariel's absence haunts the space: his frayed green backpack and scuffed walking shoes sit on the plastic couch where their owner should be. Atlas has gone to a separate room to sleep; every few seconds, we hear coarse cotton sheets rustling as he tosses and turns.

Unlike us, other uninjured Dovetailers have returned to daily life. Civilians have come up from the bunker, most of them shaken but not broken by the Committee's attack.

The broken ones have lost family and friends to death or injury, and trying to put even one heart back together takes patience. Umbriel and I have rehashed every explanation for why Wes went rogue, and every way we could have stopped him. Everything that could've happened to Ariel, and every question about when we'll hear news of him. Having polluted the air with our worry and anger, we sit blankly, listening to the puttering of the air filters and the faint buzz of the flickering orange bulbs.

When the door light blinks green in the middle of the night, we catch each other's eyes, dreading what could be on the other side.

I open the doors with my thumbprint to find Rose hovering in the hallway, the skin around her eyes pink and swollen. Tears glue her snowy lashes together.

"It's my fault," she blurts, taking my hand and holding on tight.

Bewildered, I pull Rose inside the apartment, hoverchair and all, so that Umbriel can help me make sense of what she's saying. How could she be responsible for anything that happened in the tunnel? She didn't even enter that death trap.

"Ariel," Rose murmurs, wiping her eyes. I grab a rag from the kitchen counter and hand it to her. "It shouldn't have happened. It couldn't have, if not for me."

"Go on," I say.

"S-soon after you all touched down on base, Wes met with me. Privately. He told me about a man, a rogue soldier who nursed a— a vendetta against him."

"Lazarus," Umbriel mutters through his teeth.

Rose nods. "Wes told me he feared for his life. He begged me for everything I knew about the Committee's plans concerning this Lazarus person—oh, Phaet, he seemed so frightened, he was almost crying. He needed to avoid Lazarus in battle, but he didn't want you, his commanding officer—or anyone else, for that matter—to think he was a coward. So he pressed me until I promised him confidentiality."

One by one, the pieces fall into place. Each *click* in my mind makes it harder to breathe.

"He tricked you, Rose," Umbriel says.

"I tried to help," Rose continues. "I kept his secret. Our team never learned about the exact timing of the Committee's assaults, but we found documents delineating the Pacifian chain of command. Searches for *Lazarus*, *Penny*, or his Lunar name turned up nothing. But I found out that regardless of the timing or location of an attack, a skilled bounty hunter was slated for the front lines, among a contingent of Pacifians with propulsion packs. It sounded like Lazarus, so I told Wes."

"That's why Wes led us toward the troops with the packs," I say.

"He was supposed to run from Lazarus, not try to kill him or . . . or . . ." Rose's fist shakes around her hoverchair's joystick, and the entire contraption shivers in midair. Sighing, Umbriel pries her fingers loose so that she can float steadily once more.

"Don't blame yourself for what happened to Ariel, Rose." I think back to the first months of my friendship with Wes, when he'd convinced me he was from Base I. The possibility that he was Earthbound didn't even cross my mind. "Wes is an excellent liar."

Rose stares at me, seeming to study every movement in my face. "You sound like a girl who's suffered because of him."

"I'm a girl who'd be dead without him." I remember the falsehoods he told to get me into Saint Oda and Battery Bay, remember the pinch of his lips after he was done. He did it because my life—and his too—was more important to him than upholding the truth.

"Say what you want to defend him, Phaet," Umbriel huffs. "But he's an uptight one-man death factory."

This is the first time Wes's lies have hurt someone close to me. I shouldn't forgive him. But part of me considers everything separating us unimportant.

"His comrades can't trust him with their heads," Umbriel says. "How can you trust him with your heart?"

I sink down onto a kitchen stool. Rose coasts over so that she sits beside me; she seems to know that her nearness alone is a comfort.

"I'm not jealous of him, Phaet. Not anymore." Umbriel doesn't seem to care that a near stranger is listening. He keeps hitting me with difficult truths. And unlike in training, I can't dodge these blows. "I just want the best for you—and that doesn't include liars like him."

⁕ — ⁕ — ⁕

They've put Wes under house arrest for insubordination, only let-ting him leave to complete his shifts in Medical. In the days since I've seen him, he's scrubbed his and Alex's apartment spotless; the copper furniture gleams under the orange lights.

Alex is away, on nighttime guard duty. I rap my knuckles on Wes's bedroom door, knowing he's awake: light leaks out around the edges. "Rose came by earlier tonight," I call.

Wes opens the door then, blinking at me. Half of his hair lies flat against his scalp, and he's rubbing his eyes.

"I was milliseconds away from a good nap, Phaet." The words are slurred. Through the doorway, I see his crumpled white sheets, the messiest things in the tiny, immaculate room. A sheathed dag-ger rests on the floor next to the bed.

"The lights were on." I don't apologize for waking him. Um-briel, Atlas, and my siblings probably won't sleep tonight either.

"I can't fall asleep when it's dark," he says. "The shadows take on bizarre shapes. Alex gives me his electricity ration just so I can keep my wits about me." He sits on the bed and pats the spot next to him. "What's going on? Come in."

I remain standing. Although I want to comfort him, I can't let him off so easily.

"You went after the most dangerous fighter the Committee has," I say. "With four new recruits in tow. Two are dead, and Ariel's in enemy hands. Why, Wes? Was revenge that important to you?"

I regret the question as soon as it leaves my mouth. Wes runs a hand through his hair, and I notice broken skin over his knuckles. *What's he been punching? Glass?*

"Murray would've wanted it," he says halfheartedly.

I shake my head. We both know better.

"No, you're right." Wes's eyes grow unfocused, as if he's look-ing at some place far away. "What am I becoming, Phaet? I went after that butcher not knowing what I'd do to him. Only that I'd make him suffer—that I'd hurt him. Torture him. I've never wanted to do that before."

Although I've felt the same violent impulse, I've never acted on it. Not like Wes. "How do you feel, knowing that you've changed?"

Wes's expression is pleading. "Afraid. Since . . . Murray, the one thing I thought I could control—myself—has disobeyed me. Am I like *him* now?"

"You haven't fallen that far yet." Although I doubt my own words, I say them as if, by doing so, they'll become true.

Wes shakes his head. "We both know that I've stepped off that ledge. You're looking at me differently, Phaet."

Slowly, I sit next to him on the hard mattress. He doesn't reach for me. There are some things a hug can't fix. He'll have to redeem himself in my eyes. In Umbriel's, and in Dovetail's too. But he won't get a chance unless we undo as much damage as possible. Although he's falling, he hasn't yet hit the ground.

"Keep your eyes open, Wes," I whisper. "I'll throw you a rope."

35

THE NEXT DAY, MY BODY'S IN THE DARK INFO-
Tech control room with the leadership, tallying our losses from the
tunnel and scouting new strategies. My mind is in an even darker
place, imagining what's happened to Ariel and the other fifteen soldiers listed as missing. Seventy-nine troops have been killed and a
hundred sixty-eight wounded, most of them Dovetail. As awful as
their fates are, at least we know for sure what's happened to them.

"How do you think the Pacifian commander reacted to the Committee using his soldiers and then killing them?" Asterion says.

Costa puffs out his chest. The watery "hair" on his head swirls
in violent eddies. "Commander Jang is a typical play-by-the-rules
Pacifian. Sticks to his word—in this case, that's being the Committee's puppet—even when someone personally offends him."

His voice is full of disdain, a product of decades of diplomatic
struggles with the Pacifians.

"Ms. Rose, how broad is our monitoring of Jang's communications with the Committee and the General?" Asterion asks.

"We've bugged the external handscreen they gave him as
well as the HeRP he was assigned," Rose says, scrolling through
the computer in front of her. "The Committee only sends him
directives—it's pretty much one-way communication."

Yinha scoffs. "Which is to say, exactly what Rose expected."

"Jang might suspect we're watching him," I say. "We know the Committee's hackers have accessed some of our communications. We just don't know which ones."

"So you have to get creative," Asterion says. "Rose, access Jang's private residence too. Security pods, personal devices, anything."

Rose makes a note on her handscreen. "Will do. I'll tell you if anything shows up."

The doors open, and a strawberry-blond middle-aged man with an ill-maintained beard and mustache comes rushing in. "Sorry about the interruption," he says. I recognize his voice. He was the one berating Cygnus on our flight down to Earth. "We've located the missing troops."

Asterion starts. "They're alive?"

"Prisoners on Base I," the man replies. "May I show you?" He feeds a chip into Dovetail's main HeRP, and we crowd around the monitor. I watch the blinking icon, terrified of what he's found.

Security pod footage. Sixteen prisoners strapped to electric chairs, arranged in a four-by-four square. Four—the unluckiest number, according to Chinese tradition. Seven of the sixteen are Dovetail; nine are Batterer. I spot Ariel's mop of curly brown hair and have to bite my tongue to keep from crying out. The memory of my own brother's torture washes over me, and I shut my eyes tight, unable to watch. The faint crackle of electricity echoes in my ears, almost causing me physical pain.

"Hold on," the hacker says, sounding surprised. "Someone's trying to talk to us."

I dare to open my eyes.

"The communication is unencrypted," says Asterion, reaching for the HeRP, which beeps with a voice message notification.

He reaches forward to play it, but Yinha stays his hand. "It could contain a virus."

"Relax, Yinha." Rose shakes her head. "Wouldn't have made it past our firewall if it did."

Asterion switches the machine to offline mode, just in case, and presses Play.

"We know your hackers have been peeping around the Pen, Dovetail." Hydrus's familiar, oily voice slithers out of the speaker and into my ear.

Rose narrows her eyes at her underling. "We've got to be more careful," she whispers. "You should ask Cygnus about that."

The bearded man winces. "We'll put additional proxies in place, ma'am."

Hydrus's laugh emanates from the HeRP; his message isn't over. *"You complain so much about our old 'snooping,' but you're even worse! Why don't you all give up fighting? Perhaps our new world would be so harmonious that no one would have to spy."*

He's lying. Eavesdropping kept the Committee in power for a century, and if we handed over all our territory and the Batterers' too, they'd just expand the operation to Earth.

"Not convinced?" Hydrus says. *"At least you will be able to watch the rest of our prisoners' interrogations, and when they are no longer useful, their executions."*

My breath hitches. Nearby, I hear Alex's low growl.

"Perhaps we will broadcast their deaths to Battery Bay. Show your allies how weak you are, how little you value the lives of their troops, how you exploit the Batterers for your own ends."

A *click* ends the message. How dare the Committee suggest we're using our allies the way they're using the Pacifians?

There has to be a way to save the sixteen. I catch Andromeda's eye, then think of her daughter. Callisto. Jupiter.

"We have prisoners of our own," I say. "Jupiter Alpha. Skat Yotta. Hopper Gamma."

"Are you proposing a prisoner swap?" Sol says. "Miss Phaet, if we give up their important prisoners, they won't keep us on the map." She lets the image of nuclear attack sink in.

"The Committee won't bomb the Dugout," I say. "We're so close that they can't poison us or blow us up without damaging their own turf."

Yinha and Costa solemnly nod.

"That's still an insane risk you are proposing," Sol points out.

"Let's first see what the Committee terms in such an exchange would be," Asterion says. "Andromeda, you know them best. Strike a deal."

Taking a deep breath, Andromeda begins recording a voice message, suggesting a swap of our sixteen for Jupiter. Smart—he's the lowest in the Committee's chain of command, and the least valuable. There's maternal feeling here too, I think as I watch Andromeda speak. With Jupiter off-base, Callisto might have less conflict in her heart.

"Not suitable, my old friend." Cassini replies this time, his voice weak and croaky with age. "We demand General Alpha's son, Skat Yotta . . . and Hopper Gamma." *Click.*

Andromeda's quick to respond. "Jupiter and Skat. No questions asked."

This time, the Committee takes a minute to reply. "Jupiter and Hopper," says Nebulus Nu in his usual buttery tones.

"That changes zilch. Strategically, Skat's worthless," Yinha says, the old resentment of her former boss creeping into her voice. "He's just sucking up our food and oxygen."

Andromeda counters: "We will give you Jupiter, Skat, and fifteen square kilometers of territory anywhere on the lunar surface."

From her face, I know every concession hurts.

The Committee responds immediately. "Forget the territory,"

Cassini croaks. "We will capture it ourselves. Hopper is valuable beyond measure. Skat is . . . not. If you do not return Hopper to us directly, we will take her back ourselves. We look after our own, as I'm sure you understand."

Andromeda looks deep into Asterion's eyes, then mine, and puts down the recorder. "We can't give up Hopper. I'm sorry, but . . . we must consider other options for retrieving the missing troops."

Asterion crosses his arms and stares down Andromeda. "We cannot jeopardize the sixteen loyal soldiers trapped on Base I because of one elderly Committee favorite. We will trade Hopper and Jupiter for the sixteen."

"We will lose more if our prisoners die than if Hopper makes it to Base I," Yinha says. "She's been in solitary confinement and hasn't learned anything useful."

"She's a better hacker than I am," Rose admits. "But my team can take her on. My vote's with Yinha."

"And mine," Alex says fiercely.

"Me too," I add. We're both thinking of Ariel.

Her expression unreadable, Andromeda tallies our votes in her head; it's five versus one for the prisoner swap. Whatever she thinks, our side has won.

Andromeda picks up the microphone and presses Record. "Hopper Gamma, held on Base IV, and Jupiter Alpha, on Base II, in exchange for the sixteen prisoners, effective immediately. We expect our personnel to be returned unhurt."

Tense seconds tick by while we wait for our enemies' confirmation.

"Very well. Offer accepted." Cassini's voice crackles up from the speakers. I can almost see his leering face. "Thank you for cooperating, Andromeda. The rebels' savagery does not suit you."

"Neither did yours," Andromeda shoots back, and cuts the connection.

＊ — ＊ — ＊

The Dugout Penitentiary's highest-security area is all black bars and mildewed concrete floors. Two stories of cells surround a small rotunda, a floor plan that enables the guards to watch all the prisoners at once. Mirrors line the walls, so it looks like there are infinite pairs of Batterer guards bundling infinite Jupiter Alphas out of his cell.

He still gives off the impression of bulk, despite having lost at least five kilograms and several patches of dark hair while in custody. Perhaps it's the aggressive beady eyes, which remind me of the wolves I saw at night on Saint Oda.

Callisto Chi brushes past me, Yinha, her mother, and the other observers to approach Jupiter, watching him as she would a caged beast.

"Why are *you* here?" Jupiter springs at her. He's unexpectedly strong, breaking his guards' grip on his elbows. But his magnetic handcuffs yank his arms back and over his head, securing him in place.

Callisto watches him struggle with pity in her eyes. "I came to watch you go."

"Why didn't you break me out? Why didn't you *try*? You had six months of chances. Don't pretend you didn't get the messages I sent you."

A Pygmette pulls into the rotunda. Jupiter watches the tiny ship with a mixture of relief and disdain.

"I got them." Callisto stands straighter, her hands clenching and unclenching at her sides. "You're convincing when you want to be, Jupe. I never saw that side of you when we used to argue."

"Shut up," Jupiter spits. Maybe he doesn't want to remember that they used to matter to each other. "Have you gone soft like a rebel? After everything the Committee's done for you, you became one of *them*?"

"Oh, I considered helping you. I knew they'd reward me." Callisto glances at the rest of us, takes in the lack of surprise on our faces. "But then what? How could I go on helping them after what they did to the Singularity?"

"That base had to go," Jupiter says, shrugging. I shake my head—he's spent months in prison with nothing to do but think, and he hasn't changed his violent views in the slightest.

"No." Callisto shakes her head. "That crossed a line."

"You've killed people too," Jupiter mutters. The guards prod him up a shallow ramp and into the cargo hold of the open-top Pygmette. They close the back door, leaving Jupiter's head and neck visible.

"People who threatened me. People who stood between me and what I wanted." Callisto looks at me, and I remember that dark Defense hallway, her face as she tried to stab me to death. "But never anyone who couldn't fight back."

"Think you're too good to make easy kills?" Jupiter says. "Those are the best. Don't even have to get your hands bloody."

Callisto reaches over the Pygmette's door and slaps him, her infinite reflections in the mirrors moving with her. The sharp *crack* of skin on skin echoes through the rotunda, on and on and on. All goes silent, and everyone watches Jupiter's face transition from pain to shock to unguarded fury.

"I'll kill you." Jupiter spits on the ground at Callisto's feet;

there's blood in his saliva. He lunges forward again, straining against the cuffs chaining his wrists to the cargo hold. "If I see you again, I'll *kill* you!"

"Enough." Andromeda, who has stood on the sidelines, steps forward, arms extended, reaching for her daughter. Callisto swats her hands away. She walks up to Jupiter until their faces are a breath apart, as if she'll kiss him. But she doesn't.

"Good-bye, Jupiter."

"This isn't good-bye, Callisto. You'll see me again, and before you know what's happening, I'll—" The Batterer guards slam the Pygmette's top hatch shut on Jupiter and his threats. When the ship leaves, trailing hot exhaust, I see that Callisto's eyes are wet.

"There, Dovetail." She faces her mother, Yinha, the other observers, and me, and points at the exit. "He's gone. Nothing else to see here."

36

THE OMNIBUS HOBBLES INTO THE HANGAR, its Dovetail pilot steering despite the blood flowing from multiple cuts on her face. As Umbriel, Atlas, Alex, and I pull a half-conscious Ariel out of the hatch, I count a bumpy red gash across his forehead that oozes pus, a black eye, bruises on his forearms, and a broken ankle. Moans and horrified cries from the friends and families of the other soldiers getting hoisted out of the ship hound us as we rush out of Defense and into the Dugout's main hallway.

Umbriel supports Ariel's shoulders and I his feet. Together, we rush toward Medical, Atlas in the lead and Alex in the rear. When we jostle Ariel one too many times, he faints.

"What have they done? What have they done?" Atlas looks over his shoulder, repeating his question again and again.

Dovetail's cleared out valuable single-occupancy rooms in the emergency wing for Ariel and the other prisoners. The leaders don't mean to imply that their lives are more important than those of the soldiers lying on the Medical lobby floor, but Ariel and the fifteen others might have valuable intel; it's essential they recover quickly.

We enter Ariel's room through an old-fashioned door with rusty hinges and a squeaky knob. The claustrophobic interior measures only three meters wide and five long; a creaky cot with stained sheets takes up most of the floor space. Although the sheets look clean, whoever washed them last couldn't scrub out all of the bloodstains.

Taking care not to bump Ariel's head against the flickering lamp dangling from the low ceiling, Umbriel and I set him down on the cot.

"What's all this for?" Umbriel holds up a plastic sack the size of his head. It's filled with clear liquid. Tubing dangles from the bottom, and each conduit ends in a sharp needle of a different color. "Ariel needs help. *Now*. Why haven't they sent someone?"

"Phaet?" Atlas yanks the contraption out of his son's hands and offers it to me like a sacrifice. "You were a top Biology student—please, do something."

"I never got trained." I squat by Ariel's bed, searching a panel with about twenty different buttons for one that'll send a distress signal. "Alex?"

"Wes patched everyone up back on Oda, so I'm rusty." Alex wrings his hands. "We need a Medic."

"You've got one." The voice is accented, soothing, familiar, and in this case, unwelcome. Wes, emergency kit in hand, takes two unsteady steps into the room.

"They sent *you*?" Atlas says, striding toward Ariel's bed.

"They had no choice," Wes says. "Other Medics are occupied elsewhere. Mr. Atlas, I can't take back what I did. But please, let me correct some of the damage."

"Leave us," Atlas says, pointing to the doorway behind Wes. "Please leave, and send someone in your pl—"

"Dad!" Umbriel cries.

Ariel's chest heaves—he seems to cough up blood, but due to his unconscious state, he fails to spit it out. Atlas's expression shifts from anger to panic.

"We don't have time to argue," Umbriel says. He turns to Wes, deep black eyes meeting steely gray ones.

Alex crosses his arms. "You'd better get started, mate."

※ — ※ — ※

Three tubes of antiseptic ointment and meters of medical tape. Two gaping chest incisions and a carbon-fiber splint to secure Ariel's broken rib. Several spine-tingling cracks as Wes sets Ariel's broken ankle. All the while, as calmly as if he were treating a scraped knee, Wes orders Umbriel, Atlas, Alex, and me to sanitize equipment, hold tools in place, and measure our patient's vital signs.

Two hours later, the treatment concludes. Ariel hasn't woken, but his indicators are holding steady. Looking at him now, bandaged, swathed in white sheets, I can almost forget the effort it took to bring him back. When he wakes, will he still be the boy with whom I grew up? Maybe. The Committee had him for a shorter time than Cygnus . . .

"Crisis averted," Wes declares. He strips off his white face mask and gloves, tosses them on a wall shelf, and collapses in a chair.

"I didn't know someone so good at hurting people could also heal them," Atlas says, sounding grateful in spite of himself.

"If I could, I'd only do the latter." Wes rubs his eyes, and lowers his voice. "No, forget that. I wish people would stop needing the healing."

"Earlier I told Phaet you were an uptight one-man death factory," Umbriel admits, and Alex snorts.

I nod, verifying the statement, and Wes chuckles. "Flattering," he says.

"I should've left out the *uptight*." Umbriel looks sheepish. "Maybe the *death factory* part too."

It's the only apology Wes will get from him, and to my surprise, he accepts it with a bow of the head.

The bed creaks. Ariel is stirring. All of us crowd around to watch. His fingers twitch, one leg kicks, and he cracks open his eyes. I inhale and exhale hard, unsure whether to believe he's back. Atlas shakes his head in wonder, and Umbriel cries tears of relief. Their long arms pull me into a hug that's almost painful, and soon all three of us are laughing.

"Where am I?" Ariel's voice is a croak, but he speaks with the same clarity and care that the Ariel of my memories did. "Dad? Umbriel? Phaet?" He pushes himself to a seated position and grabs his chest, wincing as his rib moves inside of him. Then he notices Alex lounging against the wall and smiles.

"Easy now, Ariel." Wes rises, and Ariel stares at him in confusion. "Took us almost two hours to tape you up."

"Not something Wes is keen to oversee again," I add.

Umbriel moves to his brother's side. "You're in the Dugout, Ariel." He looks at Wes with guarded appreciation. "Kappa here gave us a crash course in how to use all these gadgets." He points his chin at Wes's open medical kit, at the devices strewn about.

Ariel's eyes widen as he takes in the cast on his foot, the bandages covering much of his body. "Wes, all of this is yours . . ." He puts one cloth-covered hand over his heart and bows his head in a gesture of thanks.

Wes shrugs. "It was the best I could do, short of rewinding the clock and making sure you never ended up on Base I in the first place."

Umbriel catches his eye, and they nod at each other. I half expect Umbriel to drop a scathing truth-bomb, telling Wes he's been forgiven too easily, or that our standoff isn't over, but he keeps his mouth shut. Probably for Ariel's sake—or mine.

Knuckles rap on the door, cutting the tense moment short. "Pardon the interruption," says a bossy female voice.

Sol. Ridding my face of a frown, I open the door. Sol, Yinha, and Bai walk inside, crowding the tiny room. The temperature and humidity seem to spike, and I feel sweat beading along my hairline.

Bai? Usually he's not with the leaders—shouldn't he be in the lab? His hands shake and his Adam's apple bobs as he swallows repeatedly. He might be frowning behind his mask, which looks glaringly out of place even in a Medical ward. Everything about his appearance makes the back of my neck prickle—and I'm not the only one. Wes, Atlas, and the twins seem to avoid looking at him.

"Good to see you, Ariel." Sol brushes past a frowning Atlas and takes a seat near the bed. "Skipping patrol again?" she says to Alex, who groans.

"Can't a Dovetailer catch a break when his friend's a patchwork of bones and bandages?" Glaring at Sol, Alex shuffles backward out of the room. The door slams shut behind him.

Ariel seems to deflate. "Friend," he whispers, so quietly that I barely hear him. "Right."

I suddenly feel even worse for him. His feelings for Alex are unrequited, just like his brother's were for me. But unlike me, Alex doesn't show signs of liking . . . anybody. It's a small mercy to Ariel, I suppose.

Sol turns back to Ariel, ignorant of everything that just transpired. "We heard voices from this room and knew you'd woken. Tell us everything. Yinha, while he's talking, note down key facts and any appropriate courses of action."

"Cool," Yinha mutters, opening a document on her hand-screen. Her mouth tightens, though.

Sol plows on, heedless of the effect she's having. "Ariel, did the Committee try to pry information out of you?"

Ariel's expression darkens. "They questioned us one by one. For my interrogation, they brought my mother."

"*Mom* was there?" Umbriel exclaims. Beside him, his father's face blanches, and Atlas puts a hand on Umbriel's shoulder. *Take it easy*, he seems to say. But how can anyone be calm at the mention of his estranged wife?

Caeli Phi. Disgust fills me when I remember the "friend" who ratted out Mom, the woman who still has Mira Theta's life to account for.

"Maybe they thought having her tell me she loves me would give them better access to my head. Or make me switch sides. She begged me to live with her. She's got a huge, temperature-adjustable bed just waiting for me."

"But you resisted that—that *woman's* pleas." Sol bristles with anger, losing some of her usual composure. If she and I have anything in common, it's this: the wish that Mira Theta was still here. Sol's confidant; my mother.

Ariel nods, swallowing hard. "She said that Umbriel shamed her by helping Phaet in her 'terrorist activities,' but that I still had a chance at redemption."

"Sorry to hear that," Sol says. When people show emotions, she deals with them the usual Lunar way: by giving their feelings as little attention as possible. "What else did they want to know?"

"Everything." Ariel clears his throat. "The identities of the hackers giving them so much trouble in orbital space. Names of undercover Dovetailers on Bases III and V. Dovetail's next move, and whether it will be a biological attack."

"They think we would do *that*?" I blurt, unable to contain my anger. Attacking loyalists with pathogens would make us worse than the Committee, because we know what it's like to be on the receiving end.

Ariel shrugs. "Since we've developed a blanket defense, the Committee has concluded that we also have offensive capabilities. The drones aren't secret anymore."

"You're the third person who's said that," Bai says. Now I understand why he's here. "I'd hoped it wasn't true."

"They don't just know about the drones. They've got them. That shipment from Base IV to II, the one we thought was destroyed? Turns out several drones survived. They've captured them and are studying them."

Bai shakes his head, eyes shut tight.

Sol leans forward. "Did they explicitly discuss the drones?"

"No, but I could infer their meaning. I'm used to listening for clues," Ariel says. I nod, the memory still fresh: many months ago, when he was working as a Law secretary for the Committee, Ariel kept his ears open for anything that could help with Mom's trial. "They knew the specifics of how the models functioned."

"What did you tell them, Ariel?" Sol demands. "About our plans?"

"I don't *know* about your plans," Ariel says. "One good thing about being a private, I guess. I don't think anyone else spilled anything important."

"They have the drones . . . that means death. I know it." Bai begins pacing. His breath quickens, whooshing through the mask over his mouth.

"Bai," Yinha says, "so the Committee has a couple of your babies. It's a minuscule defensive capability they'll never need, because Dovetail was never going to try to infect them in the first place."

"I know." Bai sinks into a chair. "When I thought about how many people the drones could save . . . When I saw how intricate the design was, how beautiful, and how *possible*—I had to follow through. But now . . . I have a terrible feeling. If I'd known they'd fall into Committee hands, I never would have made them." He slumps forward, buries his head in his hands.

"Please, Bai, calm yourself," Sol says. "We have other things to worry about."

Bai ignores her. "The Committee—they've taken so much from me. First my leg, then Ida. Now the things I created in her memory. What's next?" He looks at Yinha. "You?"

The drones mean so much to him. As much as a person. At the realization, I'm overcome with pity. Beside me, Yinha melts into a chair, then stands back up, thinking better of it.

"Come on, Bai. Let's go." She takes her brother's arm, raking her eyes over the people in the room. "Actually, all of us should go. Ariel needs to rest up, because as soon as he's out of bed, he'll be back in basic training."

Ariel groans softly.

"Don't give me that attitude, Private," Yinha says. "Normally I'd allow you fourteen weeks' leave, but Dovetail needs every able-bodied person to fight. And you should brush up on your skills so that you don't get captured again."

Ariel smiles weakly at her. But beside his sister, Bai is shaking his head. "Yinha, you could teach them how to shoot the stars out of the sky. But it still won't be enough to protect us."

It's not the fear in his voice that makes me go cold inside. It's the resignation, the calm acceptance that even though we don't know *how* things will get worse from here, they will.

37

IN THE COURSE OF THE FOLLOWING WEEK, Battery Bay and Dovetail troops begin mingling in earnest, sharing combat tips during drills and meals in their free time. Within two days, Ariel leaves Medical in a hoverchair and begins checking and refurbishing Lazies in his family's borrowed apartment. The bruised skin on his face fades from purple to bile green, and his broken rib and ankle begin to heal.

Alex visits him regularly, but Ariel doesn't act as exuberant around the Sanctuarist as he used to. There's more physical distance between them now, and even so, Alex still seems uncomfortable. Gradually, the expression in Ariel's light brown eyes fades from brokenhearted hurt to grudging acceptance.

I hardly see the Phis, my siblings, or Wes, who remains under house arrest, since I'm occupied with back-to-back meetings. Three hours into today's gathering, Asterion calls a break and leaves to buy rice-and-cashew porridge from Market.

The leadership is cooped up in a deserted math classroom in Education, discussing supply distribution between Bases II and IV; we've arranged the dingy desks in a circle like schoolchildren. We switch our location each time in case the Committee's spying on us.

As the other leaders turn to small talk, Yinha props her elbows on the table, drops her chin into her hands, and closes her eyes. Things must be stressful at home—I haven't seen Bai out in public all week.

"Yinha," I whisper, tapping her on the shoulder. "Everything okay?"

"Is this about Bai?" Yinha snaps. Exhaustion has made her cranky.

I nod.

"Just ask me things straight, would you? Thought we were good enough friends for that. Anyway, Bai's . . . not really here anymore. Like Cygnus, you know?"

I do know, and I wish she didn't have to experience the same thing.

"He's physically in the apartment all day, but his mind's gone into hiding. He's only talked to me once, to ask about staging a rescue mission for the drones. I think he understands that they can't help the Committee much. But he takes it so *personally*."

Asterion returns, balancing a steaming pot in his gloved hands. The food snatches Yinha's attention away. Dovetail's leadership pooled our ration points to buy the bland porridge, and she'll fight to get her money's worth of calories.

As we're ladling out the liquid into identical mugs, the doors to the room slide open again, and a teenage boy shuffles inside. My little brother. I rise from the table and walk over to him.

"The enemy's surprised us." Cygnus's hands ball into fists; he doesn't look at me or anyone else. "We've been trying to crack the wrong things all along. The coding fight for the tactical bomb clusters and the communications satellites was a distraction."

What? Asterion drops the full porridge ladle on the floor, splattering the precious liquid everywhere. No one, not even Yinha, volunteers to clean it up.

"The International Space Station," Cygnus says, his voice a near-whisper. "That's the real problem. I first saw a wobble forty-five minutes ago and didn't think anything of it, but it's turned into a sort of swaying."

"The ISS is a defunct satellite." Rose's hoverchair rises from the table. "We can't hack its controls—there *are* no controls."

"I think I saw a booster pack attached to it," Cygnus says.

Rose begins jetting back and forth across the floor, as if she's pacing. Yinha leaps to her feet, chases the other woman down, puts one hand on Rose's heaving shoulder and the other on her cheek. "Rosie. Shh. We'll handle the ISS. Tell me straight: what do you think will happen?"

Rose shakes her head, looking past Yinha. She stares at my brother with pleading eyes, as if she can't say the words herself.

"The ISS's orbital radius is decreasing," Cygnus says. "It's approaching Earth at an increasing rate. Some kind of retrograde force is acting on the satellite—and it's *not* an accident."

Fear condenses into a stony mass in the pit of my stomach, and I put a hand on Cygnus's shoulder.

"Nothing's ever an accident with the Committee." Yinha takes her worn black jacket off the back of her chair and shrugs it on. "Andromeda, Asterion, Minister Costa: excuse us. Phaet, we need Wes, much as I hate to admit it. Find him, and meet me in the hangar. You have three minutes."

No one moves. Yinha's already come up with a plan. For the rest of us, the situation hasn't yet sunk in.

"Why are you still standing around, Stripes?" Yinha barks, snapping at me for the second time today. *"Move!"*

I let go of my brother and sprint out the doors.

＊ — ＊ — ＊

The Earth pulls us into orbit half a kilometer behind the massive ISS. My memories failed to do the satellite justice; it's wider and longer than the Free Radical's Atrium, with broken wings and several modules bound together by just a few screws. The wings are missing even more solar panels than when Yinha and I paid the station a visit on a nighttime flight, so long ago.

How things have changed. Then, we were on an adventure. This time, the ISS is something to fear.

"Pig A3 in place?" Rose says through the intercom. We've brought a small fleet of Dovetail and Batterer craft along with us.

"Confirmed," I say.

"Observations on the ISS?"

"There's a thruster unit attached," I say. "Firing in the direction opposite orbital path, forcing the satellite into lower altitude."

"Committee ships hovering around." Wes sits right by my side. There's nowhere I'd rather have him. If he wants to run off again, he'll have to take me with him. "A Colossus. And seven Destroyers."

That can't be good. Whatever the Committee is planning for the ISS, why does it need so much protection?

"Ships are distancing themselves now," Alex points out. He's in Pygmette A5. "Possibly coming for us."

"Blast it," Yinha says from the Destroyer she's piloting.

"ISS orbital radius decreasing," Rose says, "and decreasing faster."

All eight of the Committee's ships beeline for the Dovetail and Batterer conglomeration, paving their way with laser fire. Two are headed for us. *Breathe in, breathe out.* I watch the violet streaking forward through space, and I turn, twist, and flip our ship accordingly, relying on reflexes. Blood rushes from my head, and my world goes fuzzy and lopsided.

"Hold steady!" Wes shouts, frustrated in his efforts to fire at our enemies.

I straighten out our flight path—a huge risk—and have to jerk our ship leftward to evade a laser directed at our right wing. But it gives Wes the opportunity to fire two perfectly aimed missiles. They turn the Committee Destroyers into clouds of fire and smoke, reducing our enemies to dust.

The rest of the Dovetail front line isn't as lucky. Pygmettes A1 and A8 have gone offline, as have Destroyers R33 and T2. But at least the sky is quieter, and clearer. Hundreds of meters away, the Committee's Colossus sulks toward the Moon, its lights sputtering on and off. Someone must have scored a hit.

"The thruster that the Committee stuck on the ISS has been turned off. It's detaching . . . now," observes a Batterer soldier.

"Now that gravity alone is acting on that thing, let's figure out where it's headed," Rose says. "Cygnus, want to step in?"

A long pause. I imagine my brother recovering from the shock of the explosions that played on his screen a moment ago.

"Cygnus?" Rose repeats, her voice softer this time.

"Uh, okay," my brother says. "Way to make me the bearer of grit news."

Beeps and other computer noises replace their voices as they run various models.

"Oh no," my brother says when it's done. "Nononono."

"Cygnus, come on," Yinha says. "Spit it out."

"It's . . . it's complicated," he whispers, his voice growing unfocused. He's shutting down, and I wish I were in the control room to help him.

Rose takes over. "The ISS is spiraling down toward Earth. On its way, it will collide with the Vela, a medium-sized satellite in high Earth orbit, and get deflected fifteen degrees eastward. Both satellites will crash into the more crowded geosynchronous orbit altitude and collide with smaller satellites there."

"So Battery Bay can kiss a bunch of our communications capabilities good-bye," huffs the Batterer space forces' commander, Chief Airman Roy.

"That's not all," Rose says. "According to our models, the Vela will hit the Australian desert, which is uninhabited. But . . . the ISS and several smaller satellites will land roundabouts nineteen degrees south, one hundred seventy-eight degrees east, at terminal velocity."

Someone wrenches the microphone from Rose's hand. "No," says Costa. "We cannot allow anything to land there. Roy!"

"Yes, sir."

"I need two more fleets of ships, now! And, Yinha, whomever else you can send!"

"Got it," Yinha says. "I'll call on everyone who can fly a ship straight."

I think back to the map of Earth in the control room, matching the coordinates to the ones in my mind, and know where the satellites will crash-land before anyone says it out loud.

"I'm so sorry, friends," Rose murmurs. "The target . . . it's Battery Bay."

Whatever's been recovered of the beautiful park, the skyscrapers, the teeming aerial food stands, the *people*. The island city's chaos seemed self-perpetuating, even invulnerable, but it'll fade into an eerie calm if we don't stop this . . . abomination. This satellite cascade.

The intercom echoes with shouts of "No!" and "Our home!" as the Batterer space crews react to Rose's revelation. Wes mutes his headset, pain pulling his mouth into a tight line. "Alex and I shouldn't have been the only ones to leave Battery Bay." His voice is a whisper. "Should've brought the rest of Oda with us when we lifted off."

"No, Wes . . ." I reach for his hand; we knot our gloved fingers together and then untangle them, as we must, to retake our respective controls. "No one's safe anywhere. Not from *them*."

The Committee. Four men who abuse the people they can control and obliterate the ones they can't. Behind us, an armada of Dovetail and Batterer ships approach, but I don't know if it's sufficient to end what's been set in motion.

"Battery Bay will figure something out," Alex stammers to all of us. "The city can pick itself up, move somewhere . . ."

"It can't move far enough in twenty-four minutes and thirty-seven seconds to escape the satellite cascade," Rose says. "The red zone is several hundred kilometers across. Currently, the island has taken shelter on the landed side of a gigantic barrier reef—"

"One of the last remaining on Earth," calls a Batterer soldier.

"And it's low tide," says another. "Battery Bay can't make it out to the open ocean. Our high command has warned the navigation team on Earth, but they've only just fired up the engines. Your Committee knows the city's not going anywhere."

They knew the Batterers and Dovetail were keeping a close eye on the bombs orbiting Earth, so instead of sending a nuclear missile to annihilate the island city, they pushed the largest satellite a smidgen off course. No one would detect it, they thought, until it was too late.

It might be too late, but we need to tell ourselves otherwise. Battery Bay will *not* go the way of the Singularity. We can't let it.

"Fire everything you've got," Yinha orders us. "Deflect the satellites, or destroy them. There's nothing else we can do."

Wes looses missile after missile at the shifting ISS. Dozens of other ships follow suit. The missiles explode, doing surface-level damage, but the ISS stays true to its course.

A glittering icosahedral satellite approaches in the foreground—the Vela. Alex's Pygmette chases after it, scalding it with a laser until patches of it glow orange. But the Vela is still whole and should it crash, its impact on Earth will be massive. We have to blast each satellite apart, not turn them into superheated missiles that'll cause even greater destruction.

We need more.

"Pig A3, watch out!" Yinha calls. "Projectile on your right!"

I don't waste time looking behind us, instead pulling a loop-the-loop that slams Wes and me into our seats. A loyalist missile jets underneath our ship at its zenith and collides with the ISS, knocking off a dangling module. *Way to go, Committee.* That module equates to several kilotons of mass that won't smash into Battery Bay. I allow myself a deep recovery breath to celebrate the narrow miss.

But I've let down my guard too soon.

In the next instant, three things happen at once. The main body of the ISS smashes into the Vela, sending fragments flying into space and knocking the smaller satellite toward Earth. Loyalist ships' missiles incinerate Dovetail's sole Omnibus ship, sending up a vermilion flare that burns for a moment before the vacuum outside snuffs it out. And an armada of sleek Militia ships speeds into sight behind us—Committee reinforcements, fresh from Base I.

As my headset bursts with Dovetail's cries of despair, the hope seeps out of me, bit by bit, and I search in vain for a reason to hold on.

38

"NEVER MIND THE ENEMY SHIPS!" SHOUTS
Chief Airman Roy, above the noise of his jostling spacecraft as it
dodges enemy fire. "You Dovetailers have superior weapons—use
those to stop the cascade. We will cover for you!"

"Cover?" Wes yells as I twist our ship in a corkscrew. "How
can you cover us from that?"

Behind us, dozens of Batterer crafts aggregate, facing the enemy
ships head-on and spraying them with bullets and the occasional
precious missile. It's a shield—a shield made of our allies' bodies
and the thin-walled old spacecraft encasing them. If they were
fighting Pacifian ships, I wouldn't feel so sick with worry, but none
of those blocky spacecraft are in sight. Maybe the Committee
didn't trust their spacefaring skills . . . or the Pacifians have refused
to help after the Committee's brutal bombing of the metro tunnel.

"No, Roy!" I let out forward exhaust to slow us down. "We
won't leave you all behind. That's abandonment."

"Not quite," Roy says gruffly. "It's partitioning."

Moment by moment, the sky around our ship becomes darker
and clearer as the Committee ships' barrage of lethal armaments
thins out. It makes our flight easier, but I know that the Batterers'
spacecrafts, which we've left behind, are taking the brunt of the
assault.

"It's not right!" I say, amidst enthusiastic agreement from Yinha, Alex, and several other Dovetailers.

"Listen up." Roy sounds impatient. "If we die for our city, then we will have done our jobs. I know all about you Dovetail pilots' accomplishments, about the weapons and skills you have that my troops do not. We are giving you the space to do what you need to do. In other words, we trust you to help save Battery Bay. Do not put that trust to waste. Understood?"

I nod, and then remember that Roy can't see me.

"Understood," I say, full of guilt for what will almost certainly come. The Committee sacrificed hundreds of Pacifian troops when they tried to take the metro tunnel—*how is this any different?*

I have a horrible feeling that the outcome will be the same: Earthbound troops marching or flying into grave danger and dying in droves. But today, the Batterers had a choice. And they're fighting to defend *their* families, *their* city—not ours. Dovetail must respect their decision.

Foreboding and gratitude clash within me as I push our Pygmette closer to the ISS, dodging other satellites and chunks of debris still in orbit. Like an automaton, I tap the joystick in different directions, making myself queasy and causing Wes's face to turn green with spacesickness. If we flew a straight path, a collision would kill us within seconds. As we approach geosynchronous orbit, where old Earthbound civilizations put the majority of their satellites, the space around us becomes a minefield.

Nine Dovetail ships follow us—but within five seconds, it's eight. Another Pygmette, trying to dodge a loyalist missile, careens into a spent satellite and explodes. I cry out before I can switch off my headset. Dovetail's lost one ship and two lives.

But what about the Batterers? How many of them have perished since I last looked back?

"Eyes on the road, Stripes!" Yinha shouts.

I return my eyes to our path to see both the ISS and the Vela crash into clusters of defunct comsats, which begin curving toward Earth as well. Gritting my teeth, I decrease our speed, wiggle the Pygmette's joystick to dodge the rubbish in our way, and chase the satellites around the Earth. Now that we've descended into geosynchronous orbit, the time to circumscribe Earth is twenty-four hours. Looking at the continents and oceans speeding by beneath us makes me dizzy with the enormity of what we're trying to do.

In spite of our turbulent flight path, Wes continues shooting at the ISS and its smaller compatriots. One explosion, and the tiny Echo-3 splinters. Another, and the Astra 49 loses a solar panel. I watch the destruction with a mixture of satisfaction and resignation. Wes's aim is good, but we need about four of him at four sets of controls.

I crank the engines harder as we meet with air resistance in Earth's upper atmosphere. *The atmosphere*—we've arrived too soon. There's no hope of changing the falling satellites' paths now, of yanking them from Earth's gravitational clutches—all we can do is shoot them into pieces small enough to spare Battery Bay from being flattened.

The falling satellite chunks begin to glow as atmospheric drag scalds their surfaces. Friction will eventually stop the fragments' acceleration downward—but it won't be enough. Terminal velocity will turn them into virtual bombs.

Wes scores another hit on the ISS, taking off an antenna unit. *Good. Rip that thing apart.*

A squat Batterer ship comes zipping into view, hurling missile after missile at the ISS, like a mosquito pestering an elephant. For a second I'm elated. Then I count one, two, three, four ships following it. And no more.

"We got the loyalists off everyone's backs," a Batterer fighter says into our headsets. It's a woman this time, not Chief Airman Roy, and her voice lacks the ringing tones of victory. I shudder and look in the rearview camera, at the empty space behind us, where the skeletons of angular ships glint against the dark sky.

"At what cost?" I ask.

"The ultimate one," she says quietly. "Three quarters of the fleet is gone."

I fight down the sadness that's breaking my concentration. That's breaking *me*, opening a throbbing crack straight between my ribs. I knew what was going to happen when the Batterers stayed behind, but there was no way to predict how the pain would feel until I actually lived it.

"It's a cost each of us was willing to incur," the woman says. "No one was fooled into dying for our home, understood?"

Taking a deep breath, I nod and say, "To all of us in the sky today—destroy the satellite cascade. Shatter them. Our comrades didn't die for Battery Bay to fall."

The remaining fighters, Dovetail and Batterer alike, train our wingtip weapons on the intact satellites, streaking the atmosphere with lasers, missiles, rockets, and torpedoes. Giving the Earthbound at the surface a light show.

Do they think that they're seeing shooting stars in the daytime? I wonder. *Or do they know better now?*

Down below, Battery Bay glistens a million different colors, a sickeningly obvious target. It's flanked on one side by Australia's emerald-hued northern coast, and on the other by the sparkling ocean, which is a beautiful turquoise color I hadn't imagined nature could dream up. Wes's family is down there, on that floating city. Sear, too, and our gruff taxi driver, and the revelers at the Moon Festival. This is for them.

We don't let up our assault until Yinha calls out, "Stop!" She's afraid we might start hitting human-inhabited territory rather than satellites. Now we must watch the metal pieces fall.

The first fragments make impact on and around Battery Bay. Gray clouds of debris rise, and fires catch. As the air above the city thickens with soot and brightens with flame, pockets of the city itself go dim, and I know that the lives within have been extinguished. Fewer than we'd worried we would lose, but still far, far too many.

The majority of the satellite slivers don't crush Battery Bay. They slice into the vibrant turquoise sea instead, cutting through the tan ropes of reef crisscrossing the coastal waters and ripping apart marine cities of coral that took millennia to grow.

One of the last remaining on Earth, the Batterer soldier said.

I should feel grateful that the reef took the brunt of the damage, but that gratitude is tempered by the knowledge that we've shifted the burden of death to nonhumans, to the spotted and striped fishes, spiraling and scalloped shells, and other strange creatures whose ancestors were on Earth before the human species even appeared.

"Look at this," I say to Wes. "Look at all of this."

He can't. After taking in the patchily burning city and the dying reef, he turns and directs his steely gaze at me instead. Hugs me, holds me tight, presses his cheek against mine. Touching him grounds me in this tiny ship teetering above Earth, reminds me of the specks of goodness that endure amidst so much evil.

For a moment, I shut my eyes, blocking out the horrors of the world around us, and pretend he's the only thing that's real.

39

MINISTER COSTA says, patting me on the back. "You'll need it, for tomorrow."

Costa's water-hair sits like putty on his scalp. His teal suit is wrinkled and sweat-stained. Today, the Batterers lost many of their best pilots and their space forces commander—and Costa had to report it to his people. To his credit, he hasn't talked about the extensive damage that Battery Bay sustained; he's turned all his attention to ending the Lunar branch of the war as quickly as possible.

The leaders and I sit in the InfoTech room, from which Rose's team of hackers watches everything happening on the Moon. Protests on Base III, Committee rallies on Base V, and Dovetail construction on the Free Radical are among the many scenes playing on the HeRPs.

Tomorrow. Costa's words wring out the last of the energy in my body. I'll do as my superiors ask me, but at some point, I worry that I'll hit a wall and stop functioning.

"If you're planning skirmishes tomorrow, can you write in a coffee break?" Alex asks.

"Skirmishes aren't what we have in mind," Andromeda says. "We discussed our next move while you were all . . . out there. The

Committee's attempt to destroy Battery Bay has backfired, to say the least. A fifth of their own fleet was destroyed today. And Base III's uranium miners took advantage of the chaos to start an insurrection against occupying Militia forces."

Put like that, our situation sounds promising, and victory seems within reach. Yinha sits up straighter, seeming to shake off her exhaustion. Seeing her move lifts my flagging spirits.

"No Pacifians were fighting today," I say.

"I dug into that," Rose says. "Tried to find Pacifian voice records, or text documents—seems the Committee hasn't been involving them in key decisions."

Costa sneers. "Unsurprising. Commander Jang may consider himself a leader, but he's as obedient to the Committee as the rest of his countrymen are to the Pacifian Premier." He wrinkles his nose in distaste. "Let us move on. As a response to today, Battery Bay's voters have agreed to send three thousand additional troops to the Moon. They are en route now. The ones that were already here have left the Dugout in rovers to set up behind the mountains north of Base I. The peaks of eternal light, as you call them."

"With the lunar eclipse tomorrow, the peaks will be shrouded in darkness for four hours," Asterion says. "The Batterer troops stationed there may approach invisibly."

"The loyalists won't have a clue," Rose adds. "My people are wiping the rovers' signatures from the Committee's satellite images every time those things pass over. And after the eclipse ends, there'll be a pretty big solar storm that could keep the Committee on Base I for a few hours."

"There won't be a better time to end this war," Asterion concludes.

The enormity of what we are about to do, the *immediacy* of it, twists its way into my brain. Suddenly, I recall what my siblings looked like before the war started—their innocent faces, so obviously enamored with life. *Things could be that peaceful again.*

"All our engineers are repairing equipment and preparing vehicles and weapons for tomorrow," Asterion says. "We've sent messages to our brothers and sisters on other bases and moved all civilians into the bunker. By this time tomorrow, Base I will be Dovetail's, III and V will join us, and the Moon will be free."

He surveys the room, takes in the chaotic scenes playing on each HeRP, perhaps envisioning how each could end. "Or we will all have returned to dust."

40

DEEP BENEATH THE VOLCANO, IN THE UN-
derground bunker, eighty-year-old electric bulbs illuminate the
worry on thousands of Dovetailer and Batterer faces, old and
young alike. The old light bulbs are strung together in rows on the
low ceiling, like a sky of flickering orange stars. Many people have
gone to bed for the night, tossing and turning on thin cots stacked
three on top of each other. The scene reminds me of the camaraderie
of the Militia bunks, but on a larger scale and in a direr situation.

Dug out of dark gray rock, the underground bunker zigzags for
kilometers beneath the base. In an emergency, it could hold the
residents of Bases I and II combined. Impossible to bomb from the
lunar surface, airtight, impervious to solar flares and meteoroid
storms, it's everything one could want in a secure location. But if
soldiers or toxic gas were to breach the bunker, it would turn into
a mass murderer's paradise.

Dovetail and Batterer soldiers are still descending via the endless spiral staircases; I'm glad to see them reaching out to one another, keeping each other from falling.

Although the strategy meeting for all troops didn't last long,
our mission tomorrow weighs heavy on all our minds. Our many
tasks seem impossible: invade the base from above, while mini-
mizing civilian casualties. Because I've escaped Governance once

before, I've volunteered to go after the tyrants with Wes and Alex. Yinha let Wes off house arrest again, knowing that leaving him in the Dugout would waste his skills.

Even though we're only three people strong, our mission doesn't have room for a less experienced team member's mistakes. A single slipup—like Umbriel's several days ago—could cost us our lives, and so we've decided not to let anyone else join us.

Another small group, made up of Battery Bay's best sneaks, will attempt to capture the Committee using a different route. But we all know they're unlikely to make it halfway up the Committee's tower. The burden's on us.

We will flush out the Committee and force them to negotiate with Dovetail.

Put like that, our plan sounds ludicrous. Something or someone could capture or kill us before we get close to them. And would the Committee ever agree to peace talks? Since when has the Committee ever listened to anyone but themselves?

"You and your friends picked the most dangerous job, Phaet. No surprise there, but . . ." Anka sits beside me on the cot, picking at the hangnails on her dry fingers. "Do you know how it feels for me, having to sit here while you try to sneak onto Base I?"

I put my finger to my lips. Cygnus is sleeping—or trying to sleep—in the cot below. He lies on his side, pressing one ear into the thin mattress and covering the other with his hand. This innocent-looking, fragile boy saved Battery Bay. My brother, who can't keep the nightmares away but made sure millions of children could still have sweet dreams.

"It's not about wanting to fight the Committee," Anka says, "even though you know I hate them. It's about wanting to be with you every second. In case something happens and I can help out."

Anka feels restless too. I feel a pang of guilt for putting her in this situation—wanting to contribute to a battle she'd be better off avoiding. Thankfully, at thirteen years of age, she can't join or be drafted into the invading Dovetail force. Her actions won't cause me the same anguish the twins have caused their father. The Phis sit two rows down from us, deep in conversation; Ariel's still off-duty. Umbriel looks as if he's going to be sick, even though he has one of the easier tasks: standing guard outside the bunker tomorrow.

"Anka, you can help Cygnus by being here." My suggestion almost sounds like an order. Back in Shelter, she put herself in danger whenever she felt a situation was unjust, narrowly escaping debilitating injuries on several occasions. I can't stomach the idea of anyone or anything hurting her again. "Remember, make sure Cygnus is always wearing earplugs. But if you hear strange noises from above or Dovetail announcements, take them out so he has all his senses and can protect himself. If the loyalists breach the bunker—"

"I *know* what to do tomorrow," Anka snaps. "But what if tomorrow goes by, and you don't come back?"

"If I 'bite it,' as they say in Militia?"

Anka bows her head. "Yeah."

My death is a real possibility, as ever-present as my shadow. My brother and sister know it, though I've always skirted the issue with them. Now I picture the Moon without me. Strangely, the mental image doesn't induce panic or fear. In fact, the Moon looks the same as it does now. Maybe we don't notice ourselves and our impact in everyday life, but we underestimate the effects we have on others? I study the angles in Anka's face and the new curves on her body—she's always changing, and I find something new about her every day to take pride in.

I squeeze my sister's shoulder, clear my throat, and tackle the subject in the most practical way I can. "Cygnus can have my old e-textbooks—they're buried in my handscreen's memory chip. Umbriel . . . You can give him my infrared glasses so he'll always see people coming. And you can have my Lady of the Lab figurines, if they're still intact. Remember how I never let you play with them?"

"Yeah, but I'm too old now."

"Not too old for this." I take the spare Lazy from my belt and press it into her hand. Anka's jaw drops. Enabling her to defend herself with something more substantial than knives is one of the many reasons I needed to see her before we launch. "The switch on top turns the energy generation on, and the trigger fires it. Easy."

Anka's slim, wide-knuckled fingers wrap around the grip and squeeze it hard. The weapon looks huge in her hand. "Beaters use these for burning people. For killing them. Umbriel said he'd never touch one. Would using this thing make me as bad as the Beaters are?"

"It won't be easy," I say. "But I'd rather you live to hate yourself than die with a clean conscience."

She turns the gun over in her hands and then places it gingerly by her side. "I'll . . . I'll use it if anyone comes after me or Cygnus."

"One more thing. Keep calm, Anka. I won't be here, so all of *them*"—I tip my head outward, gesturing at the Dovetailers—"may look to you."

Anka scoffs. "Keep calm? I'm not some kind of sage, like you are. I only know how to shout."

True. I remember my fears that Anka was Mom's true heir—not me—because of her articulate speech, her anger, her power to move people. But as it turns out, we carried on Mom's legacy, together. "That's what Dovetail needs. In case I—"

"Okay, that's enough." Anka holds up a hand. "Sorry I brought it up. I'll cover for you if you die. It's not like I haven't thought about it a million times already, okay?"

A head of messy black hair peeks out above the cot we're sitting on. Cygnus has given up on trying to sleep. "Anka, you okay?" He strains to pull himself up.

While Anka buries the Lazy underneath her blanket, I heave Cygnus onto our cot—all one-point-eight meters of him. Despite his impressive height, my fifteen-year-old brother weighs as much as a prepubescent child. I want to curl up around him to protect him, even though I know I won't be able to stay forever.

"I'm fine," Anka lies. "We were . . . contingency planning. For if Phaet goes the same way as Mom tomorrow."

Cygnus flinches at her bluntness and turns to me. "If this'll be the last time we see you, then let's talk about something else. Something happier."

"This won't be the last time." I take my brother's hand, hold it tight to my heart. I drop a kiss on Anka's forehead and sling my other arm around her shoulder. "I miss Mom, but I'm not ready to join her yet." With my brother and sister in my arms, I'm at home in this dim, yellow-lit bunker, and I'm happy. Happier than anyone should be. "You both give me something to come back to."

41

I SPLASH COLD BASIN WATER ONTO MY FACE.
Sleep eluded me until early this morning; finally, I snuck out of bed while my siblings slept, to get ready in the bunker's empty unisex public restroom. When I was still a star Primary pupil, I arrived to morning class ten minutes early every day without fail. Why shouldn't I be punctual to battle too?

I've put on my uniform with the hidden mirrors, but I haven't yet picked out weapons or fixed my hair. A pile of my gear sits atop a teetering black plastic bench at the end of the row of washbasins. Unlike the rest of the bunker, the restroom's concrete walls have been painted a glaring shade of white in a futile attempt to bring some brightness underground. Beneath the flickering yellow lights, my skin looks greenish; in the cracked mirror, even my loose black-and-silver hair hangs limp and dull.

Look alive, Girl Sage, I tell myself. *How do you expect people to follow a ghost?* Though appearing alert is surely a lost cause, I hop up and down to get my blood flowing.

The primitive hinged door creaks open. Every muscle of mine tenses. *It's someone who needs to use the toilet,* I tell myself. Drying my face on my stretchy black shirt, I stand up straight and look behind me.

Wes walks my way, already dressed in full combat attire—

typical. He's even more punctual than me. He turns his helmet over in his hands as he approaches. When he gets closer, I notice the bruise-like imprints under his sleepy eyes.

Is something wrong? Sudden worry kicks me harder than caffeine ever could.

"Morning," he says, wrapping me in his arms. Entwined, we step farther into the walled-off restroom. The door swings shut.

"What's happening?" I touch his upper back before I can stop myself. "Did I miss anything important?"

"Besides me?" He cracks a tired smile.

I grimace, embarrassed that I can't even greet him sans stress. One of his hands riffles through the tangles in my hair. I lean inward, settling into him. Into the quiet contentment I haven't felt since that night on Battery Bay.

"I knew you'd be up." Wes pulls back to get a good look at me. I don't quake under his gaze like I used to. Whatever I look like, whatever I *am*, is enough. "Up and possibly upset."

"Who wouldn't be, after yesterday?" I say. "Now we're about to tear up more people and places. Part of me doesn't want to find out how this'll play out. But I want you next to me when it ends."

Wes grimaces. "I won't go rogue again, like I did in the tunnel. I'll stay, for you and the people we both care about."

"Even if Lazarus appears?" I say to make sure.

Wes exhales for a long time, as if trying to expel the anger from his body. "If I fight him, I fight him with you."

I nod, torn between crushing him in a hug and leaving him the space to reconcile his grief and anger with his responsibility toward me.

Wes looks at the assortment of weapons spread out on the bench, sparing me from making a decision. "I'll help get those ready for you."

Wes sits, while I step in front of the mirror and start wrestling my hair, thinner and grayer than ever, into a braid. It's hopelessly tangled from my tossing and turning last night, and I don't have a comb. My face twists into a scowl, but then I laugh out loud. What serious soldier worries about her hair before a battle? A strange sensation of reassurance overtakes me. The Committee hasn't changed me completely; the neat, detail-oriented part of me remains.

Looking in the mirror, I watch Wes's reflection peer down the barrel of a Downer gun; he takes a silicone cloth from his pocket and wipes away specks of dirt. His movements hypnotize me—the shifting of his forearm muscles as they hold up the weapon, the valleys that form between the tendons on the backs of his hands when his fingers contract. When he finishes polishing and loading the gun, he puts it down and starts sanding one of my favorite daggers. It has a twenty-two-centimeter blade, straight and symmetrical, ideal for close combat and throwing.

I finish braiding my hair and tie it off with the same elastic I've used for months. "You're a lifesaver, literally," I say. "Remember the Militia instructors saying that your equipment is all that stands between you and your enemies? Well, I put off doing a proper checkup last night. Procrastination at its finest."

He stands, holding the dagger in one hand, and crosses the floor to stand behind me. "They also said to trust no one else with your stash." He's close enough to rest the side of his head against mine.

My pulse picks up and my leg muscles tense, even though I know he'd never hurt me. *Why do we react to fear and excitement in the same way?*

"Those are all Militia fibs." I watch my lips move in the mirror. "I've trusted you with more important things."

I whirl around a hundred and eighty degrees as Wes raises the dagger. He holds it so that the flat of the blade rests on my mouth. His hand stays steady—the mark of an expert fighter—but the rest of him trembles.

One centimeter at a time, I lean forward, and the dagger drops away. Wrapping my arms around his waist, I kiss him hard; I tangle my fingers in his petal-soft hair, feeling the small swells on the surface of his skull. Everything that makes him *him* is right underneath my hands. My heart thuds faster and faster, as if I'm sprinting—alive, alive, *alive*, it seems to say. But for once, I feel like I'm running toward something, instead of away.

"We're being absurd," he whispers, sheathing the dagger. "We've both lost people we love . . . we know how that feels."

I put a finger on his lips. "And we haven't tried to stop caring for each other."

"We've done the complete opposite. But that's all right by me." He kisses each knuckle on my hand, and his touch fills me with so much emotion that I feel like I could burst.

When he looks in my eyes again, his face is serious and his mouth tight, filled with unspoken words.

"Since my sister died, I've thought about how nothing she did seemed rational—taking the lamp-lighting job when she could hardly walk straight, deciding to marry Lazarus when she knew that he was such a resentful person. But now she makes more sense to me. She did whatever she thought would make her happy. That's how she got the most out of her twenty-three years on Earth."

Finally, he's mentioned Murray. I have to pick my words carefully.

"You see what was best in her," I say. "That takes real love."

Wes nods, but there's a grimace on his face. "I didn't spend enough time with her while she lived," he says, letting go of me.

"That's the last thing I want to happen with you. So—cheers to our absurdity, Phaet."

He finishes with the subtle smile that never gets old. Silently, we gather our things. I coil my braid into a bun and clip it in place, and then we exit the gloomy restroom, our arms around each other, and start climbing the stairs out of the bunker.

We might not return to that place. But at least we've left one happy memory there, even if no one will ever see its light.

* — * — *

Wes and I march down the Dugout's widest hallway, palms pressed together and fingers clasped. It's our secret, the only thing that keeps me from feeling like I'm walking to my execution. We're in a dense pocket of Dovetail pilots; behind us march the ragtag foot soldiers, our passengers. About half have broken out tattered Militia uniforms from years past. Others wear the teal Batterer getup or civilian robes with extra pockets sewn in.

I imagine Umbriel guarding a staircase that leads down to the bunker, dressed all in Phi green, too-wide utility belt hanging off his hips. Will he muster up the strength to hurt, to kill if he must? Or would he rather be a victim?

Dovetail and our much larger cohort of Earthbound allies have agreed on a two-pronged attack. Dovetail forces will swoop in from above, beat back the Committee spacecraft, and fly into Base I Defense with the help of our undercover agents already stationed there, who'll open the hangar doors for us. We'll clear out Defense for the brunt of the attack, which will come from the Batterer soldiers, racing downhill in their rovers from the peaks of eternal light and straight into Base I under the cover of the eclipse.

A narrower, darker tunnel splits off from the Dugout's main hallway. From here, a straight path leads to Defense. Although we've patched up the vacuum seal, there's the same crumbling concrete, the black-and-white paint peeling off the walls' Lunar flag motifs. The sad box of a space is too small for the Batterers' many antiquated ships and Dovetail's few modern ones. To transport everyone, Dovetail will fill our three Omnibuses and one beat-up Colossus to full capacity.

This time, leadership has assigned me to pilot a Destroyer, the model with which I'm most comfortable, and take along a hand-picked team of four. Asterion's daughter, Chitra, climbs into the flight overseer's seat, closest to the ship's rear. Despite her family's tragic history with spaceflight, she has proved a competent, careful crewmember in training drills. Nash and Alex take the wing weapons. Wes sits copilot, and I take the controls. My fingers are numb, as if anxiety has drained all the blood out of them.

"Put that frown away, Dove Girl," Alex drawls, checking my reflection in the windshield. "It's not healthy for us to see."

"What he means," Nash says, "is that if *you're* losing your grit, Stripes, then we have no chance."

Chitra's big brown eyes widen in apprehension, and I suspect she's remembering her sister. How has her father reconciled Vinasa's death with sending his only remaining daughter on Dovetail's most hazardous mission yet? *Well . . . Chitra is doing what's expected of her.*

"Phaet, remember the third Militia evaluation?" Wes asks, and I look away from Chitra's face. His eyes gleam. *Steel,* I think. That's how strong I've become. "Fly like you did then. Like I know you can."

That was two years ago, I think. *My first time off Base IV.* Wes and I have accomplished so much together since then, cheated death across the Earth and Moon. If people could serve as good luck charms—if I believed in good luck charms—he'd be mine. I'd tell him now, if there weren't three other people listening.

I pull us into the airlock, telling myself that nothing can take my life as long as he's guarding it.

＊ — ＊ — ＊

"Watch out!" Yinha says into our headsets. "Enemy engaged."

Far ahead of us, her ship, Pygmette R88, executes a flawless barrel roll to dodge loyalist missiles. Less than four minutes after Dovetail's launch, the Militia has sent up its own fighter ships. Dozens of spacecraft dart above Base I; we distinguish friend from foe by the red stripes painted on the Dovetail vehicles. Base I's hemi-polyhedral structures, swathed in darkness, seem all too far away. But our easy visibility won't last long. Moment by moment, the Moon is slipping into Earth's shadow.

"The Committee sent ships up quickly," Alex mutters. "Too quickly."

I steer our Destroyer behind a Dovetail Omnibus, using the larger ship to shield us from lasers and projectiles. Beside me, Wes fine-tunes our movements, glancing nervously at the peaks of eternal light. Only their tips are still sunlit. As soon as the eclipse reaches totality, the Batterers will descend upon Base I. And they'll do it whether we've breached Defense yet or not.

A missile meets the Omnibus' left wing, and the craft swerves, knocked off balance by the damage. It retreats higher above Base I. I'm counting on the hull's self-repair mechanism to fix enough of the damage to get the craft back on track.

"Watch out for more slugs," Yinha says, referring to the missiles. "The enemy's sent up another fleet of Destroyers."

"We're going upstairs to regroup," I say, and fire our thrusters downward.

"Got you covered," Yinha says.

Our Destroyer swoops up. Here, several satellites continue in their irregular path around the Moon. Committee ships bathe in our exhaust.

When we reach five thousand meters, I stop our ascent and look down upon a dark, dark landscape. Not a single peak of eternal light is lit by the sun.

We're running out of time.

"Batterer rovers beginning descent now," Rose says in our headsets. She's in the Dugout, keeping track of the invasion's many arms.

Hearing her voice makes my heart thud, driving home the stakes of our mission: we can't fail Dovetail, can't fail the thousands of Batterer soldiers who'll be discovered by the Committee and destroyed out here if we don't open up Base I Defense for them.

"I'm not getting anything from our people in Base I Defense," Rose continues, and the stress I'm trying to suppress rises to a fever pitch. "The Committee must've . . . must've found them and . . . removed them."

No! It's bad enough that we lost Dovetailers, and even worse that they were ones so central to our plan. They can't clear the way for us, and now we'll fail to do so for the Batterers, who are picking their way down from the peaks of eternal light.

"We'll have to get into the base some other way," says Nash, gripping the right wing weapons controls.

"Hold on," Rose says, "we're trying to hack the hangar control switches . . ."

Trying isn't enough. If Rose's team can't open the hangar, we'll all be stuck out here. The attack will be a failure. Fragments of plans bounce around in my mind, none of them coherent enough to work.

"Watch out, Dove Girl!" Alex says. "Satellite coming up at a hundred seventy-five degrees—"

I see the dilapidated thing, a hexagonal prism with two solar-paneled rectangular wings sticking out the sides, whip through the loyalist crafts that have followed us, scattering them. It careens toward us from behind, and I swerve out of the way.

Then, impulsively, I twist the ship around to follow the satellite. I remember it from my studies—it's a twenty-third-century remote sensing craft called the Lunar Remote Imager, or LRI. Five hundred kilograms of metals and polymers that drifted into irregular lunar orbit over decades of disturbances. Neither side has touched the dead satellite; it was too volatile to use for weapons storage or landscape mapping.

The Committee turned the ISS into a weapon. Why shouldn't we do the same with the LRI? I look from the satellite to Wes, and he nods.

"Let's feed the Committee their own medicine," he says.

"Sage, please, have you thought this through?" Chitra asks in a tiny voice.

"Not much time for thinking," I say. "Nash and Alex, get out the carbon fiber net. Yinha, you free?"

"Yep."

"Prepare to perform a magnetic latch." I push the throttle, and our ship accelerates, closing the distance between us and the LRI. "Let's snag this thing."

42

"THIS IS A LUNATIC MOVE," NASH MUTTERS, but in spite of her doubts she punches buttons to ready our net. Measuring four by four meters, the carbon-fiber web was designed to catch and discard meteoroids that wandered too close to the base. Repurposing it for an attack shouldn't be much of a stretch.

We match the satellite's speed, and then gain on it. "We're going to catch the LRI and smash it into Base I Defense," I say. "The kinetic energy should be enough to—"

A voice message from Rose interrupts me. "No success trying to hack our way into the hangar. They've put too many layers of protection around the controls."

"Rosie," Yinha says. It's the second time she's used the nickname. "It's okay. You tried. Our turn now—we've got this."

Do we? I grip the Destroyer's controls hard, trying to hold my hands steady lest my friends see me shaking. Yinha accelerates until she's hurtling alongside the satellite—and then pounces. The Pygmette latches on with a lurch. We don't hear the *clang*, but I wince anyway. The impact had to hurt.

"Ah!" Yinha screeches. She fires the Pygmette's front thrusters, slowing herself and the satellite down.

I pull our Destroyer ahead of her and turn it around to face backward. My teammates have our net at the ready, dangling on the metal repair arms below our ship.

"Accelerating . . . now!" I fire the front thrusters.

The Pygmette and LRI smash into the net, throwing us forward. Making use of the momentum, I take us in a wide circle until we're facing Base I. Then I push the ship baseward at ninety-four meters per second.

Several kilometers from our destination, I slam on the backward thrusters, throwing Yinha and the LRI. The satellite barrels toward the lunar surface, Yinha's ship glued to it like a tick. It rotates in a corkscrew motion that makes me nauseated even from here. For one moment, I let myself be grateful that she, not I, is in that Pygmette.

"Aim for Defense!" I call to her via headset as we follow behind. It's more to soothe myself than to direct her. If she can't do this, no other pilot ever could.

Silence from Yinha's end. As she adjusts her aim, helium exhaust trails out of pipes on her ship's rear, front, and sides.

Less than a kilometer away from the base, she unlatches her Pygmette from the satellite. The LRI picks up speed, drawn by the Moon's gravity and the grav-magnets on Base I. No air resistance slows it down.

Kinetic energy increases with the square of velocity . . .

With the energy of a small bomb, the LRI smashes into the Base I hangar's ceiling. Metal chunks fly; sizzling gas jets out of the puncture wound. Twisted broken ships glint somewhere in the cloud of debris.

"Look at that gritstorm . . ." Yinha breathes into her mouthpiece.

"Looking isn't enough," Alex says.

Before the dust settles, we dive in.

⁕ — ⁕ — ⁕

Dovetail ships swoop into the destroyed hangar. Carcasses of Committee ships cringe against the walls, pieces of ceiling embedded in their hulls; on all sides, pressure-suited Militia flee the area. Because we blew apart the airlock, gas is leaking out of the hangar and into space. If we leave our ships and our pressure suits sustain enough damage, the vacuum will kill us.

The loyalists know this too. They're flying or running haphazardly through the hangar doors, into Defense's interior. *Those doors won't be open for much longer.*

"Follow them!" I call to Dovetail. "To the Defense lobby!"

Heeding my orders, our side's ships fly over the fleeing loyalists' heads and through the hangar doors as they close. Enemy projectiles hit us from the front. When the doors are nearly shut, the last Dovetail ship, an Omnibus, rams into them, puncturing a hole as it joins us.

But again, the Committee's ready: a solid metal gate descends from above, sealing off the hangar in front of us.

Dovetail taxis into the lobby to unload. As we exit our ships, we duck under the wings or behind the fuselages for shelter. The place is a fracas of shouts, laser fire, and screeching alarms. The faceted ceiling once displayed hundreds of military leaders' photographs. Now several panels have crashed to the floor, and soldiers of both sides trample over them. Decorative black and silver ribbons, slashed and torn, hang from the rafters. No battle manual would advise unloading in such chaos, but this won't be the first time my team has defied convention.

Per the plan we agreed upon, Yinha steers her ship back outside to facilitate the Batterer charge instead of disembarking like the majority of Dovetail's troops. "I'll contact you if there's very good news or very bad news," she says, and hangs up with a *click*. I watch her go, worry creeping into my heart.

Do what you promised to do. Wes, Alex, and I unbuckle the straps securing us to our seats, preparing to separate from Nash and Chitra and carry out the next part of our task. Alex climbs the ladder to the hatch first; Wes steadies him with one hand so he can open it.

"Hey, Stripes." Nash fixes her deep brown eyes on my face, looking as serious as I've ever seen her. Chitra watches our every move, beads of nervous sweat pooling on her forehead. "Make those five grit-bags hurt. I don't care how you do it. Make them wish they'd done something with their lives besides ruin ours."

She doesn't say good-bye. Maybe she's afraid that if she does, she'll never say hello again.

Alex exits the ship, and as Wes pulls himself out, he reaches a hand back to help me up the ladder. When my head emerges, the sounds and sights and smells of battle assault my senses. Violet lasers, bullets, and grenades, flying through the air and burning everything and everyone they touch. My eyes smart, my inner ears throb, and my nose and throat sting. I drop to ground level, where Committee troops have already surrounded Alex and Wes. Keeping his back against the ship, Alex slams his armored elbow into a Militia soldier's solar plexus. Wes runs forward to club another's head before the man can attack Alex from the side. We gather together, backs to one another. Slowly, painfully, we fight our way toward the Defense exit.

"I'll open up a path for you guys!" Nash seems to have taken the Destroyer's pilot seat. The hull sheds its outer shell and the wings fold in as she switches to its indoor combat settings; she takes a zigzagging path above the Militia's heads to avoid their lasers, several other ships trailing behind. Our ship's wing weapons fire shots at the enemy's foot soldiers, opening up pockets of space on either side of us.

We have to push through this. The sooner we force the Committee to negotiate, the sooner this will all end. If we fail, the Batterer team will have to get to them or die trying.

Fighting off enemies as we go, Wes, Alex, and I exit Defense. The expansive Main Lane—Base I's primary thoroughfare, now clogged with gray-suited Pacifians—stretches out before us. Instead of fighting our way through to Governance, where the Committee is stationed, we turn down a smaller side hallway that our side has already captured. At its entrance, Dovetail units fend off Militia forces. As the rovers arrive, Batterer soldiers come rushing in to help them hold down the territory.

They're all covering for us, clearing out the route we'll take toward the Committee. We have to keep going, have to succeed, or risk wasting their efforts.

Farther down, the hallway grows emptier. Dovetail troops are stationed every few meters. Windows to the dark outside are spaced evenly along the walls, and more black and silver ribbons crisscross the ceiling.

About thirty meters in, we receive an update from Chitra, who is still in Defense with Nash. "Seven Batterer rovers have entered the hangar," Chitra says. "Fourteen more are still out there."

We began with twenty-two rovers. "Casualties?" I whisper, my anxious steps punctuating my voice.

A brief silence, and then Nash speaks. "One rover got blown up outside the hangar. There were eighty-four troops in there. Things look bad, Phaet."

Fighting back nausea, I run onward with my team. There are

no friendly soldiers holding down this territory; we're treading on enemy ground.

Fifty meters down the hallway, near its terminus, we find what we were looking for: a low metal grate separating the hall from a ventilation tunnel. Alex and I guard Wes's back as he melts the edges of the grate with a continuous violet beam from his Lazy. As a cluster of gray-suited Pacifian foot soldiers turns the corner and sprints down the hallway, Wes kicks in the grate. Because the grav-magnets above our heads attract metal, it sticks to the ventilation tunnel's roof.

"Come on!" Wes helps Alex crawl inside, and I follow. Wes wrenches the grate from the roof, lines up the glowing orange edges with the edges of the hole, and holds it there while the material welds itself back together.

Before the Pacifians can shoot him through the grate's openings, I reach over Wes's shoulder, tranquilizer in hand, and plug them in the neck with Downers. One, two, three, four Pacifians collapse, unconscious.

Once the grate has cooled and looks solid again, we take off, crawling through the tunnel. By the time more Pacifians arrive, we're ten meters closer to the Committee stronghold. We move silently, breathing through our noses to avoid making noise. Two rights, a left, and a right take us underneath the Governance Department.

There's a massive opening, a vertical shaft tens of meters in diameter with whirring carbon dioxide–oxygen filters stacked in the center. Walls plated with steel, it stretches upward for hundreds of meters; I can't make out where it ends.

"Holy Father of . . ." Alex swears, peering out of the tunnel and tilting his head back.

This is it. The highest tower on Base I, topped by the Committee's conference room, where they nearly drowned Umbriel and me last year. "Can't wait to see my old friends again," I mutter.

"Then what're we dallying for?" Alex steps out of the tunnel and onto a balcony that rings the shaft's circumference. A narrow bridge leads to the air filter column.

Cautiously, Wes and I follow. My knees seem to lock with each step—the Committee must have at least an inkling that we've gotten this far.

"I don't feel so good about this," Wes says before he steps out.

"Our friends out there don't feel so good about fighting off loyalists while you make up your mind," Alex says. "Come on, Carlyle."

Wes nods and crawls out of the tunnel. But the instant both his feet touch the balcony, a force from above slams us down to the floor. I'd scream if the impact hadn't knocked all the wind out of me.

Someone has quadrupled or quintupled the current through the electromagnets in the ceiling, increasing the "gravity" of the vertical shaft. The magnets repel the water in my body, gluing my limbs down, almost nailing my chin onto the ground. I can barely lift my fingers. My skull threatens to cave under the pressure. My companions' outlines swim in my vision; their shouts and groans echo in my ears.

Then the barrage begins.

43

THE PRESSURE SEEMS TO CRUSH EVERYTHING in my head out of existence. Forcing thoughts through the morass is nearly impossible. A laser misses my shoulder but superheats the air through which it passes; my skin burns. There must be soldiers above us, but due to the immense gravity, we can't even lift ourselves off the floor. Their blasts are reflected by the steel grates and fans above us, so that the whole shaft glows violet. Who knows when they'll hit us?

Steel. There's a sizeable horizontal strut a meter or so above me, meant to support a fan higher up. I move only my eyeballs to check for Wes and Alex. Wes digs his fingers into his scalp, and Alex retreats into the ventilation tunnel from which we came. Gravity seems normal there, but Wes and I are too far out to make it back.

I wrench my jaws apart and fight the lung-crushing pressure in order to speak. "Wes—Lazy. Burn."

"Right," he chokes out.

Lifting my Lazy requires every muscle fiber in my arm—it seems to weigh more than a human being. I dig my elbow into the floor and fire a steady stream at a point on the steel bar until it glows red. Then I force my wrist to bend, adjusting my aim, slicing the metal as if the laser were a knife. Wes does the same at another point about two meters down the strut.

As the metal melts, the magnets attract the ferromagnetic material. It rattles, straining against the slivers of steel that still connect it to the rest of the strut.

"Now!" I shout.

Grabbing Wes's hand, I heave myself toward the ventilation tunnel. We progress a centimeter at a time. Above our heads, the metal segment wrenches loose and accelerates to a lethal speed. As it pulverizes the spinning fan in its path, crashes and clangs fill the vertical ventilation shaft. Fan blades, loose screws, and gigantic grates shoot up, accelerating toward the ceiling, toward the exposed electromagnets above. Then they strike, slicing through wires, truncating the current that powers the grav-magnets.

Zap! The ceiling flashes white, blinding us. For a second, it's as if we've brought lightning to the Moon. Then the immense pressure lifts, and I feel as if I could rise like a cloud. I spread my limbs out to enjoy the sensation of moon-grav, and laugh. Gathering our legs under us like springs, Wes and I push off from the floor and soar the last two meters into the tunnel's shelter. Moon-grav pulls us gently down.

But even in moon-grav, one-sixth as strong as the default base setting, falling metal lands hard. Pygmette-sized solenoids tumble past us, and keep on falling to the shaft floor dozens of meters below, accompanied by the scrape of fan blades, the jingle of nuts and bolts.

After the dust settles, I peek upward into the vertical shaft. Instead of a network of balconies and guardrails, I see only sheets of crooked metal. The air filtration column leans against the opposite wall of the cylindrical shaft.

A wave of satisfaction inundates my body. I've destroyed part of my enemies' lair, imposed a real physical threat upon them. Maybe even cut off some of their oxygen supply.

"So much for a silent entrance, Dove Girl," Alex remarks.

I smile grimly, proud of what we've accomplished but dreading what will come. *They definitely know we've made it this far.*

But who is "they"? Jupiter could be stationed above us, or his father, the General. Or if the universe decided to be unusually cruel, Lazarus.

"Phaet's changed her style," Wes agrees.

Our first few steps into the ventilation shaft are more like leaps. Wes volunteers to climb first. He jumps five meters into the air and attaches himself to the underside of the tilting central air filtration column like a spider. His fingers grip the handholds carved into its side, which once functioned as a ladder for maintenance workers.

"Come on, Phaet," he calls. "Like the climbing wall in the trainee gym."

I manage to jump even higher than him. Soon, Alex joins the climb, and the three of us scurry upward.

Another *zap!* The Committee's soldiers, still shooting at us from above. Fortunately, the gigantic toppled pillar blocks their Electro-stun pellets, diffusing the electricity, and the insulating material in our gloves and boots prevents us from receiving shocks. I climb faster, propelled by a simmering desire for revenge, and conquer floor after floor.

Near the tower's zenith, I grab a dagger from my boot and tuck it into my sleeve. The cool carbon blade taps against my skin, comforting me. I've used this trick since my trainee days, and the weapon feels like part of my arm now.

"Everybody stand back—Beaters, that means you!" Wes pulls the pin of a homemade grenade and tosses it over the lip of the highest balcony. In the aftermath of the tooth-rattling explosion, he vaults over the guardrail, a Lazy in one hand, and Alex and I scramble after.

A line of five helmeted soldiers faces us, barring the tunnel that presumably leads to the Committee's conference room. Their leader steps forward: a tall curvy female wearing a CORPO-RAL badge. She fires a violet warning shot into the wall, then lifts her visor to reveal pale, bloodless skin and electric eyes the same color as the lasers from her gun. Showing us her face is its own intimidation tactic.

"Rebel fools," Cressida Psi says. A smile parts her livid red lips. "I can arrest you quickly, or kill you slowly. Which one do you choose?"

44

My mind plays back scenes from my family's old apartment, from Base IV Shelter. Lips tight, shoulders hunched, I glare at Cressida through my visor as if that alone could take her down.

Alex rushes Cressida while Wes circles around her from behind. I move to join them, but a laser blast narrowly misses my left leg. One of Cressida's soldiers—a wobbly-kneed private—advances on me. I charge him; he fires again, and I scrunch my fists so that my uniform's mirrors deflect the shot, which burns into his ballistic shield. He stumbles back, hands over his face. I lunge and grab him behind the knees. Aided by the low gravity, I swing him in a semicircle and toss him off the balcony, into the ventilation shaft. He reaches out in vain to slow his fall, but within moments, his body lands hard on the shaft's floor. And he doesn't move.

With every heartbeat, I hate what I've done more and more. *Did it have to end that way?* I wonder, arms and legs frozen with horror. *Did I have no other choice?*

"Phaet, look out!" Alex shouts.

Another private rushes me, scimitar in hand, her too-big helmet hastily fastened. Determined to be gentler this time, I sidestep her and rip off her helmet to reveal a narrow face with wide-set, fearful eyes. I punch her in the jaw, disrupting a nerve and knocking her out. When she wakes up, she'll hurt so badly that she won't be able to scream, but at least she'll be alive.

Still feeling queasy, I sprint across the balcony to where Alex fights Cressida and another soldier. Alex is armed with a long piece of handrail, and he's taken off his helmet for better visibility. He spins the pole in both hands, landing blows whenever his opponents try to rush him. I watch for a lull in his motion so that I can throw my dagger. But nothing opens up.

Wes pulls his own knife out of a fifth soldier's back and stands by my side. "Let Alex deal with them."

Cressida and her sidekick rush Alex from both sides. He takes two steps, holding the pole out in front of him, and then vaults upward so that he's balanced on one end of it, two meters off the ground. His opponents collide with each other and bounce back, stumbling.

Holding the pole horizontally, Alex falls. Landing, he twists so that one end of the pole throws Cressida's underling over the balcony. The other knocks Cressida into the wall. She slumps against it, legs lying limp. Wes slaps cuffs around her ankles and wrists.

When Wes straightens, he's holding the glass truncheon that was once attached to her belt.

Finding herself alone and surrounded, Cressida raises her visor and spits at Wes's feet. Her violet eyes exude disdain.

So I raise my visor too and step in front of her.

"Use this. She deserves it." Wes hands me Cressida's truncheon, and I put my dagger back in my boot. The same weapon with which she beat Mom and Anka, a year apart, for her own amusement.

"Still looking for Mommy?" Cressida says to me. She struggles once, twice against her bonds.

I give her my signature silence. She's unworthy of words, or of my brutality. With my left hand, I draw my tranquilizer gun and shoot a Downer between her mocking violet eyes.

∗ — ∗ — ∗

I know we've ducked into the right ventilation tunnel when another alarm starts to screech. Single file, we crawl forward as fast as we can. The gravity settings, thankfully, remain normal. Behind me, Alex has put his helmet back on to block the noise. In case of a head-on assault, I carry Cressida's ballistic shield. It was barely narrow enough to fit into the tunnel. Wes brings up the rear with a second stolen shield.

As we make our way forward, passing grate after grate without meeting any obstructions, a familiar doubt takes seed in my mind. *This is too easy.* The Committee *knows* that two elite spies and a former captain are heading toward them, yet they only stationed one of their top personnel in our path. Cressida is an able fighter, but the privates she led were as green as Umbriel and Ariel. Did they spread their troops over every possible route to their stronghold? They didn't know we'd come through the vents.

"Hold on!" Wes hisses from the rear.

I stop moving. The sudden halt makes me dizzy—and that's when the sound of vomiting hits my ear.

"Alex?" I whisper.

Alex's chin hovers just centimeters above the floor. His chest heaves. "Keep crawling, Dove Girl, it's not a big deal." He retches again.

"It is." Wes rests his head against the side of the tunnel. "I'm also going to lose my breakfast soon."

"Something's not right." I crawl ever faster. But my limbs feel heavy, almost as heavy as they did under the altered gravity settings.

"Let's get out." For once, Alex's voice is urgent. Not languid. He stops crawling at the grate I've passed and takes out his Lazy.

"Beaters out there," I point out.

"Carbon monoxide in here." Alex fires a continuous laser at the grate's edges, making it glow orange. "New Kingstown"—his home before he emigrated to Saint Oda—"ran on Pacifian coal. Fumes it gives off don't smell like anything, but they'll suffocate you all the same. I know what CO poisoning feels like."

An orange rectangle gleams at the edges of the grate. Alex kicks it outward and tosses a lit grenade after it for good measure.

Pow! The explosion knocks several black-booted feet out from under their owners. Before the soldiers can pull themselves up, all three of us tumble out of the ventilation tunnel and into a dim, expansive corridor. I scoot to Alex's side—his chest heaves as he fills it with gulps of air—and put an arm around him, in case we need to flee. But Wes has us covered. Even though he's pale and dizzy, he props himself up on one elbow and shoots Downers into the fallen soldiers' necks, where their uniforms are thinnest.

Gradually, the world around me stops spinning, and morphs from muddy to crystal clear. The ceiling soars five meters high; black, white, silver, and gold tapestries with astronomical motifs hang from the walls. Air from the carbon dioxide and oxygen filters blows against the fabric, and it billows up as if some goliath is breathing on it.

We've made it to the Committee's hallowed halls, the closest thing Base I fanatics have to a holy place. It's encouraging to have gotten farther than our enemies meant us to. But the deeper we go, the more vulnerable we become.

"Nice place they've got here." Alex manages to stand up on his own and bounce on his toes. "We're good to go."

"Careful now," Wes warns. "I remember Micah"—the deceased Sanctuarist agent who was stationed on Base I—"saying something about automated lasers in the walls."

Our group progresses with caution, tiptoeing down the dark and narrowing hall. Because I have the best armor, I lead the way. A set of ornate silver doors glints at its terminus—our destination.

Sure enough, before we can go too far, a purple laser jets sideways across my field of vision, perpendicular to our path.

"I'll go first, to give us an idea of how many lasers there are." I hold a hand out to stop my teammates, passing Wes my stolen shield.

Clenching my left hand into a fist, thumb under fingers, I sprint through the hallway. I shut my eyes so the flying lasers don't burn my retinas; still, I see red behind my eyelids. Chunks of my suit heat up; if it weren't for the mirrored scales, I'd be dead within half a second.

And then—all clear. I've reached the silver doors. High-resolution carvings of galaxies cover them from floor to ceiling—

I hear the blow coming before I see it. I throw myself forward and land on my hands and knees. Beaters must've entered the hallway through a hidden door. Sure enough, there's a pair of black Militia boots behind me and arms holding a long, curved sword made of carbon fiber. A scimitar? Not the most useful weapon, but an impressive one. The Committee even makes a show of their bodyguards, it seems. I execute a forward roll, coaxing a dagger out of my boot in the process.

The bodyguard is not alone. A second scimitar-wielder stands over me, his blade whistling toward my neck. I duck, extending a leg to trip him. It works; he falls. I drag my blade across the back of his legs to keep him down, feeling nauseous all over again as blood spurts and tendons snap. Writhing on the ground, he struggles to right himself, but it's useless: he can't contract his legs anymore.

Running footsteps approach—my remaining opponent rushes me, blade raised above her head. I throw the dagger in my hand. It spins over itself and traces an arc. Then the blade sinks into the gap between the woman's thigh and knee plates. She falls. I stick her and her fallen partner with Downers, and their flailing ceases. I pull my knife out of her leg with a *squelch*.

Anyone we know? I wonder, flipping up their visors. It's a man in his early twenties and a slightly older woman, both with orange-tinged skin and sweaty, slick blond hair. They look like wax figures, their wide eyes staring at nothing in particular. I don't recognize them.

In the next instant, I remember that no one's covering my back and whirl around, fearing another attack. The only other people in the hallway are Wes and Alex, who's giving me a thumbs-up. *Phew.*

"If you use the shields, you can run through the lasers," I tell the boys. "They fly from side to side."

"And they're aimed at the vitals, above knee level . . ." Wes mutters into his headset. He puts up the shield so that it faces outward, and Alex does the same; they're mirror images of each other. *Go.*

Watching the two Sanctuarists dash through the laser barrage is harder than doing it myself. This is crazy. Suicidal . . . Wes hoists his shield as high as he can, but he's a head shorter than Alex; the left side of Alex's helmet remains exposed.

They make it. But the top of Alex's helmet has melted onto his visor, staining it black and making it impossible to see through. Swearing, Alex yanks the smoking contraption off his head and takes one from a fallen soldier. "It'll do more harm than good at this point."

He stretches his neck, tilting his head back to get the full impression of the Committee's ornate silver doors—the front entrance to the conference room where Umbriel and I nearly died. He shrugs, apparently unimpressed by the magnificent sight, and heaves up the burly body of the male soldier. "Do the honors, Dove Girl."

My victim's a sergeant; as an officer, he'll probably have fingerprint access. I grab his limp hand and press his thumb to the scanner. The huge doors slide open. Instead of the hexagonal conference room I remember, before us is an ancient-looking mahogany door with a traditional Earthbound lock. The doorknob is burnished copper, spherical, carved out like the Moon with all its craters.

"Thought I wouldn't have to do this after leaving Earth." Wes reaches into a pocket and pulls out a short length of copper wire. He fits it through the keyhole and squats down so he can listen for clicks.

Alex and I stand guard, watching Wes's face. We switch to our Lazies in case we don't like what we find on the other side. As I remember from Militia, Wes's expression gives nothing away, but the occasional twitch of his mouth hints at irritation. What if lock picking turns out to be his one weakness? We'll have come all this way for nothing . . .

I suddenly wish Umbriel were here—if he could contribute anything to our impossible task, breaking and entering would be it. But just as my thoughts become desperate, Wes removes the wire from the keyhole, takes a deep breath, and twists the sculpted Moon doorknob. "We're in."

45

THE DOOR BANGS OPEN, AND WE DASH INTO a hexagonal room flush with images of carnage. Half the faceted ceiling's three- and six-sided screens, which once showed security feeds from all six bases, are taken up by footage of the chaos on Base I. Entire departments—Recreation, Residential, Education— have gone up in flames, but what hits me more than any of the bombastic fires and explosions are people's faces.

Our people, looking terrified and helpless. Abandoned. Dovetail and Batterer foot soldiers, uniforms streaked with blood, haul comrades with broken or missing limbs to the battle's fringes. Units have scattered, pierced by unstoppable surges of Militia troops or surrounded by swarms of Pacifians. Ships switched to indoor settings crisscross the space above the foot soldiers' heads, engaged in their own duel. I glimpse Yinha's chaotic flying style as her Pygmette swoops through the air. She's trying to rally our forces and reinstate order.

Clustered along the sides of the Main Lane and adjacent hallways, Base I civilians don't seem to favor either side—they scurry about, seeking safety, nothing more. As they fight toward their residences, parents huddle children against walls or under benches and tables, using their own bodies as shields. For my own sanity,

I avoid thinking about the little ones that didn't clear out before the shooting started.

All the hopes I've gathered leave me in a flood of despair. Dovetail and Battery Bay have pulled out all the stops, and we still can't defeat the Militia and Pacifia. With every injury and death on our side, Wes, Alex, and I lose negotiating power over the Committee. If those tyrants have no reason to listen to us, they'll kill us. And then they'll kill everyone we've been trying to protect.

The thoughts are drowning me. So when I surface, tearing my eyes away from the images and searching our surroundings, I discover, to my relief—and then my utter dismay—that the Committee isn't here.

*　—　*　—　*

"Come in, Dovetail," the General says. Troops surround him on all sides, their Electrostuns raised. Clustering together, the three of us rush in, sidestepping electric pellets and releasing our own, more lethal ammunition.

"Argh!" Alex shouts as electricity crackles across his right foot. The rubber of his boot neutralizes the charge—but what if the pellet had hit him somewhere else? In tandem, Wes and I lower our weapons, knowing that we can't win, surrounded like this.

"We've been expecting you," says the General. Although his voice chills every cell in my body, his tone is warm—as if we were old friends instead of "criminals" he's tried to kill time after time.

Hulking and invincible, he sits at Hydrus's place at the Committee's hexagonal conference table. Jupiter flanks him, looking at his father with admiration and at everyone else with smugness. Two unfamiliar senior Militia officials sit with them, as well as a straight-backed man dressed all in gunmetal gray; I peg him as a high-ranking Pacifian officer. The last seat is empty.

At least a dozen Militia and Pacifian bodyguards line the room's perimeter, their laser blasters and long rifles pointed at us. Outnumbered and outgunned, the two Sanctuarists and I form a triangle with our backs to one another, hands on our utility belts. Our enemies' peacefulness is disturbing: they've waited here for us, without a care in the universe, as their allies downstairs and across the bases carried out wholesale slaughter.

"Traitors," the General spits. He stalks forward, his son following closely. I'm torn between backing away in fear and rushing forward, weapons raised, to end him. "Traitors and thieves, come back to beg your superiors for mercy . . . or to lop off the hand that brought you up? The Committee has no time for such nonsense."

"No," I say, forcing my voice to come out steady. I'll try to taunt the General; by insulting those to whom he's unfailingly loyal, maybe I can induce him to tell me where they've gone. "The Committee are cowards. Where are they when their people are under attack? In hiding, too afraid to face us?"

But the General sees through my strategy. Before I can raise my weapon, he lunges forward so quickly that he seems to glide. Grabbing me by the chin, he lowers his face to mine. His hot breath smells like dried blood. "You will never find them, girl."

Wes points a Lazy at him. "Hands off, or you'll never see them again either."

The General forces my head into a painful twist as he yanks his hand away from my chin. He rounds on Wes, breathing heavily through his nostrils—and breaks into deep, joyless laughter that makes me shiver.

"*You.* Threatening *me?*" says the General.

With his boulder of a fist, Jupiter knocks the Lazy out of Wes's grip and grabs his wrist. He sneers through his visor.

"You Earth-born scum, a traitor twice over," says the General. He turns to his son. "Thank you, Jupiter. But I can handle this one."

Jupiter hands Wes's arm to his father like a baton and reluctantly retreats, sitting once again at the conference table. Then the General squeezes, forcing Wes's hand back and down until pain spasms across his face. Pain that I feel more acutely than when the General hurt *me*.

Alex has backed about three meters away to get a good shot; he stands frozen in place, laser blaster raised. I know he's tempted to pull the trigger—we both are—but we know better than to assault the General with over a dozen of his allies in the room.

"Such a waste of talent, Phaet and Wesley," the General says. Shaking his head, he lets me and Wes go, and turns his broad back to us. "When I pinned your Militia insignias to your lapels all those months ago, you swore to uphold the bases' order and advance our civilization. Not destroy it."

"You're destroying the Moon yourself, Alpha," Wes blurts, and I almost slap a hand over his mouth. The General might kill him in a burst of fury. "The Moon and the Earth and everything in between. At this rate, your Pacifian lapdogs won't have a city to return to."

The Pacifian commander stiffens at Wes's remark, and I panic, not knowing how I will defend him from both men.

But the General moves first, whirling around to face us again; this time, he holds two laser blasters—one pointed at Wes's forehead and one at mine. "The punishment for treason is death—"

A low buzzing from his headset seems to interrupt him.

The General looks annoyed but keeps his voice cordial. "Yes,

Hydrus, sir, Jang is with me. We will send Pacifians to Base III straightaway. Of course the radiation-insulation suits will remain with Militia—they hardly know how to use them." The General laughs, deep and low: a sound even more terrifying than his shouts.

Sending a Pacifian contingent to the uranium mines without protection from radiation? It sounds like another suicide mission. All three Pacifians glance at each other, their expressions blank, without a trace of worry or indignation. Even though they're my enemies, I'd rather see them rage at the prospect of their comrades dying en masse—again.

"Back to the subject of your treason." The General's smile vanishes as he turns back to me, Wes, and Alex. "Should I make the end of your lives quick . . . or educational? So that other traitors can—"

"Funny word, you using over and over," says an even-toned male voice in choppy but confident English. "Traitor. Sound like *trade*-er, no?"

In our panic, we hadn't noticed the Pacifian military leader move. He walks over and stands behind the General. Desperate for help, and half-grateful to him for distracting our antagonist, I study the Pacifian. An East Asian man of average height, he's dressed all in gray canvas, not a patch or medal in sight. His jacket buttons up to his square chin, and his narrow-brimmed black cap rests on closely shorn salt-and-pepper hair. Severe rectangular spectacles betray the failing acuity of his heavy-lidded eyes, which seem permanently narrowed in consideration. This man wears his age proudly, the deep creases between his eyes and around his wide mouth like fissures in dry earth.

"Do not interrupt me, Jang," the General snarls, not bothering to look behind him at the Pacifian man. "This is official procedure."

For once, the General and I are on the same emotional wavelength—impatience is also balling up my fists and making my heartbeat flutter in my throat. People are dying below us, and it feels *wrong* to watch these leaders parley instead of fighting to defend the Lunars and Batterers.

"When Pacifia allied with your Committee, we expected a *trade*." Jang paces behind the General, who keeps twitching, as if he wants to glance backward. But he doesn't, knowing that it would give Wes, Alex, and me the opportunity to strike. Along the room's perimeter, the three Pacifian troops eye each other as though they share a secret understanding.

Their heads snap back to attention when Jang whispers something in a foreign language. The Militia forces try to hide their looks of bewilderment.

"We supposed to trade basic respects," Jang continues. "Like I call you General, you call me Commander. Like my troops share plan with you, you share plan with us."

"What's this nonsense, *Commander*?" the General seethes. "And why *now*?"

Jupiter and the two Militia officers at the conference table exchange troubled glances. Jupiter rises, a movement that seems to create vortices in the air, and begins to stalk toward us.

"But you and the Committee are more like *traitors*," Commander Jang continues. "No honor. No heart. You kill three thousand Pacifian soldiers when Dugout invasion go wrong—by bombing metro tunnel from above."

"Sealing the tunnel was our only option." Impatience sours the General's tone, and I almost expect him to pull the triggers of his two Lazies on me and Wes. "Do not force me to have this discussion again."

But Jang keeps talking, keeps demanding the General's attention.

"So now that things on Base I go wrong . . ." Halting three meters away from us—just outside the range of the General's fists—Jang presses a button on his headset and starts barking in a foreign language.

Slowly, painfully, the General turns his head to face his ally. A trickle of sweat shines on his left temple. At such close proximity, glued to the spot beside him by fear, it's all I can see.

On the screens above our heads, hordes of Pacifian soldiers turn their long rifles on the Militia. Bayonets bury into black uniforms instead of the Batterers' teal ones; Pacifian bullets pelt the Militia's ranks, as if an indomitable wind has shifted their direction. My jaw drops in amazement and horror, but even as the world spins around me, I force myself to think about what'll come next. Whatever the Pacifians have planned to do, a new order is forming, and my crewmates and I must take advantage of it to survive.

"Traitor," Jang says, glaring at the General. "I trade with you." The General lets out a howl of rage and turns one Lazy on Jang, his long muscled arm extended. But before he can fire, I slice upward at his wrist with my dagger—and his forearm snaps back into ready position. His Militia reflexes kick in one moment too soon; his finger pulls the trigger. Wes clubs the Lazy barrel sideways, and a violet beam slices through the General's forehead.

For a moment, I look into those dead eyes, still widened in surprise, and then glance down at my bloodless blade. Its sharp, unsoiled perfection brings me an odd sort of satisfaction—I ended him, ended the scourge that sickened or killed hundreds of Lunars, without even getting my hands dirty.

Then the odor of charred flesh fills my nose. I forget my surroundings, filled with the same pain that smites me every time I end a life. But someone had to do it, and best that it be me and Wes. We've been morally compromised so that our loved ones—

Anka, Cygnus, Umbriel, Wes's family—can stay safe.

The General's towering frame falls backward. Wes circles around and pulls me behind the body—and not a moment too soon. The Militia bodyguards fill the air with violet beams. We turn the General's body sideways, using him as a makeshift wall, and Alex dives behind it, dodging a laser meant for his legs.

Looking up at the ceiling screens, I see that the Pacifian soldiers have deepened their assault on the Militia, setting off explosives in addition to clubbing and stabbing their former allies.

"Either I've gone mad, or we're on Pacifia's good side now," Alex breathes. "You two all right?"

Wes and I nod.

"New plan," I say. "We fight with the Pacifians—but carefully. And we keep Jang alive at all costs. He must know where the Committee's gone. Understood? Go!"

We break cover and dash in front of Jang, throwing up our ballistic shields to protect him from laser fire. Dagger in my free hand, I swipe at every Militia soldier who tries to rush us.

My headset beeps frantically. "What the fuse is going on, Stripes?" Yinha demands, her voice barely audible above the battle's din. "Pacifians started killing Militia, and we must've gained a hundred meters of territory in as many seconds."

All's not lost yet. "Their commander mutinied," I say as my dagger finds its way between a Militia soldier's abdominal armor plates. "General's dead. We're going to find the Committee and put an end to this soon."

"Cool. Good work."

I nod, knowing she's not in a position to give a speech of appreciation. "I'd better see you by the Pillars of Liberty in the next twenty minutes. If not, I'm coming after you."

Before Yinha terminates our communication, someone yanks

me sideways as a scimitar blade whooshes past my head.

Commander Jang's fingers on my upper arm seem to be cast in iron. "*Jupiter!*" he shouts in my ear. "Look out!"

My former tormentor's face is livid, shiny with sweat and tears. "Dad! *My father!* You took him from me. You took everything!" Strengthened by grief, he wields the long, curved knife maniacally, stabbing and slashing at every part of my body. He's so strong; if he connects, he might cut through my flesh as if it's water.

I bend my knees to set up a solid foundation closer to the ground. Jupiter towers over me, leaning forward so that he can attack from above and from the front.

Where are his vulnerabilities?

His visor's up. But his head is too high for me to reach. Unless . . .

The dead General's Lazy rests by my feet. I grab it and hurl it upward: the weapon hits Jupiter's chin and forces his head back. While he teeters, I shoot a dart into his neck. He falls backward. It's the same mighty fall that his father did, like a skyscraper crashing to the ground. But Jupiter's not dead; he's knocked out. He shouldn't come to until after we're long gone.

Jang, two of his Pacifian bodyguards, the Sanctuarists, and I are left standing. I peek at the ceiling screens, and see that while our side still has the upper hand, the shock of the Pacifian mutiny is fading fast. The Militia seem to be regrouping; they form small clusters and laser-burn their way through ranks of adversaries.

Yinha contacts me again. "Stripes? Have you found the Committee yet? Overheard some Militia saying they are bringing over the remaining loyalists from Bases III and V. We'll get blasted to pieces when they arrive!"

Unless my unit forces the Committee to surrender now.

"Commander Jang, sir. You make a worthy ally." I utter every honorific possible, trying to convey trust I don't feel, lest he turn on my side next. If he could surprise the entire Lunar Militia, what might he do to us?

Jang makes a shallow bow from the waist, a movement that I clumsily imitate. Steadying my features, I look him in his bespectacled, coal-dark eyes.

"Please," I say, "take us to the Committee."

46

"GIVE ME GENERAL'S HAND, SIR," JANG SAYS, facing Wes.

Wes hoists up the General by his right arm, struggling to lift the dead weight, and presents it to Jang.

"His *hand*." Jang gestures for my dagger; I hand it over. He slices off the General's hand at the wrist and wraps the stump in a white handkerchief produced from his breast pocket. Then he presses the thumb to the bottom of the conference table. I watch the General's blood drip to the floor in horror, struggling to contain my gag reflex.

Within seconds, the table begins to sink. When the top reaches the same level as the surrounding floor, Jang and the Pacifians step onto it, and we follow, putting as much distance as we can between ourselves and the Commander. His betrayal of the General is shocking, frightening—and yet I must swallow my fear and call him an ally. After all, Wes and I are the ones that killed old Alpha. Jang just removed an appendage from the unfeeling body.

Tread lightly, I remind myself, *or Jang will be an ally no more.*

Jang wipes my dagger with another white handkerchief—how many does he carry?—and hands the weapon back to me, handle first. I accept the dagger without sparing it a glance.

And the table keeps sinking—we're in an elevator leading deep underground. The walls of the shaft turn from smooth gray metal to crumbly gray rock. As the air gets colder and drier, moisture leaches out of my skin, leaving it stretched tight and thin over my bones. Moon-grav kicks in, so all of my body feels lighter. Except my heart, which is heavy with dread.

When we must be a hundred meters under the base, the elevator sputters to a stop. We step into a narrow stone hallway that stretches out tens of meters before us. The ceiling is so low that Alex must duck to keep from hitting his head.

I turn on my helmet visor's infrared vision mode so that we can approach invisibly and still know if people are around. Wes and Alex touch their helmets, following suit. Jang and the two Pacifians take out flashlights but have the sense not to turn them on.

Moments later, four bright, human-shaped red spots appear in the center of my vision. Jang hisses something in another language to his underlings, who raise their rifles.

Before the Committee's bodyguards make sense of the situation, four shots ring out, two from each Pacifian gun. And the four figures at the hallway's end crumple.

"Go, go, go!" Jang yells, and all six of us dash forward. Nothing else leaps out to get us, and I feel a rush of satisfaction: at last, the Committee is running out of resources.

We reach the end. After stepping over the four bodyguards' prone forms, we face a pair of solid-looking black metal doors. Jang scans the General's thumbprint again, and the doors slide open into—utter luxury. A windowless hexagonal living room, an emergency light in each vertex casting an orange glow on the clean white walls. Thick gray carpet covers the floor like a layer of dead moss, serving as a cushion for silken scarlet couches that resemble gigantic pillows more than actual furniture. A steep, zigzagging metal staircase shaped like a lightning bolt descends from the ceiling.

But once again, the Committee is nowhere in sight. Instead, half a dozen Militia guards, all in black, peel away from the walls, weapons raised.

"Don't," says a familiar slippery voice, and the soldiers halt. Hydrus isn't visible, but the bunker's speaker system broadcasts his voice from all sides. He must be nearby. "Dovetail. Pacifians. Please come in."

"No, Hydrus." I've grown weary of their hide-and-seek. "You come out."

Jang edges in front of me. I'm secretly grateful to him for providing me with cover. "I will face them first, miss."

The five Committee members stroll down the stairs, dignity evident in every step. Hydrus and Cassini are first, heads held high, mouths sneering. Janus, the ancient hunchback, descends with one hand on the railing and the other gripping Nebulus Nu's shoulder for balance. Hopper shuffles down last, her thin lips pinched in anger.

The Committee forms a ring around Jang, eyes narrowed. He remains impassive, as if he could stand in their midst forever in utter comfort.

After several seconds, Hopper breaks the silence. "Jang," the old woman says. She's trying to sound furious, but the effect is more heartbroken. I almost feel bad for her. "Jang, you led *them* to us. Our enemies." She glares at Wes, Alex, and me.

Her words disgust me: of course it's all about the Committee—their safety, their peace of mind. No mention of the ambushed loyalist troops dying above our heads.

"You are Pacifia's enemy now," Jang spits back. "You Committee think we are like dogs. Obedient. Disposable. If we help you win this war, you will force us to run your filthy errands for centuries. Pacifian people are proud; we cannot bow to Lunars as if you are gods in the sky."

Hydrus scoffs. "We are not gods, but we know how to keep the human race from self-destructing a second time. With your help, we can still prevent further planetary devastation and the subsequent disorder."

Jang continues to look as unconvinced as I am feeling. Does the Committee really believe that they can tidy up the Earth after they've torn it to pieces in this war?

Hopper steps forward. "And you think Dovetail and Battery Bay won't punish you for all the abuse you gave them before switching sides?"

"Pacifia is prepared for consequences from our old enemies," Jang shoots back. "We know they will be fair. Not like the shameful 'rewards' you would give us."

"Pardon . . . pardon me," Nebulus says. "But we have shared so much. The goal of making the Earth as peaceful as the Moon. A common love of humanity. And we had an *agreement*."

Jang turns his back on the Committee, and his aides step closer to guard him. "We will not speak of this again."

Cassini crosses his arms and taps one long finger on his sleeve. "Do what you please. We won't stop you from throwing away everything you hold dear."

No reply from Jang. I decide to take over—after all, Dovetail has our own reasons for being here.

"Don't concern yourselves with *us*, Committee," I say, my voice strong. "Your own troops are dying. If you want to stop it, you will come upstairs and hand over the Lunar Bases, in front of all your people."

"Not so fast," Hydrus says. "Let us declare a truce, until each side figures out what we are really after. Let us conduct a . . . a peace talk here, if you will."

I shake my head. "After all this fighting, you want us to sit down and—and politely ask for what we want?"

"It takes manners to run this Moon," Cassini spits at me. "If that's your ambition, rebel girl, then it's time you learned some."

"Take a seat." Cassini gestures to the blood-red couches. "So that we may talk like civilized adults."

"No," I say. "Not here. We'll go before the Pillars of Liberty. Anything you choose to do will be done before thousands upon thousands of witnesses."

The Committee stares at us for a long time. Janus's eyes are furious, Hydrus's laughing, Nebulus's cold, and Cassini's poisonous. Hopper looks terrified. But in all five, there's defeat. They will agree to my demands, will take orders from another human being for the first time in decades.

It's humiliating. And by the looks on their faces, they will make us pay.

47

THE COMMITTEE HAS DIRECT ACCESS TO most parts of Base I. We step out onto a platform ten meters above ground level, directly under the Pillars of Liberty. Within seconds, Yinha's Pygmette swoops in. She swings her legs over the side to disembark and sprints toward us, gathering Wes, Alex, and me in a hug, crushing us with arms much stronger than they look.

Below the platform and down the Main Lane, swells of people—Base I Dovetail sympathizers?—jockey with loyalists for every square meter of territory, stolen weapons in their hands. Every so often, Pacifians and Militia members fire a burst of shots at one another. Now that the element of surprise has faded, and with the seeming influx of more troops, the Militia has gained back lost ground. How many more people will have to die before this ends?

A newsreel wraps around the enormous hall, spelling out in blocks of text what is happening on the other bases. The onslaught of information is the one remnant of normality amidst chaos—except that right now the screen reads: BREAKING: REBEL SYMPA-THIZERS TAKE OVER BASE III URANIUM REFINERIES.

The Graveyard's revolt has been successful, then—that explains why the Committee suddenly wants to negotiate. But how long can the bases Dovetail's taken over remain free? If we can't depose the five tyrants, then our situation will deteriorate once again.

The three Pacifians, Wes, and Alex lead the Committee to where the audience can see them. I follow closely, watching Jang and his aides out of the sides of my vision.

"Stop!" Hydrus orders into a microphone, his voice echoing throughout Base I. "Put all weapons down."

A hush falls, beginning at the front of the stage. It ripples forward, through the thousands that have gathered. Heads turn; eyes focus on us.

I face the blood-spattered Main Lane and nod. Cautiously, both sides lower their guns and sheathe their knives.

The Dovetail leadership appears on the massive screen behind the stage, their determined faces brightly lit; they look larger than life, as the Committee once did in their public addresses, except that they haven't cast themselves in shadow. Seeing Asterion, Andromeda, and even Sol and Costa makes me feel braver.

"So this is where it ends," Hydrus says. "Unless Dovetail does not cooperate."

"Tell us your terms," Asterion snarls.

"To the Earthbound: we will let you leave peacefully if you promise not to come back to the Moon."

"As if all the fighting here never happened?" Costa says incredulously. "Absolutely not."

"And so Battery Bay rejects our generosity," says Nebulus. "Pacifia?"

All eyes focus on Jang. Without speaking, he turns his back on the Committee for the second time. People whisper and point, shocked by his disrespect. He whispers to one of his underlings, a glaring-eyed young woman, who faces the Committee and says, "We do not negotiate with cowards and cheats."

"Well, then," Hydrus says. "As for Dovetail, we give you the site of Base VI as a starting point to construct a new and independent nation."

Hisses issue from Dovetailers and loyalists alike. My face grows hot with anger. We're like beggars at the Committee's feast, and they're tossing us bones they've already gnawed on. Why should we not demand what we came for? We no longer have to beg.

"If we partition the Moon into two states, they will obliterate each other," Andromeda says. "A satellite flyby bombing, poison masquerading as a gas leak . . . Without air to breathe outside, none of us can run from danger. This Moon holds no room for compromise."

A risky statement, but a true one.

"May we have a moment?" Nebulus says, gesturing to his colleagues.

Yinha nods and places both hands on her hips, centimeters away from her firearms. The Committee members huddle together in a tiny cluster, whispering, and their smallness startles me.

After they break apart, Hydrus speaks. "Dovetail, we are at an impasse. The entire Moon, or nothing, for both sides. But . . . how shall we choose the winner? Tic-tac-toe?"

On the big screen behind us, it's the Dovetail leaders' turn to cluster together, whispering. The Committee and their Militia's impatience hangs like a cloud of toxic gas over Base I.

To buy Dovetail time, I step up to the microphone.

"It's not up to you—the people at the top—to decide how the rest of us should live, and who we should live under. It never was. That's something you don't understand. The Lunar people tried to tell you so many times, first with protests, then with their votes, and now with fire: here, humankind is *not* free. And we won't rest until that changes."

"We didn't ask for a history lesson, little *Sage*," says Nebulus. "We asked to hear your side's demands."

"Here they are," I say. "My brother's mind, my sister's innocence, and my mother's life. I demand you—I beg you—to return everything you've ever stolen from any base citizen, living or dead.

"But these are things that you—even *you*, the Standing Committee of the Lunar Bases—could never do, even when you were at the peak of your power. Dovetail knows better than to ask those things of you. In comparison, our demand is child's play: *let go*."

I imagine the faces of everyone who can no longer speak to the Committee: Belinda, Mom, Murray, the thirty thousand dead on the Singularity—and of the people who still can. I imagine their spirits bolstering mine. My voice rings out louder, clearer, brighter, now that it's not entirely my own. "Let go of your dream to rule every place humankind has ever settled. Let go of your resentment of the people that have tried to stop you."

I sweep my hand across the room, gesturing at the massive, motley audience, at the rolling text on the newsreel: BASE III CITIZENS PUT OUT FIRES, CELEBRATE MILITIA'S SURRENDER.

"Let go . . . of us."

48

THOUSANDS SHOUT THEIR SUPPORT, GUSTS of sound sweeping across the base: the sound of victory, so close that I could spread my arms and ride the resonant waves of it into the air.

But the cheers quiet at the sound of muffled thumps. Hydrus is clapping into the microphone. Slow, plodding claps—one, two, three.

"A moving speech, little Sage. You have learned much. You would have made a fine politician. A fine Committee member."

Would have?

"But you will never take our place. Not you, nor anyone in Dovetail. If we cannot govern the bases, as is our right . . ." Cassini trails off. A smile twists his mouth, even as horror twists my insides. "Then nobody will."

He turns to the promenade's far end, where huge panels on the ceiling are sliding apart to reveal cavernous storage chambers underneath.

"Release the drones."

⁕ — ⁕ — ⁕

A low buzz sounds from the Main Lane's terminus, near Base I's Recreation Department. At first, I'm relieved. Since the Committee has nothing to lose, I was almost expecting them to blow up a window or bomb the base.

But no, they didn't. And whatever their plan, it is probably much worse.

A copper cloud creeps down from the ceiling, surrounding the Batterer troops, Pacifians, Militia, and Base I residents, whose screams of agony fill our ears. Even from afar, I know that these are not Bai Rho's creations. The Committee's turned Dovetail's own inventions against us, performing a last feat of scientific brilliance, as if proving that their superior minds can never lose to ours. They've warped the biodefense drones into something else, something as wicked as they are—but what?

Panicking soldiers and civilians alike flee into Culinary, InfoTech, and various scientific departments, packing the areas past capacity and then shutting the doors in an attempt to keep the drones out. People come rushing onto our stage beneath the Pillars of Liberty, their bodies' collective motion threatening to sweep us away.

Not everyone escapes. Watching on the Main Lane's big screens, which show security pod footage, I see half the drones fall like dark dust, their machinery jamming up in midair. *So the Committee's made something imperfect.* They rushed the engineering process and created a faulty product.

Finally.

It's almost satisfying to see them fall this far.

But the other half of the drones are still buoyant—and they're swarming around people, stinging them. The victims stop breathing and moving of their own free will; arms and legs rattle as if they're being electrocuted. Their skin flushes poppy red dotted with spots of cornflower blue. Their bodies wilt. Finally, they collapse. I shudder, knowing without being told that the drones are injecting abrin into their bloodstreams.

Boom. An explosion rocks the tiles beneath my feet, shaking me out of my numb horror. To my left, the cockpit of a Dovetail Destroyer has been flattened. Two soldiers within are dead. Hydrus runs toward it, another grenade raised in his hand, and the rest of the Committee follows. They scramble inside, shutting the hatch, speed into Governance, and swerve to the right. A panel of wall slides up to reveal a hidden passageway, and they jet through.

I fight down a burst of fury at the fact that they're escaping. There are more important things to do than chase them down—they've already lost, even if they live. And we won't even do that, not if we don't figure out how to escape these "drones."

We: my friends, and our thousands of allies and enemies, Earthbound and Lunar alike. We will all meet our end here.

Alarms blare, accompanied by an automated voice: *"Air filters jammed. Evacuate base immediately."*

Fuse. If the drones, faulty as they are, penetrated the air filters, that means they can slip through the tightest seams imaginable. Nowhere on base is safe.

"Hurry! Get everyone into a ship, a rover, anything!" Yinha's screaming into our headsets. "I need all capable drivers and pilots to ferry people to the Dugout—bring all available craft to make pickup!"

Jang and his two bodyguards have disappeared. Yinha and her Pygmette are nowhere in sight. She must have sped off to aid her troops, who are massed closer to the drone cloud at the other end of the hallway. How long will it take the copper death to reach us? Two minutes? One?

I grab Alex and Wes by the forearms and run toward a wall so that we don't get trampled. As we barge through a tight ring of Pacifian foot soldiers—our new allies—I lose my grip on Alex. His long arms and legs tangle in the crowd.

"Keep going!" he cries as the riptide of fleeing civilians carries him away. "Stay together, you hear?"

But when Wes and I are almost at the wall, he, too, slips out of my grip. I hear him give a shout of alarm—and pain. The crowd has parted around him. He holds his right calf, blood running through his fingers; there's also a deep gash on the outside of his left thigh. A muscular arm in a gray Pacifian uniform is tight around his neck.

"You two escaped me. Twice." Lazarus corners me against the wall, holding Wes's neck in one arm and a dagger in his other hand. "And so the Committee reduced me to a mere foot soldier." He sounds like a child mourning about never being good enough for his parents. In fact, he has *always* been that child. "Without their support, I am utterly and intolerably alone."

Indeed, Lazarus has no troops to help him. His demotion must explain why we didn't see him on our way to the Committee's hideout. No wonder I thought something was missing.

"But I did not fail to kill you," he says. "You failed to die. Even now, you are here, judging me, pitying me, puffed up with the notion that you are better than I. I cannot . . . I cannot endure it."

I swipe, parry, stab, all the while taking stock of the situation around us. Hordes of people scurry about like termites outside their nest—uselessly, without a real sense of direction. With the metro tunnel to the Dugout buried under rubble, we must escape this death trap via spaceship. People fight for room in the vehicles available, packing Lunar, Batterer, and Pacifian craft past capacity.

Lazarus uses his height against me, sending blows downward until he backs me into a Pillar of Liberty. "I will not leave the nano-drones to finish you."

I try to kick Lazarus's legs, but he swings Wes around, using him as a human shield. In one swift move, his dagger blade slips between the plates in the armor over Wes's belly, and I see Wes's eyes roll back in his head.

The scream comes from my mouth. I funnel idea after idea through my mind, trying to think in spite of the pain.

"Up," Wes chokes out. "Look up."

A ship is whining above our heads, and my head whips around to look at it.

Yinha's open-top Pygmette screeches to a halt; she fires two Lazy blasts at Lazarus. He bends like a reed to dodge them. Wes uses the distraction to twist out of his grip. Clutching his midsection, he stumbles toward me with halting steps. Every movement leaves slicks of blood on the floor. I rush forward, and he falls hard into my arms.

Shaking his head, Lazarus gives Yinha a threatening smile. "This does not become you, Yinha. I once considered you a league apart from these scum. We could have done well together."

In a rush of memory, I recall his fruitless advances toward Yinha last year. *He wanted to use her to gain Dovetail's trust, just as he tried to use me . . . or was he just craving human contact?*

"You never had a chance." Yinha's finger spasms on the trigger, but she doesn't fire.

Lazarus chuckles. "No matter. You aren't woman enough to appreciate me. And not man enough to kill me with that silly laser gun."

Yinha glares at him but doesn't fire. "I'm still human. That's more than you can say."

She can't pull the trigger. She can't end him for good, and it makes me irrationally angry. Is her humanity worth our lives?

"As I foresaw," Lazarus's hand drifts to his belt. "You miserable creature."

He throws a grenade upward, but before it hits Yinha's ship, she dives, knocking Lazarus to the floor. They grapple over her weapon; I watch, too afraid to shoot lest I hit Yinha.

Above us, the Pygmette explodes in a dense cloud of fire and smoke and flying carbon fiber. Supporting Wes, I stumble away, looking over my shoulders at the falling debris. Yinha grabs a piece of hull and slams it into Lazarus's face, knocking him out.

She doesn't need to burn him with a laser now. In a few minutes, the drones will take care of him.

"Go, Stripes!" Yinha yells, not bothering to dust herself off before running back into the fray. "Get out of here!"

"What about you?"

"I'm clearing my troops out. Get Wes to a hangar. Any hangar, you hear?"

And without a backward glance, she's gone. It's time to think hard and move quickly—Wes and I are on our own now.

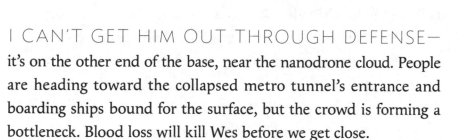

49

I CAN'T GET HIM OUT THROUGH DEFENSE—
it's on the other end of the base, near the nanodrone cloud. People are heading toward the collapsed metro tunnel's entrance and boarding ships bound for the surface, but the crowd is forming a bottleneck. Blood loss will kill Wes before we get close.

The other option is to find a ship and bust through the nearest large window, but it's a fool's hope, as ships are in short supply. *What about the Committee's emergency hangar?* I know they have one; they must keep spare craft in there.

I turn us in the Governance Department's general direction. As we struggle forward, Wes heroically supports some of his weight on his injured leg. Wincing, he presses down on his abdominal wound to staunch the flow of blood, but it's useless compared to a real bandage. *Faster!* I imagine Yinha screaming, as if this were a training drill. How could she have left us?

I half carry, half drag Wes up the stairs outside Governance, and he makes it harder by trying and failing to support his own weight. I try not to glance back at the approaching copper haze, but it's impossible. Now that I'm higher up, I see that the nanodrones have passed the three-quarters mark of the Main Lane. The cloud has thinned because of malfunctioning drones falling down, but there are still enough to kill anyone in its path.

I face forward again and try to accelerate, lunging with every step. But the screams behind me are advancing, burrowing into my skull like diamond-tipped drills. I look over my shoulder and see the whirring drones descending upon hundreds of helpless humans. They're too small to make out from this distance, but as I watch in horror, men, women, and children start to bat their arms frantically. Their faces turn red, then purple, then blue . . .

I freeze, numbed all over again by what I'm seeing. Drone attack seems like the worst way to die: suffocation and seizures, the utter shutdown of your body's cellular machinery, all while watching those around you suffer the same.

Emotions clash within me, too many to process at once. I only manage to discern pity for Bai because he made the drones, and fury at the Committee for twisting them.

"Bai was right," Wes murmurs, "to be so worried."

"Just when I thought they couldn't do anything sicker," I say.

Then his eyes cross for a moment, and renewed urgency shoots through me. I drag Wes through the Governance lobby doors, shoving past the crowd. Some people run about, unsure where to go next; others have stopped, hands on knees, to catch their breath. The drones will arrive soon, and we all know it. I have to keep moving.

"Phaet!" A voice sounds in my headset, accompanied by the sound of shooting. On a list of the people who could administer a shot of relief to me, hers would be one of the last names.

"Callisto?"

"Book it to the Committee's emergency hangar, under Governance. Mom gave me an old fingerprint mold of Hydrus's, and I used it to get in. I've got a Destroyer revved up and ready to go."

Can I trust her? Despite my doubts, I turn into a side hallway, moving in the hangar's direction.

"Dove Girl," Alex says in my ear. "I'm in the ship with her, hovering outside the airlock."

"Militia Pigs out here pestering us, so you have to run," Callisto says. "If we enter the base, they'll fly into the airlock, wreck the thing, and create a vacuum."

"It isn't far," Alex says. "Cut through the Sanitation lane on the right of the lobby, follow it down till you reach the hangar."

Someone has left a manhole open for us; Alex must have passed this way a short time ago. Wes and I crowd into a cylindrical elevator and drop down into the filthy tunnel. After the doors open, I heave us forward, every squelching step a struggle.

"Callisto," I pant. "Why?"

Callisto sighs. "I owe you one. Remember, the day this all . . . this started?" That means *the day your mom died.* "When I went mental because I found out Mom was in Dovetail? Kappa could've shot me in the Sanitation lane. You, too. But neither of you did. It's more than a favor. It's my life for yours."

That incident mattered to her this whole time? Why didn't she show her appreciation instead of antagonizing us, to the point where I wondered whether our mercy was justified?

But now I know we made the right decision. Now that Callisto's returning the favor, all of us might still have a future.

Horrible screams break out in the hallway above us. The drones have breached Governance.

Wes swears violently; his face is so pale it almost blends into the white floor.

I readjust his arm around my shoulders and move forward.

"Okay, Pig G78's attacking the enemy from behind," Callisto reports. "We're pulling into the airlock. You won't have to meet us in space."

Nanodrones buzz behind Wes and me, ever closer. I'd hoped

that the Sanitation lanes would protect us from their reach, but the bugs have infiltrated the tunnel through the tiny gaps between the elevator and the shaft. Despite the needles in my lungs, I push myself to run harder. *Move it, or there'll be stingers in your skin.*

Wes's arm chafes against my shoulders—I don't mind his strong grip, since it tells me that his body is still functioning—but his legs dangle on either side of me, slowing me down.

The buzzing gets louder, until the air around us seems to oscillate with the beating of drone wings. Wes's grip weakens.

"Hang on!" I tell him.

We take another elevator up into the Committee's blaringly bright hangar. It's much smaller than Defense's, but all too huge right now. Wes slumps in my arms. I'm supporting almost all his weight now.

"I can . . . walk . . ." he mumbles into my shoulder, pushing his feet against the ground as if to demonstrate that it's true.

When we're halfway across, I hear the faintest buzzing—but it's not just from behind us anymore.

"Step on the gas, Dove Girl, they're attacking from above!" Alex shouts in my ear.

As if invading through the ventilation tunnel weren't enough, the drones are streaming into the hangar through slats in the ceiling. I keep running, blind to the violet lasers that streak at us from behind. Mid-step, my left calf is set on fire. Shrieking, I tumble to the ground. Wes rolls off my back.

I didn't flip the mirrors on my suit.

I look behind me to see a squad of loyalist troops hunkered down in the hangar's rear, pointing laser blasters in our direction. Someone must've predicted we'd try to escape through here and sent a suicidal group of Militia to ambush us.

They manage to hit Wes's thigh too before the drone cloud surrounds them, burrowing through their uniforms' fabric. They clutch their throats, unable to breathe. Several flip up their visors in vain, thinking it'll give their lungs access to air. The bumpy red skin on their suddenly visible faces takes on a blue undertone, as if they're bruising from the inside out.

Horrified, I turn away and struggle to stand, slinging Wes's arm over my shoulder once more, but the soldiers' screams pierce through the layers of pain and concentration. My oxygen-deprived legs throb; my burnt left calf gives way. Blackness creeps in around the edges of my vision.

"Phaet, get up! We've got to try again . . ." Wes mumbles. Then he looks up at the ceiling and shouts with a strength I didn't know he still had. "God, why? It wasn't supposed to end this way!"

The copper cloud is twenty meters away.

Alex and Callisto holler in my ears: "Come on! I'm sorry, but you've got to leave him . . . it's gonna hurt, but you have to live . . ." I yank off my helmet to silence them. Right now, there's only one voice I want to hear.

Wes touches my exposed cheek, and it brings everything back into focus. His voice, his face, his big heart—he *is* everything. "Get out of here, Phaet. Do you understand? Go. I'll be okay."

By okay, he means . . . gone. I shake my head; tears fall from my face and land on his jacket.

"Your life can't end here." His eyes pierce me; his voice is stern. "People need you, Phaet."

But I need you.

His face softens suddenly, and as he blinks, tears start rolling down his cheeks. "But . . . I don't want to be alone when I die."

Even as his grip falls slack, I tighten mine around his hand. Our gloved fingers lock together like puzzle pieces, and I feel the weak *blip* of his pulse through two layers of fabric. *I could stay here, with him . . .*

"Still, I can't ask you to come with me," he whispers. He's right. My life is too important to end now, and I have too many things left to accomplish.

As the cloud descends upon us, the drones radiate heat onto the top of my head. It's like they're breathing down my neck. Why can't they allow me a few more moments with him? My mind tells me to go, but my body cannot obey.

Wes lifts his Lazy and presses its muzzle against my heart. He switches off the safety, readies his finger on the trigger. "I'll use this unless you turn around. Get home safe. Work for peace until everyone forgives one another for what's happened here."

I feel a minuscule prick on my cheek. Two. The drones have reached us, but they mean nothing compared to the words he's breathing out.

"Live long and die happy, my girl. I love you."

I leave him then, voids opening between my fingers.

50

FOUR HANDS HEAVE ME INTO THE DESTROYER.
The world has already begun to swirl. I see everything as if through a melting telescope lens—Callisto's and Alex's panicked eyes, checking on me every few seconds; the loyalist ships fleeing from us like so many flies from swatting hands. The contents of my skull swell with fever.

I don't cry. Tears release emotion. My torn-up body is trying to hold on to every feeling I associate with Wes, even this blistering pain in my chest.

". . . Dove Girl, you've got to tell me. Where did those—those *things* sting you?" Alex's voice is low and choked.

"She might respond better to her actual name, Alex."

A syringe's needle burrows into my face below my left cheekbone. It starts sucking out my poisoned blood; another needle injects a clear liquid into the crease of my elbow. Immediately, my heart beats slower. *Trying to stop the poison's spread.*

"Phaet, I'm—I'm not gonna lose you too. Can you hear me?" I lower my chin by one centimeter. "That's not good enough! Tell me, can you hang on until we're home? We're going home, Phaet."

The corners of my mouth spasm sideways: the most pathetic smile I've ever worn. Dimmer than Wes's lowest-wattage grin.

"Phaet?" Callisto says. "Say something!"

"Come on, Phaet, stay with us! Phaet . . ."

Fatefatefate. Destiny. After all that's happened, I want to chide my parents for choosing the name they did. If the Odan afterlife exists—a preposterous idea, but it helps me cope—maybe I'll see them soon.

My eyes shut, but my ears stay open.

". . . Alex, there's Destroyer four twenty-four! The one we want—the Committee . . ."

I can't miss this. Haven't I waited years to see them in pain? I wrench one eye open—a millimeter—and focus on the windshield. The ship in question doesn't lead the pack. It lingers in the middle, protected on all sides by three more vessels. *Cowards.*

They fire at us, and we dodge with a jerking motion that makes my head loll on my shoulders. We send a flock of missiles at the ships; in true loyalist fashion, they scatter, leaving the Committee undefended. Two more missiles are all it takes to destroy them. The ship explodes in a small red cloud, its obliteration accompanied by no booming fanfare. Hull fragments jet toward the guard ships, and they swerve predictably. Alex and Callisto take them down.

A series of silent flashes, and my enemies are dead, their bodies' burnt cells permanently dissociated.

But the sight brings me no satisfaction. They died too perfectly. They suffered one moment of agony, though they deserved many more. And they expired outside the public eye, as they would've wanted. How ironic, that the Committee members lived ostentatiously but died anonymously. The opposite of Murray, a side casualty in their endless war.

So . . . unfair. Cold hatred breaks through my fever . . . not of a person, but of the situation. Of the past few hours. My soul's numb—frostbitten—by the fact that I'll spend my entire life, whether it lasts a minute or a century, with only the memory of *him*.

People call my name, seemingly from kilometers away. I hear the voices of Wes, Murray, Mom, even Dad—or my mind's fabrication of them. *Fatefatefate. You belong here.* As the voices grow louder, I feel closer to the dead than I ever did.

I cozy up to the cold, and the sensation of nothing becomes everything.

*— * — *

One copper wire, thin, endlessly long. To what—or whom—will it lead? *Him?*

My dream-eyes spark with unshed tears. I lean forward until the wire is level with my eyes and raise the magnifying glass in my hand.

Wings twitch. The wire's formed of reddish-brown mosquitoes, lined up in rows. They clutch each other's abdomens with their front legs, strengthening their hold by inserting their proboscises— the feeding tubes—inside the bug in front of them. I leap backward, quivering with revulsion, but their beady eyes find me and zoom in. They are camera lenses.

If I could scream, I would. Even in my sleep, I can't shake the impression that someone, somewhere always has eyes on me.

"You're sleeping, and the world keeps going," says a girl's voice. *I love her*, I vaguely remember. "We've made a list, so that we can tell you everything when you wake up."

The name comes to me. *Anka.*

"They're drafting a constitution." The deeper voice is Umbriel's. "Didn't even wait for Mira Theta's girl to see it."

I will my blood to flow faster, my heart to pump with greater gusto—as if conscious effort could control my autonomic nervous system.

"They're rebuilding the Singularity in another crater on the Far Side," Cygnus says. "And Base I. About half the people there got to the Dugout before the drones got them."

"But we're on Base IV," Umbriel says. "We knew you'd want to wake up here."

Home. Home! I struggle to shake off the shroud of sleep. They're so close . . .

"Mhm," Anka says. "We miss you so, so much. Wake up, big sister . . . wake up, won't you?"

Doors slide open; footsteps approach. "She's not ready," says an authoritative male voice. "Her body hasn't recovered from the toxin yet. I'm sorry to do this, Miss Anka."

"No!" Anka's voice becomes indignant. "Don't keep her from us any longer."

I picture Umbriel restraining her. "You know Phaet needs this . . ."

Something pinches my forearm. Chilly liquid enters my bloodstream, and cold once again blocks off my senses.

⁎ — ⁎ — ⁎

". . . blood pressure rising, pulse accelerating." An unfamiliar woman's voice. "She'll wake soon—no, don't touch her. Or you could disrupt the dialysis."

"And then she'll have a harder time recovering." A young man's voice. He sounds clipped, rushed—a Medical assistant, perhaps. Instinctively, I picture *him* in a white coat, speaking patiently to me, and the jab of memory jolts me further into consciousness.

"Psh. If she dies, I'll kill her." *Yinha*—she's alive! And her voice sounds so nonchalant; it's morbidly funny, and morbid things no longer scare me. Death feels like nothing but an impatient friend I've put off seeing.

Laughing hurts, but I do it. I sound like a congested coal engine.

"She's waking up," Anka says. "Someone tell Umbriel!"

My eyes crack open. Stung by white light, they take in the elliptical intensive care room and the wireless devices lodged in my body to measure my vitals. A large, colorful screen shows my heartbeat, blood pressure, respiratory rate, and temperature. I also see my cells' average rate of protein synthesis, which indicates how quickly they've recovered from the abrin. The two Medics, noses and mouths obscured by masks, adjust my bed so that I'm reclining at a thirty-degree angle. Then they retreat to the far wall.

Anka and Cygnus lean over the glass barrier, probably breaking some Medical guidelines about proximity to patients. Yinha paces in a small portion of floor space. Seconds later, Umbriel skids into the room, completing the picture. He opens his arms wide, as if to hug me, and then seems to remember that I can't lift mine yet.

"Phew. You're up in time for the new constitution's ratification ceremony." Yinha's smiling in spite of herself. "It's in four and a half days."

"Psh," Umbriel says, "it's not like they would hold the proceedings without her."

"Fine. But are four and a half days enough to get her looking like the Girl Sage again?"

How bad is it? Supporting myself on my elbows, I raise my head off the pillow and struggle to a sitting position, nearly hitting my head on the top of my glass bubble. *Ouch.* Too much leg movement, too soon.

"No, don't look, Phaet," Umbriel says, moving closer. "You don't want to see . . ."

Yes, I do. I catch my reflection in my bed's glass barrier—and it's mesmerizing. I'm fascinated, not repulsed, by the changes in my appearance. This is how war has marked me. My face has shrunken and my skin has turned the color of old soybeans, except for two shiny scarlet splotches on my cheeks where the drones pricked me. Each blemish must measure a full centimeter across.

Even my eyes have changed. Dull, unblinking, and opaquely dark, they'd haunt me if they belonged to someone else.

But most strikingly, a silver tide has washed out every black hair on my head. Millions of comet tails, with no empty dark space between them. It's the fullest night sky I've ever seen, and I'll carry it wherever I go.

Amazing, how it completes me.

51

OVER THE NEXT FEW DAYS, I BOMBARD MY brain with all sorts of stimuli. They don't fill the empty space in my heart, but if I keep my mind occupied and don't think about *him* and the life we'll never have, the emptiness manifests as a muted ache.

A carousel of friends and family stop by my bedside. Anka and the Phi twins sneak me my favorite rice candies from Market, but I can't stomach them. Asterion, Andromeda, and Callisto bring me a small sprig of purple sage blossoms. They use a graduated cylinder from Chemistry as a vase.

Alex, the only person on the bases whose grief over Wes might compare to mine, is absent. He has left for Earth, to "clean up that garbage dump of a planet," Yinha says. I envy him. He can translate feelings into action, as I'm so accustomed to doing, while I'm a passive observer stuck in bed.

"Poor guy—he has to tell Wes's parents," Yinha says with a sigh.

I don't envy him that. Telling Wesley and Holly Carlyle, who have already lost their vulnerable daughter, that their indomitable son is no more will destroy them. Wes's life had just begun. Parents mourning their children reverses a natural rhythm as old as humanity—a reversal that's *wrong*.

My brooding seems to alarm Cygnus. "Grits, you're reminding me of me when I had nothing to do."

A day later, he and Umbriel remove the HeRP from the room's one table and install it on the ceiling. The Medics remove the glass lid of my coffin but tell me not to leave the bed. Now I can watch live updates on the Earth situation while lying down. My family's no-nonsense display of affection helps thaw my brittle heart.

※ — ※ — ※

Three days after I wake, Pacifia and Battery Bay conduct peace talks. Although people have gathered in the Atrium to watch the live feed on the big screens, homemade drinks in hand, my siblings join me in my Medical room.

On the HeRP screen, we watch Pacifia's Premier, an East Asian woman with crimped black hair and dangling fist-shaped earrings, shake hands with Prime Minister Sear. Thousands of people have crammed side by side on the widest boulevard on Battery Bay under a cloudy, pre-monsoon sky to watch. The Premier's wide, red-lipped smile droops at the sides so she looks more feral than compliant, more likely to throttle Sear than to parley with him.

And yet, with their tattered armies standing behind them, the two leaders sign treaty after treaty. Both alliances agree to bilateral disarmament, a peace summit once a year, and economic and humanitarian aid to war-torn areas. I feel sorry for the Earthbound, who must repair their ruined planet because of a war started by the Lunar Standing Committee. And I'm angry with the Committee for dying when it was convenient. For heaping the fallout from a world war onto innocent people's shoulders.

Speaking of innocents, the Odans are absent from Battery Bay. They've gone home. Or have they? Within the next hour, the screen shows a panorama of razed forests, scorched meadows, and collapsed rock formations. No bacterial lamps cast blue illumination over the cracked, bloodstained footpaths. Instead, multi-drill mining rigs spread their arms over swaths of land like gigantic spiders. As Wes and I feared, Battery Bay has come to collect payment for saving the Odans' lives last year. His homeland will become a mining settlement for natural gas, iron, and zinc.

The unmistakable shape of Koré Island's peak and the presence of familiar faces indicate that this wasteland is, in fact, Saint Oda. The Odan people stolidly watch bulldozers, cranes, and armored trucks ravage the once-beautiful landscape. Only some of the adults cry for what they've lost. The children regard the scorched earth with puzzlement. These young ones can't recognize their old home.

Up here on the Moon, I don't feel I have the right to cry with the Odans. All the guilt in the world won't change the fact that I'm partly responsible for this . . . this crime.

The video's focus shifts to a group of men patching up a collapsed tunnel. Alex, wearing a beige shirt soaked with sweat, strains to lift metal supports into place. He stares straight ahead and doesn't make eye contact with anyone.

I should be with him. But my tumbledown shell of a body can't leave this sickbed.

Someone steers the video camera closer to Alex, who notices it, slams a strut into place, and glares into the lens. "Get out!" he shouts, striding toward the camera. "Get out and—"

The scene cuts to a familiar vista overlooking the cliffs and sea; gray clouds shift over the Odan harbor, rearrange themselves around pine tree branches. A lumpy shadow takes up the middle of the shot. It's a family, all tangled in one another's arms, kneeling, shivering with sadness. A father, a mother, two girls, their grandmother, and a pony-sized black hound. In front of them are two square blocks of petrified wood, the ancient trees' xylem and phloem replaced with swirling patterns of black, white, and rust-colored stone. Two memorials, for the boy and girl who didn't make it home.

It's impossible to breathe.

"Anka, she's shaking." Cygnus's fingertips are light on my fore-head. "Should I get her another blanket?"

"No, that's not it." Anka shuts off the HeRP. "She needs a good cry."

"Oh," Cygnus says. Confusion washes over his face. Then he wraps my free hand in his fingers and says something that he might've learned from watching Umbriel comfort people. "Let it out, Phaet. No one will ever know except for us."

The mattress dips as my sister sits beside me. She pushes silver hair off my forehead, the way our mother used to. And like Mom, she bends down and kisses the spot she's cleared.

I haven't felt so safe since both our parents were here. Surrounded on all sides by my family's love, I let myself feel. Grief fills me up, and then ebbs with each sputtering breath.

"You did so much to save us from dying, big sister." Anka's voice cracks on a swell of sadness. "But how do we keep every part of you alive?"

52

AS THE DAYS STRETCH ON, MY BODY GETS stronger. My laser-burned leg begins to feel pain, and then sensations other than pain. The splotches on my face disappear, and my skin loses its anoxic pallor. Medics move me from intensive care to a recovery room. The walls, floor, and ceiling are stark white, as Medical rooms always are, but someone has hung colorful ribbons over my bed. Even though the tinted glass window blocks out sunlight when I'm sleeping, the intrepid decorator has put up a yellow window shade printed with the black outline of trees.

The volume of traffic in and out of this room is higher than the ICU's. Yinha and my old Militia friends stop by, as do people I haven't talked to since Primary. I bear their presence with a smile until it grates on me—then I call a Medical assistant to shoo them away and dose me with sleeping meds.

One evening, the carousel of visitors brings someone I've hoped to see since I regained consciousness. Alex has returned.

When he staggers in, slack-jawed and bleary-eyed, I'm standing with my hands against a wall, digging my heel into the floor to stretch my calf. Something tells me that forces other than lack of caffeine are responsible for his exhaustion.

I nod at him in greeting.

"Good evening to you too, Dove Girl," Alex says. "I'm relieved

to be back. Couldn't take it over there." He flops into the chair be-
hind the Medic's desk; his head droops, and he stares at the ceiling.
"Most people are sad over someone. All of 'em are livid about the
Batterers paving over Saint Oda."

I sit on the edge of my bed to face him, stretching my ham-
strings now.

"Coordinator Carlyle ignored me. His wife wanted to know
every detail about what happened to . . . to Wes. Me? I tried not to
get riled up when the Batterers knocked over the lighthouse where
he and I used to go climbing. But two days ago, the developers
started building a rig right over my parents' old wheat field—that
was the last straw, and I don't mean that as a pun."

I nod, pretending to understand the depth of his pain. But I
can't. I still have a family and a recognizable homeland.

"Earth's got nothing for me," Alex says softly. "Nothing. I don't
want to live in a place where I see what's missing instead of what's
there. I'd rather be here, where things can get better, not worse."

My mouth hangs open. Why would someone from a beautiful
Earthbound city choose to live on the Moon instead? Somewhere
without the salty ocean and the sun on his face. "But you lived in
Saint Oda for so long," I say. "There must be things worth remembering."

Alex takes his paper notebook out of his jacket pocket. The
cover hangs on to the spine by a corner; several pages flutter away,
but he catches them in midair. "Every memory I need is in here."

"What do you plan to do with that?" I ask.

"Remind people of everything we've lost." Alex leafs through
the notebook, reading over his own words. His narrow, irregular
scrawl fills page after page. "So that a war like this one doesn't happen again."

"That's . . . optimistic," I say. Both of us have seen and done too much to believe that "peaceful" is humanity's default setting. "Do you think you can change people? Even the best of them turn to force when they have everything to lose."

Alex snaps the book shut and fixes his eyes on me. "Then we ought to create a world where they don't have to worry."

※ — ※ — ※

Forty-seven hours later, the Girl Sage leaves Medical, withered but alive. That peaceful world Alex was talking about? We'll make it real, starting today in the Free Radical's Atrium. The vast dome is bustling again after months of fearful stillness.

"Remember, you don't have to say anything if you don't want to." Umbriel walks behind me, arms extended, ready to catch me should I stumble on my way up the stairs. Andromeda, who waits for me on the Atrium's second level, offered me a hoverchair like Rose's for the ceremony, but I declined.

With each step, I fight gravity—and grow more conscious of the several thousand eyes watching my struggle. Alex stands guard at the top step, Yinha across from him. He nods to Umbriel and me, a somewhat betrayed look on his face. Had Wes lived, he might have helped me climb the stairs. Or we might have clutched each other to keep from falling. I know Alex isn't the only one picturing what could have been.

I reel in sadness before it has a chance to surface. *This day belongs to the people*, I tell myself, *and my parents, because their dream is finally a reality.*

Defiant, I look out at the audience. The Batterer troops are gone. They have returned to Earth and joined their comrades in tidying up the mess. Instead of their teal uniforms, I see Anka's beaming face, Cygnus's toothy grin, and Ariel's starstruck eyes.

Atlas Phi towers above his neighbors, sobbing for everyone to see. Even Caeli Phi has stepped out, escorted by guards from Dovetail.

Noticeably absent are Yinha and Bai, the latter of whom is in Medical. According to his sister, Bai ingested jequirity seeds after watching the footage from Base I. I can't decide if Yinha's alerting Medical and saving his life was cruel or kind. Even though he was just a pawn in the Committee's plans, Bai's existence will always remind me that Wes is no more. And every mention of Base I will remind Bai that he'll live forever in people's memories, but in infamy.

Callisto, who stands behind her mother, nods to me as I take the stage. The Lunar Republic's new flag lies folded in Asterion's arms. Elections won't happen for another six months at least, but the new independent presses predict he'll win a legislative or executive position. Asterion unfolds the flag lengthwise; Andromeda and I each hold one corner. Together, we fling the heavy cloth over the edge and let all thirty square meters of it unfurl.

Five gold stars in a circle on a silver background. A red star in the center commemorates the bloodshed on the Singularity—that was Anka's idea. Some journalists labeled the flag "dazzling to a fault" and "extravagantly optimistic," but they missed the fact that we *need* "dazzling" and "optimistic." By the volume of the citizens' cheers, the wattage of their smiles, I know we've picked the right design.

Here you go, my friends. Silver, red, and gold ripple against the blank white Atrium wall. *Here's your sunrise.*

53

THE OTHER BASES STAGE THEIR OWN RATIFICATION services, and they require my attendance for each ceremony. Within a week, I'm piloting a Pygmette en route to Base I, Yinha next to me, in case I bungle a maneuver in my compromised state. Andromeda wanted me on the Omnibus with the rest of the Dovetail entourage, which left the Free Radical this morning, but I need the autonomy. Steering my own ship gives me control over some portion of my life.

As we coast above Mare Tranquillitatis, a black basalt plain ringed by bumpy peaks, Yinha taps my shoulder. "Can we touch down for a second? I want to show you something."

Yinha's surprises never fail to astonish, so I nod yes and land the Pygmette in the middle of the sea, near a small area sectioned off with steel wires. We taxi over, following Yinha's directions, suit up, and step outside.

"The first human ever to set foot on the Moon," Yinha says. "Almost four centuries ago now. This is all he left behind."

We walk to the steel fence. The first footprint is bigger than my two feet put together. It looks like a striated bacterium, an engorged version of the simplest, oldest organism. There's also a rectangular plaque and a narrow circular hole where some kind of staff or flag used to be.

That was the beginning. Before me lies evidence of the first human ever to tread on regolith, to brave the vacuum-sealed desert that we call the Moon. Centuries later, his legacy gave the bases' founders hope—the knowledge that they could send up massive numbers of people, could build and settle here.

But the original Committee soon laid down the law. They did it to safeguard everyone from the hostile outdoors. But from there, they made the short leap to ruling, fighting, and murdering, all in the name of survival.

We can't let that happen again. Protecting people from nature is not an excuse to prey on them. The Moon's new leadership, whoever it comprises, has to remember that distinction. In the years ahead, I'll do everything possible to remind them.

I look down at the footprint—so innocuous, so unaware. This ancient Earthbound man wouldn't be able to comprehend the era he ushered in. But it's not his fault that so much destruction happened here. It's not any one human's fault.

Still, I wonder.

Should we ever have come?

Epilogue

ACROSS THE MOON, THERE WAS PLENTY MORE public mourning, followed by plenty of public fanfare. After my initial victory lap around the five bases, I participated in neither, drawing concern and criticism from the newly freed citizens of the bases—I mean, of the Lunar Republic.

My silence lasted six months, which seems short in retrospect but was long enough to concern people. They couldn't understand why I felt so empty, why I had nothing to say about the Earth's peaceful state, the Moon's improving quality of life, the countless fictionalizations that people wrote about my ordeal.

Truth was, talking about anything other than death—the thousands of deaths, including Wes's—seemed frivolous. I couldn't contemplate the subject without grief blocking off my throat. Not even Alex, Wes's other mourner, could get a response out of me. What could I have said? Rumor holds that Wes watched me run toward the Destroyer, even as the copper drone cloud descended upon him and pumped him full of poison. That he wanted me to be the last thing he ever saw.

I wouldn't know; I could never watch the footage.

Year by year, the pain ebbed away. Eventually, there came a day when someone made me feel as I never thought I'd feel again, and it didn't seem like an insult to the memory of a boy I loved when I was seventeen. So the man became my family, and now I have someone with whom to spend the many years Wes wanted me to live.

And my husband isn't all. These days, a smaller set of fingers warms the spaces between my own. Their owner walks by my side now, her strides exactly half as long as mine.

Dawn, my little light. Biology says I bestowed life upon her, but in my soul I know it was the other way around. She gave me the strength to do ordinary things again, and that makes her extraordinary.

As we leave the light-filled Primary lobby, Dawn waves goodbye to her friends. At six, she's active and gregarious, with very specific clothing preferences. Today's outfit is green overalls dotted with silver spaceships. Dawn's short black hair curls at the ends; eight freckles zigzag across her nose on skin a shade darker than mine. Her father and I didn't say a word when we first saw them; we simply looked at each other and understood. When she began biting her food with the sides of her mouth instead of the front, it became even clearer: Wes might have left the universe, but the universe hasn't forgotten him.

"Ms. Phaet! Thank you for getting those agar plates." One of my tenth-year Primary students, Columba, catches up to us. She smiles down at my daughter. "I'm gonna grow the most diverse bacteria colony in class."

I laugh, shaking my head. Columba, a lanky girl of fifteen with multiple ear piercings, reminds me of my own overachieving tendencies. She waves to me and zips off on her maglev scooter, probably to get a head start on homework.

Dawn and I step into the Free Radical's colorful main corridor, which is now covered by murals that flow seamlessly together. They portray subjects as varied as a little girl blowing bubbles, a giant zipper with tulips in place of teeth, and the words YOUR VOICE HERE with an arrow pointing upward. Occasionally, we pass patrol officers leaning against the wall, watching passersby or admiring the artwork. They wear narrow-brimmed, bulletproof caps instead of helmets, leaving their faces open for observation. My daughter has never seen fully armed Beetles with gleaming bug-eye visors, and for that I'm grateful.

"Can we see Auntie Anka's big bird? Please, Mommy?" Dawn pulls me to a stop in front of my sister's best-known mural: a dove in profile painted entirely with children's handprints. My daughter was three when she covered her palm in silver paint and contributed a feather low on its left wing. Her uncle Umbriel gave her a piggyback ride when she was done.

Now Dawn's much larger, six-year-old hand hovers over that original print.

"Look at how you've grown!" I say. "Now let's get home before Daddy does. It's a race!"

We never linger long in front of the painting. I always come up with some reason to move on, before Dawn asks me why it's called *In Memoriam: Young Doves*. She'll notice the plaque someday, and read it. She'll ask about the war, my role in it, and the "young doves" who I knew and loved before they died. I won't know what to say. But I suppose it's better to try to explain before she hears about it in history class.

We pass the shiny new Transit Department, which has replaced Defense. There are queues out the door for base-to-base spaceship rides and the daily Moon-to-Earth shuttle. I catch a glimpse of Yinha, hugging a pale woman in a hoverchair whose platinum hair tumbles down her back. Rose now oversees base digital communication, keeping cyber-channels open for all kinds of traffic.

Yinha strides toward a side entrance to Transit, notices me—or rather, notices my distinctive hair—and nods before stepping inside. Advancing into her late forties has made her features sharper, her steps quicker. As soon as the shuttle opened, Yinha stopped training Lunar Armed Forces recruits and became a pilot. Callisto Chi took over her old job. The population has swelled, and without the constant need for policing the halls and soldiering on Earth, enough people enlist of their own free will that service is no longer mandatory.

While Yinha's passengers wait, they examine a video advertisement for *Eternal Light: Battle and Rebuilding in the North,* a new essay collection by Alex Huxley about his experiences observing the reconstruction on Base I. Although I admire Alex's work and feel endless pride in his success, I've decided not to read this new text. He accepts it. I'm "too close to the material," as he would say.

Dawn watches the screen intently as the next advertisement starts. "And there's Uncle Umbriel!"

My best friend, his curly hair as untamed as ever, appears on the screen in front of the cracked Pillars of Liberty on Base I. Old magnetic handcuffs, which the Militia used for routine arrests, bind his wrists and ankles. After hopping and weaving behind the columns, he slips them off, passes them behind his back, and steps into a glass tank that looks almost exactly like the one in which the Committee tried to kill us via drowning.

The screen blacks out, leaving viewers to wonder if he will escape (spoiler alert—he will). DON'T MISS THE ULTIMATE UMBRIEL SHOW! say white letters across the screen. BUY YOUR TICKET TODAY! Though old memories sicken me every time I watch the routine— Dawn loves it, so I have Anka take her instead—he's told me that every performance helps him heal, allowing him to break free of the Committee again and again.

After Umbriel's advertisement ends, Dawn and I walk onward

to our apartment complex and take the cylindrical elevator to floor eighteen. My daughter opens our green front door with her thumbprint, just as I've taught her.

Even though years have passed since I last saw one, I scan the foyer for security pods. As expected, nothing buzzes around the bamboo coffee table or the plush lime-colored couches. Dawn's father thinks my lingering paranoia makes sense in light of my experiences, but I'm trying to kick the habit. InfoTech has debugged every Lunar residence; Cygnus oversaw the cleanup project to its completion, which got him promoted to Department Chief.

"Mommy, will you help me fly?"

At the sound of her voice, everything else in the world crumbles away—everything but my girl.

"Always, Dawn." To avoid spoiling her, I try not to indulge her when she begs for sweets or new toys, but I never refuse to do this.

I lie back, my silver hair fanning out on the floor. Dawn sits on my shins and puts her palms on mine. Laughing, she rises up, lets go of my hands, and pumps her arms like wings. With me here, she has never fallen, and never will.

Our apartment doors slide open. Unlike in years past, I feel elation instead of cold fear. Dawn's father walks in, puts his shoulder bag down, and watches us. The love on his face fuels our flight, and I lift Dawn higher, making zooming noises with my mouth.

"I'm flying, Dad, I'm flying!" she cries.

Our daughter's ringing voice produces the loudest squeal of joy I've ever heard, and my eardrums revel in the sound. In the world we've built, there's no need to shush her. And no limit to how high she'll soar.

Acknowledgments

How could I possibly thank everyone properly at the end of this half-decade-long journey? That's a tough question. But as for who to thank? That's easy. The following people have been guiding lights, and may they shine here like the stars they are.

At Writers House: Simon Lipskar, thanks for your unwavering support and guidance as I grew from a clueless teenager into a less clueless adult. Genevieve Gagne-Hawes—with your editing, you've made the books so much better, and with your friendship, you've made my life so colorful. Cecelia de la Campa, with your patience and tireless work, you have helped Phaet fly across the world. Julie Trelstad, you showed me the wonders of Author Internet, and for that I am so grateful.

At Penguin Young Readers Group: Kendra Levin, where would these books be without your careful eye and your faith in them? Ken Wright, it's been wonderful to see the series grow under your watch. Julia McCarthy, you have made the paperback editions something to be proud of. Krista Ahlberg and Jody Corbett, I am so grateful (and relieved!) that you both copyedited the manuscript as carefully as you did. Marisa Russell, thank you for working tirelessly to get the books to as many readers as possible. Elyse Marshall, you are seriously a road warrior; I was so lucky to travel with you. Melinda Quick and Angela Cruise, thank you for bringing the books to schools and students. Thank you to Colin Anderson for breathtaking cover photography; to Cara Petrus and Maria Fazio for beautiful cover design; and to marketing and sales for reaching as many readers as we have.

Author friends: Sabaa Tahir, Alison Goodman, Rachel Hawkins, April Tucholke, and Alwyn Hamilton—we toured together for only a few days, but you all made it an unforgettable experience. Tommy Wallach and Danielle Paige, may we have many more fun times together in the future! Arvin Ahmadi, thanks for the shots of much-needed wisdom. Christopher Paolini, as always, you are not only a wonderful friend, but also an example to me in so many ways.

To my hosts around the country, thank you for welcoming me with open arms: Poly Prep Day School, John Witherspoon Middle School, Princeton Public Library, Science Fiction Association of Bergen County, Barnes and Nobles across New Jersey, Labyrinth Books, Kirkwood High, Main Street Books, St. Charles-City-County Library District, Red Balloon Bookshop, Tucson Festival of Books, SUNY Oswego. Getting to meet book lovers is truly the best part of my job.

At Columbia University: the E3B Department, especially The Drew Lab, for encouraging me in every pursuit, whether scientific or literary. Special thanks to my orgo and math instructors for making my final year so enjoyable. Finally, thanks to my amazing friends—computer geniuses, tae kwon do fighters, musicians, writers, artists, eco-warriors—who brought me food and hugs when things got tough. May we all escape Butler in one piece.

I am also indebted to the friends who inspire me and support me from afar. I miss you dearly.

Larry, Mom, and Dad, you make it better just by being here. Love you always.

And readers: we have now landed. Thank you for coming on this crazy ride.